THIS SIGNED E

THE

PROMISE

OF

STARDUST

by

Priscille Sibley

HAS BEEN SPECIALLY BOUND BY THE PUBLISHER.

Priscille Sibley

LIMITED SIGNED EDITION FOR TARGET BOOK CLUB

Club Pick

Dear Target Guest,

I'll let you in on a secret. I cannot walk past a book aisle without stopping to browse. I think I have a bit of a book addiction. On more than one occasion, my oldest son has had to grab me by the elbow and pull me away with the admonishment "Mom, we didn't come here for books!" In response, I typically just smile at him and then, while he looks at electronics, DVDs, or something else nearby, I find my way back to the books. Perhaps in the same way you came into Target for something else, maybe a bottle of eye drops, maybe a scarf, but you wandered over here looking for a good read.

The Promise of Stardust is my first novel, and I am very honored that Target has selected it for its February Book Club. I am especially pleased that Target gave me the opportunity to communicate directly with you in this letter. Like many authors, I have a "day job." I'm a registered nurse and I work in a neonatal intensive care unit where I take care of newborns—some of them premature and others full-term but sick. Most of my patients recover and grow into healthy children. But not all babies and their families have happy outcomes; we cannot save every child, no matter how hard we try. There are times when I find myself wondering about the limits of medicine and how far we push—and how far we *should* push—those limits. I don't pretend to have the answers, especially since over the course of my nursing career I've witnessed many miracles. Sometimes a child we didn't expect to live . . . does. Sometimes that child even thrives.

The Promise of Stardust is the story of a family entrenched in a medical crisis, but it is also a love story. The family is divided not by hatred, but by what each member believes is in the best interest of the beloved woman who was his or her daughter, wife, and friend—a woman who can no longer voice her own wishes.

The story may cause you to take sides. It may make you question what you would do if your family faced such a dilemma. Although *The Promise of Stardust* is a work of fiction, my experiences as a nurse played a huge part in my ability to create and present both sides of the family members' argument. I hope that by the time you read the last page, you will have your own questions and that you'll bring these questions with you to your book group. If you're not yet part of a reading group, I hope you use this novel as motivation to join or start one!

There are many books to choose from, and I just wanted to let you know that I sincerely appreciate your selection of *The Promise of Stardust*. Once you're done reading it, I'd love to hear your thoughts. Please visit my website and drop me a line at www.priscillesibley.com.

All the best,

Priscille Sibley

Priscille Sibley

Advance Praise for

THE PROMISE OF STARDUST

"A literate and incandescent Nicholas Sparks-like love story complicated by intense moral and ethical questions."

—*Kirkus*

"There's nothing like devastating moral quandary to spark reading, and this trade paperback original would be a great book club choice."

—*Library Journal*

"In this brave novel, *The Promise of Stardust*, [the members of] a family making choices about death with dignity find themselves in uncomfortable opposition. Author Priscille Sibley explores with compassion and insight, how political and personal needs align and shift as a husband, a mother, and a father navigate the needs of a family member in crisis."

—Randy Susan Meyers, author of *The Murderer's Daughters*

"Sibley explores an ethical dilemma in a way that might lead you to question your own beliefs. Woven with elegance through a twenty-year love story, the novel takes numerous twists and turns that will keep you turning the pages."

—Catherine McKenzie, internationally bestselling author of *Spin, Arranged,* and *Forgotten*

"Sibley's debut dissects the ethics of a patient's right to die with dignity. . . . The journey is heartrending and tragic."

—*Publishers Weekly*

"*The Promise of Stardust* is a riveting story of a family ripped apart by an impossible choice. You will live these characters' lives like they are your own, and race through the pages of this engrossing, deeply moving novel."

—Kristina Riggle, author of *Keepsake*

THE
PROMISE
OF
STARDUST

Priscille Sibley

WILLIAM MORROW
An Imprint of HarperCollinsPublishers

P.S.™ is a trademark of HarperCollins Publishers.

HarperCollins books may be purchased for educational, business, or sales promotional use. For information please write: Special Markets Department, HarperCollins Publishers, 10 East 53rd Street, New York, NY 10022.

FIRST EDITION

Designed by Diahann Sturge

Library of Congress Cataloging-in-Publication Data has been applied for.

ISBN 978-0-06-226990-4

13 14 15 16 17 OV/RRD 10 9 8 7 6 5 4 3 2 1

For Tim, who has given me his heart and
the courage to write. And for Robert, Cole, and Ethan,
who have taught me why it is important to never give up.

As for me, to love you alone, to make you happy, to do nothing which would contradict your wishes, this is my destiny and the meaning of my life.

—Napoleon Bonaparte

THE

PROMISE

OF

STARDUST

✦ 1 ✦

The Emergency Room Call

Late that night—on our last night—we lay in awe, mesmerized again by the Perseid meteor showers as they transformed stardust into streamers of light. They were an anniversary of sorts for us, a summertime event Elle and I cherished, and we fell asleep on the widow's walk of our old house, my beautiful wife curled up beside me, her head resting in the crook of my arm.

If only I stayed home in the morning—if only I'd looked over at Elle and realized nothing I could or would ever do was more important than keeping her safe. If only—Jesus—

I've heard patients' families play the "if only" game. In the eleven years I've been a doctor, I've come to expect the denial and the bargaining. But reality is cold and hard and, all too often, irreversible. I did not stay home and neither did Elle.

I was already at my office, studying an MRI that showed what I suspected was a glioblastoma and wondering how much time I could buy my patient by excising his malignant tumor, when my receptionist buzzed me. "The hospital is on line three. Said it's urgent."

"Thanks, Tanya." I picked up the phone, still staring at cross sections of the temporal lobe. "This is Dr. Beaulieu," I said.

"Hi, Matt. It's Carl Archer." The emergency room doc cleared his throat. "You need to come over."

"Page Phil. He's covering the hospital."

"He's already here. I need *you* to come in. It's your wife." Carl's voice sounded as tight as screeching tires. "She's had an accident."

His tone, more than his words, conveyed the gravity. And its weight kept many questions tamped down in my throat. If Phil had already arrived, were Elle's injuries neurosurgical? Or perhaps my partner simply happened by the ER. Maybe he was standing there telling Elle jokes to distract her from something minor. *Please*, I thought. *Don't let her be dead.*

"Is Elle all right?" I asked.

Carl cleared his throat again. "It's serious. Come now. I'll see you in a few minutes." The dial tone sounded.

I leaped out of my chair and charged through the waiting room, past a woman standing next to her wheelchair-bound son, barely turning to my receptionist to say where I was going. After sprinting the four blocks to the hospital, I arrived at the emergency entrance in a cold sweat. I pushed through the double doors and headed straight to the trauma area. My partner, Phil Grey, stood next to a red code cart, its drawers open. He wore sterile gloves, a gown, and a surgical mask. An IV pole, decked out with a dozen IV bags and pumps, stood against the gurney. Lines of all sorts sprang from the patient's extremities. Not Elle. Please, not Elle. The ventilator hissed its accordioned wheeze as it pumped oxygen into the hose coming out of her body. The nurse stepped aside, and I saw Elle's face, white as the bed linens, dried blood caked in her blond hair. The only indicator that she was still alive was the tracing across the cardiac monitor.

Her body was rigid and arched, her toes were pointed, and her hands were curled under. The position is called decerebrate posturing, and it is an indicator of severe brain damage. I dropped to my knees, knowing whatever happened had devastated her brain.

I can't say exactly what happened next. Maybe someone dragged me to my feet. Maybe I staggered up of my own volition. Phil said something about Elle and a fall from a ladder, something about a grand mal seizure in the ambulance. And Carl was hovering and saying something about a full cardiac arrest and a Glasgow score of five. Something—about being down for only four or five minutes. Something—about her fixed and dilated pupils. Something—about her CAT scan. Something—about surgery.

I touched Elle's cold contorted hand. People were staring at me, pitying me. People I worked with. People I didn't give a damn about. I pulled a light pen from my pocket and checked Elle's pupils. *Come on, Elle*, I thought. *React. Prove my gut reaction wrong. Prove. Them. All. Wrong.*

I flicked the light across my wife's green eyes, which weren't green at all but black. Her pupils were blown and huge.

I checked her reflexes and found nothing but more evidence that the accident had destroyed Elle's brain.

I met Phil's eyes, eyes filled with tears. "Let me show you the CAT scan. I just put in the ICP monitor. Her pressure's high. We started steroids and mannitol. I want to get her downstairs right now. I'll do everything. D'Amato is scrubbing in with me. The OR is all ready for her."

For a flitter of a second, I thought I would scrub in, too, but then my sensibility returned. I could no more cut into her brain or watch anyone else do it than I could turn into a superhero.

Phil held up the CAT scan that showed the bleeding compressing her brain tissue. I steadied myself against the wall. This could *not* be happening.

Less than twelve hours before, Elle and I had made love on the widow's walk. I must still be sleeping there, having a nightmare, worrying about Elle leaning against the rickety railing. I had to force myself to wake up. As I glanced around—taking in the textures of the emergency room, the definition of the lines on Phil's face as his logical mind planned out his surgical approach, the axle grease on the gurney's wheels—I renounced reality in favor of believing it a vivid nightmare. Powerlessness pounded my denial like a drum. I wandered back into the trauma room as the nurse I now recognized looked up from checking one of Elle's tubes.

No. This was real. And my wife, the girl I'd been in love with since I was seventeen, the girl who I had loved as my closest friend for an even longer time, had fallen and cracked her head open. Even the best neurosurgeon I knew, my friend and partner, would never be able to fix the damage.

For a minute, I stood frozen, remembering how much Elle did not want to suffer through a lingering death like her mother had endured. Phil shoved a consent form on a clipboard in front of my face. "Sign, so I can take her to the OR. I don't need to explain this to you," he said.

"We should let her go." I turned and bolted into the bathroom, where I heaved my lunch. It felt like everything else I'd ever eaten came up in that scummy hospital toilet, too. Make no mistake; it is possible to turn inside out.

Phil opened the door and found me throwing up. "Matt, I need to take her downstairs. Now. We don't have time for bullshit. Listen, horrible as this is, you know as well as I do, she probably won't make it, but you'll hate yourself if we don't try." He shoved the clipboard in my face again.

What did I promise Elle on our wedding day? That I would love, honor, and respect her. I had to respect her wishes. She wouldn't want this. I knew the odds. I knew the consequences.

I grabbed the clipboard and scribbled my consent anyway.

He disappeared through the door, leaving me behind, regretting every betrayal I'd ever made of her. It was selfish to want her to live, knowing the kind of suffering she would have to bear, knowing her brain could never truly recover from a neurological insult this devastating. That was the trouble with being a neurosurgeon; I knew her prognosis. I could not be lulled by blind hope. Nothing and no one could save Elle. But I needed her. I needed Phil to save her even if it was impossible.

I splashed water on my face and returned to the trauma room. The nurse was setting up the portable ventilator so they could move Elle to the OR. "Can you give me one minute alone with her?" I asked.

The nurse sidled around the equipment and then touched my elbow like a visitor at a funeral home does a mourner. "We need to get her to the OR."

I put my hand on Elle's. The frigging IV was in the way. I bent down and kissed her cheek. I couldn't kiss her mouth because of the endotracheal tube that was sticking out of it like an elephant trunk. "I love you, Peep. I've always loved you. Understand, I can't live without you in this world. Come back to me. Please."

Orderlies, a respiratory tech, and two nurses came through the door. They unlocked the gurney's wheels and pushed Elle and the shitload of life-support equipment.

Left behind at the elevator, I walked around in circles. I had to tell our family, her father and my mother, and I had no idea how. I removed my cell phone from my pocket and stared at the screen alerting me that I had a voice mail from Elle. I held the phone to my ear.

"Hey, it's me." She sighed softly. "Can we do something tonight? Maybe we could take a walk on the beach? Listen, I know we made up afterward, but I am *so sorry* we argued yesterday. Let's spend a little quiet time together this evening, talking and holding hands and . . . I love you *so much*." She paused for a moment and then sounded like she was smiling when she continued. "Give me a call when you get this, and we'll make plans for later, okay? I can't wait to see you! Bye."

I couldn't breathe. Elle. Jesus. She had to be all right. Phil would get in there and the damage wouldn't be as bad as the CAT scan indicated. I started muttering out loud. Elle was brilliant. If anyone could recover from a brain injury, she could. I'd work with her. She was resilient. Maybe I was misreading everything. I held the phone to my ear, listening to her voice again as I followed a current of people back to the ER. Carl was staring at me as I approached. I wanted to look at the CAT scan again. This was insane. *Please, tell me. Tell me it's not as bad as I think.*

"I—I'm not sure what you said before. I guess I'm in shock. What exactly happened?" I asked.

Carl rubbed his forehead. "According to the rescue squad, they picked her up at her brother's house. He's out in the waiting room, by the way. Evidently, she hit her head on a rock after she fell about ten feet off a ladder. Your brother-in-law can probably tell you more about what happened. She had a long seizure on the way in, maybe ten minutes. She was in respiratory arrest when the EMTs got her here. They bagged her. We had trouble tubing her, and she went into a cardiac arrest, but we got her back fairly quickly."

"How long was she here before you called me?"

"Twenty minutes. We were busy, trying to save her," he said.

I swallowed while I tried to gather my thoughts. He wasn't

saying anything encouraging, and the mirage of my denial evaporated. "Where's her CT scan?"

"Phil took it with him."

Right. I'm not thinking clearly. "I have to talk to Elle's brother," I said.

As I turned toward the waiting room, the hospital CEO approached me and stretched out his hand. "Dr. Beaulieu. I heard that your wife is on her way to the OR. I hope it goes well." He hesitated a bit before adding, "I don't know if you're up to it right now, but the press wants a statement."

"The press?"

"The accident was on the police scanners," Carl said. "If Elle McClure is rushed to the hospital, it's news. She's a local celebrity. Maine's like a small town. They remember her from NASA."

For a moment I was still at a loss, then I realized Carl was talking about the Space Shuttle. Elle was an astrophysicist, a college professor now. But four years ago she had actually flown in space and been part of a NASA mission, one which had garnered worldwide attention.

Carl fiddled with his stethoscope and nodded toward the CEO. "Listen, we can't tell them anything, HIPAA laws and all that, but when you're ready—"

"I can't right now. Excuse me." I had to talk to Elle's brother. I pushed my way into the waiting room, a twenty-by-twenty-foot square with plastic benches and a flat screen mounted on the wall. Christopher stood with his back to me, studying the contents of a vending machine. I tugged on his shoulder, and he spun around.

"Matt, finally." Christopher's gaze frantically darted between me and the double doors of the ER. "No one will tell me anything."

"What happened?" I asked.

"Is she all right?"

"Not really. What the hell was she doing on a ladder?"

His mouth hung open for a moment. "Elle dropped by, and Arianne and I were washing windows, and the baby was hungry, so Arianne went inside to nurse her, and Elle said she'd help out, and she took over for Ari on the ladder, and I went back inside, you know, to work on the same window, make sure there were no streaks—and then Elle fainted. But she's going to be okay, right?"

Fainted? The word registered on some back shelf in my mind. I tried to steady my voice and focused on the "Triage" sign hanging above the door. I couldn't look Christopher in the eye as I pictured the CAT scan again. She'd arrested. Given her appearance and the decerebrate posturing, she had significant brain damage. I admitted the unfathomable to Chris and to myself. "No. I don't think she's going to be okay." The room's temperature felt like it dropped forty degrees. "Where's your father?"

"Wait. What do you mean?" Christopher asked.

"It's a bad head injury. Really bad. Where's your father? Does he know she's hurt?"

Christopher shook his head. "But she didn't even fall that far. She cut her head and everything but—you're a neurosurgeon. You can fix her, right? Did you see her? Did you talk to her?"

"She's not conscious," I said, trying to stay composed. "I saw her. I—listen, Phil took her to surgery. Call your father. Tell him to come in." I blinked a few times. "Chris—she probably won't make it."

"What?"

"It's bad." I turned around and walked away.

Maybe it was cold to leave him with the prognosis, but I had someone else to tell. My mother. This would kill her. Or me.

My mother was an obstetrical nurse—had been for almost forty years—but I didn't know if she was working that day. I took the elevator to Labor and Delivery, passed security, waving my hospital

ID, and went to the nurses' station. A couple people recognized me, smiled hellos, and one said, "Hi, Matt. Linney's on break, but I think she's in the lounge."

I turned and beat my way past a laboring mother pushing an IV pole down the hall. She paused, evidently in the grip of a contraction.

Galloping laughter emerged from the nurses' lounge as I pushed open the door. Mom sat at the table, holding a mug of hospital-grade sludge. She took one look at me and stopped short. "Who is it?" she asked.

"Elle. She had a fall." And just like that, I was sobbing in my mother's strong arms. Thirty-seven years old and I might as well have been one of the newborns wailing his first sounds of life. Except this felt more like a death cry.

✦ 2 ✦

The Surgery

I paced the hospital corridors like a video Pac-Man, sweeping each cybersquare, counting the linoleum tiles, cornering and turning when I hit the wall.

My mother walked with me, asking me inane questions like "Why would Elle faint? Has she been sick?"

It didn't matter why—only the result of the fall mattered. "I doubt she fainted. It's more likely Christopher was supposed to be holding the ladder steady, and instead, he went to take a piss."

"Matt, really."

"You know what he's like. He's what, twenty-eight, and he still gets Elle to wash his windows because he's too afraid to climb his own goddamned ladder. Besides, you'd put it past him to walk away when she needed him?"

Mom grabbed my sleeve. "You're upset, and you want someone to blame."

I tugged away as I turned into the next corridor. "The only time Elle's ever fainted was when she hemorrhaged—when we lost

Dylan." Even for someone like me, a doctor, it was astounding how much blood a woman could lose in childbirth when things went wrong. And things went very wrong. "She doesn't faint," I said.

Mom came to a halt. "She passed out in her father's driveway once."

I stopped abruptly and turned toward Mom. "When was this?"

"She was pregnant, before one of the miscarriages, early on. She made me swear not to tell you because she didn't want you to worry. She's not pregnant again, is she?"

I hesitated for a moment before I answered. "No. She isn't." While I resumed pacing, I considered how my mind had yet to assimilate the situation, how for one instant my heart raced again at the possibility of having a child—at the thought of a family—but Elle wasn't pregnant. I wouldn't let her risk her health after the last time. But we'd argued about trying—yesterday—just yesterday.

I'd dismissed the idea with a single syllable. "No." I was good at no. But I could still see Elle standing on the widow's walk. The sun shining on the river backlit her like a halo, making her hair look as white-blond as it did when she was a little girl. Over the years her hair had darkened to the shade of honey, but her eyes were the same green they'd always been, a color that could be as warm as sex or as paralyzing as anger. And she was angry.

I leaned up against the jamb of the attic's doorway, watching her, the sole of her instep, the curve of her bare calf, the way her hip turned slightly toward me, the narrowing of her waist. Even angry she was beautiful, maybe more beautiful. She didn't look much different than she had as a girl, determined and certain of her convictions.

"Life is all about taking chances, or you may as well curl up in a cave." She sighed, then came to me and reached up to touch my face with her fingertips. "I'm sorry. I know that losing the baby devastated you. And me. But we should try. I'm thirty-five, Matt. I don't have forever. I want to try one last time."

Time.

Less than twenty-four hours ago, she wanted me to take a chance. Now time was lost. Elle was lost. I was lost.

After they brought Elle back from the OR, I knew from the expression on Phil's face as he led me into the intensive care unit's on-call room what he was about to tell me. "Matt," he said, steepling his fingers almost as if he were praying for my forgiveness. "I couldn't do much. She had subarachnoid bleeding and shearing." He stopped for a moment to take a breath. "It's a mess. With all the cerebral edema, her brain stem should have herniated. I removed part of her skull, stopped the bleeding, evacuated what hematomas I could get to, but everything from her frontal lobes to her parietal lobes is shot . . ." He rambled on with the details.

I didn't respond. I couldn't.

"After the anesthesia wears off, we should verify brain death," he said. Then he stammered a bit before adding, "I—I can't believe I'm asking you this. But do you . . . well, would she want to be an organ donor?"

I nodded. She'd signed the form on her driver's license; however, it occurred to me Elle's autoimmune issues might disqualify her.

"I'll take care of talking to the New England Organ Donor Bank," he said.

I tried to compose myself as I yanked open the on-call room door. I needed to see Elle. Even though I understood the traumatic damage, my wife was not like any other patient to me. I couldn't see this as a clinical situation. Phil could lay out the most wretched scenario, but they were only words. Hell, I'd reported the same ones to families more times than I cared to recall.

I was collapsing inward, like one of those black holes Elle spent so much time studying. Had studied. Her existence, in the most pragmatic of ways, had ceased. The proof: Phil's surgical report, a CAT scan, and my wife's flaccid form stretched out in the intensive care bed in front of me. I stared from the doorway as nurses adjusted her monitor wires, set her IV pumps, and cleaned away the antiseptic from her shaven head.

I gathered a breath, bracing myself against the inevitable. There is no definitive test for brain death. Doppler flows, corneal reflexes, apnea testing, a series of criteria, physical responses—or her lack thereof—are what we use to establish it. I stood, a little wobbly, but somehow I stood, barely drawing air. I needed time before I could accept this. Elle had no other significant injuries. Why hadn't she smashed an arm or a leg? Even if she'd broken her back or her neck. Why did it have to be her head that hit the rock?

Phil's hand on my shoulder startled me. "Do you want me to talk to your family?"

"No. I'll go to them in a minute." What was another minute or another year? At least for now, they had hope. Hearing his report would end everything. I slipped in and took Elle's hand. It was so cold. They hadn't bothered to take off her wedding band down in the OR. At least that much of me was with her while Phil operated.

"Excuse me," one of the nurses said. "I have to check her IV."

I backed into the corner of the room by the wash sink. I slipped off my own ring and read the inscription. *My love, my life, Peep.* I placed it back on my finger and stumbled down the corridor to the ICU's waiting room.

I paused before entering. Our families were inside—correction: our family. The plural had changed to the singular when Elle and I married. Not that there had ever been much differentiation between the Beaulieus and the McClures. Elle and I grew up in side-by-side Victorian houses, and both families passed easily from one kitchen into the other. At either place we were home.

And now our family was sitting in the ICU waiting room. Elle's father, Hank; her brother, Christopher, and his wife, Arianne. And my mother. I had to tell them we had lost Elle. One by one, their eyes found me standing in the doorway. Her father drew his fist to his mouth. Christopher jumped up. And my mother drew a hesitant breath then fell forward, folding onto her own lap, and she wept silently. My mother loved Elle; she had always loved Elle.

I sat beside Mom and rubbed her back. Emotionally, I was in a sensory deprivation chamber or in a tunnel with no light, and I didn't believe I'd ever see light again.

Words dribbled out of me, slowly at first, mechanical words, rehearsed words, a mere substitution of Elle's name for some other poor schmuck's. "Elle suffered a devastating and irreparable brain injury. It damaged her center for consciousness. She won't wake up. She signed the organ-donor box on her driver's license." I watched their faces, grappling with the news. "After the anesthesia wears off, two doctors will determine if she meets brain-death criteria; the odds are she will, and if her autoimmune issues don't disqualify her as a donor, well, she'd want to donate her organs. The donor team will probably come within the next twenty-four hours."

Christopher shook his head, whimpering, "No. No. It has to be a mistake."

My father-in-law stared at me, disbelief leaking from his every pore. "You're not going to do anything about it, to save her?"

"I can't. No one can." I stammered inside my own denial of the evidence.

"People come out of comas," Hank stated with such assurance it sounded like a truth.

"She won't. It's not exactly a coma. Comas usually stem from more localized injuries. Not that they aren't serious, but Elle suffered a massive head injury." My voice faltered. My mother took my hand in hers as I continued. "Elle wouldn't want to live like that anyway. There's profound damage to almost every part of her brain."

"You're going to give up? I won't allow it." Hank pounded the arm of his chair.

I stared at a corner of the ceiling. "This isn't giving up. And it isn't something we allow or disallow. I wish it were. I'm going to sit with her. If anyone else wants to come in—to say good-bye—give the nurses a half hour to settle her first."

"Oh my God." Christopher was shaking like he was going to collapse, and his wife put her arm around him.

Hank bolted over and blocked the doorway as I stood to leave. "There's no way you're going to let my daughter die. I'll get a court order."

When I tried to sidestep him, he slammed me up against the wall. His breath smelled of whiskey. How the hell had he gotten liquor at the hospital? More to the point, when had he fallen off the wagon? As far as I knew, he'd been sober for the last twenty years. But it didn't matter. I didn't know when he'd started drinking again, and I didn't really give a shit.

I grabbed his wrists and yanked them away from my shoulders. "I'm not *letting* her do anything. If there was *anything* I could do, I would. I love her, but the second she fell, it was too late. And she didn't want to die the way her mother did, and you know it."

My mother pushed her way between us like a referee in a contentious prizefight. "Come on, Hank, sit down. Matt's right. Elle made a living will—years ago. After Alice passed away. As soon as Elle turned eighteen."

Mom always thought fast on her feet, and this sounded like something Elle would have done, but Mom was lying. Elle let everyone know she believed her father had mishandled her mother's illness, but she would have told me if she'd made an advanced health care directive. Still, I was grateful for my mother's fabrication.

My mother sniffed. "God, have you been drinking?" she asked Hank, her voice rife with frustration.

He shook his head. "Just one."

Mom's eyes filled with pity or anger, hard to tell which, and she spun away from him.

"Dad!" Christopher said. "What are you doing? Jesus Christ. Call your sponsor. We'll go find you a meeting."

For a second I saw Elle in Christopher's eyes—the way she always tried to keep her father under control—and then it was gone. Hank swooped up his suit jacket and stormed past his son. Christopher retreated and became a man-child again, sitting next to his wife. I wondered how he would ever survive without Elle to take care of him.

I wondered how I would.

Even when the nursing staff was not in Elle's room, they could see inside because instead of Sheetrock there was a glass wall between Elle and the nurses' station. In the past, and from the detached perspective of a physician, I'd thought of ICU rooms as fishbowls, but now the fishbowl metaphor seemed more darkly apt than I'd ever considered. Somehow, I pictured Elle floating to the top, belly-up and lost, or maybe it was me there, disembodied and displaced. I couldn't focus or make sense of anything. Cognitive dissonance had taken over. I kept whispering to Elle and begging her to wake up. I knew what was happening. I could not accept it even though every prop tethered me to this unreality. One minute I was looking at Elle's intracranial pressure monitor, and the next my mind shot into fantastical asides like—fishbowls.

Supposedly, right before you die, your life flashes before your eyes. I wondered what Elle was thinking about, the best way to keep the streaks off the windows? Should she spray Windex directly on the storm window or on the paper towel? Her legacy: the streakless window.

Or was she thinking about us?

Grief has stages, five if you buy into the Kübler-Ross worldview: denial, bargaining, depression, anger, and acceptance. For me, the first four were superimposed upon one another, but I wasn't close to accepting anything. Currently, anger took top billing, anger at her, anger at her brother. I couldn't even begin to tell anyone how angry I was at Hank. Fury. Blind raging fury. I would have put my fist through the wall, a fucking glass wall, but some level of reason persisted. They would have made me leave the intensive care unit—leave Elle. They would have had to kill me to do it, of course, but that had its appeal; I'd be dead then, too.

On the exterior wall, the ICU's double-paned window overlooked the ER's ambulance bay and it didn't open, which was a good thing since I was considering the best way to kill myself. *Shake it off, Matt. The window's not high enough to jump out of anyway.*

The sun vacated the sky, and the full moon was making a stealthy appearance up high. *Come on, Matt, find a loophole. Some miracle surgery, some drug regimen no one has ever considered. Find a frigging innovation, and save Elle.* I'd put in twenty years of education and seven more of indentured servitude to the medical community. For that, I needed restitution. I was desperate for a stroke of genius that would bring Elle back to me.

A deep void was beginning to replace my anger, and deflated, I paced the ICU cubical, occasionally glancing out through the glass walls to the nurses' station. I didn't know what I expected to see. Elle, maybe. The body lying on the bed wasn't really my brilliant wife. Her clever mind. Her compassionate heart. I took her hand

in mine and sat in the tangerine leatherette chair at her bedside.
Please, wake up.

After a while I flipped the little television onto CNN. Another
story about the debacle in Iraq followed a story about an earth-
quake in Peru. Just when I reached to shut it off, Elle's picture
popped onto the screen. One from a NASA celebration. She was
dressed to the nines in a spaghetti-strapped peach dress that fit
her like she was born in it. Her hair was longer then, down to her
midback, and she looked more like a Hollywood ingenue than the
hard-core scientist she was. *Was?* I'd used the past tense.

I upped the volume.

"Former astronaut Elle McClure is in a Maine hospital this evening after an accident. A spokesman for the family released the
following statement: 'Elle McClure Beaulieu is in intensive care
pending the results of tests. Her family requests prayers on her
behalf.'"

I had not requested anything. I'd made no statement nor authorized anyone to do so. Video of her EVA, or space walk in layman's
terms, popped up on the screen.

"You may recall that Dr. McClure rescued fellow astronaut
Andre Jabert on the 2004 mission to upgrade the Hubble Telescope. A micrometeorite penetrated Jabert's space suit, and
McClure pulled him into the shuttle before his suit fully depressurized. His injury forced *Atlantis* to make an emergency landing,
but Jabert survived and has flown on a subsequent NASA flight.
McClure left NASA four months later and returned to her home-
town to marry neurosurgeon Matthew Beaulieu. She currently
teaches at Bowdoin College and consults at both MIT and NASA."

The press kept obituaries prepared for all people of note. They'd
pulled hers and read it.

"She *did* teach. Get it right. It's all past tense now," I mumbled,
switching off the TV.

I spotted Elle's OB/GYN standing beside the nurses' station, talking to Phil. I nodded in acknowledgment.

I couldn't concentrate, and I resumed thinking about death by carbon-monoxide poisoning, death by Vicodin overdose, or death by blowing my brains out—one of which would occur after I buried Elle. I was also considering ways to make my suicide look like an accident, considering whether that might be easier on our family.

The thing was, I could almost hear Elle sneering at me. "It is always consoling to think of suicide: in that way one gets through many a bad night." She'd been fond of quoting Nietzsche; at least she often cited his less misogynistic lines. She picked and chose. Come to think of it, she didn't like his atheism either. Those lines were mine to banter around, particularly on the rare occasion she headed off to church early on a Sunday morning and I wanted to sleep in.

Where was God now?

Equipment rolled up to the doorway, but I didn't glance up again until I heard my name.

"Matt? Can I come in?" Blythe Clarke, Elle's high-risk OB, stood before me, shrugging into her lab coat. As always, Blythe wore a pink ribbon in her otherwise stark white hair.

I would have preferred to endure torture than make small talk. I was afraid the next time anyone said he was sorry I'd punch him—or her—in the nose. Still, I murmured, "Sure."

To my surprise, she pushed a portable ultrasound machine to Elle's bedside.

I narrowed my eyes, wondering what the hell Blythe was doing. Elle had not sustained any other significant injuries. Phil stood at the doorway as Blythe set Elle's chart on top of the machine then pulled up a stool next to my chair. "You know we run pregnancy tests on all female trauma patients."

"She isn't." I pinched the bridge of my nose. Aside from that moment or two with my mother, I'd held myself together. I couldn't waste these last hours with Elle crying. There would be time later.

"Actually, the pregnancy test in the ER was positive," Blythe said. "And the beta hCG indicates she's close to eight weeks along."

Phil cleared his throat. "Somehow we overlooked it before we took her to the OR. I don't know how that happened."

"No. She can't be," I said, remembering the pregnancy test beneath the bathroom sink, the one she bought last month, the one she didn't take because her period started on her way home from the store. That was only a couple of weeks ago. Besides, we'd been careful.

"Has she been taking the baby aspirin?" Blythe asked.

"Yes." After Elle's third miscarriage, Blythe figured out that Elle kept losing babies because she had an autoimmune disorder. Aspirin really is a miracle drug; it even treated Elle's APS.

Blythe passed me the lab printout.

I gripped the paper. Elle *was* pregnant. "Seriously? She had a period a couple of weeks ago. This isn't a mix-up?" I asked.

"Maybe she had breakthrough bleeding, and that's why you didn't know. I want to do an ultrasound to see if there's a fetal heartbeat. After what's transpired today, there's a good chance she may have miscarried."

I raked my hair, still flummoxed.

Blythe beckoned a nurse, who closed the drapes and bedside curtains, darkening the room. Then Blythe took a wandlike ultrasound probe and covered it with a sterile cot and transducer gel. "Matt, I need to do an internal exam. Do you want to leave?"

"No, but, Phil, do you mind?"

He ducked away.

The nurse, barely out of college, raised Elle's right thigh and draped her perineum. Blythe inserted the probe into Elle's vagina.

Anxiety jacked up my heart rate. How many X-rays were done that day? How many teratogenic drugs did the emergency room pump into Elle? What might that have done to a developing fetus? At the same time I remembered reading a journal article about one brain-dead woman who carried a baby to a good outcome and I wondered if it was possible.

"There," Blythe said, pointing at the monitor. "A heartbeat."

I narrowed my eyes and approached the ultrasound machine. The little flicker on the screen fortified me. "She's really pregnant."

"I'd say about eight weeks is right." Blythe pointed, marked it, and saved the results to the hard drive. Drawing a deep breath, she turned to me. "I can make some phone calls to find out how this would work. I've never treated this kind of situation but, at a conference, one of the presenters talked about a case. The family didn't know the woman was pregnant until after a motorcycle accident. She stayed in a persistent vegetative state throughout the pregnancy and still delivered a healthy baby."

I remembered to breathe only after stars started bouncing around the periphery of my vision. "Given Elle's history . . . do you think it's possible?"

"Maybe." Blythe shrugged. "Phil said her pituitary gland and hypothalamus looked okay. So if the injury didn't destroy her pituitary, her body should be able to regulate her hormone levels, maintain her body temperature. But I don't know, Matt. It's hard to say."

"She's been pregnant four times; she's never gone to term."

"The last one was close. The reason the baby died had nothing to do with anything that we'd expect to recur."

The blood drained from my head, remembering Baby Dylan's lifeless body in my arms.

Blythe rested her hand on my shoulder. "I'm not trying to tell you what you to do. But I do think you should have all the facts before you decide to withdraw Elle's life support."

✦ 3 ✦

After the Surgery

Mom entered Elle's hospital room carrying two cups of coffee and a bag with sandwiches from a shop across the street. I set it aside. For some reason, people try to fill you with food when you're filled with grief. I didn't need food. I needed a reason to keep living.

"You have to eat, Matthew."

I shrugged and continued to stare out the window, agonizing about what Elle would want me to do.

Mom set the sandwich on my lap again and turned toward Elle. "Do you think she's in pain?"

"No. She's . . ." Elle was brain-dead. She wasn't experiencing anything anymore, and I was so lonely for her that nothing could ever take up the hollow space she'd left vacant.

Mom bent down and kissed Elle's cheek. "Do you think she might still be able to hear us?"

"No." Her temporal lobes, the parts of the brain which hear, were saturated with enough blood to create their own Red Sea. She couldn't hear. Or see. Or act. And still I'd spent most of the last hour whispering to Elle and asking her what she wanted me to do.

Touching my shoulder gently, Mom said, "It's late. Let me drive you home."

"I can't."

My mother pulled up a chair beside mine, in the already crowded space between the bed and the wall. "It took me hours and hours to leave when your father passed away. But she's not here, if what you said is right—that she's brain-dead—she's not here anymore. You don't have to stay."

I didn't want to start crying. Not about Elle. Not about Dad. Yet the mention of his name nearly undid me. And the longevity of grief, the endlessness of it, settled into my future reality. Besides, I was hoping Elle's spirit lingered nearby, even though I didn't believe in bullshit like that. "Listen, Mom, you can go. I'm fine," I said flatly.

I could feel it in her exhalation, her desire to do what mothers do. She wanted to take me away from this sadness, but she couldn't fix this.

Probably in an attempt to remove me from this place, if not physically, emotionally—to pull me into memory, to a happier time—Mom said, "I keep thinking about when Alice and Hank brought Elle home from the hospital when she was a baby."

I nodded, not paying my mother much heed. Elle would probably miscarry, but everything she'd ever said about being pregnant and babies screamed she'd want me to try. In fact, almost everything she'd ever said indicated that.

Almost. Elle didn't want to live in a vegetative state, but at the same time she had risked her life for things she deemed bigger than herself—like on the Space Shuttle.

Mom reminisced. "Her mother put Elle in my arms—well, in

your arms, Matt, because you were sitting on my lap. You don't remember it by any chance, do you?"

"I was two and a half. How could I?" Although I'd heard the story enough times, how I had held Elle when she was just three days old.

"We thought you were deaf. Did you know that?" Mom was talking to herself as much as she was to me. She needed to distract herself from Elle's condition, too.

"You thought I was autistic." My pediatrician said something was profoundly wrong with me because, until the day the Mc-Clures brought their new baby over, I'd never spoken. My parents had taken me to a dozen specialists, none of whom could find a damn thing wrong with me other than I didn't speak.

Mom wiped a tear from her cheek. "I didn't believe any of it. I knew you'd be fine, and when Elle started cooing, you said, 'Peep.' You called her Peep for the longest time. Until you two started dating."

I nodded. Sometimes I still called her Peep, usually as a term of endearment, rarely in front of anyone else. I twisted my wedding band. *My love, my life, Peep.*

"Your father said you couldn't stand being upstaged by the little baby girl."

"It was probably more like I'd been waiting around for her to show up. I can't imagine this world without her in it." I shuddered, on the brink of crying.

My mother nodded. "Me either. It seems impossible, Matt, but you do go on. I did after your father died. You will, too."

"She's pregnant," I said.

My mother's eyes widened. "Pregnant?"

I nodded. "It looks like eight weeks, but we didn't know. She hadn't missed her period."

"Oh my goodness. That *is* why she fainted, then."

"Maybe." I shook my head, thinking the pregnancy had done this to her. By getting her pregnant again, *I* had done this to Elle. "I found out a couple of hours ago. Part of the trauma workup."

"I'm sorry, honey." Mom put her hand on mine. "Too many losses."

"Blythe Clarke thinks it might be possible to save—the baby. She's on the phone, talking to perinatologists all over the country. A couple of similar situations made it to term."

"Matt—Matt, you can't be serious. There is *no way* Elle would want to be kept alive like this."

"I haven't made a decision yet, but I think she'd want me to try," I said.

Mom blinked rapidly. "She signed a living will."

I leaned forward. "I thought you were bullshitting about that."

"No, she signed one. Don't you remember how much she hated that they kept her mother going for so long?"

"I know, Mom, but Alice had cancer and was suffering. Elle's not in pain. Don't you think she would want the baby to live?"

Mom squeezed her eyes shut, then a moment later covered her face with her hands. "If it means staying on life support for months? No, I don't. I can't let what happened to Alice happen to Elle. Oh my God, it's not even reasonable to think this pregnancy could succeed. She's had so many miscarriages."

"That was because of the APS. It's treatable."

Mom pressed her lips together and drew in a deep breath. "Honey, you treated it last time, and you still lost the baby."

"Not from the APS."

"But he still died." Mom reached out and took my hand. "I'm so sorry, but he did. And it almost killed Elle. I think it almost killed you. I don't want you to get your hopes up just to have them crushed again. Let Elle go peacefully."

"She'd want me to save the baby."

Mom stood, looked out the window, and sighed. "It's too early. Are you sure *you* don't want to save a piece of Elle?"

"Of course I do, but I'm pretty certain she would want me to put the baby first."

Mom shook her head. "It's hardly a baby at this point. Matt, for heaven's sake, you don't even call it a fetus until it's eight weeks."

I glared at my mother. I did not need a lesson in embryology.

"I know," she said. "My heart is breaking. And I'd do anything if I thought we could bring Elle back. You're shattered, but try to put on your doctor's hat. What do you think the odds are that she could carry a pregnancy now when she never could before? A hundred to one, a thousand? I love her. She's like my daughter, you know that. I want her to wake up and—" Mom's voice broke. "And that isn't going to happen. Letting go is hard. But she made me promise I'd never let anyone do this to her."

"She's my wife."

"I'm well aware, but you're grieving, and you aren't thinking straight." My mother's expression conveyed regret but also absolute immovability.

Panic rose in my gut, not because I was afraid of my mother, but because she is the most relentlessly stubborn person I've ever known. "When did Elle sign this thing? Where is it? Doesn't it say something about pregnancy?" I asked.

"It was a long time ago. I don't remember that specifically, but I'll dig it out and take a look."

Blythe Clarke returned to the room, stopping short when she saw the stern expression on my mother's face. "Hello, Linney. Matt, I have more information when you're ready."

I stood and stepped around my mother's chair. "Go ahead, Blythe. I told Mom Elle's pregnant."

Blythe pulled a PDA device from her lab-coat pocket. "The

pregnancy looks viable so far. The outcome will depend on how stable they can keep Elle."

"But she's only eight weeks now?" Mom asked.

"Yes," Blythe said.

Mom squeezed her eyes shut. "I can't let you do this to Elle. Not for months and months." Mom reached for her purse. "I'll be back in a couple of hours," she said. As she exited the room, she moved so fast I felt like I was in the ebb of a semi traveling down the highway.

Blythe stared at me. "What does she mean?"

"Tell me what you learned first."

She hesitated a moment before she replied. "I found about a dozen anecdotal cases. I can't make any promises. It's August. If we can keep her alive until Christmas, the baby will be twenty-six weeks."

"That's awfully premature."

"Yes. I'd like to see her make it to February, but by Christmas, the baby would be small, but most likely it would live; it would have a chance anyway."

I pictured the NICU and the preemies there, not mini, chubby-cheeked versions of the full-term variety, but sick little things, thin-skinned and struggling. "My mother said Elle had a living will or an advanced health care directive. I never heard about this until now."

"Hmm . . ." Blythe furrowed her brow as if she were puzzled. "I'm on call tonight, so I'll be around. You can page me anytime. Otherwise I'll stop by in the morning."

"Okay," I said as she walked away.

Lost in my thoughts, I must not have noticed my brother Mike walking up the hall. He said, "How is she? I raced over here as soon as I heard."

"Come in if you want," I said.

He glanced down at his grease-stained mechanic overalls. "How bad is it?"

Unable to find words, I shuddered.

Mike grabbed me and pulled me into a hug as if I were a little kid. And he started to cry.

"Come on," I said, taking his elbow. I led him out of the room. Even if Elle couldn't hear us, I couldn't say "brain-dead" in front of her. While we walked down the long hospital corridor, I told him Elle was pregnant.

He blew out air like the wind had been knocked out of him. "But months? Are you sure you'd want to do this for months?"

"There's a chance. So yes, I guess I am. Yes. I'm certain we should try," I said, not at all certain about anything except that I felt devastated.

✦ 4 ✦

Day 2

In the morning when Phil entered the hospital room, I straightened and rubbed the kink in my neck as my partner performed a neuro exam on Elle. Periodically, I'd checked her pupils and reflexes during the night. She hadn't improved, and as a doctor, I did not expect a miracle. As a husband, I wanted her back, so I kept looking for a glimmer of hope.

"Melanie's outside," he said. "She'd like to sneak in and see Elle."

I nodded. Although the Longfellow Memorial's ICU usually enforced the family-only visitation policy, something told me the nurses wouldn't balk when the neurosurgeon's wife broke the rules. "Tell her to come in."

Phil went to the door and beckoned. When Mel entered, she looked as if she might cry, but instead she swallowed hard and opened her arms wide to me. "I'm so sorry," she said. She held on for longer and tighter than would normally feel comforting, and still I wished she wouldn't let go. She offered what little comfort was within her power. Was I hungry? Did I need anything from home? What about clean clothes?

Mel sat next to Elle and took Phil's hand as if she needed his strength. "Phil says you can't hear me, but . . . Oh God . . ." Her lower lip quivered and she looked up at Phil. "Isn't there something you can do?"

Phil seemed to deflate and shook his head.

Melanie pressed the back of her hand to her mouth for a moment. "Okay, listen, Elle, we love you. Don't want you to worry about Matt—or any of us. We'll watch out for him. I promise." Mel stood abruptly and folded herself into Phil's arms.

An hour later Christopher came into the hospital room. Shaken, he had declined to see Elle the previous day.

"Hey," he said as if we were tossing a baseball back and forth, then his jaw tightened. "They shaved her head."

"For the surgery," I said.

His eyes shifted to the floor. "This isn't fair."

Fair? The statement was so typical of Christopher, but this wasn't a playground with referees.

"It never occurred to me that she might faint," he said.

"You want me to absolve you and say, 'Christopher, these things happen'? Okay. Accidents do happen. But this one wouldn't have if you'd gone up on your own goddamned ladder."

He grabbed the bed's footboard. "Heights never bothered her. She's never afraid of anything."

I shook my head and led him out of the room. Elle couldn't hear me. She couldn't hear her brother, or any of us, but at any second I might blast Christopher for being such a pansy that he had to ask his big sister to act as his handyman. And I didn't want her to see me beat the shit out of her precious Christopher.

Elle.

I stopped in the hallway and looked back through the glass wall at her stilled body, her eyes closed, swollen from the surgery and the fall. Even if she could open them, she couldn't see me.

No wonder my patients' families struggled with denial. I understood the physiology of Elle's injuries. And none of this made sense to me. I couldn't grasp the shift in my world.

"Matt? Did you hear me?"

I turned toward Christopher and shook my head. "What?"

"Why did you drag me out here?"

For a second grief overpowered my anger and then, like a demon, my rage resurfaced. "It's not true that Elle was never afraid. She just hid her fears better than most people."

"What was she afraid of besides ending up like my mom?"

I stared at him for a moment. Elle was afraid of a slow death. How the hell could I even consider keeping her on life support? Because, I told myself, she was willing to risk her life to have a baby. "Not realizing her dreams."

"It's not the same." His mouth tightened, and he avoided my gaze. "She was only afraid of dying like my mom. What time are they going to turn off the machines? I—I should be here."

"They aren't. I changed my mind."

"Why? Did Phil think of something that could save her?" Christopher's eyes widened, and hope fell across his face like sun breaking out of a storm cloud.

Oh God, I wished I could reach out and grab a fistful of his blissful ignorance. I shook my head. "There isn't anything anyone can do."

His mouth tightened, and he seemed to search the corridor, my face, and then the palms of his hands, which he then pressed against his eyes. "My dad wasn't making any sense yesterday. He never did when he was drinking."

I shuffled my restless feet, remembering the days when Hank

was falling apart, when Chris was barely eight, their mother was dying, and Elle thought she had to carry the lot on her young shoulders. "I'm kind of surprised you even remember your father's drinking days," I said. Hank had been sober for a long time—at least until yesterday.

"I was old enough. You'd be surprised what I remember. You can't make Elle go through what my mom did."

I peered through the glass at Elle again, horrified by my decision to keep her on life support. "It's not the same. She isn't in pain. And she's—pregnant. If we can keep her stable long enough, we can save the baby."

His jaw dropped. "What? Not again. How many times now? Four? Five pregnancies?" He clenched his hands as if he wanted to strangle someone, me, most likely. "Damn it. I told you last time you'd better not get her pregnant again. She almost died last time." He turned toward the room. Chris started shaking with anger or grief.

I didn't know what to say, so I said nothing because this time she'd suffered brain death. Because of me.

It was rare for Christopher to act protectively of Elle. She was seven years older. But after her last pregnancy he pulled me aside. At the time I'd agreed with Chris. Trying to have a baby again would be too risky.

"She didn't tell me she was pregnant," Chris said.

"We didn't even know. It's early."

"Are you saying we'd have to keep her on life support for nine months? I don't think so. Elle didn't want that. I don't want that. I already watched my mom die that way."

He took off down the hall, blasting through the ICU double doors with me in pursuit. He was halfway to the elevator when I grabbed his arm. "This isn't about what you want, Chris. It's about Elle. It's about the family she wanted."

"Wait, you're making me feel guilty because Elle fell off the ladder, but you got her pregnant again? Asshole!"

The elevator doors opened and my own mother strode off, looking a bit frazzled. Tendrils of her gray hair fell around her face. "Christopher, honey." She kissed his cheek, then quickly turned her attention to me. "I found it, Matt. It took me half the night, but here it is." She passed me a form, a fill-in-the-blank living will, named as such, not titled "An Advanced Directive."

I scanned it quickly. It actually had boxes to check.

Do you want to have a respirator to help you breathe if you are unable to do so?

Yes ☐
No ☒

Do you want the use of a feeding tube if you are unable to eat?

Yes ☐
No ☒

It had no pregnancy clause. *Shit*.

Elle's teenaged handwriting crossed the page with negative responses to every single question. In one simple sentence she wrote, "I do not want to ever be kept on life support unless it is likely I will recover." Then her signature stretched across the bottom, all the loopy *L*s and *E*s. Making matters worse, Elle had taken the time and the effort to get the document notarized.

I rubbed my eyes and tried to unearth a memory. In the ER after Dylan's birth, did the hospital ask Elle if she had an advanced directive? It was policy for them to ask. Wouldn't I have paid attention if she'd said yes? Then again, I was probably too preoccupied by our son's lifeless body. I'd have to check the medical records. "It doesn't matter," I said. "This is too old. Her legal status must have changed when we got married. I'm her husband, her next of kin."

"Matthew, you have to know a living will isn't about next of kin and it has nothing to do with marital status. It's about who she designated, and that's me," Mom said.

"What do you mean?"

Mom flipped the paper over and there on the back Elle authorized my mother to make any more specific decisions if Elle could not make them for herself. This document gave Mom Elle's medical power of attorney.

I held my hand up in an effort to stop her. "Ah, no. Elle's pregnant. You know how much she'd want a baby," I said.

"I'm with Linney," Christopher said.

"We're not taking a vote here." I crumpled the living will.

"Give that to me," my mother said.

I held it tight in my fist, wondering how far this situation might devolve. My mother scolding me as if I were a two-year-old? Me stomping my foot? At some point one would think we could move past these dynamics where she thought she could give me the eye and I would fold.

"We're not going to keep her on life support. I'm paging the nursing supervisor," Mom said.

"Why do you need a nursing supervisor?" I asked. Jesus, I didn't want this to become something which would cause hospital gossip.

"Because Elle picked me to watch out for her, and you are seriously considering keeping her on life support, and that's not what Elle wanted. It's just wrong to keep her in this state, as an incubator for something that isn't even a baby yet. Women are more than vessels for offspring."

My heart was pounding in my chest so hard I was seeing spots. "She's not an incubator. She's the baby's mother."

"Honey. Be realistic," Mom said, her voice noticeably less combative. "It's barely a fetus, and even if it were further along in its development, God knows what kinds of things happened to it yesterday. The CT? The X-rays of her back? The drugs? You aren't thinking straight. You're too upset." Mom held out her hand, palm upward, waiting for me to pass the living will back to her.

I didn't.

I was certain Elle had never considered this scenario. "I know all that, and I am worried about the X-rays and medications, but—"

"But nothing," Christopher said. "Stop it. You're not going to keep her alive." He turned and marched off.

My mother touched my arm, and I withdrew.

Elle's nurse was staring at us as we barreled up to the nurses' station.

"Get the nursing supervisor. I want to talk to her. I want to talk to the CEO, and the hospital attorneys. I need the ethics committee to convene. I want to talk to the head of Medical Records. Now," I said.

The nurse paled.

"Never mind," I said. "I'll make the calls."

Five minutes into the ethics committee's meeting, the hospital chairman, attorney, and pastoral council were embroiled in a heated debate. My mother slapped the crinkled document on the table. "The purpose of the living will is to avoid this sort of thing."

"In Maine," the hospital attorney, who was a pudgy guy with ears that stuck out like butterfly wings, said, "whatever a patient states when he has capacity—in other words, when he can speak for himself—overrules *anything* else."

I pulled out Elle's medical records from our son's birth. "But

right here, they asked her if she had an advanced health care directive. She said no."

"Well, she did. Obviously." Mom tapped the living will.

"Elle signed that half her life ago," I said. "She never would have
considered these particular circumstances."

"And how would you know? She wouldn't even speak to you at
that point," Mom said.

It was true. For a few years, when Elle and I were in college, we
were not on speaking terms. "She changed her mind about me,
and about a lot of other things, too. It was seventeen years ago," I
yelled.

The hospital CEO stood. "Stop. The hospital is not going to
take the liability for this decision, not when it's in dispute. I don't
know what the legality is on this."

"It really isn't about what the family wants or doesn't want,"
the attorney said. "It's about what this patient wanted. That's the
bottom line. What concerns me is that we have two conflicting
documents."

The CEO drew a deep breath and said, "Get a judge to decide.
Get a court order."

✦ 5 ✦

Day 2

I pulled out the business card: *Jake Sutter, Attorney.* The previous spring Elle and I ran into Jake in a movie-theater lobby. He handed me his card and said, "Give me a call. We should get together for a drink soon." Until yesterday, when I had to search for our insurance information, I'd forgotten I'd stuffed his card in my wallet.

Telling his receptionist I was Jake's college roommate yielded an appointment in a week's time. Telling her I was Elle's husband fared better: one minute on hold, and then straight through.

"Matt? Holy smokes. I heard the news. How is she?" Jake asked.

"Not good." I lunged into the story and talked for five minutes before I stopped for air. "I'm not sure how to handle this, legally, that is."

A moment of silence preceded his words. "I do know how to handle it, but first, let me tell you how sorry I am about Elle. Yvette wanted me to reach out to you last night when the news broke, but I thought you'd be at the hospital, and it sounds like you haven't left Elle's side."

"No," I said, "except when I attended the ethics committee's meeting."

"What the hospital's attorney said is right to some degree. A judge will want to determine what Elle would want under the circumstances," he said. "This could be tricky, but I know exactly what to do. When can you come to my office? I'll clear my schedule." As always, Jake thought he knew everything, and this time I hoped he was right.

"I don't want to leave her. Can you come here instead?"

"Ah . . ." He gulped. "This isn't something we could discuss easily in a hospital room."

Damn, I'd almost forgotten how much he hated hospitals, and I didn't have time to deal with his medical phobias.

Jake and I landed in the same college dorm room because someone putting freshmen together that year thought geography would give us something in common, but we didn't have much beyond that. Jake was the son of a former Maine governor, and I was the son of a blue-collar worker from one town over. His neighborhood was considerably more upscale than mine. Nevertheless, we were both ambitious, so although we were never buddies, we were compatible as roommates. We kept in touch for a while afterward, but once I was in med school, I found it difficult to talk to him. If I so much as said the word *blood*, he turned a little green and he said if God wanted us to see blood, He wouldn't have given us skin.

"Look, this involves a slew of medical issues," I said. "If it isn't something you're comfortable with, can you give me a name of someone who—"

"Come on, Matt. My job is not at the bedside. I'll be in the courtroom. Yeah, hospitals set me on edge. All those people complaining and the smells and— When my wife was in labor with Janey . . . I couldn't stand to see her like that, suffering. Maybe I'm too sensitive. So no, I don't like hospitals. I don't know how you do it. But I can deal with the verbal and written part."

On a different day, at a different place and time, I would have laughed at the way he characterized himself. He truly thought he was a righteous man, but whenever people told me they were "too sensitive" to take care of someone injured or sick, the hypocrisy drove me crazy. I was a pragmatist with a do-something-about-it approach—help people instead of looking away—but for this situation it didn't matter if Jake was sensitive or not. I didn't need him to hold Elle's hand, or mine for that matter. I needed someone with the expertise to beat my mother in court. "Jake—"

"Shoot, you're my friend. Under the circumstances I'll come there. How about this?" he said. "Find a place where we can talk freely—a waiting room—no, an office would be better. I'll walk you through what you'll need to know going forward. No obligation. Feel free to consult another attorney. I'll tell you what questions you should ask, but no one else in Portland has the experience I have."

Although Jake never suffered from modesty, in this he was understating his platform. I doubted anyone else in Portland, Maine, had argued cases in front of the Supreme Court of the United States. "Okay," I said.

I arranged for the use of a conference room off the ICU. At ten past seven, he walked in minus his usual strut, wearing a hand-tailored suit, Italian shoes, and a bead of sweat on his upper lip.

"Have a seat." I laid the photocopy of Elle's living will before him. "And here's a copy of her hospital admission record from last winter."

He positioned himself at the head of the wood-grained laminate table and exhaled. "Last winter?"

"We lost a baby in February. He was stillborn."

Jake stared at me for a moment before he made what I first

thought was a lame attempt to sound sympathetic. "Matt. You've been through—"

I cut him off without even looking up. "Elle initialed the box, stating she didn't have an advanced directive. See here?" I pointed at her scrawled letters on the hospital form. For the first time I really looked at her penmanship. I wasn't a handwriting expert, but even I could see how weak she was when she'd put her mark there. She was so out of it that night that she might not have known what she was signing.

Jake shifted in his seat and his eyes weighed me. "You doing okay?"

I glanced at him for a second, nodded, and then averted my gaze. I couldn't cope with another layer of grief even if he was willing to listen.

Respectfully, he moved to the other piece of paper. "Even though this says 'living will,' it's not exactly. A living will is an isolated set of instructions. It falls under the category of advanced directives, but its scope is narrow, a set of instructions the patient wrote with no margin for unforeseen circumstances. Elle gave a set of instructions, yes, but she also gave your mother her durable power of attorney for health care. So this so-called living will falls under the broader category of an advanced directive. The important thing is that Elle made certain choices for herself, but she also designated someone else to make decisions, which were not covered on the form. That says to the court Elle recognized some circumstances could not be anticipated, and she trusted your mother to act on her behalf. Now, I have to tell you some things you aren't going to want to hear."

I pulled out a chair and dropped onto it. "You don't think I have a case."

"You've got a case. A very big case. The thing is you're a private guy, and this *won't* stay private. Reporters have set up camp outside the hospital already, and it will get worse because this could knock the block off *Roe v. Wade*."

"How? This isn't about abortion."

"Not to you. To you this is about your wife and your unborn child, something that is highly personal. Legally, though, it is about the rights of an unborn baby versus his mother's, and that will have far-reaching implications. Right to life. Right to die. Rights of the unborn. *Roe v. Wade*. But let's put that aside right now." He leaned back in his seat and chewed on the inside of his lip.

"In this state," Jake said. "Probate court hears these matters. There's no jury, only a judge. It's what's called a bench trial. If Elle weren't pregnant, this would be a clear-cut matter of what she expressed in this advanced directive." He tapped the paper. "It doesn't matter that this document is old as eight-track tapes or that she was single at the time. She made it pretty clear that she didn't want to live if she were terminally ill or in a persistent vegetative state." He lowered his gaze to the documents before him and ran his manicured fingernails against the grain of his five o'clock shadow. "You said you didn't know about this advanced directive?"

"Not until this morning. But I knew Elle felt that way. Before I found out she's pregnant, I agreed to take her off life support—" My voice broke hard and I buried my face in my hands.

"It's okay." Jake squeezed my shoulder, waited while I collected myself, and then asked if we could continue.

"In a lot of states, this wouldn't be an issue because pregnancy automatically revokes a woman's advanced directive, but Maine isn't one of those states. As long as she has an AD, it stands."

I was about to ask which states, momentarily thinking maybe we could move her to another hospital in another state, but that probably wouldn't work. Elle wasn't stable enough. And my mother would fight me.

"Is it your child?" he asked. "I mean, if they tested the DNA?"

"Of course it's mine. Elle wouldn't—"

"That's not what I mean. I need to know that *genetically* it's yours. You didn't have a sperm donor or anything?"

"Why the hell are you asking me this?"

"Answer the question, Matt. Genetically, it's yours?"

"Yes."

"Good, in case that comes up. In the meantime, I'll need to file papers, which will request the court to adjudicate Elle as incompetent. Here in Maine we use the kinder-gentler term, 'incapacitated.' Nicer connotation, but it means she's incompetent to act on her own behalf. So, I'll need affidavits from her doctors, explaining her condition."

I nodded, then he continued on, explaining that he would ask the court to name me as Elle's guardian. However, that did not mean I could make her medical decisions. He pointed at the document labeled as Elle's living will. "Once the judge sees this, he may uphold it."

"You think my mother has the right to turn off Elle's life support?"

Jake tipped his head side to side as if he were weighing the matter. "We have the hospital records to dispute the validity of the older document, but yes, it's possible the judge will let your mother make medical decisions for Elle." He drew a deep breath. "Which is why I wanted to make certain the baby is yours. If we need to, we can go at this from an entirely different angle. If the judge rules in your mother's favor, I want to ask the court to give you guardianship of your unborn baby."

"Okay. That sounds good. What does it involve?" I asked, sitting up straighter.

"It's complicated. You know I've worked on Pro-Life cases?"

I nodded. "My mother will claim this is about Elle's right to die. And I swear to let her go after she delivers, but—"

He interrupted me. "I promise we'll use every legal strategy to make certain your child has a chance to live. Letting Elle go afterward is an entirely different issue, but the most pressing one facing us *right now* is keeping her on life support until the baby is born, correct?"

"Yes," I said, answering his rhetorical question.

"Let me explain. You see, the court doesn't recognize the human rights of babies before they are born—or it hasn't until recently. And the court will only give guardianship to someone it recognizes *as having* human rights. The unborn don't have a voice. So we have that hurdle, but I have a plan. I convince the judge. He rules in our favor. The ruling establishes a precedent—"

I coughed. "Forget precedents. This is about Elle and the baby."

"*Your* baby," he said, almost as if he were questioning the baby's paternity again.

"Yeah," I said.

"And trust me, saving this child is important to me, too, but setting a precedent by getting the judge to give you guardianship will be important to the Pro-Life movement. That's why this is a much bigger case than you realize. Your only concern is your wife and your child, but the entire Pro-Life movement will come to your aid. Lawyers sympathetic to the cause will offer us any help they can. Write an amicus curiae. Research. Anything."

"Write a what? Forget it; never mind. Why would the Pro-Life movement care? Elle *isn't* having an abortion."

A patronizing smirk simmered behind the finger that touched Jake's upper lip. I'd seen that expression on his face many times. He was aiming for a posture of sincerity, and he would have fooled me with it if I hadn't known him since college, if I didn't know the ambition he possessed.

Jake said, "No, but don't you see the parallel? Terminate Elle's life support, and you are terminating a pregnancy, too. Let me see if I can explain this better. The Fourteenth Amendment grants rights to persons. All rights. If the court grants you guardianship of your unborn baby, it makes an unborn baby a person— legally—a person with rights. Those rights will trump *Roe v. Wade* and privacy. If *Roe v. Wade* is overturned any other way, the states will regain the ability to decide the abortion issue, one by one."

"I reiterate. I don't give a damn!"

He glared and kept talking. "Okay, fine, but if the court gives you guardianship, it will have larger implications. Even if the judge decides against us, we can appeal it. Which will buy time. And if it fails in appeal, we can go all the way up. We can ask for a writ of certiorari."

"A what?"

"A writ of certiorari, a cert petition. It means we're asking the Supreme Court to review a lower-court decision. If the Court gives you guardianship, the United States government would, in essence, grant a fetus personhood, then all fetuses would have rights as persons. And any action that destroys a fetus would be considered a murder. Abortion would be outlawed *everywhere*."

"That's a hell of a stretch, and all I want is to give *this* baby a chance," I said.

"Do you remember the Scott Peterson case?"

"What the hell does any of this have to do with Elle?"

"Bear with me. Do you remember it?"

I leaned back in the chair and glared at Jake. He was like this. He'd go off on something, and in school I'd walk out of the dorm room, but I didn't have that luxury now. "Peterson? The bastard who killed his pregnant wife? Sure," I said.

"He was convicted of killing both his wife *and* his unborn son. Afterward, Congress passed the Unborn Victims of Violent

Crimes Act. It was a huge step forward because it protected the unborn. The authors of the bill were Pro-Life. Unofficially it's called Laci and Connor's Law."

"Oh, for Christ's sake. Dump the minutiae and get to the point."

"I am. That law protects the unborn, and it gives us a legal leg."

I grunted something innocuous, but equating what was happening to Elle in any way with the Scott Peterson case pissed me off. I wanted to stop this circus before the roustabouts started putting up the big top.

"If we go for guardianship of the baby, we will get Pro-Life backing—"

"And if you try to make this about abortion, you'll bring down the opposition of the National Organization of Women, who are probably just as radical as the right-to-lifers. You're going to turn this into a circus." My mother was a member of NOW. She was, for the most part, a reasonable person, interested in furthering opportunities for women, but there were a couple of hotheads in her chapter, ones who would, given the opportunity, boil abortion-clinic protesters in oil.

Jake sat there resolute, sneering at my mention of NOW. "The Pro-Life movement is a humanitarian effort," he said. "But let's not debate that one. There's more. Using guardianship is a risky tack. Here's why. There've only been two cases.

"The first one in Florida involved all the hot-button issues: a mentally disabled woman and a rape. The State tried to gain guardianship of the unborn baby. Long story short, the appellate court denied appointing the State guardian on two grounds: one, the State had no standing, which is why I wanted you to assure me Elle's baby is yours, and two, the Florida courts have no statutes, no laws on the books, to give a fetus a guardian."

"So the woman had an abortion?" I asked.

"Actually, no. The case stalled long enough for the baby to be born. And I'm willing to use the same tactic. I'm a principled man, a man who goes to church on Sunday, a man who holds my faith as my priority, but I'm also a realist, Matt. The State didn't win the battle, but they won the war. The baby lived—" He held up his finger. "One baby, and I'll take saving *your* baby. But the larger issue here is that a ruling that gives you guardianship could save more than a million children every year. I'm very sorry this happened to Elle, but—"

I clenched both my fists. "Don't you *dare* make a martyr out of her!"

He fell silent long enough for me to think he couldn't come up with a rebuttal. Or maybe he knew if he tried I'd kick him out. "Understood," he said. Then he began rambling on about a Pennsylvania case. "The judge ruled in favor of guardianship, but I don't believe it would have withstood an appeal."

I got up and paced the small conference room. "So this strategy, asking for guardianship, has a fifty-fifty chance? At best?"

Jake blinked a yes. "But we can do better because, as you said, this *isn't* an abortion case. You're trying to preserve what remains of your family, your child. As a father, you have rights, or at least you will after the baby is born. This is a particularly compelling situation."

I leaned on the table, palms pressed down. "But my rights don't kick in until after the baby is born unless you can get the world to change and get me guardianship?"

"Exactly," he said.

I glanced over at the copy of Elle's shaky handwriting on the hospital admission record from our son's stillbirth. "And what about the fact she said she didn't have an advanced directive?"

"I will definitely use that first. But you have to realize, Elle's brother will probably testify, and the judge may be swayed by what he says."

"Christopher? How do you know what Christopher has to say about this?"

"He was on the evening news."

"He what!" Blood pounded at my temples.

"Sit down."

I complied, dumfounded that Chris had the audacity to go to the press.

"The local news got him first, but it played on the networks tonight. Essentially, he said that his sister's injuries were fatal, but you were keeping her on life support because you had some misguided desire to save her. He said Elle had explicitly expressed her wishes that she be allowed to die in her living will. He *said* that although she was the bravest person he'd ever known, she was afraid of being kept alive this way."

"Shit," I said.

Jake grimaced. "Do yourself a favor, and watch that mouth of yours—at least in front of the cameras. The press is going to be all over this. It will be important how you present yourself."

"And you think that 'golly gee whiz' is going to ingratiate me?"

Jake shook his head. "I believe you when you say that under these circumstances Elle would stay on life support. We'll use everything including that there are states which prohibit the removal of life support when a woman is pregnant, but I want to you to understand I'm trying to protect you. Some people will vilify you for going against her wishes. It may look like you're willing to let her suffer for months. The fact is you are going against the wishes she expressed in her advanced directive."

I gulped down the meaning of his words, which burned like swallowing lye.

"You need to look like you're half grieving husband and the other half saint." He pushed a folder at me. "My fee agreement. This one's the retainer."

I gawked at the plethora of zeros and whistled. I had eight years' worth of Ivy League school loans, and I hadn't been in private practice long enough to pay them off much less sock that amount away.

"I can do this, if the judge gives us half a chance and doesn't immediately act on her advanced directive, Matt. I promise you that I'm your best bet."

"I don't have this kind of cash. Hell, I don't have a checkbook with me if I did."

"Don't worry about the retainer," he said. "I'll forgo the retainer. We're friends. I want this case because I believe in it. We can even talk about a reduced hourly rate, depending on how long the case runs. Just sign here." He shuffled a few pages and then pointed at the blank signature line.

I drew a deep breath and picked up the pen. "Before I do, there's one thing you need to understand. I'm not interested in your political agenda, Jake. I don't want Elle to be anyone's poster child."

"You'll change your mind before I'm done with you."

Jake didn't get it. He never got it. People weren't things to be used for the greater good as *he* saw it. "No," I said. "If you represent me, the case is about *this* particular situation, not about your Pro-Life cause or your ambition to get into the governor's mansion like your father."

"I'm not interested in being governor anymore. Yvette doesn't want to be a politician's wife, and I stopped trying to convince her years ago. My sole interest is in saving your unborn baby." Jake tapped his index finger near the blank signature line. "I have the chops to do this. I'm an expert in constitutional law. I commute to Boston to teach First Amendment law at Harvard, for heaven's sake. I'm a member of the Christian Legal Society. I get called on to consult on Pro-Life issues on a regular basis."

An odd memory snapped into my mind's eye, something from

freshman orientation when everyone asked the same three questions: What's your name? Where are you from? What's your major? Jake always answered in an odd way. He always said, "Jake Leahy Sutter, I am from the right wing, and I am majoring in a course that will lead me to the Supreme Court, preferably to the chief justice's seat."

"You always wanted to be a judge. You believe this will get you to the bench?"

His eyes narrowed and he leaned back in his seat. "Come on. There's no way I'm ever going to get the robes. My record is too Pro-Life. It's a litmus issue. I refused to walk on the fence of political indifference."

"Fine. Jake, do I have your word that you'll keep the focus on Elle and the baby? Yes or no?"

His tongue pushed at the inside of his cheek and he nodded.

✦ 6 ✦

Day 3

Pro-Life advocates were already picketing the courthouse where a judge would decide my wife's fate. No. I had to stop thinking like that. Elle's fate was decided when she fell. I was fighting for the baby's life—our baby's life. The strange thing was that Elle didn't even look pregnant. I hadn't felt the baby kick. The baby was a blip on an ultrasound. And still I knew, if she could, she'd already be reading *Goodnight Moon* to her belly.

I straightened my tie and pushed past the throngs of network reporters shoving microphones in my face.

"Dr. Beaulieu, how's your wife doing?"

"Her brother said she won't survive. Would you comment?"

A guy I'd known in high school yelled at me, "Matt, just one question about Elle."

"No comment," I said. They'd heard Christopher's version. I wouldn't provide more fodder for what should be a private matter.

Pro-Lifers held signs on either side of the door: GIVE LIFE, DON'T TAKE IT. SAVE ELLE.

Even though they were technically siding with me, I avoided eye contact with the activists. They were not picketing on my behalf, and certainly not on Elle's. They came with their own agenda, and our tragedy was merely a way to promote it.

I continued through the courthouse doors hoping that once I was inside, someone would keep the reporters and protesters away. No one did.

Next door the federal courthouse had metal detectors, but Cumberland County District Court might be the only courthouse in the country without them. Reporters trailed me across the rotunda, yelping their information-hungry inquiries.

Jake met me halfway to the courtroom, turned to the reporters, and said, "Surely you recognize this is a difficult time for Dr. Beaulieu and his family. We have no comment, but when we do, I'll hold a press conference, and you can ask anything you want."

To my surprise, they faded back. Admittedly, their eyes continued to loom on me as if they were anxious for the disclosure of a dirty secret.

At the end of the marble checkerboard corridor, my mother stood next to Christopher, looking like she'd been crying. As Jake and I passed, I almost pitied her. Almost. She was in pain, but we were waging a war. Love can conquer, but it can also divide.

The reporters found Chris, and he dove into conversation with them.

I turned to Jake and spoke in a hushed voice. "How did the right-to-lifers find out about this?"

"Come on," Jake said.

"Did you encourage them to show up today?"

"I didn't need to. Ever since Elle's brother held his press conference, the reporters have been all over this case, and the Pro-Life people are rallying on their own."

"But how did they know about the court case?"

"I'm sure they're watching the court docket just like the report-ers. I would be. They're trying to stop women from being brutal-ized, children from being murdered," he said.

I gritted my teeth. "Jake."

"I know. Not my fight this time." He flattened his lapel. "You look terrible, by the way. When did you sleep last?"

"I'll sleep when you get the judge to keep Elle's life support going."

"That's what we're doing here." Jake stopped outside the court-room entrance and whispered, "This could take a while, so you need to pace yourself. Translation: sleep. Frankly, I'll be happy if justice moves about as fast as my grandmother who has Parkinson's disease. The longer it takes, the further along Elle is in her preg-nancy, and the better it is for us. And pray the judge has a heart and a *Catholic* mother." Jake wagged his eyebrows. "Hey, you're Catholic. Tell your priest I want him to testify."

"My priest?"

"You're exercising your religious beliefs." He took a step closer to me and spoke softly. "Catholics have the Pro-Life part right. I want you to look devout even if you are a heathen."

Raised Catholic from Baptism through Confirmation, the Sac-rament of Marriage with a full Mass thrown in for good measure, I wasn't a churchgoer or even certain if I believed God existed. Elle did, though. She even went to Mass from time to time. And I liked the idea of a benevolent God and believed in the do-unto-others aspect of Christian doctrine. Philosophically, I bought in. Spiritu-ally, I remained skeptical. If God didn't exist, and if heaven and hell were myths, I'd lost Elle forever. I suppose I wanted to believe in God the way a kid wants to hold on to Santa Claus.

Jake glanced down at his buzzing BlackBerry and turned it off. Following his lead, I did the same, noting another voice mail mes-sage from Melanie.

"I've never understood," Jake said, "why Catholics pray to saints or worship Mary, but at least your church believes life begins at conception." He grinned. "Besides, it's about time you got something out of them besides eating fish on Friday."

I didn't have the energy or the inclination to clarify Catholic doctrine. "So you're going to *use religion*?"

"Of course. Religious freedom is in the Constitution, or haven't you heard?"

Christopher and my mother pulled open the courtroom doors and disappeared behind them. My mother, too, was a Catholic, but a typical American cafeteria Catholic. And she believed in a woman's right to choose.

Jake patted my shoulder as we walked through the doors. "Take a deep breath. Hopefully, the judge won't rule that Elle's living will is valid before giving us a chance to present our case."

I searched the gallery for Elle's father. No one had seen Hank in days. In one of those incongruous mental sidetracks the mind takes before it truly accepts someone's death, I thought, *Elle will be frantic about her father.*

Floor-to-ceiling oak paneling lined the courtroom walls. Mom hadn't retained a lawyer, so she sat alone on the side designated for the RESPONDENT, but Christopher was behind her whispering in her ear.

Jake and I took our seat at the table labeled PETITIONER. He flipped through papers he pulled from his briefcase, while I avoided Mom's stare. Usually, my sixty-three-year-old mother could pass for fifty, yet with the morning light shining through the transom, the thinness of her skin struck me. She was getting old and she looked like hell, but I doubted I looked much better. It occurred to me that if this didn't work out—if the baby died along with Elle—my dropping dead from exhaustion would save me the trouble of killing myself.

The court officer entered the door. "All rise. The Honorable Martin Wheeler presiding."

On his cue, the judge entered and took the bench. Like a swell in the ocean, we stood; we sat. The middle-aged judge shuffled papers in front of him, pulled out a pair of rimless glasses from a leather case, and cleaned them with a tissue as he spoke. "The first case is In the Matter of the Guardianship of Elle Lenore Beaulieu. Her husband, Dr. Matthew Beaulieu, filed a petition for guardianship, and Elinor Beaulieu, who is also seeking guardianship, has filed an objection to Dr. Beaulieu's petition. The court should note that Elinor Beaulieu is Elle Lenore Beaulieu's mother-in-law. The names are similar."

My mother raised her hand. "I can explain. Alice, Elle's mother, named Elle after me. But everyone calls me Linney, so you can call me Linney if it makes things simpler."

The judge pressed his lips together, and I expected a rebuke or a lesson in courtroom etiquette. Instead he sounded as patient as a kindergarten teacher when he said, "Yes." He spelled out each of their names and made my mother, Elinor, Mrs. Linney Beaulieu for the record. "Do you have legal representation, Mrs. Beaulieu?"

My mother shook her head. "No, I just filed the papers like they told me to do in the probate office. Elle wrote a living will. She didn't want to live this way."

"Technically it's an advanced directive despite what it says on the form. But, we'll get to that and your affidavit shortly," Judge Wheeler said. "The first official action is to establish that Elle Beaulieu is permanently incapacitated." He shifted in his seat and summarized the doctors' affidavits, describing the details of Elle's injuries and prognosis. The judge looked up and asked Jake to agree that Elle was permanently incapacitated. Then he asked the same of my mother.

"Yes, Your Honor," Mom replied.

"See how easy it is to agree on something? Let's do more of that in the future," the judge said. "Elle Beaulieu is deemed incapacitated and may be referred to as 'the ward.'"

I swallowed hard, squelching my impulse to puke. "The ward" was another step in Elle's dehumanization, like "the corpse" or "it."

Judge Wheeler set aside a document. "In the Matter of the Guardianship, we have a dispute. However, although guardianship papers were filed, the issue under contention seems to be what Elle would want under these circumstances. Dr. Beaulieu acknowledges that if his wife were not pregnant, he would have discontinued her life support. However, he believes that in this situation Elle would have wanted the pregnancy to continue even if it means keeping her on life support for the duration of her pregnancy. He agrees to discontinue her life support after the baby's delivery."

The judge looked over his reading glasses. "Mrs. Linney Beaulieu's petition indicates she believes differently. In her certification she states that she and Alice McClure, Elle's mother, were lifelong friends. Linney was involved in Elle's upbringing, and was, in fact, Elle's godmother. After Alice McClure's death Mrs. Beaulieu continued to have a close and loving relationship with Elle. During Alice McClure's terminal cancer battle, she lapsed into a three-month-long coma. Hospice nurses attended her in the McClure household during that period, and the effect that that had on the then-teenaged Elle was that she developed a profound belief that terminally ill persons should not have extraordinary measures taken to extend their lives. Elle signed this so-titled living will as soon as she reached the age of majority and designated Mrs. Linney Beaulieu to act on her behalf should Elle ever become incapacitated. If given guardianship, Mrs. Beaulieu would instruct Elle's physicians to discontinue her life support so Elle might die peacefully."

Wheeler paused, set down the court records, and folded his

hands on his desk. "Mrs. Beaulieu, were you aware of Elle's pregnancy when you wrote your petition?"

"Yes. But she's in the earliest stages of pregnancy. For the fetus to have a real chance, she'd be on life support for months and months—"

A dowdy-looking woman stood up in the gallery and shouted, "It's a baby, not a fetus. A baby!"

My mother craned her head around.

The dowdy woman sneered in Mom's direction and yelled again. "Elle is carrying a baby!"

"Order." Wheeler's voice lowered to a resonating timbre, and all heads swung back toward the judge. He reached for his gavel, and I felt its authority although he didn't use it. "This is a court of law, and if someone in the gallery speaks out of order, I will have him or her removed from this courtroom."

Jake clenched his pen like he was going to use it to stab his legal pad. I moved my attention to the judge and tried to solve the inscrutable mystery sandwiched between the lines on his face. I didn't know if the woman had angered him or if he'd scowled as a show of power. Within five seconds the furrow between his brows disappeared and a gentler expression appeared.

I'd always thought of a judge looking a certain way, soldier straight, neatly groomed, middle-aged or older. But Wheeler's hair was rather long and curly—poorly masking a receding hairline. His shoulders were rounded, his jawline soft. Yet in the moment when the woman called out, the judge still managed to summon a posture of authority.

He thumbed through the papers before him and pulled out Elle's living will, which showed the crinkled damage I'd done it. "This 1991 document is an advanced directive signed by Elle McClure Beaulieu. She was at that time eighteen years old, which made her a legal adult. And here," he said, pulling out another form," "is a hospital admission record that Elle Beaulieu signed this past February. Her initials indicate she had no advanced health care directive. This discrepancy could mean she nullified the 1991 document. However, her brother, Christopher McClure, wrote a certification of support, stating that he and his sister discussed right-to-die issues innumerable times, and she did not want to be kept alive on machines."

Wheeler's eyes scanned the courtroom. "This is not so much about guardianship as it is about what Elle Beaulieu would want done on her behalf under these tragic circumstances. I will grant temporary guardianship to Matthew Beaulieu while we attempt to resolve this matter in upcoming court sessions. Mr. Sutter, how many days do you estimate you will require to present your case, and how many witnesses do you intend to call?"

Jake scratched his chin as he flipped through a calendar. "I anticipate about five days," he said. "I will be calling Dr. Beaulieu, her husband; medical experts, including Dr. Philip Grey; and personal friends, clergy . . ."

I attempted to shake my head imperceptibly at him, trying to advise him against putting my partner, Phil, on the stand, but Jake didn't notice.

The judge scribbled down the names and then glanced up. "I have another trial scheduled for next week, but we can get started on September first—no, that's Labor Day. We'll continue on September third." His attention fell on Mom. "What about you, Mrs. Beaulieu? How much time do you need to present your case?"

"I don't understand how this all works, but can't you get to this sooner, Your Honor? Elle wouldn't want to be on life support all that time."

Wheeler shook his head and spoke in a matter-of-fact tone. "Mrs. Beaulieu, I realize you feel a sense of urgency; however, my docket is full with cases other parties feel are equally urgent. I suggest you retain counsel to help you prepare for the hearing."

"Your Honor, the majority of states revoke advanced health care directives when a woman is pregnant. Move to—"

"Mr. Sutter, Maine is not one of those states. Court dismissed." He grabbed his files and walked out of the courtroom without a backward glance.

Damn. I stared at Jake. He'd barely said anything. Why hadn't he asked the judge to give me guardianship of the baby?

Jake snapped closed his briefcase. "Get that conference room again. Book it for as long as you can. We'll need her medical records, and I need to talk to these doctors. And to you."

I whispered, "You don't want Phil to testify."

"We'll discuss that later. In *private*." His words sounded clipped and angry.

"Matt," my mother called.

All the muscles in my shoulders knotted. I turned my back on her and walked out.

✦ 7 ✦

Day 3

The ICU's glass walls permitted no privacy for Elle—but now someone had drawn the curtain around her bed. I returned from court unable to see her as I strode toward her room, and all I could think was she had died without me beside her.

I swung back the curtain and startled a young nurse with a water basin and towels. "Oh, Dr. Beaulieu. I'm about to give her a bath."

Breathing had become a deliberate act. For Elle, mechanical ventilation opened her lungs eighteen times per minute. Me? Because of a sponge bath, I had forgotten to inhale as if I'd lost the most fundamental drive to sustain my own life. *Just a sponge bath.*

"Ah, yeah, yeah. My name is Matt, by the way. Let me wash her," I said.

"You don't have to."

"Please. I want to take care of her." There was so little I could do for Elle now. And so much I still wanted to give to her: a life in which we grew old together with children and grandchildren and family dinners. And all I could give her was a sponge bath.

"All right," the nurse said. She set down the basin, checked Elle's IV, then left.

The moment I saw Elle in the emergency room, I knew the situation was dire. But even after a couple days of staring at her like this, her appearance was a blow. Death isn't a shrouded figure. It's a depletion. I couldn't feel her anymore. In the flimsy privacy the drawn curtain provided, I hung my head and wiped away tears.

"Hey, Peep." I kissed Elle's right cheek. Her left eye was still swollen closed. "Did you miss me? God knows, I miss you. Try to hang on, please," I whispered. I looked at her belly. There was a baby who was part Elle and part me; a baby I wanted to love, but who in the wake of my grief, felt like a stranger from some other part of the world. Yet, in the past, every time Elle was pregnant, she took my hand and put it on her belly.

Hey, I could almost hear her say. *Say hello to the baby.*

I reached out and gently put my hand on Elle's lower abdomen. "You, too, kiddo," I said. "You hang on, too."

I squeezed water out of the washcloth and continued to talk to Elle like she could hear me. "I expected the judge to be some gray-haired bozo. But this guy looks a lot like Tom Hanks, back when he did *Big*. Without the sense of humor. Not that anything about this is funny. I couldn't read him at all. He told Mom to get a lawyer. It would probably be better for us if she didn't, though."

Gently, I cleansed Elle's face, taking care with the endotracheal tube sticking out of her mouth and the feeding tube jammed down her nose, each a blight on her beautiful face. I knew we'd remove the ET tube and put in a tracheotomy in another day or two, but I also knew that even without the tube sticking out of her face, Elle still would never look like herself again. She wasn't behind those eyes anymore.

Phil had removed a section of her left parietal skull to relieve pressure from the cerebral edema, which left her head misshapen. And her hair—for a planned craniotomy, the nurses typically shaved a minimal amount of hair, but the OR didn't have time for cosmetics. They shaved Elle's entire head. After just two days, blond stubble was shadowing her crown.

For a while she had highlighted her hair, but after we married, she let it go back to its natural color, a warm shade of blond. She didn't want to use anything potentially toxic when she might get pregnant. "No dyes in my food or in my hair," she said. She wanted children, healthy children, and she'd obsessed over doing everything right.

Now, instead of eating pure foods, we were pumping steroids and potent diuretics into her to reduce her brain swelling. The X-rays had sprayed her with radiation.

I immersed the washcloth into the tepid water and wrung it out, then slipped off her hospital gown, taking care with her IVs. Elle was an athlete; she even ran marathons, and she had an exquisitely fit body. I soaped the washcloth and bathed her powerless form, already losing its tone.

Phil Grey rounded the curtain, and instinctively, I pulled a towel over Elle to protect her modesty.

"Ah, sorry." Phil stood there, blinking and looking uncomfortable in his OR scrubs.

I nodded. "How was the surgery?"

"Uneventful," he said. "I talked to D'Amato. He says their practice can help cover while you're on leave. And he sends his best."

"Thank him for me. I'll reciprocate later."

"He knows you will." Phil scratched his cheek and averted his gaze. "How was the meeting with the judge?" he asked.

"Okay." I dropped the washcloth in the basin then stood and

pocketed my wet hands. "He set a hearing date. My lawyer wants one of the ICU docs and Blythe to testify. Maybe you."

"Are you sure you want to do this?" His brow furrowed.

I wasn't certain of anything, but I was afraid to express doubt—even to my partner, who might say just that if he took the stand. "Yeah," I said. "This is the right thing." I turned toward the window. "Would you let Melanie go if you were in my place?"

Phil exhaled loudly. "Yeah. I think I would. Ethics 101. Do no harm. Elle didn't want to be kept alive. And you're going to lose her anyway."

"I've already lost her." I looked away. "I know the odds are overwhelming, but Elle would still try to save the baby. If you testify, what would you say?"

He thought for a moment then shuddered. "The truth. Medically, so far, she's stable. If she does survive, she'll remain in a persistent vegetative state—maybe even for years. Are you prepared for that? If she lives indefinitely?"

My head was pounding as ruthlessly as it would with a fever. "After she delivers, I'll let her go."

"Do you remember how long it took the courts to let Terri Schiavo die?" Phil asked. "When that story was all over the news, Elle was pretty upset. She didn't agree with the Pro-Lifers."

"This is different. In the Schiavo case, the parents were in denial. They thought their daughter was responding to them. I know better."

"But Elle's father doesn't. You said he's opposed to taking her off life support."

I paused to wonder about my father-in-law, his sobriety, and whether or not his opposition would become a problem if Elle survived that long or if she miscarried. "I'll deal with Hank when I need to—if he ever shows up again." On top of everything else,

I was also growing more concerned about Hank, beginning to wonder if he'd drunk himself to death or gone off a road somewhere.

"One way or another," Phil said, "in the end, you'll have to say good-bye to her, and by then, all you'll remember is how she became, not how she was."

"I'm stating the obvious here, but she's pregnant. So one way is not the same as the other. She wanted a baby."

"*She* wanted a baby? What about you?"

I met his eyes. Sure, I wanted a child with Elle; we both wanted a family. But alone? Did I want to raise baby alone? I felt so alone. I nodded.

Phil's nostrils flared as he exhaled. "Okay." For a minute or two longer, he rambled about her clinical status. "Melanie wants me to bring you home for dinner."

I shook my head. "Thank her for me anyway."

He looked, for a few seconds, as if he might try to persuade me and I began to compose my rationalizations, but then he said, "Okay." He left without further ado.

Because the water had cooled, I changed it and continued to bathe her. She didn't look pregnant; her belly was still flat. Maybe her breasts were a tad fuller. I marveled as I always did, at her tiny feet, and for the smallest moment I indulged myself in possibility, and my mind conjured an image of Elle holding a newborn baby. Then the moment ended.

I dried off my hands, pulled out my cell phone, and replayed Elle's last voice message. "Hey, it's me," she said.

8

Day 3

Usually, we discontinued life support within hours of a brain-death determination. The longest I'd ever kept anyone "alive" was the previous Christmas. A teenager, braving her first ice storm as a driver, went off the road and hit a tree. Her father, an army reservist deployed in Iraq, rushed home on an emergency leave. We kept the girl on life support long enough for him to say his good-byes. The elapsed time from the skidding tires to calling her time of death was four days, seven hours, and thirty minutes.

Elle would need five or six months in order to save the baby.

Jake took over the ICU conference room to interview all of Elle's doctors, and Phil was first up. He didn't think we could do it; Elle's body could start shutting down at any moment. At least that's what I heard him tell Jake as I stood next to the window staring blankly out at the rain clouds building on the horizon.

I'd known Phil since my neurosurgical residency. He was a year my senior, brilliant, compassionate, and uncompromising. He believed in salvaging people—when there was something to salvage. He believed in the dignity of life. And he believed in self-determination. His own. His patients'. Elle's.

More than that, Phil knew Elle personally. No, you're not supposed to talk about your patients outside of work, but Phil and I were friends. We socialized. Sometimes we talked shop at home. Wives were present. And Elle and Melanie expressed their opinions. When you're a neurosurgeon, quality-of-life issues arise and eat at you. They ate at me. Ate at Phil. And now as he explained Elle's condition to Jake, Phil made it clear that he didn't think we could save the baby in Elle's womb.

Maybe clinging to the idea that some part of Elle could live on was irrational, but the night before the accident Elle insisted that sometimes a person had to take chances. She was, of course, talking about getting pregnant again. I fought with her because another pregnancy would be *extremely* high risk. Hell, I didn't want to risk Elle's life, but that was before. She was already brain-dead. And as unlikely as it may be, the baby was still alive.

And I could hear her—really hear the echoes of words she said in desperation the night our baby Dylan died. Her words of pleading, begging me to save him, even if it killed her.

That night almost did kill her. That's why I didn't want to try again. That's also why Elle used a diaphragm ever since that night. We were careful, *damn it*. She wouldn't have fallen, and she wouldn't have fainted, if *I* hadn't gotten her pregnant again. *If*, instead of relying on her stupid diaphragm, I'd had a vasectomy after Dylan died.

She wanted a child then, and she would want a child now. It was the only thing I had left: giving her the baby everyone wanted me to forget. I was doing the right thing. I was. And it pissed me off that the family thought they knew Elle better than I did—or that I was some slobbering fool who couldn't face the reality in front of me. That I couldn't let her go. I didn't want to let Elle die, but it was too late to save her.

I blew out of the conference room and headed straight to the only private bathroom on the floor and closed the door behind me, taking refuge in the quiet. In the darkness I sank down and into the grief I was fighting so hard with reason. If I disintegrated, they would dismiss me. If I lost my credibility, they'd side with Mom. If I turned into the blubbering widower, no one would believe me capable of logic. But what if I was wrong? I began banging my head against the ceramic tile wall once for every emotional thought I had. I didn't know how long I could keep up this pretense. I wanted to die. I wanted to kill someone.

With the back of my hand, I wiped away the snot running out of my nose. I kicked the wall under the sink as I banged my head. Again. And again. And again.

My foot went through the drywall.

Ah, shit. I shook my foot loose and stood, feeling for the light. Shit.

I tried to bend the Sheetrock back into place, but it crumbled. I crept out of the bathroom and straight into Jillian Waters, the nurse manager, who was staring at me.

"I—uh, put a hole in the wall."

She stuck her head through the bathroom door and then turned to me. "Nice one. Are you okay?"

I struggled to find my voice, but it cracked when I said, "Yeah."

"Listen, go take a walk. I'll let maintenance know. Not that you did it, but well . . . Do you want me to call someone for you?"

"No. No thanks."

I trolled down one long corridor after another, hit a staircase, walked up a flight, circled the loop of Orthopedics, hit the staircase, up another flight to Telemetry, repeat, Pediatrics. I was halfway around when I saw the twelve-year-old boy I'd operated on the night before Elle's accident. He was sitting in a wheelchair, and his parents were pushing him in my direction.

I stopped and feigned a professional smile. "Hello. You probably don't remember me. I'm Dr. Beaulieu. I did your surgery."

The boy raised his hand in a half wave.

Mrs. Nguyen squatted, eye level with her son. "Dr. B. said you a strong boy."

The boy nodded, twisted his lips, but his tongue struggled to wrap itself around his garbled words. I couldn't understand him.

The father held out his hand and shook mine. "Dr. Grey is very happy with Mark's progress. The speech therapist said he could start on Monday."

"Good, very good," I said.

"We're sorry to hear about your wife's accident. We saw you there, in ICU room next to Mark's, but you looked busy," Mrs. Nguyen said.

I nodded. "I haven't been seeing patients, but I'm happy you're doing better, Mark." And I was glad he was doing well, but at the same time I didn't really want to be there talking to them.

Mark waved again.

I waved back this time. "You're doing great, kiddo. I'll come by later," I said, although I had no immediate plans of taking up my normal life or making rounds.

"Doctor, Mark says he's seeing double," the father said.

Damn. I'd only stumbled onto Pediatrics. I wanted to walk away, let someone else handle it. "Give me a few minutes to chase down an ophthalmoscope, and I'll meet you in his room."

Handmade get-well cards decorated Mark's wall, drawn by a younger sibling, a sister, judging by the smiley faces, sunshine, and purple daisies. Or were those echinacea? Elle loved echinacea.

Mark's mother plugged the boy's IV pump into the wall outlet while I examined him. Funny how the mothers always did that, jumped right in, learning whatever they needed to know to take care of their children.

That's when I realized that the baby inside Elle would never have a mother to do those things for him. I'd have to do them. I'd have to be father and mother.

Mark's neuro exam was good. Cognition was difficult to assess because of his speech difficulties. He had aphasia, a neurologically based language impairment, receptive as well as expressive, from what I could tell. When I asked him to point to his mother, he failed, and her eyes welled with tears, but he probably didn't know what either the word *point* or the word *mother* meant. He might have known who she was.

I squatted, eye level with the boy. "We know you're having trouble understanding us, but I think you'll improve." I smiled, hoping that my tone and my smile would reassure him. I glanced up at his father. "How'd you know Mark was seeing double?"

"Earlier today, he said, two, two, *hai bà mẹ hai cha*. And he reached for my hand, next to my hand."

"You speak Vietnamese at home?"

Mrs. Nguyen leaned toward me. "But we speak English, too."

"Before, when I first met you in the hall, was he speaking Vietnamese?"

"He said hello," she said.

"Okay. And now he's responded with a mishmash of the two. In Vietnamese, ask him if he can point to his father," I said

She did, and he pointed appropriately. Relief flooded her eyes.

"Good. He understands," I said. "There's still cerebral edema, swelling in his brain, but I would expect this to improve with time, with therapy. In the meantime, I'll let Dr. Grey know."

When I returned to the ICU, Phil was examining Elle.

"Did something happen?" I asked.

"No," he said, pulling off his gloves. "The nurse wanted me to take a look at her incision. I removed one of the sutures and put a steri-strip on it. It's nothing."

I peeked at the occipital incision and nodded. Innocuous erythema. Okay. I needed to refocus. "The Nguyen kid is having double-vision issues on top of his aphasia. His exam is in keeping with your last progress note," I said.

"I'll order an MRI."

"Already done. I ordered it stat. They were taking him down when I left."

"Okay. I'll check the results. About Elle, you didn't like what I was saying in the conference room—to your lawyer."

"No, not much." I rubbed my eyes. "Clinically, I understand why you said what you did. The odds are against us. Against her. Against getting a live baby out of this. So? Don't you get it? I have to try." I shook my head at him. "Go take a look at the Nguyen boy. Just go."

Phil slogged out, glancing back at me.

Damn it.

"Hey, Peep. Remember that kid I operated on the day before the accident—instead of spending those hours with you? He's doing pretty well, considering, but so you know, I would never have left you for a minute if I'd known we were almost out of time."

The silence, punctuated by the hiss of the ventilator and beeps of the hospital, condemned my pretense. "I miss you, Elle. Jesus, I miss you."

I headed back to the conference room. The intensive care doc, Clint Everest, was still answering Jake's questions. He was one of those lanky guys with little to no hair and didn't care who knew it. Instead of a comb-over, he buzzed it down to nubs. Although we were about the same age, he gave the impression he'd done it all and seen it all. Board certified in both intensive care medicine and immunology, he always took the autoimmune cases, lupus, Guillain-Barre, Addison's. He was giving Jake a primer in Elle's autoimmune issues, which were relatively minor, except when she was pregnant—like now.

I knew the material and didn't feel patient enough to listen in on the remedial version. "If you need to talk to me, I'll be with Elle," I said.

"It's getting late," Jake replied. "I'll come in to talk to you in the morning."

I wandered back into Elle's room and took the seat next to her bed. Her hand was starting to gnarl into a contracture. In the past I'd written orders for physical therapists to come and deal with things like this, delegating the neurological sequelae away. But not now. I couldn't just look elsewhere. Elle's brain had sustained too much damage for any neurosurgeon to repair, but I could try to keep her body healthy. I pulled open the drawer of the bedside table, rummaged for the hospital-supplied lotion, took her hand in my own, and began working the muscles for her.

In one of the deeper catnaps I'd slipped into, I heard my name being called. "Dr. Beaulieu?" Deb was one of the charge nurses on the night shift and one of the sharpest nurses whose path I'd ever crossed.

I shook my head awake. Elle was still beside me. "Yeah. You know, my name is Matt."

"Right," Deb said. "There's a woman on the telephone. Keisha? She says she's in New Zealand, and she can't get through to your cell but that you'd want to talk to her."

I was already out of the chair and on my way to the nurses' station while Deb finished her story about being afraid the woman was another reporter.

"No, it's okay," I said.

The unit secretary pointed at a line and I picked up. "Keisha?"

There was a moment of delay before Keisha's soft Bahamian accent came through the line. "Matthew, tell me the news reports are wrong."

I sank into the chair and stared into Elle's dimly lit room. "She fell," I said. "I don't know what to tell you. I don't know what you've heard."

A whimper on the other side of the world can sound as cataclysmic as two planets colliding. "Say she's not really dead."

I exhaled and told Elle's dearest friend about the baby.

✦ 9 ✦

Day 4

Hank stood in front of me, stroking Elle's forearm. She'd never resembled her father. She looked like her mother, fair-skinned and fine-boned, while he was dark and rugged. Rather, he used to be dark before his hair thinned and turned gray, but that only served to make him look more distinguished. Hank had always carried himself with certainty, pressed, ready, and confident. At least that's how he appeared for the last twenty years.

Unlike how he was—before he stopped drinking. His world was different then, rumpled and edgy.

Today Hank's eyes shifted back and forth, although his clothes were still sharply creased. He could neither maintain eye contact with me nor keep his voice steady when he looked at Elle, but he told me he'd been on a binge these past few days and that he'd drunk enough to make him pass out in a bar and land in a Brunswick hospital. They released him sober and repentant. He turned to me with downcast eyes. "I don't know what to say except I'm sorry. I know she'll be disappointed in me."

"She'd tell you she loved you. Just don't repeat the mistake," I said, squelching my anger.

"I fucked up again," he said.

Again. Yes. Again. For a couple of years, he'd fallen deeply into the throes of alcoholism—when Elle's mother was sick and for a while afterward. We were losing Alice, but at fifteen, Elle was trying to cope with her own grief, take care of Christopher, and deal with her drunken father. Those were times all of us forgave, although none of us forgot. He'd made matters worse for everyone.

But he got sober, and in many ways he became someone I deeply admired, working against his demons, helping out others in AA. And he became my father-in-law and, in spirit, a father to me.

He wet his lips. "Is it true? What the papers say? She's pregnant?" I nodded.

"And now you're fighting for her life in court?" He squeezed his eyes shut and waited for my reply as if he were praying.

I considered my answer. "I'm fighting for the *baby's* life, Hank." For a second I could see Dylan. My son would be six months old now, babbling and sucking his thumb. I fought for him, and I failed. For Elle's sake, this time had to be different.

"I'll help you," Hank said. "Do you have a good lawyer?"

"Jake Sutter. He's excellent. I went to school with him."

Hank grimaced. "The one who was at your wedding? Short guy, gravelly voice? The one who never stops talking politics?"

"That would be him. He argued a Pro-Life case in front of the Supreme Court when he was just a few years out of law—"

"Did he win?"

"No, but it was a five–four vote, which means he convinced some of the justices."

"Is he expensive? Is he charging you?"

"Both. But it doesn't matter; I have to do it." I mumbled something more about how this would bankrupt me, but that money didn't mean anything. Not now.

"I have money, Matt."

"I didn't mean to imply—"

"I can pay him. Who knows? By the time the baby is born, maybe Elle will wake up." Hank pointed at her. "So we understand one another. I'm fighting for *my baby's life.*"

"I appreciate your help, Hank. Really, I do. And I'd like you on my side, but listen . . ." I struggled to find the words. I needed to be clear, but I didn't want to send him back to the nearest bar. "I'd give anything if Elle would wake up, but she won't." I hung my head, visualizing the trauma Phil described in Elle's brain. Not in some patient's. In my wife's.

She would never wake up no matter how much I wanted her to, no matter how Hank denied the reality of her condition, but this wasn't the time to dissuade my father-in-law of his delusions. The house was in Elle's name. Her grandfather had left it to her. I would have to ask Jake if I could sell the house if I only had temporary guardianship. Yeah, I was a hotshot brain surgeon, but I was still paying off my school loans. So money, in the pragmatic sense, did mean something: the power to fight. But more than that, I needed someone on my side. "I might need your help, depending on how long this goes on. The medical expenses, Jake's fees. I hate to ask. I *won't ask* unless I can't swing it on my own." I could probably get loans, barter with the hospital. I'd figure it out.

"She's my daughter," he said, "and I can afford to take care of her. Having money has only meant one thing to me: I could provide for my family."

"That's supposed to be my job, taking care of her." We had always taken care of each other. Elle. Me.

"I was lucky in real estate. Just lucky. So shut up. We're a family. The bills will get paid," he said.

One of Elle's monitors gonged. Her pulse oximeter dropped to eighty and then to seventy-five as her color deteriorated to an ashen gray. I increased the oxygen coming from her ventilator, then I picked up a stethoscope and listened to her lungs.

One of her nurses rushed in.

"She needs suctioning," I said as my thoughts raced. The constant cacophony and moment-to-moment crises of intensive care were familiar, and I understood that endotracheal tubes frequently clogged up and needed this type of housekeeping, but Elle wasn't a patient to me. She was my wife. So I watched the nurse's face for cues. Would I need to step in and replace Elle's endotracheal tube? Or maybe I ought to call in the intensive care doc.

The second hand made a full and slow rotation on the clock before Elle's oxygen level climbed to an acceptable level, and finally I breathed again.

The nurse looked up at me and smiled. "She's okay."

"Right," I said, noting that Hank had backed away and was gripping the counter by the sink, looking paler and older than he had moments before. "That kind of thing happens all the time," I said, hoping he couldn't tell how worried I was.

"Matt, I want a drink," he said. Before I had time to protest, he said, "But instead, I'm going to call my sponsor. Again. After which, I'm still going to need a drink."

I got in his face. "Don't. I need you sober. I need your help to get through this. And not because of the money."

He rubbed his eyes, smearing away the tears. "She's really going to die, isn't she?"

"Maybe the baby will survive," I said. I patted his shoulder, and he cried the same way I'd seen him cry in Elle's arms when her mother died.

I didn't cry with him. I couldn't fall apart in front of my colleagues. But inside, another layer of my denial dissolved as I thought about Hank's words: "She's really going to die, isn't she?"

No, Hank, I thought. *She's already gone. We already lost her.*

Phil walked in for morning rounds and handed me a small cooler packed with food from Melanie, apple slices and a PB&J sandwich with the crust cut off. He raised an eyebrow. "You can kind of tell we have preschoolers in the house. Here," he said, passing me the newspaper he'd had tucked under his arm.

The headline of the *Portland Press Herald* read:

PREGNANT ASTRONAUT BRAIN-DEAD
Family Waging Court Battle

Phil leaned against the wall as I skimmed the article. My weary brain interpreted the journalist's words with flat surprise. She reported the courtroom events with little to no embellishments, and I was grateful for that minor indulgence. Still, the translation of Elle's life into black-and-white newsprint brought a concrete texture, heavy, solid, and subject to popular discussion.

"Damn," I said.

"It's in the *Boston Globe*, too. Probably in every major paper. The networks are going for a more sensational version."

"Which is?"

"This is being done against Elle's will. Playing up her brother's contention. The Pro-Life pundits are spewing their vitriol with equal intensity. Turn on the news; you'll see."

I rubbed my neck, glancing at the darkened television mounted to the wall. "It's not unexpected."

Phil drew a deep breath. "You should go home and sleep today. This is my fault. If I hadn't insisted on doing the surgery—"

"Would you stop? Just stop and think. If you didn't do the surgery, the baby would be dead, too. The only reason I'm doing this is for the baby."

Phil looked away. "I'm sorry this is happening," he said. "You didn't want me to operate at first. I feel responsible you're in this situation. And the media . . ." He flicked the newspaper.

"Damn it, Phil. I said stop. The news involvement is unfortunate. Jake told me to expect the case might get ugly." The exposure was collateral damage. More and more the war analogy made sense to me. I was at war, and at stake was saving what was left of Elle: the baby. I realized I was a desperate man, and a desperate man is a dangerous one—and a reckless one. I didn't care if my reputation or my livelihood fell apart. I didn't care if it killed me or destroyed my relationship with my mother and my brother-in-law. I had nothing to salvage if this baby didn't survive. I was clinging to the baby as if it could save me instead of the other way around.

Phil shifted his feet. "Okay. I won't try to change your mind, but you look exhausted. She's stable. Her blood gases are good. Why don't you go home and sleep for a while. You haven't really slept since it happened. Maybe that will help."

The concept of sleep was a seductive one even if I resented Phil's insinuation that I wasn't thinking clearly. I also knew he was right—I wasn't thinking clearly—but I was scared to leave Elle, afraid someone would turn off her life support in my absence. I'm sure I seemed irrational to Phil. Admittedly, I usually believed in the quality of life being as important as its longevity. And I knew I might not approve of my stance in his shoes.

Telling myself that Elle would want me to save this baby didn't change the fact that I also knew she'd be appalled she was in that bed unable to control her bladder or her bowels. There was nothing pretty or dignified about the way she was dying. And it didn't matter that I believed she would throw herself at the base of the Space Shuttle at launch time if it meant saving this child. I'd made the bed she had to lie in. Staying with her was my duty. "I'm sleeping now and then," I said.

"Here and there doesn't cut it. You look like death. Listen, Matt, we should trach her and put in a PEG. Clint will do it. Do you want him to give you the risks and benefits talk or can you just sign it?" Phil set a consent in front of me for the tracheotomy and a PEG, a surgically placed feeding tube.

I drew the consent closer and scribbled my signature.

Phil nodded. "Go shower and shave, and when you come back, it will be done. You are not staying to watch."

"That's fine."

"By the way, I upped Mark Nguyen's dexamethasone. His cerebral edema was worsening. Thanks for getting the ball rolling with the MRI."

"Sure." I stood, and for a moment the room wobbled.

"You need to sleep. Grab a few hours in the on-call room. You want me to write you a script?"

"No." I needed to keep a clear head. When I returned an hour later, the room seemed even more silent. Elle's mouth no longer bore the elephant's tusk of an endotracheal tube. Instead, they'd cut open her throat and inserted a trach. Her beautiful neck, the hollow where I'd kissed her so tenderly, now hosted a tube.

I pulled a picture of her from my wallet. As always, her eyes glimmered as she smiled back at me. I couldn't remember a single instance when she didn't look like she knew something I didn't, and the mystery of what always held me captive.

But not now. Now she didn't react at all and her eyes were— vacant. I cleansed her cracked lips with water and smoothed Vaseline on them. "It's all right, Peep," I said. But the words were lies, and I said them not for her benefit but for mine.

✦ 10 ✦

Day 4

I slipped out an employee exit and left the hospital without the press or the Pro-Lifers accosting me. I walked fast, urgently, barely taking note of the adjacent park. The hospital is situated on a hill that overlooks the western end of Portland, and on a clear day the White Mountains are visible. Today the air was heavy with the promise of an afternoon thundershower, and still, it felt good to be outside and *moving*. After a few minutes I slowed down and breathed and looked around.

Although it was only mid-August, a few stray maples were masquerading in autumn colors. I bent down and picked up a prematurely fallen maple leaf with red and gold striations. It was beautiful and sad, a little like Elle. Damn, I saw her everywhere. My exhaustion was making it difficult to focus.

I was supposed to meet Jake to discuss the case. Despite his aversion to hospitals, he and his wife lived nearby, and when I reached the far end of the Promenade, I saw them standing arm in arm and staring out at the view. Both were dressed in muted shades of linen, casual and neutral. Yvette nearly disappeared into him. Back at Columbia, I thought Jake set his sights on her because of her stature; she made him look tall—a short guy with a shorter girlfriend. She was pretty enough, but always so quiet she made me uncomfortable.

Elle once described Yvette as "diminutive." At the time I raised an eyebrow at Elle. Anyone else would have said "short" or "tiny" or maybe "petite," but no, Elle summoned a less common adjective. "Think about it," she said. "She's like a perfectly proportioned doll. Even her voice is small."

"You never struck me as one of those catty women," I said.

"I'm not," Elle said, stretching her back as we finished our morning run. "They're a perfect example of how opposites attract. She's shy. He's not. She's sweet. He's . . . never mind. I'm not going to win this one. I do sound like a catty woman."

I pulled her to me and tipped her chin up. "Are we opposites?"

Elle cocked her head to one side and measured my question. She slipped her arms around me. "Well, the attraction is strong, but no, we're kindred spirits and need each other to be whole."

Looking over at Jake and his wife nestled together, I experienced the sharp pang of envy. Whether they loved each other the same way—or in some different way than Elle and I did—they still had each other. All I had now was loneliness. And its weight bore down on me with such heaviness I wondered if I could even lift my feet to return to the hospital and to Elle.

Before I could decide whether I should interrupt them, Jake waved, and then Yvette looped her arm through his as they strolled toward me. He shook my hand, and she barely made eye contact. "Bring Matt to dinner," she said to Jake.

I shook my head. The last thing I needed was to make polite dinner conversation. "Thank you, but I have plans," I said.

She smiled, but there was pity in her expression as she reached out and touched my elbow. It was the warmest gesture she'd ever made toward me in all the years I'd known her. "I'll let you boys talk," Yvette said. They kissed and she wandered away.

As soon as she was out of earshot, Jake dove into his plans. After talking to Phil, he'd decided he would not make a good witness for our side.

"Would any of Elle's friends tell the judge that all Elle wanted was a baby?" he asked.

I told him about Keisha and that she'd been on sabbatical down in New Zealand. "But she'll be home in a couple of days."

"I need to talk to her before Friday. I have an appointment with your priest after he does a christening tomorrow afternoon. The Church wasn't much use in the Schiavo case, but then, she wasn't pregnant."

"You realize we aren't devout Catholics," I said. Even Elle only attended Mass a few times each year.

"You need to start going to services, if only for appearances. When were you there last?"

The last time I'd been inside a church was six months before. "Dylan's funeral," I said. "We had a Mass for him. Just the family."

"That's too long," he said. "Catholics have Last Rites. Has she had Last Rites?" It was like he was groping for anything. Even Last Rites were a ploy to him.

"No," I said. "*Her name* is Elle. I didn't even think about it. And by the way, it's called Anointing of the Sick, not Last Rites."

"Fine," he said a little more respectfully. "We need to establish that you and Elle are practicing Catholics. So it would be good to have the priest come in. I know you were never very religious, but you two were married by a priest."

"Elle wanted a church wedding." And she might want to be anointed, so for her sake, not Jake's, I would call the priest. "She went to Mass occasionally—without me—usually."

"Has she been to church since the funeral?" Jake gestured toward a park bench.

I dropped onto the weathered park bench and looked out at the view, but fog was rolling up the embankment. "Good Friday. She always did the Stations-of-the-Cross thing, something she did with her mother." Something Alice made a big deal about. Even all these years after her mother's death, Elle still attended church on Good Friday and then she put fresh flowers on Alice's grave.

"My associate told me priests are sticklers about saying someone is a member of the congregation if they aren't. I need to be able to put him on the stand." Jake sat beside me and took a rubber band off a stack of index cards and started flipping through them.

The funny thing was everything he said about Catholicism was off by a degree. I never heard a Catholic call it a congregation. It was a parish. It was Mass, not services. Reluctantly, I realized these things, these Catholic terms, were ingrained in my identity; I was tied to Sunday mornings, the Eucharist, and bowing my head during the Nicene Creed: *by the power of the Holy Spirit, He was born of the Virgin Mary* . . . no matter how much I resisted.

"Moving on, when you testify," Jake said, "for expedience, I'll ask you about her neurological status instead of asking those questions of Phil. You're as much of an expert as he is. You'll tell everyone that a person in her condition is incapable of experiencing pain. Or awareness."

I nodded. She wasn't in pain. She wasn't afraid. I kept trying to reassure myself.

"If they make any case that your testimony is tainted by your closeness to the situation, I'll get another neurologist or neurosurgeon to back you up. Then you'll summarize your relationship with Elle and tell the court about your efforts to have a baby, about how she still wanted to have a child even after multiple miscarriages. That will say something about what she'd want done on her behalf." Jake flipped through three more index cards. "Given the judge's abrupt dismissal of the fact other states revoke advanced directives during pregnancy, I won't use that issue for now."

Although I believed Elle would want me to keep her on life support, I wasn't certain how I felt about the blanket revocation in other states. I had to think about that one, but I wondered how many women were aware. "Can you ask the judge to ban the press from the courtroom? Our life together doesn't belong on the front page," I said.

He leaned toward me. "I know you're a private man, but—their presence is good for our case. The more this is in the public eye, the harder it will be to ignore the baby's plight. Politicians may even rally and pass a statute about pregnant women and advanced directives. It's true the judge won't decide this case on public opinion. But he'll want to look good; he'll want his rulings and procedures to be above reproach. He doesn't want to get overturned on appeal. This could work in our favor or against us because I want him to exercise a measure of judicial activism if we petition for fetal guardianship. I have it on good authority Judge Wheeler's been lobbying for an appointment to the court of appeals. The better news is the people he's talking to lean to the right. Unfortunately, that means they are constitutionally conservative, too. We just have to hope Pro-Life trumps that."

Jake flipped to an index card with a calendar printed on it. "In three weeks, Elle will be in her second trimester. My understanding is most miscarriages happen in the first three months."

"Not with her autoimmune disorder. With APS, miscarriages tend to come later." I swallowed. One was at twelve weeks, one at fourteen—and one at nineteen. Then Dylan's stillbirth. "You haven't interviewed Elle's OB/GYN yet, have you?"

"No. Dr. Clarke is coming to my office Monday morning."

"I'm more concerned about Elle's overall status, her life support. The longer she's on it, the likelier other complications will develop," I said.

A couple of women, holding a bouquet of Mylar get-well balloons, strolled down the walk. Jake stood and beckoned them. "These are some people I want you to meet, Matt. This is Sherry O'Reilly and Patricia Kent from Children from Conception. Are you familiar with that organization?"

I drew a deep breath as I rose. "I told you. This isn't about your cause."

"If you could just give us a minute of your time, Dr. Beaulieu." The woman who spoke had the round cheeks of a retired nursery school teacher. "If you just listen, you'll see how this can help your wife and preborn child."

I turned away from them, intent on holding my temper. Yet after stomping less than ten feet, I spun back. "For thirty or forty years the antiabortion movement has made a spectacle of their continued inability to overturn laws. Why the hell do you think you can help?"

"Because it's always easier to see an isolated situation and empathize with it," the one who looked like a nursery school teacher said. "People talk about a woman's rights, and it seems to me that in this case, a woman has lost her rights. If she hadn't fallen, your wife wouldn't have had an abortion, would she?"

"No. That's not the issue, though," I said.

"Sure it is. There's a lot of chatter about your situation in Pro-Life circles already. What we want to do is organize, form a comprehensive plan that will include everything from contacting legislators to prayer groups."

"We can rally the best legal minds to look for a loophole," said the other woman.

I glared at Jake. "The thing is," I said, "you're all begging the question. This isn't about what Elle would want done if she were healthy. The case is about what she would have wanted done if she were brain-dead." *Is brain-dead*, I thought.

"Yes," I said to the women. "I believe she would have wanted me to save the baby. So go ahead, pray. But stay the hell away from the court. You are only going to aggravate the judge. That's what happened when that woman called out in court."

Then I directed my attention—or was it wrath?—at Jake. "You saw Wheeler's face. And as you pointed out, he's the one who will decide. And the fact is, I don't want any part of your circus. This is about my wife and my baby."

Two blocks later, with Jake on my heels, I stopped and faced him. "You ever ambush me like that again, you're fired. Fuck it. Maybe I should fire you right now."

"You're making a mistake," he said. "You want to save one life. And we can, but quite possibly we could crush legalized abortion, too."

"Last warning," I yelled, not caring who might overhear. "I will not allow you to use Elle to serve your agenda. Take my terms or leave me alone."

Jake shook his head. "Matt, Matt, Matt," he said as if I were a naive child. "You think you can find someone more prepared than I am? Or maybe you're thinking *you* can waltz into the courtroom and earnestly ask the judge to keep Elle on life support all by yourself?"

"That's not what I said." Although the thought, however fleeting, had occurred to me.

"Grow up," Jake said. "This is the law. It works on precedents. And statutes. And obscure rulings. Case law. We need to give the judge a reason to keep Elle on life support when she so clearly stated she didn't want to ever be put on machines. I'm acting in your best interest. I'm trying to avail you of every legal opportunity. Are you really so blind you can't see what I'm doing?"

I studied him with his puffed-up ego and his arrogant superiority. As angry as I was, I wondered if he could be right, that I was naive. Saving Elle's baby—Elle's?—ours—would take a medical miracle. Was I being realistic? Probably not. And yet I was willing to do the one thing that terrified my wife. And I was worried about our lack of privacy? I was worried about making this a circus? Which of us, Jake or me, was balancing on a thinner tightrope? I didn't give a damn about *Roe v. Wade*. I didn't believe in forcing women to bear children they didn't want. But saving the baby in Elle's womb wasn't about an unwanted child.

"Come on," Jake said. "Let's go to your office and discuss how we're going to save your baby." He held up his hands as if he were about to fend me off. "I have my priorities straight. This case. How about you? What are you willing to do?"

I swallowed, trying to moisten my very dry throat.

He tapped my shoulder and pointed toward my office, and we started down the path.

Jake lifted the framed photograph of Elle from my desk. "She looks angelic in this one."

She could look like an angel, but that was too simplistic a description for someone who could banter with an unmatched sarcastic wit or enrapture me in bed. Her depth and compassion simmered with a kaleidoscope of other attributes and a few faults: backseat driver, never put a damned thing away, and she tended to laugh at her own jokes. And because she could count cards in her sleep, she cheated at twenty-one. I loved her. I would always love her. Our relationship was no one's business but ours. I didn't want to justify anything to Jake. Or to a judge. Or those do-gooders in the park. And especially not to a courtroom full of the media. But to some degree Jake was right: to win the case I had to put up with the trappings.

"She could be both angel and devil," I said, wearing a path down the newly installed Berber. I'd always been a pacer, and away from Elle's hospital bed, I was feeling trapped and nervous.

He glared pointedly at me. Even when we'd roomed together at Columbia, my restlessness annoyed him, and I suppose we knew each other well enough from those four years that I could read him without words.

"Fine." I dropped into a chair.

Jake pulled out his handy stack of index cards again. "You look terrible."

"You said that yesterday."

"Well, you still look terrible." He nodded as if to say he'd expressed the appropriate amount of concern for his client, and now he could move on. He shifted both in his seat and in his direction. "Let me get a couple of things out of the way. Did Elle have a will?"

"Yes."

"Bring me a copy. I need to see it. To the best of your ability, give me a rundown of her assets."

"We made wills mostly to designate a guardian when Elle was pregnant—the last time. My brother Mike and his wife were supposed to be guardians."

He scribbled something down. "And her assets?"

"The farm was in Elle's family for more than a century, so it's in her name, but it goes to me in the event of her death, to our children if we both died. If we both died, and in the absence of children, it goes back to her brother. We have the usual life insurance policies, and some savings, stocks, CDs, but not a fortune. I've only been in private practice for four years. I'm still paying off school loans. And Phil and I needed to invest in the practice, purchase medical equipment and office supplies. We decided to buy the building."

Jake looked up from his cards. "What about her income?"

"People think because being an astronaut is prestigious that the money is there, but no. NASA doesn't pay a hell of a lot. People work there because they dream about quasars and discovering microbes on Mars. She isn't tenured at Bowdoin yet. *Wasn't* tenured. We're not rolling in the dough, but we're frugal, and we put a little away. We have joint savings accounts."

"I have to ask this," Jake said. "But do you have anything financial to gain by having Elle live a few more months? Like a prenup that said you don't inherit anything unless you've been married X amount of time?"

"Jesus Christ, no. You're seriously suggesting I'm doing this for the money?"

"No, but someone could raise the issue if you had something to gain."

"We didn't have a prenup."

"Works for me. Get me her will—so I have a copy. Next, did you discuss an advanced directive when she made her will?" He turned the page on his legal pad.

"I went with her. To make a will in my name, too, but I don't remember talking about an advanced directive." I searched my memory. "Come to think of it, the hospital called me away for an emergency. I went back to the attorney's office the following day."

"Talk to the attorney you used. Find out if he discussed it with her. Before we get into your relationship with Elle, what were her personal beliefs? She believed in God. What was her opinion on abortion?"

"We are not doing this again." I glowered at Jake.

He shook his head, and we sat in silence for a few minutes, the clock ticking on the wall. "I won't set you up again that way, which doesn't mean I don't want to explore using Pro-Life support, but I won't blindside you, even if I think we could accomplish something incredibly important."

"You're an asshole, you know that," I said.

"I'm your attorney, and you have to listen to me about this. We have to convince the judge about the kinds of decisions Elle would make on her own behalf. Her core beliefs are relevant. How she would feel about her unborn child *is relevant*. So how she felt about babies before they are born is important."

I stood and wandered over to the window. The fog had grown so dense I could barely see the opposite side of the street. My view of the future and perhaps my ability to tell whom I could trust were also clouded. All I knew was that I needed his help. I didn't know how to find another lawyer who would have a chance of winning the case.

"How did she feel about abortion?" he asked.

I told Jake a half-truth. "She wasn't *in favor* of abortion."

"Do you have anything in writing?"

"In writing? Why would she have anything in writing about abortion?"

He exhaled loudly. "She could belong to a group through her church."

"No. She wasn't involved with any of that."

"Did she contribute to any Pro-Life organizations?"

"No."

"Was she involved with *any* charities?"

"Breast cancer, it killed her mother. And we sponsor four children in Guatemala through Save the Children." Every time we lost another baby, we sponsored another child.

"All right. But we need something that shows she was Pro-Life, that she believed life started at conception, that this baby would have already been real to her. Maybe during her college days she took an ethics class, and the papers are stowed away somewhere."

"As an undergraduate, she majored in physics and astronomy. Her doctoral thesis was on magnetohydrodynamic waves."

"What?"

"Something to do with plasma physics—neutron stars—I think."

Jake shook his head. "She must have taken liberal arts classes when she was an undergrad at Bowdoin. It's a liberal arts college."

"I don't know. We weren't exactly talking back then."

He scratched his chin. "That's right, the two of you split up freshman year. How could I forget the way you moped around afterward listening to that U2 song? What was it? 'I'm Losing You'?"

"It's called 'The Sweetest Thing,'" I said. But like the lyrics, I was losing her. Only this time it was so much worse.

"That's right. Listen," he said. "I need you to go through her things—if she still has her college papers. Anything she wrote down, *anything* that indicates she would put the baby first."

In my mind's eye, I saw Elle sitting on the dock by the tidal river that flowed by our property, her feet dangling in the water, her diary in her hands. I saw her curled up by the window seat on winter nights, glancing up at the falling snow then writing in her journal. I remembered Elle just a few nights ago, cross-legged, writing tomes under the lamplight by the French doors to the widow's walk.

"What?" Jake asked.

"I don't know." I rubbed my eyes with the palms of my hands, wondering what she'd written in those journals for all those years. She once told me she started journaling when I was a foreign exchange student in high school. Letters. She began journals by writing letters to me, letters she never mailed. She said she still wrote "Dear Matt" instead of "Dear Diary." But she never showed me any of these diaries, nor any of the entries. And a little intimidated, I never snuck a look. One time I asked what she was scribbling about and all she said was, "Some people meditate. This is how I work through my day. It's like talking to my best friend. And you're my best friend, but think of it this way, I spare you my whiny side."

Maybe I hadn't wanted to know if she was whining about me. God, I missed her. I would have given anything to hear her, even to hear her bitch or tell me I was full of shit.

"You all right?" Jake asked, bringing me back to the present.

I glanced up at him. "Sure. I'll see what I can dig up, but I don't know if I'll find anything that will help. Listen, the truth is, politically, Elle was Pro-Choice."

Jake let his head flop backward and covered his eyes. "No. I don't want to hear that."

"I said *politically*. She didn't want to force her beliefs down anyone else's throat. She didn't want to hear about dead babies in Dumpsters or young women bleeding to death by someone with dirty hands and a coat hanger. But Elle would never have aborted—no matter what it cost her." I didn't want to confess to Jake, but if it came out during the proceedings—and it could because my mother knew—I didn't want Jake blindsided. "When Elle was fifteen, and I was seventeen, I got her pregnant."

Jake's eyebrows flew up, and he leaned forward. "What happened to the baby?"

I drew in a deep breath and told Jake about the daughter Elle and I lost a long time ago.

✳ 11 ✳

Twenty Years Before Elle's Accident

In late May of 1988, I returned home after spending my junior year of high school as a foreign exchange student in Wales. I thought I'd grown up over there, as if getting laid for the first time transformed a boy into a man. Later I would realize losing my virginity could not conjure an adult spirit. I was the same bubble-gum-snapping, seventeen-year-old kid who had left ten months earlier, the youngest of four boys, filled with bravado. I told myself I could finally stand up and be counted as a man instead of the family's pipsqueak.

Home hadn't changed much, a bit perhaps. My brother Mike had gotten his own place, and Mom had redecorated his room with this god-awful floral wallpaper, but otherwise not one fork or dinner plate had shifted location in the cupboard.

Next door, however, Alice McClure, my mother's best friend, was dying, and she was relying heavily on Elle for all sorts of things, from watching her little, seven-year-old brother to keeping track of how much beer Hank was consuming.

Before I'd left for Wales, Elle had always followed me around like an annoying puppy with those big moss-green eyes of hers. I would have been at the top of my class if Elle hadn't skipped two grades and landed in mine. She was one of those child prodigies, and I was merely brilliant. She was competition, and I tolerated her. The girl next door. A neighbor. A friend of forced proximity.

Yet strangely, I'd missed her more than anyone else while I was gone, especially after her once-a-day letters stopped coming without explanation. Within hours of my return, I sought her out. Not because I recognized the truth: I loved her more deeply than I would ever love anyone else. I didn't yet. I hadn't emerged from my childish narcissism.

No, I banged on her back door because she hadn't appeared at the airport along with the rest of the family. I gave her a second chance to welcome me home and invited her to the party a school buddy was throwing in my honor.

Elle didn't conform to the mold well enough to fit with the in-crowd. Even so, she came reluctantly because I asked. While I was grabbing a beer, high-fiving the hordes who'd come to celebrate my return, I realized Elle was gone.

Her father's parting dispatch was that I should look after her. Shit, I thought. I found her twenty minutes later out on the lawn staring up at the night sky. Of course she'd be stargazing with or without her telescope. I should have known to look there first.

"It's too crowded for me," she said.

I dropped down beside her and lay back with my arm tucked behind my head. "Where's Orion?"

She chuckled. "You can't see Orion in a summer sky." Without hesitation, she pointed. "There's Vega, Altair, and Deneb, the summer triangle, each one the brightest in its constellation."

I glanced over at her. She was holding back. She probably knew an encyclopedia of information, complete with the solar mass and luminosity of each star.

"I've seen a couple of shooting stars, too," she said.

"What did you wish for?"

She grimaced and shook her head. "It would take a miracle to get what I want."

"Which is?"

"Never mind. You can't tell someone your wish or it won't come true." Her voice snagged like a fishing line on a lily pad, and she couldn't yank it in. She sat up and turned away. Her voice broke again. "I'm heading home."

I put my hand on her shoulder and tugged her back to me. Her face was warm and wet, and I wondered how I'd missed that she must have been crying.

"What is it?"

She said nothing but clung to me. It had to be about her mother.

"They can cure breast cancer, right?" I asked.

"If they catch it in time, sure," she said.

"They did, right?"

"It's in her bones."

And suddenly the Barbie-doll blond wig that covered her mother's head concealed something other than vanity. In a letter Mom wrote back in January, she told me about Alice's cancer. There would be chemotherapy and radiation, Mom said, but I hadn't grasped the full implication. Alice might die. Alice. God. "That's bad? If it's in her bones?" I asked.

"Terrible. Don't tell anyone, okay?" Elle was trembling. "She's trying to be brave."

And so was Elle. Intrepid. Even as a teenager.

I kissed her forehead, a caring gesture, nothing more. "Let's see if we can see another shooting star," I said.

We eased down on our backs to the grass, side by side. I took her hand while I scrutinized the sky, searching for some way to make her feel better. Some way to make me feel better. I had nada. The night was supposed to go differently—be fun. Me. My friends. A party.

Elle and I were close enough to one of the citronella torches that, after adjusting to the darkness, I could make out her face, and I found myself staring at her. Her braces were off her teeth, and she'd grown beautiful in my absence.

Once in a while a kid or two came out on the lawn and wandered around. None of them said a thing to us. We said nothing to them. Or to each other. After a bit, Elle's breathing grew soft. In the distance, the heavy bass of a Billy Idol song boomed out from the house. We were detached from the sound, and the activity slipped farther away until I was dreaming. Something. Like all dreams, it melted.

When I awoke, my face was millimeters from Elle's. I pushed the dial to look at my watch. It was a little past ten-thirty. "Wake up," I whispered.

Instead of rearing, her breathing deepened. I let my lips brush hers as much out of curiosity as out of lust. That's when her eyes fluttered open. With our lips touching so gently, I wondered if I was the same guy I'd been in Wales, the one who thought of sex as a target.

God, Elle's lips were soft. At any moment I expected her to burst into juvenile laughter the way her little brother did when she tickled him right before we left her house earlier that night. She was a kid, too, but she didn't laugh.

And for the first time she didn't look like a kid. I ran my fingers along her cheek, wondering why I'd never even considered kissing her before.

Her breathing quickened as her lips held on mine, the pressure increasing hesitantly. I tried to slip my tongue into her mouth, but I guess the dare was too much. She shifted away from me and brought the pads of her fingertips to her mouth, and then, with her eyes locked on mine, she reached out and touched my lips as if she were bringing the kiss back to me.

I didn't have any idea what I should do next. I wanted her, but this was Elle.

She stood, looking equally uncertain of herself. "It must be late. I'd better go home."

I rose and tucked a strand of her hair behind her ear, intending to kiss her again, seriously this time, but she backed away.

"Elle." What was I supposed to say? That I didn't want her to leave? She had to. She was past curfew. "I'll walk you home."

We didn't talk about the kiss. We didn't talk at all for a few minutes.

The trees, tall oaks, maples, and pines, blocked the night sky from view as we strolled down the street. I tripped in a pothole, and feeling like a klutz, I tried to laugh it off. "I should have brought a flashlight." My arm brushed against hers, half intentionally, half because I couldn't see. I wanted to take her hand, but she'd broken away from my kiss, and the possibility of changing a relationship so rooted in established roles seemed as dangerous as anything I'd ever dared to do.

After another block, she halted.

I turned to her, needing to touch her again.

"Matt?" Her voice whispered through the inky air. "Does that count as a kiss?"

"What? That? Well, um, I guess. What do you mean?"

"I've never kissed anyone before. Does that count as a kiss? Did you mean to kiss me?"

"Yeah. Not at first, but yeah. I wanted to kiss you. Is that weird?"

Elle slipped her hand in mine. "No, it was nice."

"What about a second kiss?" I inched closer, leaning over her.

A car pulled out of a driveway, and like guilty schemers, we released each other's hand and strolled awkwardly the last two blocks home.

The TV lit the living room of her house with a blue hue. "It's after eleven," I said. "You're late. I'll come in with you and explain."

She opened the front door. Her father was conked out on the sofa.

"No need. I guess he fell asleep," Elle whispered. "Night, Matt."

I pecked her mouth and tried to tug her back onto the porch for more, but she pulled away again. "I can't. Good night," she said. The door slowly closed in my face.

Through the window, I could see Elle rounding up beer bottles from the coffee table in front of her father, flipping on the kitchen light, and disappearing into the back of the house.

In Wales, I'd had sex with a girl I didn't care about—much. I could have—but she was more interested in conquest than even I was. This newborn fascination I had with Elle couldn't be like that. We had to care about each other or it would be disastrous. Even at seventeen, I knew that much. But here's the thing: I did care. That's what made it scary. I already loved her—even if I didn't love her like that. For days, I tried to convince myself it was a stupid crush.

Besides, Elle was just a kid. Then I'd rationalize she would be fifteen in twelve more days, then eleven. Then it didn't matter much; Elle's mother ended up in the hospital with a blood infection, and her grandfather dropped dead from a stroke. If that weren't enough, I was hit by a car.

Actually, Hank ran me down, not on purpose, but he did. He'd been drinking, and I was out jogging after dark. A downpour started, and somehow Hank hit me and broke my leg, my left tibia. He drove off, unaware. My folks figured it out the next day. His car had pulled into the driveway minutes after it happened, and then Dad found fabric from my running shorts embedded in Hank's bumper.

For Mom and Dad, my injuries presented a moral dilemma. Hank needed to stop drinking before he killed someone, especially since that someone could be me. Dad thought a drunk-driving, hit-and-run arrest might make Hank wake up to the reality he'd become an alcoholic. Mom worried about how sick Alice was and what would happen to Elle and Christopher if Hank went to prison. One dying mother, one jailbird father would likely land Elle and Chris in foster care. There were zip relatives—only my parents—and technically they weren't related.

My parents opted to handle the situation themselves. They confronted Hank, and utterly remorseful and relieved my broken leg would heal, he went to his first AA meeting, offered to pay my college tuition, and stayed sober—briefly.

With the adults preoccupied, Elle and I stole plenty of opportunities to make out when no one was looking. No one was ever looking. No one even noticed we were smitten with each other. Why would they? Everyone assumed we had the same old relationship.

Whether love at first sight is a myth or a legitimate phenomenon, I can't say, but falling in love with Elle was as unexpected. I wish I could say it was a pure, chaste kind of love, and that I would have waited forever to make love to her. But I was seventeen. I'd already felt the curve and grind of a girl's pelvis beneath my own. I knew Elle was too young. I did. But I couldn't explain the hunger I had for her. And only in retrospect did I realize how big a mistake I was making by pushing her into sleeping with me.

I was working the graveyard shift at L.L.Bean's mail order,

sleeping away the mornings, stealing the afternoons with Elle when she didn't have to watch Christopher, and trying to put my hands places she continued to resist.

Elle had been her grandfather's favorite, and he left his house to her for when she grew up. It remained vacant and available for our meetings. We took advantage. With all the awkward fumbling complicated by the cast on my leg, we rolled around on the sofa, and once I got her into a bedroom and half undressed before she said no. Our parents showed no indication of knowing or outward concern. Hank was still going to AA meetings. Alice, although still hospitalized, had improved, and my folks were busy watching Christopher and working their own jobs.

In mid-August, Elle paid close attention to the weather forecast because the Perseid meteor showers were coming, and a cloudless sky was crucial to see shooting stars. Up on her grandfather's widow's walk, she lugged out the telescope. The hospital had released Alice the day before, and the families were having a quiet afternoon picnic down by the riverfront. Alice, Hank, and my folks gathered down below in the gazebo, and Christopher was running around with his hyperactive arms flailing away. One place Elle and I were always safe from Christopher was up on the widow's walk because the kid might run around flapping his wings, but he would never fly. He was terrified of heights. Her grandfather's house sat on over a hundred acres of land that rose up over the Harraseeket River. Most of it was forested except for the lawn that sloped down to the riverbank. The farmhouse, as we called it, was really an octagonal Victorian, a onetime fad of architecture. It had a wraparound porch and a widow's walk where Elle loved to watch the nighttime sky.

"You don't need the telescope to see shooting stars," I said, rubbing my shin. With my cast finally off, I felt compelled to scratch at even the slightest itch.

"Shush, don't tell my parents that I don't need Gramps's telescope. They'll make me stay home and watch from the backyard."

"They can't hear us up here." I pulled Elle back into the attic, where I could kiss her. I pinned her against the wall, slid my hand up under her shirt, and snapped open her bra.

"Matt, no; don't."

I ignored her, kissing her neck, her ears, anywhere which had previously elicited a reaction.

"My parents. They might come looking for us."

I slipped my hand onto her breast.

"Matt, tomorrow night. Not now."

"Tomorrow?" I stood erect. Well, my posture was not my only anatomically erect feature.

She trembled a little then met my eyes with her own less-than-certain-looking ones. "If you can get protection—I'm staying here tomorrow night for the Perseids. Alone. Can you, you know, sneak down here? You're off, right?"

For a moment my breath left me. "Seriously?"

She nodded. "I want to—sleep with you."

"God, I love you, Peep."

"Me, too," she said. "We just have to be careful."

And we were. But as it turned out, not nearly careful enough.

✦ 12 ✦

Twenty Years Before Elle's Accident

In September of '88, I started my senior year of high school, but Elle had zoomed past me. Bowdoin College had allowed her to audit classes the previous semester since Freeport High School no longer knew what to do with her, and she impressed the hell out of the college. The dean of admissions looked at her age, grades, and perfect SAT scores, and the school admitted her for the fall semester. Since she was too young to drive, I volunteered to pick her up in the afternoons, but it was another excuse to be alone and to sneak more time down at her grandfather's house.

As the weather grew colder, so did Alice's prognosis. Fully aware of the inevitable outcome, Alice decided to stop cancer treatment against the wishes of her husband.

Elle's tears didn't surprise me. She wanted more time with her mother, and she cut classes, stayed up half the night studying, and generally neglected herself to get it. Even so, we found time to be together. Rather than distance developing, we found something else—intimacy, I suppose. I swore I could feel her pain, and I wanted to carry it for her. We were children, but we were a family, the two of us, and I could only foresee one future: we would get married—someday.

On a mid-November afternoon, at her grandfather's house, we started a fire in the woodstove and cuddled up on the sofa. Elle wasn't feeling well. Everyone had noticed that much. Mom kept saying, "The girl's run-down, trying to do all the housework for Alice and carrying a full load at college. Why doesn't Hank hire a housekeeper? He can afford it."

I stroked Elle's hair. She bolted upright and ran into the bathroom. Through the oak-paneled door, the sound of retching followed. An irrational idea hit me. Although I knew cancer wasn't contagious, the tendency did run through families. But then, feeling like a dolt, I realized it was the chemo that made a person puke, not the cancer itself. "Peep?"

"Go away."

"Can I come in?"

"No!"

"Elle, you're sick. Do you need to go to the doctor?"

The door creaked open, and pale as the ceiling, she crept back to the sofa and plopped her face in her hands.

"What is it?" I rubbed her back.

Her eyes widened to the size of saucers. "I didn't pay attention at first." Her chin quivered. "But I think I'm pregnant."

Elle didn't want me to go in while the doctor examined her. So there I sat, conspicuously killing time in Planned Parenthood's outer office, reading material on STDs. I didn't have one of those. I used a condom every time I had sex. Every single time. I switched to literature on contraceptives. On condoms. On how to use them properly. I knew how. I went through boxes of them. The stupid thing was, I never read the directions. I learned like every other guy—by word of mouth. You waited until you got hard and rolled it on. When you were done, you threw it away and made sure your parents didn't find the wrappers. Except these directions had a tidbit about making sure you were still hard when you pulled out.

With the girl in Wales, I couldn't get out fast enough. With Elle, I liked to stay inside her. And once, the condom came half off when I pulled out. It didn't completely, so I thought we were safe. *Christ.*

The door to the inner office opened and a woman in a lab coat beckoned me inside.

Elle sat in one of those creepy hospital gowns on a table with stirrups. At least she didn't have her feet in them. Her head hung low, and she didn't meet my gaze.

"Do you want to tell Matt, or do you want me to?" the doctor asked.

Elle bit her lip and stared at her hands, which she had knitted together so tightly they were turning white.

"She's about ten weeks pregnant," the doctor said. "You have options. You'll have to decide quickly if you want to terminate. We have about a two-week window. You can keep the baby. Or you can consider placing it for adoption. I urge you to talk to your parents."

Elle stood and grabbed the back of her gown. "No. My mom and dad cannot know about this. Not now. Not ever." She ran into the bathroom and slammed the door.

For a moment I just stared and then I felt the doctor's eyes on me. "Her mother is very sick," I said as a way of explanation. Then it hit me just how dire the situation was.

"I want you to talk with one of our counselors."

"Sure," I said.

After the doctor exited, Elle emerged, wearing her clothes and a panicked expression on her face. She dropped her shoes onto the floor and jammed her feet into them. "Let's go."

"The doctor wants us to talk to—"

"I can't. Not now. I have to think. Please, Matt. Take me home."

I didn't take her home. Once we climbed into the car, I had another idea, and I turned onto the interstate. Internally muttering self-recriminations, I drove. In silence. I'd promised to take care of her, to be safe when we had sex, and I'd been so frigging arrogant, so certain I knew exactly what I was doing. And she had trusted me.

An hour later, I pulled off an exit near a beach town. The overcast day had that raw, November feeling. It was gray and the leaves were gone. We parked next to a boarded-up beach motel and started down the sand. The wind blew off the Atlantic, chilling, not quite freezing. I took her hand in mine as we walked the wide beach. "We can do anything you want to do," I said.

"I don't want to be pregnant. Do I look pregnant?"

I shook my head. But her breasts were bigger, and her belly had a fullness that hadn't been there before. I'd chalked it up to maturity, to growing curves. "You want to have an abortion?"

She turned toward me. "How could I do that? My mom's dying. I keep begging God to save her, and you want me to turn around and kill a baby?"

"No, Peep. I didn't say that." I didn't know what I thought. Or what I said. Or what I wanted. I wanted her not to be pregnant. "My parents'll help us. Right after they kill me, that is."

"I'm fifteen. I can't have a baby. I have to take care of Christopher. I promised my mom." Elle started to cry, not in little whimpers but in consuming sobs. I took her in my arms, and we sat on the cold sand, huddled together.

Our dreams were disappearing, medical school for me, MIT and NASA for her. And then, there was the more immediate. Alice would have to know. And my parents; I'd be disappointing them in incalculable ways. Hank would wish he'd killed me instead of just breaking my leg when he ran into me. It was a bigger mess than I could believe. However, part of me, a minuscule part of me, was in awe that we had made a baby. One I didn't want, but we had made a baby.

"How long do you think I can hide it?" she asked.

"You can't hide being pregnant. It's going to get pretty obvious."

Elle tugged at the front of her bulky sweater, the style of the time. "Eventually. But if I can hide it for a while, if my mom doesn't have to know—I mean—I don't want her to die, but they said two or three months—and if I can hide it for that long, she wouldn't have to worry about me, too. How could I do this to her now?" Elle started crying again, this time with her hands cradling her lower belly.

I nodded. "What then?"

"I'm not ready. I want one someday—but not now. I want to go to MIT. I want to—" She started shaking like she was freezing cold, like she was terrified. "What if we put it up for adoption?"

"Give it up? No. I don't know." I stood and reached out my hand to her. We walked to the end of the beach, where the river cut through the sand on its way to the ocean. "What if we get married?"

She clapped her hand over her mouth.

I should have gone down on one knee. I knew you were supposed to do that when you asked a girl to marry you. So I did, feeling stupid on top of feeling guilty. "This is forever, right? So let's get married."

She knelt beside me and buried her face in my chest. She held on for minutes, and I started thinking how crazy this was. How she and I would be getting married and playing house.

"I love you," she whispered. "You know I love you, right?"

I nodded.

"But, Matt, how could we get married? We're not old enough. I'm not old enough. I'm not ready to get married—or to have a baby. Part of me wants to. I want all those things, just not yet. Not now."

I didn't know what to say, so I said nothing.

"Do you really want to get married and have a baby now?" Elle asked.

We broke apart just enough to look into each other's eyes. I shook my head.

"Me either. What are we going to do?" she whispered.

A red ambulance strobe lit our street. Elle opened the car door before I came to stop. "What are you doing?" I yelled, slamming on the brakes.

She jumped out and ran full sprint toward her house, and I followed after her.

The ambulance crew was strapping Alice, pale, pasty, and wigless, onto a gurney while my parents looked on.

"Mommy? What happened?" Elle grabbed Alice's hand. The ambulance crew hoisted the stretcher into the back of the truck. Elle tried to climb in, but my mother took Elle's shoulder and pulled her off to the side. The word *seizure* filtered through the darkness. Elle tore away and up into the back of the ambulance. She kissed her mother's forehead. "Mommy, I love you."

"We need to take your mother to the hospital. You have to get out of the ambulance now," the rescue-squad driver told her.

"Come down, Elle," Hank said. He was carrying Christopher, and he turned and walked away, as if Elle should obey him, as if she didn't need her father every bit as much as Christopher did.

Sniffling, Elle climbed down and into my arms. "This can't be happening. Not all at once."

I held her close and whispered, "It will be all right. It will be. I love you, and I swear, I'll take care of you." Without thinking, we kissed, and when we pulled apart, I caught my mother's surprised gaze.

My father stood on the porch, studying me. "Where the hell have you been? You and Elle should have been home hours ago. We were worried."

I shook my head. "We went for a walk. What happened?"

Elle shimmied away from me and dashed across the yard, following Hank and Christopher with Mom in pursuit.

Dad's eyes traced Elle's path. "Alice had a convulsion on the kitchen floor. What's going on with you and Elle?"

"I love her."

"Love her? Since when?"

I shrugged. "This summer."

He drew a deep breath. "Son, she's too young for you. She's fourteen."

"No, she turned fifteen in July. And you don't understand, Dad. I really, *really* love her."

Something about the way my father's eyes focused made me realize that I revealed more than I intended to. Dad rubbed his balding forehead. "Matt, don't even think about it. She's too young. You're too young. Don't. I mean it, don't."

I glared, but in a couple of months, it would become obvious his warning came too late. Every dream either of us had ever held was coming to an end.

The next day I dragged Elle back to Planned Parenthood, where, after an agonizing session with a social worker, we obtained the name of an adoption agency and a clinic for Elle's prenatal care. We had a plan, but life didn't get easier.

After Alice's seizure, the hospital released her on anticonvulsants and a new regimen of pain medications. Elle and I weren't the only ones with a secret. In silence, Alice had been suffering an escalating level of pain.

As if she'd waited for the family to have one last holiday together, Alice didn't wake up the morning after Thanksgiving. No one could rouse her. Again, an ambulance arrived, but this time Elle seemed resigned. She was the one holding her brother as he clung to her neck. Hank paced back and forth, listing all Alice's medications to the rescue-squad EMTs.

I tried to take Christopher from Elle, but he wouldn't let go. I kept thinking she shouldn't be lugging around her eighty-pound brother when she was three months pregnant. I finally got her to sit on the steps with him on her lap.

"There, Christopher. It's okay. She's sleeping. The hospital will wake her up," she said.

"But I want Mommy."

"Don't worry. I'll take care of you. Come on, I'll make us breakfast," she said, leading him inside.

Over the Thanksgiving weekend, Hank begged the oncologist to restart Alice's chemo, but they wouldn't. Instead, he told Hank that Alice could stay in the hospital to die, or Hank could take her home for hospice care.

Thus, the McClure house became Agony Central.

Alice had fallen into what the doctors described as a "light coma," but that's not what it seemed like. She lay on a rented hospital bed in the middle of the living room writhing most of the time. Because she wasn't sufficiently conscious to eat or drink, they kept her alive by jamming a feeding tube up one nostril and pumping formula into her stomach. And worse, because she was unable to use a toilet, the stench of urine and feces took residence in the house.

Anytime the hospice nurse wasn't actively trying to take care of Alice's physical needs, turning her, changing her, filling a bag that poured into her feeding tube, she tried to fill the gaps of silence, chatting endlessly. Monotonously.

I sat in the corner on an overstuffed chair, pretending I wasn't there, my nose in a book, my ears covered by Walkman head-phones, the music sometimes off and sometimes on. I tried to blend into the wallpaper. There, but not there.

In contrast, the nurse, a woman with round cheeks and a rounder backside, tried to blend into the family, doing her best to mother the kids. "When are you going to put up the Christmas tree?"

Elle glanced up from whatever book she was reading to Alice. "What?"

"Does your mother like Christmas, Elle?"

Elle pressed her lips together, seemingly wholly lost for words.

"Maybe she'd like a tree. What do you want for Christmas, anyway? Girls your age usually want clothes," the nurse said.

"I guess," Elle said, rising. "Do you really think we should deco-rate?"

"You should do everything; bake cookies, mull cider, every-thing you would ordinarily do."

Elle looked across the living room at her little brother, who sat building a fort with LEGOs. "Hey, Christopher, do you want to help me make cookies? I'll let you lick the spoon."

"Yeah! Yay!" He ran into the kitchen.

Alice moaned, as she did so often, and the nurse stood.

"Can't you give her more pain medicine?" Elle asked.

The nurse glanced at her watch. "Not for another hour."

"This isn't fair," Elle said.

"Suffering is never fair. Not for your mother. Not for the sick and not for kids like you."

* * *

During the afternoons I tried to do my homework at the Mc-
Clures' so Elle wouldn't be alone, but we talked less and less. We
had no privacy, and talking about the school holiday parties, about
who was dating whom, or about the basketball team's last game
didn't penetrate Elle's veneer. Most of the time it was like she
didn't hear me.

When Hank was around, it was pretty obvious he was drinking
again. His speech tumbled, and he tripped over things that weren't
there. I tried to ask Elle about it, but she only shrugged.

One evening I heard my parents arguing. "Talk to him!" my
mother yelled.

"I have." Dad dropped into his armchair. "I've dragged him to
AA meetings, even threatened him with calling the police about
what he did to Matt. If Hank is determined to drink himself to
death, how the hell do you think I can stop him?"

Mom hissed and stormed out of our house and into the Mc-
Clures'.

A few minutes later Elle knocked on our door.

"Matt," Dad yelled. "Ellie's here. Why don't the two of you take
off for a while, go see a movie. Go ahead, take the car." He picked
up the keys, clenched them in his hand, then added, "Behave yourself."

We left, taking our freedom and clinging to each other. Elle
and I hadn't stopped having sex. It seemed more imperative now,
like instead of being about wanting to touch her, making love was
the reassurance and steadiness that we would survive together. I
needed her. And when we were together, she showed me that she
needed me, too.

That Christmas was a pathetic sham of a holiday. My mother had
to work, and my father, brothers, and I all planned to descend on

Aunt Beth's for Christmas dinner. Mike and I went next door to invite the McClures to come with us.

Elle ushered us through the kitchen door and gestured we should sit at the table, offering us hot chocolate and Danish.

"Not sure there's time for that, Elle," Mike said. "Just came by to see if you guys want to come with us."

"We can't. There's no nurse today. I have to take care of my mom," she said.

Her father was in the living room, drooling into the sofa's cushion. Even on Christmas Day. *Damn him.*

Elle gave me a hug, and as she stepped back, the hair covering her cheek slipped aside, revealing a deep purple bruise.

Mike stood at the door. "We have to get going, Matt."

"What happened here?" I lifted Elle's hair to get a better look.

"Nothing." She replaced her hair to cover her cheek, patting it down.

"Something happened," I said.

She swallowed and whispered, "Daddy took us to Midnight Mass. He was—drunk."

"Wait, you got in the car with him when he was drinking?" My eyes darted to the driveway, expecting to see a smashed-up car.

Elle tugged on my sleeve. "I know, but I didn't realize how much he'd had. He made a scene at church, and the deacon asked us to leave. Anyway, Daddy took a swing at the guy but cuffed me by mistake. He didn't mean—"

I flew into the living room, ready to haul Hank off the couch, and I don't know. I wasn't thinking about what I was going to do.

Mike grabbed my arm. "Whoa!"

Dad walked in and noticed the ruckus. "What's going on here?"

"Hank hit Elle," I yelled as I tried to shake Mike loose.

"It was an accident. He didn't mean to," Elle said.

"Mike, take Matt to the car. Let me handle this," Dad said.

My brother practically carried me out to the car. I was no longer a *little* brother, but Mike was the biggest and strongest of the bunch of us. He slammed me against the outside door. "Cool down. Let Dad handle this."

When Dad finally came out of the house, he said Hank was still bombed out of his mind, too drunk to talk.

"He's driving drunk, Dad. Elle was in the car with him. He hit her."

"I'll handle this, Matt. You got that? I'll handle this," he said, his voice firm.

Four hours later, as soon we arrived back home from Aunt Beth's, I charged toward the McClure house.

"Go home, Matt," Dad said. "I'll talk to him—if he's even awake."

But I shook loose from my father and yanked open the Mc-Clures' back door.

Hank was in the kitchen, cradling his head in his hands.

I dropped into the chair opposite him and pointed my finger in his face. "If you ever hurt Elle again, I will tell the police what you did to me. You're a lousy drunk and a worse father. Don't you dare touch her!"

Hank looked up, utterly blank. "What?"

Elle rubbed my arm. "It's all right," she said to me. "It was an accident. He doesn't even remember."

"Remember what?" Hank slurred.

"You had too much to drink, Daddy. And you, um, you kind of punched me. You weren't trying to hit me, you just banged into me."

"You have to get it together, Hank, or Linney and I will have to notify the authorities," Dad said as he leaned on the table, getting into Hank's face. "You're going to lose your kids as well as your wife."

Elle burst out into tears and darted upstairs with me not far behind her. My father followed.

"You can't do it, Dennis," she screamed at my father. "It's not Daddy's fault. He's upset about my mom. He's not himself." Her voice became so small, like a little girl's. "I need him."

Dad shoved me aside and tilted her chin up so he could see the bruise. "I know you do, but this can't go on. Someone is going to get seriously hurt." My father took Elle in his arms, then suddenly pulled away, looking down at her belly. His eyes shot to me. "No."

Squeezing his eyes shut, he shook his head. "No," he repeated. "I don't want to know this. Not today."

✦ 13 ✦

Nineteen Years Before the Accident

Elle didn't go back for the spring semester at Bowdoin. She told everyone else she couldn't leave her mother. She told me it was because the baby would come before the end of the term. The end of spring. The end of everything.

Panic was rising in my seventeen-year-old psyche, and I needed to talk it over with my father. Based on his reaction to Elle's belly, he knew. Based on how he'd avoided me afterward, he hated me. I knew I'd disappointed him. And I wasn't sure which was worse.

Before Elle's pregnancy, I planned on an Ivy League education. The truth was that even going to college meant I'd accomplished something huge. Although my father had been accepted at Dartmouth, he didn't attend. My oldest brother was born six months after my folks graduated from high school, and all three of my brothers had taken the trade school route. Keith was a contractor, Doug a plumber, and Mike a mechanic. All fine paths in life. Just not what *I wanted*. I wanted to prove I could do more.

Instead, I proved I was stupid enough to get a girl pregnant.

Holding on to a box of Cheerios, I dropped into the kitchen chair.

"It snowed last night," my father said in a monotone voice. It was the first time Dad had acknowledged me in days. Weeks. He picked up a spoonful of oatmeal.

He didn't need to tell me to go outside and take care of the driveway. That was understood. Three years before he'd had a heart attack while shoveling. I stood and walked over to the mudroom and shrugged into my jacket.

"Things are bad next door." He sighed after stating the obvious. There was no need for me to respond. "Your mother figures we're going to end up as Elle and Christopher's guardians—if Hank doesn't stop drinking," he said. "But your mother doesn't realize Elle is pregnant, yet."

I wondered if the knot in my gut felt anything like the lump of a baby growing in Elle's belly. I could feel my father's eyes burning into my back. I turned around, defiant if I needed to be.

He looked sad, not angry. "It's going to complicate things. I can't imagine that Alice will last much longer." Dad exhaled. "What are you planning to do about the baby?"

I stammered, unable to find words.

He stood and put his hand on my shoulder. "I'd be a hypocrite if I condemned you, but Elle is so young. You're *both* so young." Was he giving me absolution? I didn't know, but his gesture gave me comfort.

"She wants to put the baby up for adoption," I said.

A pensive expression fell across Dad's face. "When's it due?"

"Late April."

He walked over to the sink and softly said, "Giving a child up is harder than it sounds. We thought about it, with your oldest brother, but as soon as your mother felt him move—"

"Elle doesn't want anyone to find out yet. Hank's going to flip out, isn't he?"

"Yeah. I don't know. Probably."

"Elle wants to wait to tell him until after Alice—you know . . ." *Dies.* "One crisis at a time."

"Jesus. Okay." He stared through the kitchen curtains at the McClure house. "I can't believe she's still alive. The doctors didn't think she'd make it until Christmas. And we're halfway through January."

A couple of days later, Elle took my hand and laid it on her abdomen. "Do you feel that? It's the baby. I've been feeling it for about a week, but I'm sure now."

I couldn't feel anything. I was about to patronize her with a "Yeah, that's cool," but then I felt a little flutter through her skin. "Shit," I said. "No way."

She smiled as if she were utterly content.

"Wow. You're not making it do that?"

"No. She's doing it all by herself. It's so weird to think there's a new person inside me."

"She?"

Elle shrugged. "Don't worry. I know we can't keep her—or him. But, Matt, I love this baby. I dream about holding her and smelling that sweet baby smell."

The smell that popped into my head was the diaper pail at my brother's house, that sickening, sour, rotten smell. My heart pounded in my chest because I knew Elle would never give up this baby just like my mother hadn't put my oldest brother, Doug, up for adoption. In a year, Elle and I would be trudging along with a kid and no future. A sour smell was all I could imagine.

"You know what I mean about that baby smell, right?" Elle asked.

I wanted to smile at her, but I couldn't. "I guess."

"Never mind. It's just that babies smell like life, and my house smells like death."

At school, an old girlfriend, Donna, started flirting with me again. I don't know why she thought I was fair game, but every time I went to my locker, she was right there, flipping her hair, touching my hand. "The Winter Dance is this Friday. I'll let you take me if you ask nicely."

"I'm *still* going out with Elle," I said, but it occurred to me that it sounded as if I meant that to be temporary, like tomorrow I might not *still* be going out with her. I wouldn't dump Elle while she was pregnant, and I didn't plan to dump her afterward. Yet there was a sense of relief that if the baby were adopted, staying with Elle would be my choice again. I loved her, but I was scared shitless.

Donna snickered. "She's getting fat. I saw her up at L.L.Bean's the other day. You can do better than her. Take me to the dance, please?"

"I'm with Elle." I walked off, wondering how neither my mother nor Hank noticed that Elle was not getting *fat*.

Like always, I stopped after school at the McClures' before dropping my books at home. The nightmare continued smack in the middle of the McClure living room, which I renamed the dying room in my head. Once I even slipped and said it aloud, but I managed to cover with "dining room."

Alice was moaning in those low rumbles that punctuated every moment at 43 Chamberlain Street. The nurse was turning Alice so she didn't get bedsores. "Hi, Matt."

"Where's Elle?"

"Upstairs. She's not feeling well. I convinced her to take a nap."

"Oh." I wondered if it was the pregnancy bothering her and started up the steps. "I'll just check on her."

"Can I say something?"

I turned around to look at the portly woman.

"Hank is out and Christopher's still at school, otherwise I wouldn't bring this up, but it's getting pretty obvious."

My heart raced. "What?"

Her eyes narrowed like I was an idiot for trying to cover it up. "I heard her talking to her mother."

How could Elle talk to Alice? "What do you mean?"

"I take breaks, and Elle always sits with Alice when I go outside for a smoke, but sometimes I hear her talking to her mother. Listen, Elle's very scared. She looks like she's handling everything okay, but she isn't. She's just a kid."

"What did she say to Alice?"

"She promised to name the baby after her mother," she said.

I could hear my father saying my mother couldn't give up my brother once she felt him move. Elle had picked out a name. Jesus.

"It's hard to be fifteen and pregnant," the nurse said. "Even harder to watch your mother die, not to mention the bender her father is on. I know you're just a kid, too, but stick with her through this or she won't make it."

I didn't know what I'd done that would make this nurse think I would ever abandon Elle. I grunted something and continued up the steps. We were both scared. True. I'd been accepted at all the colleges I'd applied to. I still wanted Columbia, but given the circumstances, I'd be lucky to commute to the University of Southern Maine—or even to a good trade school. I was feeling resentful. Guilty and resentful. Maybe the nurse saw that.

I cracked opened Elle's bedroom door. She stirred at the sound of the creak, and then settled down into the pillows again. Her shirt rose up a bit, revealing her pregnant abdomen. That my mother hadn't noticed was absurd. Hank had an excuse. In the past few months, he hadn't been sober.

Suddenly Elle drew her legs up as if she were in pain, rising with it. "Oh God." Her eyes flew open.

I sat beside her. "What is it, Peep? Are you sick?"

"Matt? Oh." She grimaced. "Cramps."

"It's not the baby?"

She cradled her belly. "Of course not. I'm not due for months."

I accepted her explanation. "Do you need to go to the doctor?"

"I don't think so. Matt, the nurse knows about the baby. She asked me point-blank."

"I know. We have to tell your father before he finds out."

"Not yet." Her chin dropped low.

I couldn't tell if she was afraid or ashamed, and I didn't want to ask. I searched the room for something else to talk about. These days we discussed only two things, her mother and the baby. It was becoming such a hellhole. "There's the dance Friday night. Want to go?"

She lit up. "Really?"

"Yeah. It'd be fun, right? Hang out. We've never done that to-gether, gone to a school thing."

She raised an eyebrow and pointed to her belly. "What about?"

"Who cares? Everyone will know pretty soon. We may as well hold our heads up." I rested my hand on her belly. "How's the little kiddo anyway?"

"Quiet," she said.

For two months I'd watched her mother writhe. I'd learned the body language of pain, the tensing and the wash of it as it pounded into a person.

Elle's belly went rock hard, and she gasped.

"What the hell is that?" But I knew the answer to the question. My mother had talked about how a woman's belly could get as hard as granite during a contraction. "Are you in labor?"

"No," she said. "It's too ear—" She grabbed my arm.

"I'm taking you to the hospital. Wait right here."

"Maybe to the clinic."

"The hospital." I bolted down the stairs and stopped in the living room. The nurse glanced up at me. "Something's wrong with Elle. I'll be right back."

The nurse headed up the steps two at a time.

My mother's car was in the driveway. I scurried over the fence, the snowbank piled on top of it, and blasted into the kitchen. Mom was peeling carrots, humming some stupid Supremes song, "Stop . . . before you break my heart."

"I need to borrow the car." I grabbed her keys from the rack and turned for the door.

Mom swung around. "Have a horse of your own, and then you can borrow another's. I have to go to the—"

"It's an emergency. Elle. She's sick. I have to take her to the hospital."

Mom grabbed her purse from the kitchen table. "What's wrong with her? Where is she?"

I needed a lie. This wasn't something to spit out like gum. "Food poisoning. I don't know for sure. Let me have the car, Mom."

"I'll drive if Elle's sick."

I didn't know what to do, but before I could think of a response, we were pushing through the McClures' front door. Alice was so still I wondered if she'd finally had the grace to die. Mom paused for a moment to check Alice as I barreled up the steps to Elle's room, which was empty. I stepped back into the hall. Mom was three-quarters of the way upstairs.

The nurse was coming out of the bathroom. "She needs to go to the hospital. I think she's in preterm labor."

"Who's in labor?" Mom asked.

I swallowed. "Elle. She's pregnant."

Shock registered on my mother's face, but she didn't pause or hesitate. She yanked open the bathroom door and found Elle lying doubled over on the floor.

"How far along are you?" Mom squatted beside Elle.

"I'm supposed to go to the clinic tomorrow for my five-month checkup. It's just cramps."

Mom set her hand on Elle's belly to assess the contractions, and within two minutes we were on the road to the hospital. My mother put aside her surprise, disappointment, and anger to contend with the pragmatic concerns. "I have to get ahold of your father, Elle. Do you know where he is?"

"Please don't tell him." Elle shook her head. She sounded so much like a little girl for a moment that I recognized something so frank and apparent, but totally elusive to my usual perspective. She was a child. And so was I.

"We have to reach your father to consent for treatment." My mother had taken on a role I rarely saw. As a labor and delivery nurse, she'd told stories of seeing a zillion women give birth, but somehow I hadn't considered her in this context, taking over, not as my mother, but as something else.

"But I'm pregnant. Doesn't that mean I can—at the clinic—they let me—agh." Elle's face knotted in pain again.

"Where is your father?"

Through gritted teeth, Elle said, "I don't know—somewhere getting drunk."

That seemed a little optimistic on Elle's part. "Getting drunk" suggested Hank had been sober at some point during the previous day. Or week. Or month.

When we arrived at the hospital, my mother grabbed a wheel-chair and pushed Elle directly upstairs to a labor room. Three nurses who worked with Mom appeared somewhat baffled.

One cracked, "So are you rounding up girls off the street now, Linney?"

"This is my son, Matt. And this is his girlfriend, Elle McClure. She's pregnant, in her nineteenth or twentieth week, and she's having contractions. What OB is on call?"

"Blythe Clarke's covering. All the regular OBs are at some con-ference."

"Thank God. Call her. Elle, change into this." Mom handed Elle a gown and ushered me out into the hall.

Mom's expression hardened. She whispered, "Why didn't you tell me? I taught you about birth control. And if you didn't listen about that, then she still could have had an abortion. Jesus, she's fifteen. Your whole life just went down the tubes, Matt."

I figured this wasn't the time to tell her I did my very best to ignore her when she gave that particular lecture, or that I'd used birth control—just not properly. Nor was it the time to tell her that Elle had dismissed an abortion outright. As angry as my mother was at me, I was angrier at myself, and at that moment I didn't give a shit if my mother never forgave me. I was sorry I'd hurt her, probably embarrassed her in front of her coworkers, but I only cared that Elle was okay. "Is she going to be all right?"

In a frustrated gesture, Mom threw her hands into the air then returned to the room. I followed.

The nurse was strapping two belts around Elle's belly. "I've got to find the baby's heartbeat." The nurse had a disklike device, and she was tracing it around Elle's belly button up, then belly button down. Side to side. Its speaker made a gooey, swishing sound. The nurse, who wore an uneasy expression, looked up at my mother.

"Any bleeding?" Mom asked, taking over the search, continuing to move the probe as it made its scratchy white noise.

"No, just cramps." Elle drew a breath. "Like now."

"That's a contraction, sweetheart," Mom said.

"But it's too soon," Elle said.

Her reaction flabbergasted me. I didn't understand how she could still be in denial. Because Mom talked about her work, I knew under certain circumstances they could stop premature labor, but not always. Sometimes babies came so early they spent months and months in the NICU.

Mom continued her search for a heartbeat. Elle and I had heard its pitter-patter plenty of times at the clinic. Right now there was no such sound.

Mom swallowed. "The doctor at the clinic, where is he finding the heartbeat?"

Elle pointed to a spot on her belly.

"Is the baby moving?" the nurse asked.

"No, not since yesterday," Elle said.

Mom's jaw tightened and she turned to the other nurse. "Go get a portable ultrasound."

"What's wrong?" I asked, but I was thinking, *What* else *could go wrong?*

"Sometimes it's just hard to find a heartbeat," Mom said.

"Is that why the baby's so quiet?" The pitch of Elle's voice rose. She had figured out, as I had, what was happening. Not only was she in labor; something was wrong with the baby. I circled the bed to get to a place where neither hospital machines nor people would come between us. She buried her face in my chest, and I buried mine in her hair.

The nurse rolled an ultrasound machine to Elle's bedside. And in walked Dr. Clarke, pink ribbon in her hair like she was trying to signal she was a girl. Although her hair wasn't as white in those days, she still looked ancient to me. "So what do we have here? Hi, I'm Dr. Clarke. Have you been getting prenatal care, sweetie?"

"At the clinic in Brunswick," Elle said.

Blythe shot questions. Elle and I filled in the details again. Prenatal vitamins, check. Blood tests, check. Everything fine, check. Nineteen weeks.

"Okay, let's have a look." She rolled the ultrasound transducer over Elle's belly. A circular image appeared.

"That's your baby's head." The doctor's eyes darted back and forth from the screen to Elle's face.

"This is the chest." She swallowed.

My mother squeezed her eyes shut.

Dr. Clarke drew a deep breath. "How long since you felt movement?"

"Last night at bedtime."

Dr. Clarke put one hand on Elle's and pointed with her other. "This is your baby's heart, and I'm so sorry, but it isn't beating."

Elle scrutinized the screen. "But . . . but . . . it has to be beating. Are you saying—oh no, please. Oh God, please." The monitor graph showed a rising wave. Still, she squeaked, "You mean she's dead?"

"I'm afraid so," Dr. Clarke said softly.

So many emotions surged through me simultaneously, sadness, concern, anger, disappointment, and to my shame—relief. I felt relieved, and I was horrified that I felt that way. I took Elle's hand, and she batted me away. My mother tried. Elle reacted the same way.

"That's a pretty hard contraction. I'm going to check your cervix," Dr. Clarke said.

The nurse passed the doctor a pack of sterile gloves and offered her slimy goop.

"Out of here, Matt," Mom said, pushing me toward the door.

"Linney, can you stay with me?" Elle whimpered, and again, her voice sounded so young.

"Okay, honey," Mom said.

"What about me?"

"Wait outside for a few minutes." Mom shooed me.

Elle opened her mouth to speak and closed it again.

And so I was dismissed, useless, guilty, and sad. Elle didn't want me there. She wanted my mother, any mother, because Elle was a child. And I wanted my mother, too, but all I could think was how much Mom hated me now and how badly I'd hurt Elle. I stood at the door, eavesdropping.

"She's fully dilated. Elle, with your next contraction, I want you to push," Dr. Clarke said.

"Okay."

"Let's get an IV into her. Have the lab come up and draw her blood, and get ahold of the clinic to have them forward any medical records."

What seemed like forever passed, but it was probably only a half hour. Mom came into the corridor, touched my sleeve, and led me down the hall. I stared at her, unable to muster the questions. *Is Elle all right? What happened?*

My mother avoided my gaze until we reached the window at the very end.

"Mom?"

"Physically, Elle will be all right."

"What about the baby?"

"It was a girl. I want you to go in there with Elle, and although this is going to be very difficult, it is important that you hold the baby. If you don't, you'll always wonder."

My legs felt rubbery. I thought she was punishing me, making me look at my mistake. Then she embraced me. "I love you, Matt. Go inside, talk to Elle. I'm going to call home first. Your father should be home by now. Does he know?"

I nodded, thinking that he would probably catch hell from my mother for not telling her.

Mom exhaled. "Once I speak to your father. I'll join you while you hold your daughter."

My daughter?

Elle was sitting in the bed, pale and drawn. The nurse was injecting something in the IV bag. Elle didn't look up; she just stared at her lap.

"Hi," I said.

"Do you think we should give her a name? I didn't let myself pick one . . . well, I did. But she was going to belong to someone else. I was going to call her Allie, for my mom—but that doesn't seem right now. Do you think we should give her a name?"

I was taken aback, but I said, "Yeah." It was then that I saw the baby, tucked in the blankets on Elle's lap. The baby was so small, maybe eight inches long. I gulped.

"What names do you like?" Elle asked.

It seemed like the most absurd question. Like it mattered. We would never call her to come to the supper table or sing "Happy Birthday" to her. "I don't know."

"It should be special because it's the only thing we will ever give her."

That's when the reality of what was happening hit me. This was a baby—who might have grown up into a person. I choked up. "Okay, a name."

Elle reached out and put one hand on my shoulder.

"Whatever you want," I managed to say.

"Celina. It's a beautiful name, right? It means goddess of the moon, and—"

"That's fine." I cut Elle off because I knew I couldn't handle whatever sentimental thing she was about to say. Like every time we looked at the moon, we would think of Celina. I already knew I would.

"I think she would have been pretty. And smart, of course," Elle said.

"Brilliant like you." I drew nearer to see.

"Do you want to hold her?"

I nodded, but I didn't really.

Elle put the blankets in my hands, and I couldn't feel the weight of a baby. It was as if she wasn't there at all.

"I'm sorry, Matt." Elle rubbed her eyes.

"Why?"

"It must be my fault. Dying is all around me. In my house. In my body. Everywhere. I'm *so* sorry."

I sat on the bed beside Elle and kissed her hair. "No, Peep. This isn't—your fault." It felt like it was mine. I'd believed Elle would never give the baby up. And I'd resented that, but seeing Celina, I knew I wouldn't have been able to surrender her either.

Mom tapped on the door, slipped inside, and sat on a chair in the corner. Her eyes were red. "When you're ready, they'll take her. They need to move you to a regular room soon."

"Take her? What are they going to do with her?" Elle took Celina from me and pulled the baby close.

"Some decide to have a funeral. Most just let the hospital dispose of a fetus this early." Mom meant they'd throw her away.

"No. A funeral," I said.

"Dispose? God," Elle said. "But a funeral? I can't tell my dad about her. Not the way things are at my house. What are we going to do, Linney?" She started crying in earnest sobs.

For a few minutes, in the resonating silence that filled the room, I held Elle while she held Celina.

Finally Mom spoke. "I would like to disagree with you about not telling Hank, but right now maybe you're right, Elle. I'll see what I can do with the hospital. I'll try to get them to direct the hospital bill to our house instead of yours. And the alternative to having a funeral would be to have her cremated. Dad and I can pay the expenses. Then you can do what you want with her ashes. They would give you an urn, but you could keep her ashes or bury them, spread them on the water, whatever you decide."

"Cremation?" They were going to burn her. I felt like I was going to puke. "No way."

Elle wiped her face. "It's okay, Matt." Elle's tears started pouring down her face again. She smeared them away with one hand as she held the baby to her heart with the other. "You know that song, 'Woodstock.' It says 'We are stardust.' And we are. We come from stardust. Everything on earth is just ashes." Her voice broke.

A nurse entered the room. "We need to move you, Elle. Are you ready, honey?"

"I'll miss you." Elle kissed Celina's tiny little head and passed the baby back to me.

They were going to burn her, no matter what euphemism Elle slapped on it. Feeling light-headed, I whispered to Celina, "I'm sorry."

Mom took the baby from my hands and blinked away her own tears. "Come here, little angel. I wish I could have known you."

Every year since, I've tried to watch the Perseids. It seems so long ago now that Elle and I first stayed up to watch them at Elle's grandfather's house, our house now. We conceived Celina not long after that first night together. In the years between, I have driven for hours to find a road open and dark enough, then climbed up on the car's roof to watch the light show. Believing somehow Celina would know I was thinking of her. Other years, with no alternative, I'd watched from a New York City rooftop and only pretended I could see the fine streaks of fire.

Celina, our little spark of stardust.

14

After Elle's Accident
Day 4

"So you lost Celina." Jake shook his head. "Was it Elle's autoimmune disease?"

"Probably." I pulled a textbook from my office bookshelf that contained a chapter on antiphospholipid syndrome and set it on the desk in front of him. "Some light reading, if you're so inclined." I opened a file cabinet and pulled out a folder filled with journal articles on APS in pregnancy and dumped that in front of Jake as well. "Or you could rely on what Clint told you about APS when you interviewed him."

"There's a lot here. You do your homework," Jake said, flipping through the pages.

"It's not a neurosurgical problem. Before Elle's diagnosis, it was just a footnote in my medical education. But for the past four years, it's had my life by the balls."

"Anything else you think I should know about it?"

"It *didn't* kill the last baby."

"What did?"

"We were at home. Elle's water broke. Everything went wrong. And it went wrong very fast. I called for an ambulance, but—" My voice cracked. I started pacing again. "We didn't get to the hospital in time. Not in time for the baby."

Jake and I spent an exhaustive hour, discussing what happened and about why I was so reluctant to try to have a child afterward.

I gave him our life stories, even though he knew most of mine. I told him Elle's, the part separate from me, the part when we weren't together. The part that included NASA and Adam, although I don't think I mentioned Adam by name, only that she had lived with him.

Finally, at seven o'clock, Jake and I parted company.

✦ 15 ✦

Day 4

I walked into our empty kitchen and flipped on the light. Elle's running shoes were under a pulled-out kitchen chair, and the Boston fern over the sink drooped from lack of water. I half expected our yellow Lab, Hubble, to come bounding up to me, but my brother Mike had picked him up days ago.

The stillness.

Elle was in every room, the colors she picked for the walls, the books stacked on the shelves, the photographs of us, photographs with our friends, and the ones from her NASA days. She wasn't exactly messy, but no one would ever accuse her of being a neatnik. Objects landed where they landed. "Gravity," she'd say. "I'll get to it later." But she didn't always get around to the smaller details in life.

I used to find bills tucked away in odd places. "You're like an absentminded professor," I said once.

"I know where everything is. Everything. Granted, Martha Stewart would cringe at my lack of external organization." Elle tapped her temple. "But up here, I have a very detailed algorithm."

"Sure you do," I said, and then I took over paying our bills.

Entering our bedroom, I hoped to drown in the scent she left on the sheets, but she'd stripped the bedding the morning of the accident and left the quilt haphazardly folded on the bench at the foot of the bed.

I went into the bathroom for a set of sheets. A bag from CVS sat on the counter. It held baby aspirin and a pack of pictures from our trip to Prince Edward Island the month before. Most of the photos were of me. She loved to shoot with a long lens, catching me unaware. She said that's when you could find a person's spirit, their truth.

That was Elle, full of mysticisms and superstitions and contradictions. I loved that about her. The world might see her as a driven scientist. She was, I suppose. How many people earn their PhD before they turn twenty-two? But my brilliant wife still feared black cats crossing her path. She wished on stars—even though she could mathematically calculate the trajectory of a satellite's orbital decay and explain the chemistry and physics behind fission. And she never let an empty rocking chair move back and forth—something about it inviting a child's death. *The hollow of it.* We lost our babies anyway. All before they were born.

Why did I believe it could be different this time? That this baby would live—that Elle could be kept alive long enough to nourish it? Because this time had to be different. Because I had to give her the child she wanted. Because I could still see her holding Celina and weeping. Because part of me still carried that first baby, all of our babies, too. Because.

The baby inside Elle was only shadow on the ultrasound. A glimmer. And yet I had to make that baby real.

Dylan was a real baby; he was four pounds, ten ounces. At the hospital, they weighed his body and gave us his vital statistics as if *vital* statistics made him alive. The numbers were supposed to be something to hold on to, something concrete to grieve. I held my son in my arms. I tried to breathe life back into him. And I failed.

Maybe that was what I was trying to do now—breathe life into this baby—breathe life back into some part of Elle. I did not believe a baby would bring her back, but having one was her dream. I needed to keep her hopes and dreams alive.

I shuffled through the pictures and found one of her smiling. Her broad smile. Her smile gone forever. "What do you want me to do, Peep?"

A few days ago she said trying to have a baby was worth the risk.

Was it worth making her stay on life support? Would she think so, or was I clinging onto a delusion?

I slipped a picture of Elle walking along the red sand beach into my breast pocket, and put the remainder back in the bag, and stopped cold. There was a pregnancy test under the bathroom sink. I pulled open the door and reached for it. Not there. I rifled around. Not there. Did she take the test? Did she know? Or did she simply throw it away so we wouldn't fight over it anymore?

She didn't know. She couldn't have known. She wouldn't have gone up on that ladder if she knew.

The farmhouse bedroom was small and plain, painted in a cool gray. "Gray is restful," she'd said. It was just big enough for a full-size bed, ridiculously short for my height, but it meant Elle and I were always touching at night, which proved to have benefits.

I couldn't sleep there without her now or ever again. I picked up the quilt and a pillow, intending to take them downstairs to the couch in the living room, but instead, when I reached the attic door, I stood frozen, lost in the vastness of what had occurred in the past few days.

I dragged myself upstairs. Only five nights ago, I'd come home late after doing an emergency surgery on what should have been my day off. Elle was waiting in the attic, sitting cross-legged beneath a floor lamp reading her mother's old diaries and writing in her own.

Elle should still be here, hiding the letters under the trapdoor in the attic, where she kept them tucked away from the world. What were the odds that she wrote something about believing life started at conception in one of those diaries? Slim, but it didn't matter; I couldn't bear to look right now. This was where I last saw her, where I last held her, yet it was the first place we made love. And the last place.

But she wasn't here. And the house was silent in the way that reverberates the pulse in a man's ears.

I lit the floor lamp and stepped through the doors to the widow's walk, an apt name, for I had become a widower in all but fact. While waiting for a meteorite to pass, I spread out the quilt then sat down to look up at the night sky. The peak of the Perseids had come and gone, but Earth was still passing through the region of space. What would I wish for? To go back in time. I'd tell her not to climb up on that ladder. I'd wish for the baby to survive against the damning odds. Or I could die in my sleep so I could join Elle in nothingness. The vacuum nearly swallowed me.

I curled on my side and cried. I cried harder than I ever had.

When I awoke, the morning's first light tinted the sky. I was achy from the hard roof, from the catharsis, and from a clearer vision of what the future held.

✦ 16 ✦

Day 5

I should have expected to see Elle's writing on the steamed-up bathroom mirror. It said, THE SWEETEST THING! Almost every day Elle left a couple of words scrawled on the glass, and the next time I showered a phrase would reveal itself. Sometimes it was something from a poem. She liked Dickinson, Thomas, and Rossetti. Some days she simply wrote, "Go save a life" or "I love you."

And I'd smile then wipe down the mirror before I shaved. Today I toweled off and leaned against the wall and waited for the steam to dry. I watched Elle's love note disappear.

I turned the shower back on and let steam fill the bathroom again, but her message did not rematerialize. Instead it condensed and rained down in heavy droplets. I wondered why she wrote those three words. Was it the title to a U2 song I used to play over and over? The chances were it was just Elle's way of saying she loved me. She did. And it was the sweetest thing.

The smell of coffee and my mother's corn bread wafted upward—along with the sound of water running and dishes clinking. Immediately I knew Mom had let herself in. I stomped down the steps, prepared to throw her out. I would have, but her eyes were sad and hollowed. If we hadn't been on opposite sides of the court dispute, we might have grieved together. She might have shared with me how she found the strength to survive my father's death.

But now I sensed another loss, my mother's. Before this, before Elle's accident, Mom and I were close, for the most part. But in the courtroom, Mom had one thing right: Elle was even closer, closer than a daughter-in-law. Sometimes, she was closer than a son.

Mom turned away from me when I entered the kitchen. "Mike still has Hubble. I made you breakfast and—"

"I can take care of myself."

"I made a leg of lamb last night and packed you up a couple of sandwiches. Don't worry, I removed most of the fat, but you need to eat, and you love lamb." She wiped down the counter with a sponge.

"I can take care of myself," I repeated.

She was acting as if I were still dependent upon her for food, for housekeeping, for her moral compass, and she kept rambling on as if she were giving a teenager a list to follow while she was at work. "We should be pulling together right now," she said.

"I can't do that when you're trying to kill my wife."

Mom gasped and stepped backward. "You cannot be serious! I love Elle."

"Get out," I said. For a second I wanted to bodily remove her, drag her outside. For a second I forgot she was my mother. Pull together? She was tearing us apart. Elle and I married each other. What is the wedding rhetoric? *What God has joined together, let no man put asunder.* Sure. Try to tell that to my mother. "Get out," I said again.

Mom pretended not to hear me. Instead, she dried her hands on a dish towel, then not so furtively dabbed at her eyes. She poured two cups of coffee and set them on the table. "For ten minutes, just sit down. Eat something. I'm not ready to bury you, too. Come on, corn bread's your favorite."

"But you're ready to bury Elle? Jesus." I glared at her for a moment, not willing to let it go, trying to punish her. She held out a plate.

Hell. I didn't want to take the time to make breakfast or stop at a fast-food place, so I grabbed it and sat down at the table.

"We're not enemies, just adversaries," she said.

I didn't speak to her as I wolfed down her food and gulped her coffee.

"The reporters kept calling," she said as she slid a piece of paper across the table. "I have a new phone number; it's unlisted."

I glanced at the blinking answering machine on the counter.

"You might want to do the same." She stared into her coffee. It was rare for her to avoid eye contact.

I stood and listened to the first part of two dozen messages, deleting them as soon as the callers identified themselves. "Why can't they leave me alone to deal with this?"

"Because they feel like they own some little part of her. When she went up into space, she captured the imagination of people who wanted to believe in heroes. Because people don't want to be kept alive against their wills."

I shot my mother a dirty look.

"Being a vegetable scares people, honey. I'm sorry, but given what you do for a living, you know that."

"A vegetative state is not the same thing as being a goddamned vegetable, and *you* should know that. She's brain-injured. Badly, but she's a human being, not a vegetable." I held out my hand. She took it, and I shook her loose. "I want my house keys."

"Matthew, I'm sorry." My mother rubbed her forehead. "I

thought by now you'd see more clearly. I'm going to have to hire an attorney. I can see that after Friday. We're on opposite sides, but please understand."

"Understand what? Goddamn it, what? That you can't even consider that I'm right?"

"She was terrified by how Alice died."

"This isn't the same. Alice was in constant pain. Elle isn't. Elle is pregnant. Alice wasn't. And even if Elle were in pain, she would have sacrificed herself for the baby."

"But how do you know she's not in pain? When Alice was sick, the doctors insisted that since she was in a coma, she wasn't in pain. And you and I both know that just wasn't true. How do you know that, on some level, Elle isn't experiencing pain? She can't tell you. What if her head hurts at some excruciating level? On some primal level. What if she's trapped in that pain?"

A lump formed in my throat, and I barely was able to spit out the words. "I've studied her EEG. There's virtually no brain activity, Mom. Artifact." How I hated that word, *artifact*. The electrical artifact was all that was left of Elle's essence. "She's not there anymore."

My mother shuddered, then held still, probably absorbing the vacuum of Elle's absence. Mom slowly walked to the door and removed my house key from her purse, which was hanging on the knob. "You are blind about what you're doing to Elle. And to yourself." She set the key on the counter. "And it is terrifying me."

✦ 17 ✦

Day 6

People try hard not to stare at the victims of tragedy, but they do. They stare at broken arms and wonder how it happened. They stare at missing legs. They stared at me as I stood in the cafeteria line. But I needed caffeine almost as much as I needed air.

My cell phone rang. After the brief pleasantries, Jake went straight to the point. Had I searched our papers? Where was Elle's will?

Preoccupied by Mom's appearance and exhausted, I hadn't looked for anything the only night I'd gone home.

"It's been two days since we talked," Jake said. "We need to prepare for the hearing."

At noon, I left Hank with Elle again, and I went to the bank. In the safe-deposit box, I found our wills, birth certificates, deeds, Social Security cards, nothing but meaningless crap. Nothing was secure, our lives, least of all.

The truth was I never wanted to make a will. Elle pushed the idea at me like an unwelcome banner: we are both going to die someday. I'd seen death in all its ugly shapes and forms, and I understood the inevitability of it. But planning for it took courage, and I'd never been brave.

She was. Imagine climbing into the Space Shuttle just a little more than a year after the *Columbia* disaster. She was terrified. Happy, but terrified. And she did it.

Afterward, she told me that while they were strapping her in on *Atlantis*, she thought she was cursed, and she hoped everyone else aboard wouldn't die with her. "It was stupid," she said. "Don't laugh, but not one woman in my mom's line survived past the age of forty, not in six generations."

I knew this, had been to the family cemetery with her to see the headstones, but I teased her. "What? Some old witch cursed all the females in your family?"

"You're laughing."

Laughter was a defense mechanism. I watched her mother die. I knew Elle's grandfather, and saw the scars he carried away from the accident that killed his wife.

Elle was very pregnant with Dylan when we had that conversation. She took my hand in hers so I could feel him kick. "I'm not going to die young. We're going to watch him grow up, but on *Atlantis* I was terrified. I thought I might somehow be dooming my crewmates to death along with me."

I kissed her mouth, and then I kissed her belly. "We're going to be a family. We will live a long, happy life together."

"If I were destined to die young, it would have been on that space walk, right? Let's make the will, if only to ward off the evil spirits," she said.

So as an act of solidarity, I went to a lawyer and made a will to match hers—to appease her superstition—to make her sleep easier at night. We lost Dylan anyway. I lost Elle. The only thing I had left—the only part of *Elle* I had left—was the baby inside her.

I went home again and searched our home office, papers, checking account statements, bills, and medical records. Inside them, there was nothing that would support our contention. I couldn't find her undergraduate papers or textbooks; maybe she had them in her office at Bowdoin.

A late-afternoon thunderstorm rumbled off in the distance, and moments later the wind howled up the river to our house. I headed upstairs to check the windows and to look for Elle's journals. Then something crashed in the attic, and I hurried up the steps into the ripe oven heat. The French doors to the widow's walk, whipping back and forth in the torrents of wind, had knocked over the floor lamp. I closed the doors and bolted them, then bent down to lift the lamp, its bulb shattered from the crash. Perfect. Just perfect. I brushed away the fine glass and pulled up the trapdoor. Elle kept her diaries and her mother's inside a hollowed-out compartment in the attic floor. One of many secret compartments in the old house—a reminder of a bootlegging great-grandfather.

Alice's diaries weren't relevant. I only needed Elle's. There were hundreds, maybe a thousand letters, far more than I'd realized. I wondered where to start, if she'd ordered them chronologically or if she'd simply shoved them away. At some point she started writing in composition books, and there were maybe seventy of those. Jesus, what if she wrote about Adam and the life she shared with him, their sex lives.

I'd had other relationships, been fascinated by other women during the years Elle and I spent apart, but I didn't want to know about her. With him.

I pushed aside the thought and reminded myself that I needed to look for one thing: evidence that she recanted her advanced directive. Deep down, I knew it was unlikely she would ever have done any such thing. Elle hated, hated, hated how her mother died.

I scooped up the bound satchels and marbled comp books and

dropped them on the attic floor because my cell phone was buzzing in my pocket. I yanked it out expecting it to be the hospital. It wasn't. It was just Melanie again. "Hi, Mel," I said.

"Why don't you come over for dinner. We're cooking on the grill. Just corn on the cob and burgers. It'll be good for you to be out in the fresh air for a while."

"Ah, yeah, thanks for the invitation, but I have to find some papers for my attorney tonight. Some other time."

After hanging up, I looked at the size of the pile. I'd be there all night. Or longer, probably much longer. First, I needed more coffee and assurance Elle was still stable, so I called the hospital. The nurses said her status was unchanged, and then Hank came to the phone, confirming the same. He agreed to spend the night.

I skipped most of Elle's early entries and focused instead on the ones since our marriage. It was a little strange reading *Dear Matt*. It was stranger that at times she seemed to truly be addressing me. Most were loving. A few were not; one she'd written about a time I'd forgotten to call her when I was stuck at the hospital, another after I'd stood her up because I had gotten bogged down with paperwork at the office. Other entries were sentimental drivel. And I savored them, forgetting I had a purpose, a passage to find, something about a living will.

Around midnight I brought the letters down to the living room, and sometime after that I fell asleep, dreaming of Elle in my arms and her voice reading her letters aloud.

October 2, 2004

Dear Matt,

 In the morning, you and I will stand in front of our friends and our families and promise ourselves to each other. I'm supposed to be nervous. I'm supposed to be worried whether I'm doing the right thing. Instead, I am at such peace.

That we decided to sleep separately tonight is the most absurd choice I've ever made. Here is a truth, one thing the Catholic Church got right: Matrimony is one sacrament the priest does not give. He presides over it, but the sacrament itself is given to the man by the woman, and to the woman by the man. I marry you. You marry me. It is for that reason alone I wanted to marry inside the Church, why I made a big deal about it when ordinarily we don't attend Mass. I believe this marriage is between us more surely than I believe in anything else.

I've loved you my entire life. Never ever doubt that. Even when I couldn't see clearly, I loved you. I felt you in my soul. So this wedding in the morning is simply a seal on what I've always believed was my destiny. Our destiny. I love you, Matthew. And I will for as long as I live. For longer.

Love,
Peep

✦ 18 ✦

Nineteen Years Before the Accident

I decided I wanted to become a doctor when I witnessed my first medical miracle. I was seven. My family was picnicking at Sebago Lake, and my then ten-year-old brother, Mike, jumped off a rope swing into the water. He didn't come up for air. Dad dove in and fished him out, limp and blue. My mother resuscitated him with mouth-to-mouth, compressions, the whole CPR bit. Two days later, sporting a black eye and ten stitches, he came home from the hospital.

Not all endings are happy ones, but I didn't understand that for ten more years. Alice was dying. Everything went wrong during those last weeks. First Elle lost the baby, and then the hospice nurses called Child and Family Services.

Looking back, it's hard to believe they hadn't reported what was going on in the McClure house sooner. They may have rationalized that my folks were over there all the time or that Christopher and Elle weren't being physically abused. But Hank had started to disappear for days at a time.

The hospice agency reported the neglect a few weeks later, citing that on the date Elle lost the baby, Christopher came home from school and no one was there to take care of him. They didn't say where or why Elle was absent, only that she was. Yes, the nurse was caring for his dying mother, but she was not responsible for the eight-year-old boy. Hank never came home or called that night. The nurse reported that more often than not he appeared to be inebriated.

During the time between the miscarriage and the report to Child and Family Services, my parents also argued about calling in the authorities.

"Before Matt and Elle took leave of their senses," Mom said, "we could have taken the kids in with us, but we can't have Matt and Elle living under the same roof. We'd never be able to keep them apart."

"We can't keep them apart when the McClures live across the driveway either," Dad said. "What's the difference?"

Did I mention the radiator grille in my bedroom allowed me to hear every kitchen-held conversation? Their words flew at me like a swarm of hornets.

I still went over to Elle's house every day after school. Her lissome form returned in just a couple of weeks. I craved her, but she didn't want me. She said she was scared of getting pregnant again. We had messed up once. She wouldn't use the pill because she was afraid of getting breast cancer like her mother. The physical and emotional intimacy we'd shared evaporated as she grew increasingly distracted by her mother's condition.

"Let her go, Daddy," Elle begged over and over. "Just stop her feedings. If Mommy didn't have that tube jammed down her nose, she would—she would be at peace. Look at her! Please! She's in pain. Can't they at least give her more medicine?"

Elle pleaded with the nurses. She pleaded with Hank. But even when Hank was there, he was so bombed he didn't see what the rest of us saw. I guess that was the point.

Once, when the nurse went outside for a smoke, Elle tried to jimmy open the locked medication box. The nurse came back inside and all but threatened to call the police. Maybe that's when they decided the family was in real trouble.

"What were you planning to do?" I screamed as Elle stormed off.

"Just give my mom enough to stop her pain. This is horrible. It's as wrong as torturing someone. Why won't he let her go? Why won't the doctors make this stop? My dad can drink himself into oblivion, but he's letting my mom suffer."

"What do you want them to do? Help her die? A mercy killing?"

Elle rounded on me in the driveway. "Do you really think that would be wrong? If that were me, *I'd* want to die."

I didn't know her when she was like this; her eyes were darting around like she was trapped in a room on fire.

"I have to study for my calculus midterm," I said, charging off, not wanting to be a participant in what might follow.

Another week passed. Hank disappeared for three days.

That's when it happened.

Elle didn't even tell me he was gone. We had all but stopped talking. I found out when I came home from school. The note Mom left on the table said:

We found Hank. Dad's taking him to a place to dry out. The hospice nurse called Child Services. I'm going to Portland to see if I can keep Elle and Christopher out of foster care.

I leaped over the fence between our two driveways to the McClures'.

The nurse opened the door. "I had no choice. I'm legally bound to report neglect and abuse. Your family has been trying to keep the kids safe, but this is a mess."

Behind the nurse, I could see that Alice lingered, more skeletal than ever, and she sounded like she was struggling to breathe.

"I didn't tell CPS about Elle getting pregnant," the nurse said. "And if your parents can get custody of Elle and Christopher, I will tell the social workers it's for the best. Your parents obviously love the kids. But, Matt, you and Elle can't mess around. If something happened again, if anyone found out, the kids would both end up in foster care for sure."

"It's all right. Elle won't let me near her anymore," I said.

Take one formerly pregnant underage girlfriend and one horny high school senior, and Elle and I arrived at an impasse. My father threatened to pull my college savings. My mother threatened castration. Elle cowered away every time I tried to touch her. And Alice festered. Day in and day out, Alice did not die. She would never die.

Mom came home with Christopher and Elle around ten that night. Elle's face was red and her eyes were puffy. Christopher's face was filthy with snot.

Mom kept shaking her head no. Dad beckoned to me to follow as he carried Christopher upstairs to my room. After dropping Chris on the top bunk, Dad said, "He's scared. I want you to stay here with him."

I followed my father out into the hall. "Let me talk to Elle first."

Dad put his hand on my chest and pushed me back. "You need to get to bed. You've got school in the morning. Your mother is going to take Elle home. The nurse is over there, and the social worker said as long as that was the case, it was okay to leave Elle home."

I didn't have school in the morning. It was a Friday night, but as I opened my mouth to argue, Christopher started bawling. "It's too high. I want Elle."

"Go. Stay with him," Dad said. "Let your mother handle Elle."

I sagged and joined Christopher. "It's okay, kiddo. I'm here."

"I want Elle."

"Me, too." I pulled off my shirt and dove under the flannel sheets of the bottom bunk.

"It's too high up here," Chris said. "Can I sleep with you?"

The only McClure I wanted to sleep with was Elle. "No. There's a rail. You won't fall out."

"Please, can't I sleep with you?"

"The bed's too small," I said. Hell, it was too small for me without him hogging the covers.

"Elle would let me," he said.

Shit. Elle could probably hear him whining all the way down in the kitchen, too. So to shut Chris up, I said, "Fine."

His legs swung over, and he stepped on my arm. After a few minutes of shifting around, he settled next to the wall. I stared out the window at the McClure house until Mom walked Elle over. I expected Mom to be right back, but I didn't see her come home.

In the morning, Mom was cooking corn bread and bacon. I plopped down at the table. "Christopher snores."

Mom set a cup of coffee in front of me. A little baffled, I sniffed it. She'd never given me coffee before, although I'd drunk a cup here and there. "Is this mine?"

She didn't answer.

"Mom? Are you okay?"

She looked at me, seeming to see me for the first time. "Why are you drinking coffee?" she asked. And then, before I could answer, "You'd better hurry; you'll be late for school."

"It's Saturday."

There was a tap on the door and the nurse entered. "I'm sorry to bother you, but—" She cleared her throat. "Alice McClure died about an hour ago. Elle is inconsolable."

Even after the months of praying for her mother's peace, Elle wasn't prepared for the impact.

We never are.

19

A Year Before Elle's Accident

Elle and I were in bed together, discussing the differences between the sexes. After the usual and obvious anatomical comments, the ones lovers share, conversation turned to the psychosocial, the spiritual, the cliché. I said men were more aggressive and women more nurturing.

Elle said, "Women are stronger, more certain of themselves."

I flexed a muscle. "How do you figure that one?"

"No, no, men have all the testosterone to grow the bulging muscles—hmm, nice, by the way—and assert themselves, but men are an insecure bunch. I mean you, and I don't mean you personally, but you in the plural sense, need to control everything you don't understand. Men don't get women, so they subjugate them. Your gender won't even read books or watch films with female protagonists; it's intimidating, and if men feel inadequate about something, they hide it."

"Huh?"

"If you—and again I mean the plural you"—she wagged her eyebrows and touched me suggestively—"couldn't get it up—which doesn't seem to be a problem—but if a man had that issue, would he tell his buddies at the gym? I think not. No, he'd lay on the machismo even thicker, brag about all his conquests, and manage to convey he was a lothario instead."

"I'm being maligned."

She rolled her eyes. "No. You don't have an issue in that department. Obviously. Let me make the counterexample, a case closer to home. If a woman couldn't carry a baby to term, something which makes me feel like I'm as big of a failure as a woman as impotence would a man, what would she do? What did I do? I found another woman who has been through a similar thing, and we obsess about it together. Men can't do that. They aren't certain enough of themselves."

"Or, as I said, women are nurturers. You nurture each other. Same thing. We agree on everything. Did you ever notice that?"

She hit me over the head with a pillow.

The other woman Elle had found was Keisha Sudani. That was one of the few things the two of them had in common: their mutual inability to give birth. Keisha couldn't conceive, and Elle couldn't carry a baby to term. Yes, they were both associate professors at Bowdoin, but Elle taught physics and astronomy. Keisha taught women's studies. Elle spent every minute she could outdoors, running, swimming, kneading the earth in her garden. The only way Keisha would put her hands in the dirt would be if someone told her it would help her conceive. She'd tried everything from IVF, herbs, and acupuncture to tribal remedies in the South Pacific. She had one of those undiagnosable fertility issues. Everything was perfect—except Keisha and her husband were lonely for a child—the same way Elle and I were.

20

After Elle's Accident
Day 7

Having spent the last few months in New Zealand, Keisha came straight from the airport to the hospital, and her midnight-dark eyes filled with tears as she touched Elle's shaven head. She murmured in her soft accent, "Girlfriend, girlfriend, look what they did to you." Then, meeting my gaze, she said, "How's the baby, Matthew? And how are you?"

"I'm holding on. Everything's all right with the . . ." I almost said *pregnancy*, but stammered, "baby." That's how I was still thinking about it, the pregnancy. Elle was pregnant.

"Tell me what you need, and I'll do it," Keisha said.

"Can you testify that Elle would want the baby to live?"

"No, she wouldn't *want* it." Keisha swallowed. "She would *insist* upon it. I don't understand how your mother could even consider stopping Elle's life support, not when there's a baby growing in her belly."

My mind flashed to Elle taking my hand and putting it on her belly to feel Celina kick—to feel Dylan kick. I connected to the child inside her through her actions. Elle would never do that with this baby. And it occurred to me, I might never feel attached to this child without Elle. It occurred to me, I would have to raise it alone. It occurred to me, I hadn't even thought that far ahead.

"Matthew, are you all right?"

"Yeah," I said. "Thank you. And, uh, could you go through her office at Bowdoin? Pack it up? If you find anything that would even hint at what she'd want done in this situation . . ."

"I'll keep my eyes open." She turned back toward Elle. "This breaks my heart." She leaned over to kiss Elle's forehead. "I love you, my sweet friend."

I had two allies: Hank and Keisha. But the foes numbered higher. Christopher and his wife, Arianne, a sheepish little blond woman, came in to see Elle, stayed four or five minutes, and stormed out. All three of my brothers, one at a time, or occasionally with collective strength, paraded in to remind me about Alice McClure festering in her living/dying room for months. Doug moved to Vermont right out of high school, and since he was the oldest, and I the youngest, we had never been close. He put his arm around my shoulder. "Matty, it's over. Let her go. You don't have perspective."

"It's not over," I said. "Not while Elle's pregnant."

Or Keith, who tried another approach: Mom and the guilt I should feel about defying her. Defying? As if I were an errant teenager instead of a grown man. And Mike—he turned into a water bucket every time he entered Elle's room, blubbering about how she shouldn't be lying in that bed. I told him not to come anymore. If anyone should be crying, it was me. But I couldn't cry. I needed to act certain.

Mike still came, and I was grateful he did. He was the only one who would come and talk about something else even though he disagreed about keeping Elle on life support. We were still family.

In between the visits, all I wanted to do was sit in the corner of Elle's hospital room and hear her voice in the shelter of her diaries. Instead, people came in waves, my family, Elle's, doctors—the ones I'd chosen and the ones who were to testify for my mother.

And the priest, Father Meehan, wearing black trousers and the collared black shirt, stood in the doorway in silence. Was I supposed to confess that he was the last person I thought to call? I didn't believe Elle's soul needed saving or that some incantation would make a difference to the Almighty God, the Father, Son, or Holy Ghost. I felt like a hypocrite, using Father Meehan so that I could go into court and swear on a Bible that Elle was in God's grace and that keeping her on life support was an expression of her First Amendment rights to practice her religion. Yet I held out my hand to the priest and lied or told the truth. Who knows? In my eyes, she was a good woman, and it never occurred to me that when she died she would go anywhere but heaven. I didn't mention I was uncertain if such a place existed.

He blessed her with oil, uttered his prayers, and gave her Extreme Unction. He turned to leave, and I don't know what came over me, but I dropped into the chair and began to sob.

His brow furrowed, and he pulled up a chair next to mine. He said nothing for a few minutes while I cried with my face buried in my hands. Finally I said, "I'm sorry."

"I remember your wedding," he said. "I don't marry too many astronauts. Neither of you have attended Mass much since. She came once in a while this spring."

I pulled a hospital-issued box of tissue from the nightstand and honked my nose. "After Dylan died."

He nodded and paused before he spoke. "Is that why you lost your faith, Matt?"

"I don't know," I said. "Maybe I never had it."

Father Meehan shook his head, maybe in anger, maybe out of pity. "I spoke with your lawyer," he said. "He wants me to say Elle and you were practicing Catholics, and I suppose that's why I'm here. For show."

I swallowed. "In part. But Elle would want to give the baby a chance. She'd want prayers."

He seemed to measure my words. "What about you? Do you want to give the baby a chance?"

"Of course. We wanted kids." I hesitated. "If I sound ambivalent, try to understand that my wife is—gone—lost, and I'm so—broken, and so tired. But we wanted children. We always wanted children."

He nodded. "See, this is what I'm thinking. I understand that you're concerned about whether or not the baby will be born. And without that"— he shrugged—"you think nothing matters, but you've fallen away from the Church, Matt."

"Don't hold my lack of religious fervor against the baby," I said. "And Elle might not have been a churchgoer, but she believed in God. Maybe this would be easier *if I did*."

"I know she believed. She didn't attend Mass often, but she came in to talk more than once about the pregnancies she lost. She believed life began at conception. When I tell the court that, it won't be a lie. I'll testify—for her—for the baby. But I'd like to ask something of you."

"Anything." I was willing to make a deal with the devil or with his nemesis. It didn't matter which.

"When the baby is born, I want you to come back to the Church. Come even if you don't believe at first. Go through the motions with an open heart. Have the baby baptized. Make it a commitment to raise the baby with faith. You see, I want you to give the baby a chance, too."

All in all, it was a small concession. Who knew that the bargaining phase of my grief would be so concrete? "Church. I can do that."

Father Meehan held up his hand and made the sign of the cross. "This Sunday would be a good start."

✦ 21 ✦

Day 8

Change of shift is not a peaceful hour. The nurses forget to keep their voices down when they greet one another—as if it were just another day at the office. There's the occasional bitching about the work anticipated for the day ahead, and then the march through begins.

The night-shift nurse led the day-shift nurse to Elle's bedside, where one reported to the other while inspecting IV bags, double-checking settings and tubings and monitor waves.

I scraped my stiff body out of the recliner and headed into the on-call room. There were benefits to being on staff, including a hot shower and shave without leaving the building.

When I returned, my mother was sitting in my chair with elbows on her knees, her head cradled in her hands. My eyes darted to the ventilator, to Elle's monitor—the same settings, a regular sinus rhythm. I drew air and stood silent, waiting for Mom to look up.

But she didn't. And I realized after a minute that this was how my mother had always cried, in silence, her shoulders heaving almost imperceptibly.

"You okay?" I asked despite my deep anger, resentment, and outrage. The list could have gone on.

She startled, hastily wiping her eyes, then nodded. She was wearing her scrubs covered by a lab coat, her hair pulled up in a soft bun. "I hate this." She gestured toward Elle. "It shouldn't be like this. Elle. Elle." She repeated the name like a chant.

Part of me wanted to oust Mom from the premises. But another part of me wanted to hug her and release the grief and horror welled up behind the levee of my reserve. "No," I said. "It shouldn't be like this. But it is. Because there's still a life at stake."

"That's not what I meant . . . I want to roll time back a month. I want her to be all right again."

"Finally. Something we agree on." I felt my resolve slipping. "You're working today?"

She nodded. "Trying to, but . . . well . . ."

"Don't even try to tell me they sent you over here to check the fetal heartbeat."

Mom regarded me. "I was at work," she said. "My patient read my name tag and asked me if I was related to *the astronaut*. When I said yes, she told me to get out—said that I was some kind of baby killer. Me? I've had crazy patients over the years. One sixteen-year-old didn't like it much when I told her to push, and she grabbed me by the throat so hard she left fingerprints, but no one has ever accused me of anything so heinous as being a baby killer."

"So why are you here? You want me to tell you you're a saint? I'm not about to offer you my support. You're wrong about Elle."

Mom wasn't looking at me. She was stroking Elle's forearm. "I'm not wrong. She didn't want to die this way." She bent down and kissed Elle's forehead. "I didn't do anything when Alice was dying. I didn't stand up to Hank. I didn't push the oncologists. I didn't go over anyone's head from the hospice agency. I held my tongue like a good little subservient nurse. Back when nurses were silent. Back when we didn't assert ourselves. Back before we had a voice in the health care team. I grew up old school, as the young ones say these days. And I have regretted my silence, my passivity, ever since. I let my best friend down. I let her suffer." Mom continued to rub Elle's arm. "I won't do that to Elle. I'm standing up for her and for what is right. And I'm sorry that means I'm standing against you." Mom was trembling as she whisked past me. "I love you, Matt. Don't forget that. But I love Elle, too."

Hank was usually meticulous and fresh-pressed from the dry cleaner, but he came in looking like he'd slept in his clothes. I sniffed in his direction. He smelled like Old Spice, not like beer or any other form of alcohol. He shook his head. "I didn't have anything to drink."

"Okay," I said, barely masking my doubt.

"I didn't. I look like this because I just got off a plane. I went down to Houston last night."

"Why?"

"Adam." Hank sneered. I knew he never liked Adam, and I think it was because Adam was more than ten years older than Elle, and she was only twenty when she started living with him.

To be honest, I never liked Adam either. For eight long years he had the woman I wanted: Elle. "You went to see Adam?"

"He called me. And, Matt, he said he has proof Elle wouldn't want to stay on life support. He's coming here tomorrow to testify."

My neck muscles locked up as if someone had just slapped a neck brace on me. "Testify? What kind of goddamned proof?"

"He didn't say. Or he *wouldn't* say. That's why I flew down there. To try to get him to tell me what he had. He's been leaving messages on my machine since the accident. Finally he says, 'If you don't get that asshole'—meaning you; sorry, Matt—'to turn off Elle's life support, I will.' So I flew down to Houston, but all he said was he has proof."

It didn't make sense that Adam would interject himself after all this time. "Bastard," I said. "Forget him. If he had something substantial, he'd have said what it was."

Maybe Elle was right. Like other members of my gender, when cornered, I resorted to plastering on the face of courage.

I left Hank with Elle and went to meet Jake at my office, barely noticing the four-block walk. My receptionist had shown him in before I arrived and he was talking on the BlackBerry. I dropped down into the chair opposite his.

"Matt just walked in, Yvette. Yeah, yeah, I'll tell him. Love you," Jake said, hanging up. "Yvette said to give you a hug. You don't mind if I just tell you instead, right?"

"A hug?" Maybe she wasn't as cold as I'd always thought. "Words will do just fine," I said.

"Any problems getting out of the hospital?" he asked, referring to the press.

"The rain seems to have scared them off. Or they're losing interest. Hopefully the latter."

"I doubt it," he said, opening his briefcase.

"Keisha is going through Elle's things at Bowdoin."

"Gotta say, I like Professor Sudant. I like her a lot. Talked to her for a couple of hours. A feminist Pro-Lifer," Jake said. "I can work with that."

I handed over Elle's will and said the attorney we used had not prepared an advanced directive for Elle. Then I mentioned she'd kept a diary, partially loose letters, partially in composition books.

"And?" Jake leaned back in his seat.

"Nothing that says what she'd want to do under the circumstances. At least not yet."

He asked how long she had kept a journal, and when I told him, he said he would have his associates read through them.

"No," I said immediately. "They're private. Anyway, there's something else. Her old . . . Adam Cunningham—the guy Elle lived with for a while—he's making noise about having some sort of proof that she wouldn't want to live on life support."

Jake tapped his knuckles against his chin. "Your mother retained an attorney, and this Adam Cunningham was on his witness list. Tell me what you know about him. Had he and Elle kept in touch?"

"Maybe a Christmas card, but nothing more. In terms of his credentials, he got his PhD from Princeton, and he works for NASA as an aerospace engineer. Last I knew, he worked on safety issues like heat tiles on the Space Shuttle."

Jake picked up his fountain pen and shook it at me. "Wait. I might have met him once. Princeton. You dragged me along to a party there. Elle was with a tall guy. Was that him?"

"Probably. He's basketball-player tall." I told Jake about the duration of Elle's relationship with Adam, that eventually, like most couples, they unraveled. Later Elle told me she had never quite gotten over me, and that's why she could never commit to him.

"My associate is researching him. Will she find anything to discredit him?"

"Besides being a controlling prick? Probably not."

"What's his proof?" Jake asked.

"I have no idea. He talked to Hank, not to me. But he wouldn't tell Hank anything either. Like I said, Adam's controlling. That's how he likes to play his hand. He waves a big red flag and hides his knife."

22

Nineteen Years Before Elle's Accident

Elle and I didn't stay together the way we should have. Our relationship fell apart. We—fell apart. And mostly it was my fault. That autumn I left for Columbia University, while Elle remained home. Officially, after the social workers got involved, Hank stopped drinking, but he was still going on benders sporadically, and she believed Chris was too young to fend for himself. So instead of attending her dream school, she commuted to Bowdoin College, not a place without merit, but it wasn't MIT.

Six weeks into my freshman year, I blew it by getting so mind-fucking drunk at a frat-party hazing that I slept with a sorority girl in the same condition, and when I went home for Thanksgiving, I confessed. Brokenhearted, Elle refused to acknowledge my presence. She wouldn't answer my calls, my letters, or my pleas at her threshold for five long years.

Two years after our split she went her own way—off to her doctoral studies at Princeton, where Adam Cunningham pounced on her as fast as a hawk on an unprotected nest of baby mice.

At least, that was my impression. Not so much by what Elle told me—she told me nothing—but in how I interpreted the second-hand facts Mom spread my way. Elle met Adam as soon as she arrived in Princeton, and after that, he was always around, hovering. Elle claimed they were only friends the first couple of years. Yes, he made overtures, but she was only eighteen years old. He was twenty-nine.

23

After Elle's Accident
Day 10

I never understood why Elle stayed with Adam for eight years, but ten months before her Space Shuttle mission, they finally broke off their relationship. That should have been the end of his influence in her life, yet as I worried about the start of the hearing, I also worried about what Adam might pull and about his so-called proof.

I was at the nurses' station, shrugging into my suit jacket and talking to Clint about Elle's blood thinners, when I noticed Adam in Elle's hospital room, standing with his back to me. His hands were characteristically laced behind his head.

What next? Would hospital security let the press in to take pictures of Elle lying there, her head shaven, unable to swallow her own spit?

I charged into her room with ten days' worth of grief and anger, loaded and ready to aim. He was a target. I'd wanted to belt him for years.

I grabbed his arm and spun him around.

After his startled look disappeared, a contemptuous expression replaced it. "Elle didn't want to die this way," he said. "Why are you doing this to her?"

"What the hell are you doing here? Security is only supposed to let in the family."

"I said I was family. I used to be her family." His gaze left me and found her, a shadow of her former brilliant self.

I shuddered in the cold reality. "No. You were never her family."

"I was. Maybe not technically, but Texas recognizes common-law marriage."

"Oh, for Christ's sake," I said.

"I know 'common law' is an old-fashioned term," he said, his voice measured with his slow West Virginian accent. "But Elle and I were together for a long time, twice as long as the two of you have been married. And my point is, I know what she would want under these unfortunate circumstances."

Fear and anger, two intricately interwoven emotions, propelled me toward him. I had never been a violent guy, but I was willing to make an exception, and it didn't matter that he was a head taller. "Get out," I said, issuing my last warning.

His eyes narrowed as he looked down on me; a glint of a smug smile flashed and disappeared. "When Elle was with me, she gave me her medical power of attorney."

Although the blow was not physical, it punched me just the same.

"I wouldn't step into the middle of this," he said, "if you'd let her die in peace. But you won't. And from what I've read in the paper, you didn't even know about that old advanced directive your mother produced. So actually, this is my responsibility. I talked to your mother's lawyer, and he's filing something or other so the judge will order the hospital to discontinue Elle's life support."

The floor seemed to shimmy from side to side. I grabbed the bed rail.

"Listen, *Matt*." He pronounced my name with true disdain. "From what your mother's lawyer tells me, the advanced directive I gave him should end any speculation about what Elle wanted done on her behalf."

"You never knew what Elle wanted. Besides, a lot can happen in five years."

Or in ten days. Or in the instant her head hit that rock.

"I knew," Adam said. "And I took care of her when no one else did. She trusted me, but she never trusted you. Apparently, with good reason. I'm not disputing she married you. As insipid as it is that she left NASA and ended her brilliant career to go home and marry the boy next door, she did it. But she didn't want *this*. *This* terrified her. The idea of *this* woke her up at night. Crying about her mother, powerless in a coma. Christopher said it still nagged on her. When Elle signed the advanced directive, well, she made her own choice, and evidently, she didn't trust you to make the decisions for her. Being married to her doesn't give you the right to do anything you damn please. This is abuse, and I will end it. I have her medical power of attorney, and by this afternoon these machines will be off." He leaned over and kissed her cheek.

Almost of its own volition, my hand shot from my side. I wanted to slam him against the wall, but in a last-second act of self-control I held up my palm instead. "Let me see the document."

"Your mother's attorney has it."

The only thing that pounded harder than my heart was my desire to pulverize Adam. Maybe it was the glint in his eyes, his calculated self-satisfaction that stopped me, the idea that if I lost control, he might somehow win by maintaining his. I said, "I'm calling security, and you will leave here. Now."

"No need." He held up his hand and strutted away.

I tore my cell phone out of my trousers pocket and dialed Jake. It rang until the voice mail picked up. I waited for the beep. "Jake, we've got trouble. Call me."

For a futile five minutes we played a game of cell-phone tag. Finally we connected. "Don't worry about the common-law issue. The problem is this new advanced directive. We'll be in court in less than an hour for our regular hearing date. Rather than wasting time holding your hand, let me figure out what I can do to head this off."

✦ 24 ✦

Day 10

On our way to the courthouse, reporters trailed Jake and me as if we were the Pied Piper: our music, the inside story they coveted. They barked questions, and we answered them with deliberate silence—until one stopped in front of me, brandishing a microphone.

The clichéd blue-eyed blond reporter with glaringly white teeth and a simulated smile to go with it refused to move. "How's Elle? Is there any improvement? Has she spoken?"

Clearly, the reporter, an anchor at a local affiliate, what was her name, Paige Cartwright, didn't understand the meaning of brain death. Or maybe she was hoping to provoke a reaction. I opened my mouth to speak.

Jake grabbed my arm. "Dr. Beaulieu has no comment, but he asks for prayers for his wife and unborn child."

I wanted something besides prayers. I wanted all these assholes out of my face. I wanted privacy. And time to grieve. And control over Elle's fate.

I wanted Adam dead.

All I had was a court date. The truth was that, even if medical technology could keep Elle's body going long enough for the baby to become viable, the court might take one look at Adam's advanced directive and tell the hospital to turn off Elle's life support. Prayers? Hell, I needed more than that.

I had no patience for the reporters. They were exploiting our tragedy. Paige Cartwright practically poked her microphone in my mouth. "But, Dr. Beaulieu, if Elle had an advanced directive, doesn't that mean that you're using her body against her will? Isn't forcing her to remain on those machines for the duration of her pregnancy akin to rape?"

"What?" I yelled. "What's the matter with you?"

"Easy." Jake's hand landed on my shoulder. "We have no comment."

I stood, stunned, knowing I should back away, so entirely incensed that if the newswoman had been a man, I would have punched her. I could see the manipulation, and still, I couldn't budge.

Cartwright cocked her head to one side. "But don't you want to explain your position? I would love to interview you, Dr. Beaulieu," she said.

"You aren't serious," I answered back. "I'm trying to save my family, and you just compared that to . . ." I couldn't even say the word aloud. "You're a sadistic opportunist."

The flash of her eyes betrayed an emotional response; perhaps it was contempt or perhaps it was satisfaction. "I didn't suggest she became pregnant through rape," Cartwright said. "But forcing Elle to vegetate on life support against her will for the sake of pregnancy, which is by all reports unlikely to succeed, is akin to rape."

Jake pushed me behind him. "Don't say anything." Jake turned to Cartwright. It was easy to see even he was straining to keep his tone level, easy to see she was hoping he wouldn't or that I wouldn't.

"You're trying to provoke a sound bite with the use of that word," Jake said. "We have *no comment*."

Predatory, the reporters closed in around us.

"Merriam-Webster defines 'rape' as an act or instance of robbing or despoiling or carrying away a person by force," Cartwright said. "It's defined as an outrageous violation. Elle McClure said she didn't want to be kept alive on machines. Isn't this an outrageous violation of her will? You're forcing her to vegetate on life support. Isn't that, by definition, rape?"

Cartwright was prepared, reading from memory etched on some neural pathway. Elle could do that with her eidetic memory; she could tell the page and the paragraph of something she'd read. But all similarity between Elle and this witch ended with that one simple talent. Elle would never prey on someone shredded by grief. Elle never preyed at all.

And Paige Cartwright did it for a living.

"Get out of my way," I said, grinding my teeth.

One cameraman stepped sideways, and Jake and I shoved our way through the breach in the wall of reporters.

And still Paige Cartwright continued: "Women have been used to produce offspring, *forced* to produce offspring for tyrants. For kings. For fascists."

"There is no equating one situation with the other," Jake said, nearly as indignant as I was.

"Women in Nazi Germany were impregnated like livestock and forced to bear children for the fatherland."

"Oh, for Christ's sake." I spun around, my hands balled into fists. "This child wasn't forced on her. We conceived this child together—*in love*. She would insist that we save our baby. Now get out of my face."

"Come on, Matt. Let's go." Jake pulled at my arm.

I stood fast, glaring at the reporter. Cameras were rolling. I could almost see the glee around me. Headlines. "Husband of Stricken Astronaut Explodes When Questioned." I forced my voice to level. "Elle loved children. Loved them." I pushed through the crowd without looking back again.

At the courtroom door, Jake finally made eye contact and exhaled loudly. "I tried to prepare you. Don't rise to it, particularly *not* inside the courtroom. Not out there either. The judge might see the news. I admit I didn't see that one coming, and she used some seriously inflammatory language, but it's over. Now forget about it. We have to go into the courtroom and be in the moment. But don't comment at all next time."

I nodded but was still shaking with rage. I breathed in and out and proceeded through the heavy courtroom doors.

As Jake and I took our places, I noticed that seated next to my mother was a dark-eyed, middle-aged man, tapping his sharpened pencil on a legal pad. Adam sat in the gallery just behind them.

Jake leaned in. "Your mother's new attorney, Paul Klein. Works for a decent-size firm as a litigator, mostly involving trusts, but he used to litigate medical malpractice."

The court officer announced the judge's entry. We stood.

Once seated, Judge Wheeler shuffled papers in front of him. "First let the record show Mrs. Linney Beaulieu is now represented by Mr. Paul Klein. Next is the Order to Show Cause. Attached is an affidavit with what purports to be an advanced health care directive signed by Elle McClure. This one names one Adam Cunningham and gives him Elle McClure's medical power of attorney. Mr. Sutter, I'll hear from you."

Jake stood and buttoned his jacket. "Your Honor. The advanced directive produced by Adam Cunningham is only a photocopy— not an original. Elle Beaulieu has had no substantive relationship with Cunningham other than their mutual association with NASA for the past five years. As far as we know, she could have torn up the original document when she moved out of the residence they once shared. Furthermore, in Texas, this AD would be automatically revoked during a pregnancy."

"Yes, but if you recall, we are not in Texas, Mr. Sutter," the judge said.

"Which is why I move to exclude the document," Jake said.

Judge Wheeler folded his hands and leaned forward. "What interests the court is what Elle would want done on her behalf if she were able to speak for herself," the judge said. "I'd like to hear what Elle wrote on this 2003 document. We're putting together a puzzle here. Mr. Klein, do you have any evidence to substantiate that this advanced directive is current?"

"We do not have possession of the original at this time, Your Honor. We are trying to contact the attorney who drew up the document."

"Very well," Wheeler said. "I'll hear testimony concerning this advanced directive along with whatever other testimony each side is going to present. And since we were already scheduled to meet this morning, I'd like to hear your opening statements."

Jake wrote on the legal pad, "Grounds for Appeal."

"Just a note," Wheeler continued, "because of the change in focus, from guardianship to the removal of the ward's life support, Mrs. Linney Beaulieu is now the petitioner. Dr. Beaulieu is the respondent. Mr. Klein, are you prepared?"

"Yes, Your Honor." Klein took three steps toward the gallery and locked eyes with reporters representing CNN, FOX, ABC, NBC, CBS, the *New York Times*, and the *Boston Globe*. Along with the journalists, Paige Cartwright sat off to the side with her glower homed on me. She was nothing but a small-town reporter with a big story in her backyard. She obviously wanted to make a name for herself in front of the networks. And when she baited me with her twisted take on the situation, I made an easy mark by jumping through her goddamned hoop. I groaned inwardly and forced my attention back to the front of the courtroom and my mother's attorney.

Over the next few minutes Klein summed up my mother's position while he rolled an unsharpened yellow pencil back and forth between his palms. "Anytime the issue came up, whenever right-to-die issues were in the news, Elle clearly informed those around her she did not want to be kept alive if there was no hope of recovery." He harped on the fact that Elle had come to these strongly held opinions through her experiences with her own mother's prolonged death.

With great clarity I could still see Alice on her deathbed. Watching her die beat down Elle's indomitable spirit for a while. At the time I focused on Elle. It wasn't until I was in med school that I realized Alice's death had profoundly changed me, too. It made me cognizant of the quality of life and the impact illness made on an entire family.

My family. There were other similarities besides the physical resemblance Elle bore to Alice. Two women, a mother and a daughter, each lost her voice and the ability to choose her destiny. And like Hank, I was fighting against immeasurable odds that a miracle would come. I didn't appreciate the comparison even though I recognized its validity.

My mother's attorney had been articulating his case for seven or eight minutes when he said, "As a competent adult, Elle signed not one but two documents outlining that she didn't want extreme measures to prolong her life. The law dictates that she has an inalienable right to self-determination. Her pregnancy in no way changes this. Texas law notwithstanding, she said she did not want to ever be put on life support of any kind. Please honor her wishes. Thank you, Your Honor."

Wheeler's face showed no emotion. "The court will hear from you, Mr. Sutter."

Jake stood and glanced quickly at the press before addressing the judge. "Your Honor, Elle Beaulieu was a thoughtful woman, brilliant and complex, but she was never motivated by a single factor." He spoke as if he understood Elle's wishes, perhaps because he had pulled out phrases I had used to describe her intensity as well as her tender side. "The day before her terrible accident Elle and Matt discussed the possibility of trying to start a family. Tragically, neither knew she was already pregnant." Jake paused with his gaze fixed on mine and nodded at me.

I swallowed hard. If only I had known about the baby, everything would have been different. She wouldn't have gone up on that ladder. Maybe I would have stayed home that morning and we would have celebrated.

"We are here to determine what Elle Beaulieu would have wanted done on her behalf." Jake rubbed the nape of his neck. "She wanted to have children even at the peril of her own life." He went on to outline his case with one notable exception. He said nothing about petitioning for fetal guardianship, but that omission felt deliberate.

Jake's gaze rolled over to me, and the judge's eyes followed. "Your Honor, Elle married Matthew Beaulieu and they dreamed of building a family together. Let Elle fulfill her dream." He came to the respondent's table, unbuttoned his jacket, and sat down.

A court officer approached the bench and passed the judge a note.

"Thank you, Counselors. I need a twenty-minute recess to attend to a different matter. Afterward, Mr. Klein, you may call your first witness."

While Jake spent the recess pulling together his notes, I read an entry Elle wrote fourteen years earlier.

✦ 25 ✦

Fourteen Years Before Elle's Accident

An Entry in Her First Composition Book

March 12, 1994

Dear Matt,

   I didn't write last night. I felt too exhausted, too drained. Bereft. I can't believe your dad died or that I had to deliver the terrible news to you.

   But your brother called me and said he didn't want you to hear about Dennis's heart attack alone. Could I pick you up? New York City is on the way to Maine from Princeton after all, he said. Not exactly. And I've never driven into New York City before. But apparently Mike has, and he gave me directions to your med school apartment. So delivering the brutal words fell to me. God, Matt. I'm so sorry. I didn't want to tell you.

I have to stop trembling. I can't write like this. And I have to sort out my feelings or I won't be able to ever sleep again.

For five years I have avoided you whenever we both happened to be home at the same time—I refused to talk to you. Linney says I have a passive-aggressive streak wider than the distance from the earth to the moon. But honestly, I just felt so completely humiliated. Back then, I believed you loved me as much as I loved you. And you broke my heart, Matt. You went away to college, and you promised we would always be together. Then you slept with that girl. And you came home and said you were sorry. You said you still loved me. But how could you have _ever_ loved me and made love to someone else? It doesn't matter. It _shouldn't_ matter. Not now. Dennis is dead.

I loved your dad. My heart is simply breaking for your mom. And yesterday I had to bring you such wretched sadness. And I'm so sorry because I never wanted to hurt you. Not like this.

When my mom was sick, you held my hand. Every day. You sat with Mommy and me all those afternoons. When my voice grew hoarse from hours of reading to her, you read to her for me. I needed you back then, and you were there. We loved each other. I know we did. I thought we did.

I needed you. I don't think I've ever stopped

needing you. And yesterday I realized how petty I've been _all_ this time. How I didn't forgive you for, I don't know, growing up? Moving on?

You cried when I told you about your dad. You cried in my arms. And I wanted to take your grief away because you carried me through those dark days when my mom was sick, when we lost the baby. And I wanted to make love to you again. The way we used to when it wasn't only about sex. I thought about it for a couple of seconds while you were in my arms—while I was holding you. I wanted to kiss you. I wanted to be even closer, but too much time has passed. We were children then. But you are still such a part of who I am, a part of who I have become, and that realization crystallized last night on the drive home.

On the radio, "I Want to Know What Love Is" popped on. I changed the station. I had to. It was playing the first time we made love. That night when the Perseid showers rained celestial dust around us.

The baby, that's what she was. Stardust. God, I need to focus.

After a few minutes you said, "Peep, I'd offer to drive, but with exams, I haven't slept in two days. I'd probably kill us both."

You called me Peep. No one has called me that in years. No one ever called me Peep but you. I almost started to cry. Because of your dad. Because of our baby. Because of every loss I ever experienced. But mostly because it was like someone recognized this girl inside me again. For the first time in forever I remembered who I was.

And who you were.

I have missed you. I have hidden from the ache of your absence.

And then I met your eyes for a driver's moment, and my heart pounded so hard I thought you could probably hear inside my soul, and that scared me, too. So like a coward, I turned back to study the yellow line running down the highway and told you to sleep.

I suppose that is the sum of the last two days. I loved you. And finally, I believe you loved me once upon a long time ago. Isn't it tragic that sometimes it takes grief to understand what we have held so dear?

Love, Peep

✦ 26 ✦

Fourteen Years Before the Accident

Even all these years later, I remember that drive home and the nightmares I had. I sank into oblivion and dreamed of dismembered torsos, which probably wasn't surprising since I'd spent the previous week hovering over cadavers in the anatomy and physiology lab. Except, in my sleep, half bore my father's tattoo, a tree with my mother's name on the trunk, and each branch had the name of one of my brothers. And my name—even my name. The leaves were a fetus cupped in a girl's hands, Elle's hands, an opal ring I'd given her on her left. Then her hands melted like wax. Like tears rolling down over Celina, our tiny, tiny baby girl.

Elle's voice, real or imagined, said, "It's okay, Matt. It's okay."

I startled awake as we pulled down the street where we grew up.

"We're here." She took my hand. "Your mom won't expect you to be strong for her. Linney doesn't need that. She just needs you to be close. Let her cry, but if you need to cry, let her hold you while that happens."

Elle sounded so certain, like an arrogant sage.

"How do you know?"

"Because that's what she told me when my mom died."

Inside, the fluorescent light over the sink flickered, setting the mood with cold and hard shadows. Elle followed me into the kitchen, took the kettle off the stove, and filled it from the tap. "You want a cup of tea?"

I nodded. "Mom must have gone to bed. I wonder if I should wake her."

On cue, my mother padded down the creaking stairs. We didn't say a word. She wrapped her arms around me, then beckoned Elle over and hugged her, too.

Mom insisted Dad's funeral would not be morbid. Word went around that we were each to come up with five stories to tell about Dad—or else. Funny stories were best, but any reasonably non-sappy tale would do. I found out more things about my father in those two days than I'd known in my lifetime. For six months, when he was in elementary school, he ate nothing but peanut-butter sandwiches. In high school, he and his father helped build a house for a family who lost everything after their furnace exploded. The reason my mother, a self-confessed cat lover, never owned a cat was that they terrified Dad. Everyone insisted it was true. I found myself wondering: Why is it we know so little about the people we love until they are gone?

I stared across the funeral parlor at Elle. I didn't know she could be so vengeful that she could hold angry silence over me. And I didn't know I was capable of hurting her so thoroughly that she would change. But then she strolled up to my side. "Do you know what I'll always remember about your dad?"

Nor did I know she could transform herself back into the friend I'd known. "What?"

"That summer when you were trying out for pitcher for the

middle school team. He took me aside, and said—" Elle lowered the timbre of her voice, impersonating my father. " 'You watch him, Elle. Matt isn't the most talented kid in baseball, but he works harder than anyone else.' He was so proud of you. And then you struck out the next three players. And your dad was on his feet, clapping so hard. Then he turned to me and said, 'Well, he's got some talent, too.' God, I miss him, already." She squeezed my elbow and slipped away. "And I've missed you, too, Matt."

After the graveside service, relatives filled the kitchen while my mother busied herself, packing away casseroles into individual-size portions. She couldn't sit still or put up with more condolences, and I couldn't sit still, so I paced. I should have stowed away in my room and buried my nose in my pharmacology textbook, but I couldn't study. With the upcoming test, I figured I'd fall from the top 5 percent of my class to the fucking bottom. *One* test. If I could even afford the next semester's tuition.

Everything was slipping away. Elle left after the funeral, and I wanted another chance to talk with her. I stepped onto the back porch and into the cold night air. Across the driveway she was probably packing to return to Princeton. Floodlights hit the snow and broke the darkness as I climbed the McClures' front steps.

Christopher came to the door. He'd become such a gangly-looking mutt, with the beginnings of acne, and if I wasn't mistaken, a little hair shadowed his upper lip. "You want to come in, Matt?"

I entered, not so covertly scanning for Elle. "Is she around?" I asked.

"Nope. She doesn't usually stay here when she's up from school."

"She doesn't? Where does she stay?"

"Gramps's. It works out better, you know, with Dad."

"They don't get along anymore?"

"Elle and Dad?" Christopher's incredulous expression said more than any explanation. Apparently not. Then he offered a teenage shrug as if it could not be less important.

Completely sober for a few years, Hank strolled in from the kitchen, still wearing his neatly pressed suit and carrying a coffee mug. His eyebrows rose. "Matt, how are you holding up?"

"Okay. How about you?'

"I lost my best friend a couple of days ago. Life sucks. I imagine you're not all that okay either."

My composure stumbled, and I fought hard to avoid breaking down.

"I didn't mean to take off without saying good-bye," he said. "But I needed a few minutes with Elle before she headed out. When are you going back to New York?"

"I have a six A.M. flight. I wanted to thank you for everything, helping with the arrangements. The eulogy. Um, about Elle, will she be back tonight?" I studied him for any indication of the rift Christopher implied, but Hank didn't elaborate.

"Unlikely. If you need anything, let me know. Do you have enough money to finish the school term?"

"Yeah." I was working night shift as an orderly. I made enough to pay the rent. But tuition, that would be another matter, one I would have to address with the financial aid office.

"Your dad had life insurance. Your mom will be all right. You know your dad made me the executor of his will?"

I shrugged, a little surprised that my mother would have to rely on Hank to distribute my father's life insurance and pension.

"It's not important that we discuss it yet. I mean, I'll have to evaluate all your father's assets, but covering your tuition could be a little tougher."

"I'll figure it out," I said. "I've been taking out loans, anyway."

"Your dad was helping some?"

I nodded.

"He was so proud of you getting into med school, an Ivy League one at that. He'd want you to finish. What I'm trying to say is, I'll help out if you need it." He sat on the arm of the leather chair.

"I can't take your money, Hank," I said.

"Why not? Elle's schooling is done, or at least my financial contribution to it is. Chris is a great kid, but he's no scholar. He'll plod through a state school. Maybe, if he's persistent, he'll eventually get an MBA so he can run McClure Realty. I can afford to help you. If your pride pesters you, pay me back when you're a wealthy surgeon. Or better yet, do the same thing for some deserving kid who happens across your path."

My mind was spinning. Admittedly, I'd already run a couple of scenarios, but I hadn't considered one where I would be unable to finish med school at all.

Hank walked over to me and put his hands on my shoulders. "What I'm saying is I will see you through this, and I don't want you to worry. Dennis and Linney saved my family when I was drinking. And I'd like to help yours."

I nodded again.

"Good," he said. "Be a doctor. In honor of Alice. To honor your dad."

I wondered if I could really make a difference. Dad was still dead. Alice was still dead. Medicine didn't seem as miraculous as it once had. Not like when my mother saved Mike after he almost drowned. And if I could not save the people I cared about most, what point was there? "I'll try," I said. "I, uh, have to get back."

"Okay, son. You take care. I'll keep in touch."

When I returned home, Mom was sitting in the dining room with Aunt Beth, drinking coffee, looking weary. "Can you take the dog out for a walk?"

Lucky, our Irish setter, was curled up by the living room hearth.

He raised his head when he heard "dog." "You want to go out, boy?"

Five minutes later, in sweats and running shoes, I jogged down Bow Street with Lucky at my side. The subzero air dug into my lungs, but it didn't matter that it was cold. It didn't matter that I should be studying. I wanted to see Elle, and she was only a few miles away. She'd said she missed me.

At the fork, I turned down Wolf Neck Road, remembering all the times we had snuck down there to be alone. After I reached the driveway, I trudged out onto the field. Because of the dark and because of the frozen layer of snow, I couldn't be entirely certain if I had arrived at the right place, but I pulled a crushed rose from my pocket, one I'd picked up from Dad's funeral, and I dropped it on the garden for Celina.

It was now or never. I cut a path to the house. The dog barked as we climbed the porch steps. Before I had a chance to knock, the door pulled open, but Elle didn't answer. It was that guy she was with the previous Christmas when she had only acknowledged me in a "Matt, this is . . ." What the hell was his name? Adam, something.

"Hi," he said. "Can I help you?"

Elle bounced down the steps, wearing a pair of flannel pj pants and pulling a camisole over her head. Her lacy blue bra disappeared. "Oh my gosh," she said when she saw me. "Matt, I wasn't expecting you."

Obviously.

"Adam, you remember Matt? Matt Beaulieu, Adam Cunningham."

"Oh. Sorry about your loss, man." Adam extended his hand to me. His handshake was strong and sincere, and there was something a little south of the Mason-Dixon Line in his accent.

And I hated him.

"Thanks." I hadn't thought this through. Although, in my defense, Elle hadn't mentioned this asshole on the drive up or in any other conversation we'd had in the past two days.

Elle bit her lower lip, and squatting to rub Lucky's ears, she avoided looking at me—or at Adam.

"I'm headed back to New York tomorrow, and I wanted to, you know, thank you for driving me home."

"Sure, no problem." She stood.

"We're staying for a couple of days." Adam draped his arm around her, and she seemed to fit there, comfortably. He continued: "I drove up this morning so we could go skiing tomorrow. Ah, do you want a drink or anything?"

"Water would be great. For Lucky. In a bowl. We were out for a run. I saw the light on." What a fucking lame excuse, especially since the house wasn't visible from the road.

Adam disappeared to the back of the house. Elle shifted her feet, but didn't offer me a seat. It was as though she couldn't wait to be rid of me.

I was stuck, waiting for water for the dog. "You and him?"

"We live together, so yeah. About a month ago we started living together. We both want to work for NASA. Did I tell you I won a summer internship?"

"No. NASA. That's great." I tried to gather my breath, my pride. I tried to sound like this news that she was living with this guy didn't faze me. Instead I blurted out, "Are you happy? I mean, do you love him?"

"I wouldn't be with him if I didn't. But this really isn't any of your business." She looked away for a moment, squeezing her eyes shut. "It's been years. We haven't even talked in years."

Her anger pummeled me. I never meant to hurt her, yet she had punished me deliberately, and continued to do so now. Yes, I was wrong, but so was she. "Not talking wasn't *my* choice. I *tried* to talk to you."

She glared. "I don't want to do this. I especially don't want to do this right after your dad's funeral." She balled her hands into fists and covered her face. "I don't want to hurt you, but if I tell you how angry I've been, I will."

"Oh, Elle, come off it. You've wanted to hurt me ever since it happened. And you have. Silence is as scathing as confrontation. Get it over with. Say it. I was a bastard."

Her chin jutted out, then she lowered her eyes and softly said, "You were."

"And I'm sorry. It was the worst mistake I've ever made."

She sighed, a long and heavy morose sigh. "Look, we were young. Stupid. What happened with us didn't even mean anything. Between my mom dying, and my dad's alcoholism, and having to stay home to take care of Christopher, I was just trying to find an escape. I picked lucky you to be the vehicle. Then the baby made me understand the consequences of playing house." She stopped speaking abruptly and clapped her hand over her mouth, looking back toward the kitchen.

"He doesn't know?"

"Of course not. Why would I tell him?" she whispered.

"I don't know. I guess if—"

She stepped so close I could feel her seething words. "Do you tell every girl you meet you got your girlfriend pregnant when you were in high school?"

"No, but—"

"What do you want here? You want me to tell you I'm still pining away for you? That I waste my time, telling a great guy like Adam that I screwed you the first chance I got. Stud that you were, you knocked me up? I told him we went out. I told him it ended badly. Look, you met some sorority girl who swooned and spread her legs willingly. Good for you. At least it gave me someone to blame for all my troubles. I used you to pin all my disappointments on. Pin the tail on the ass."

It was like she'd written a completely different version of history than I had. I stood in shock for a moment, absorbing her blistering analysis, and decided that if she needed to see it that way, I'd let her. But I would not pretend that was how I remembered it. "It wasn't like that for me, Peep. I loved you, *deeply loved* you. I didn't want to break up. I wanted to be with you—I wanted—you. That girl, she got in the way—one night. One night. What happened, happened because I'd had too much to drink, and I wasn't thinking. I never planned to cheat on you."

I took Lucky's leash and headed for the door. Within seconds the night air tore into me, and I found myself shivering, not because of the temperature but because of Elle's coldness. I wondered if I'd hurt her so much that I'd made her this way or if she'd always been so jaded underneath.

"Wait! Stop. The water for Lucky." Elle padded down the front steps in her bare feet. The walk still had a layer of ice at its edge, Jack Frost etches, brittle and cold.

Adam followed behind her, pulling off his sweater, and he tugged it over her head. It hung to her midthigh. It was such a goddamned transparent gesture of possession that I wanted to kill him.

"Can you give me a minute with Matt?" she asked him.

He kissed her temple. "Sure, I'll be inside, babe."

She watched him return to the house, a house they seemed to share. "Matt," she said softly. "I didn't mean—that you meant nothing to me. But it doesn't mean anything now. Or it shouldn't. We were kids. It just seemed so powerful at the time because it was the one good thing I had to cling to. *You* were the good thing. You helped me survive the most difficult events I've ever faced."

With only the porch light for illumination, her pupils were as wide as if she'd been tripping on belladonna. If someone looked at her features one by one, they would probably have thought she was homely. Her nose was a little wide. Her cleft chin a little pointy. Her mouth—well, yes, her mouth was a perfect bow. And the intensity of her eyes had me from the time she was a little girl when we used to play staring contests on the front porch. She wasn't perfect, but she was so vibrant that she was intoxicating. I was under a spell and unable to look away.

She touched my forearm. "I do still care about you. I—I loved you. I did. And—I've missed you. God, Matt. I want to stop being angry. It takes so much energy to be that angry. Can we, maybe, talk like friends do, from time to time? I mean, I'd like to reciprocate. Be there for you now. You know, losing your dad."

"I don't need your pity, and I don't want it." I turned from her and started walking, but Lucky was still slurping up the water, and I was snagged when I reached the end of his leash.

"What about my friendship? Do you want that?" she asked.

Adam stood at the door, watching. And I wondered if she would marry him. "Does he treat you well?" I asked, looking at the house.

She twisted to the door and smiled at him. "Yes. He's patient."

"And old, Elle. Jeez, he looks like he's thirtysomething."

She lowered her gaze and shook her head. "He wants to take care of me. He waited a long time. We knew each other for a couple of years before we got together."

"I see." But I didn't want to. I flipped to the first other subject that came to mind. "What's with you and your father? Christopher said something about you aren't getting along with him."

"Daddy will be okay about Adam after he gets used to the idea we're living together," she said.

Shit. That change of subject failed miserably.

Elle's teeth began to chatter. It was freezing, yet I didn't want her to go back inside. To him. She would be with him. That night. Christ. Or maybe they had just been together.

"If you want, call me sometime," she said. "Maybe you and a girlfriend could come down to Princeton. It's pretty around there. There are millions of restaurants."

"Or you could come up to New York." *Maybe Adam could stay home.*

She shrugged.

"Sure. I'll do that," I said, never intending to. But I did.

A month later I called. And I continued to call almost every week for as long as Elle lived there. After she moved to Houston, it didn't take long for me to figure out Adam's schedule and that it was better to call when he wasn't home. Elle talked more freely in his absence. We quickly fell back into the most solid of friendships. And I rationalized that as long as she was a part of my world, as long as I had her in my life, I could survive.

27

After Elle's Accident

Day 10

I knew this much for certain: the baby would not survive if my mother won her lawsuit. And the baby *had to live* for me to justify what I was doing to Elle. For two conscience-crushing hours Mom testified that Elle would rather die than rot away in a hospital bed, and she described how Elle looked now, drooping, stiffening, flattening, unable to swallow, unable to see or hear. "If Elle knew what was happening to her she would be terrified."

I couldn't dispute my mother's argument, and truth can devour rationalizations.

Still I rationalized and told myself Elle *didn't* know what was happening, and therefore she was not afraid, and unlike her mother, she was not sensing waves of unbearable pain.

"Your cross, Mr. Sutter," Judge Wheeler said.

Jake stood, buttoned his suit jacket, and shook his head as if he were searching for words. But he knew. He liked his witnesses to feel they had the upper hand before he targeted them. "Mrs. Beaulieu, you said you had a close relationship with Elle."

"Yes."

Acting troubled, Jake tapped his upper lip with his index finger. "I would think you would want to do anything you could to help your daughter-in-law."

"Yes."

"Did Elle ever indicate to you that she wanted children?"

A flutter of recognition entered my mother's eyes as Jake laid his trap. Through a series of questions he insinuated that because Mom already had nine grandchildren, the baby Elle was carrying didn't mean all that much to her. It wasn't true, it wasn't fair, and I didn't care. Jake pounded question after question at my mother, all aimed at showing how much Elle had wanted a child, how Elle grieved when she miscarried, how she named the babies even before they were born. And when he spoke about Dylan, the sheer heaviness of my son's absence hung like a dirge. It took a few moments for me to refocus my attention to the testimony.

"After Dylan's death . . ." Jake counted on his fingers. "About seven months ago, did Elle confide in you about her desire to try to have another baby, Mrs. Beaulieu?"

"Yes," Mom said, shifting in the witness box.

"Did you discourage her from trying to conceive again?"

Mom's eyes narrowed slightly, her defenses raised like the quills on a porcupine. "We were all concerned about her health."

"Did you discourage her?"

"I told her to consider adoption. Matt wanted her to consider adoption, too."

"What did Elle say to that?"

"She knew I was right, but she was too stubborn to admit it."

Jake shook his head. "If she was too stubborn to admit it, she never said she agreed with you, did she?"

Mom hung her head. "No. She wanted to have a baby. Is that what you want me to say?"

Jake walked over to our table and appeared to be glancing at his notes, but he was simply giving Mom's response a dramatic pause.

After a minute Jake continued, "Mrs. Beaulieu, in your earlier testimony, you stated that you and Elle had discussed the Terri Schiavo case."

"Yes."

"Just for clarification's sake, Terri Schiavo was the Florida woman who fell into a persistent vegetative state after she suffered a cardiac arrest in 1990, is that correct?"

"Yes."

"Her husband, Michael Schiavo, petitioned the Florida court to discontinue Terri's life support after a number of years had passed. Her parents opposed. Are we discussing the same case?"

"Yes."

"You stated that you had a conversation with Elle regarding the Schiavo case in January of 2005."

"Yes."

"Earlier you stated Elle thought the courts should rule to remove Terri Schiavo's life support. How many years after Schiavo went into a persistent vegetative state would that make this conversation?"

"What do you mean?"

"If Terri Schiavo had been in a persistent vegetative state since 1990, and the courts were deciding in 2005, how much time had elapsed?"

"Fifteen years, I guess."

"And Elle's accident happened how long ago?"

Mom stared at her hands. "Only ten days ago, but you don't understand. Elle was terrified of being on life support. Under these circumstances, ten days is a long time." Mom's voice broke.

Jake poured a glass of water and offered it to my mother. "Are you ready to continue?" he asked her.

She nodded.

"Terri Schiavo was on life support for fifteen years," Jake said. "And Elle has been on it for ten days. And there's another difference, isn't there? Mrs. Schiavo wasn't pregnant, was she?"

Mom drew a deep breath and appeared to be holding it.

"Mrs. Beaulieu, I realize this is difficult, but—"

"No. Terri Schiavo wasn't pregnant."

"Did you ever ask Elle if she would have supported the withdrawal of life support had Terri Schiavo been pregnant?"

"No, there was no reason to discuss that."

"Did Elle ever state that under the circumstances she is currently in, pregnant and brain injured, what she would want done in her behalf?"

"Specifically? No, but . . ." Mom looked down at her hands again. "I know she didn't want to be kept alive."

"But she never discussed this scenario, did she?"

"This exact scenario, no."

"One more thing. Earlier you indicated Elle didn't want her father to make health care decisions for her, correct?"

"That's right."

"And that's because he insisted her mother be kept on a feeding tube long after she could eat, correct?"

"Yes. Alice would have died within days if nature had been allowed to take its course."

"At the time Elle's father was Elle's next of kin, but after Elle married Matt, he would be considered her next of kin, wouldn't he?"

A puzzled expression fell over my mother's face. "Um, I guess."

"Did she come to you and ask that you act on her behalf because she was concerned that Matt would not act as she would wish?"

Mom hesitated. "She probably thought that Matt would take her off life support."

Jake repeated, "Did Elle ask you to act on her behalf once she had married Matt?"

"No."

"Thank you. Nothing further." Jake returned to the seat beside me.

"Redirect, Mr. Klein?"

"Not at this time. I'd like to call my next witness, Adam Cunningham."

Judge Wheeler looked at his watch. "Yes. We'll hear from him after we reconvene at one o'clock sharp."

After speaking with Jake for a few minutes in one of the conference rooms where attorneys and clients meet, I decided to swing by the hospital during the recess.

"Don't let the reporters provoke you," he said. "No comment, no comment, ad infinitum."

I raised my hand in acknowledgment and bolstered myself for the onslaught of cameras and microphones. Alas, no one awaited me in the hollowed-out halls. Relief.

Not until I left the courthouse did I understand where the reporters had gone. Across the street in Lincoln Park, the Pro-Life protesters had set up some kind of demonstration. And curiosity getting the better of many of the good people of Portland, a crowd was gathering on this late August lunchtime. The reporters were circling, looking for a story, an angle, or a headline.

Furtively, I peeked up as I strode the circumference. I had fifty-five minutes to make it to the hospital, see Elle, get an update, and return before Adam testified. I didn't want a distraction.

Then I saw my mother, cornered between the wrought-iron fence and a circle of people holding life-size baby dolls in her face as if my mother didn't know more about infants than any of them—as if she'd never helped a baby be born.

Christ. I stopped and swallowed, glancing back at the court-house. There were security guards there. Would they leave to assist her? Did I actually have to step into this?

I inched forward, then stopped to pull out my phone to call the police. Someone shoved my mother, and I barreled forward. "Get away from her," I yelled. "Get out of the way. What's wrong with you people?"

The crowd hardly parted, but people, even angry people, yield more readily to a six-foot-two-inch man than to a sixty-some-year-old woman. Funny that these people who believed they were standing up for weak, unprotected babies were willing to attack an old woman who had brought countless children into the world, a woman who'd saved more than a few babies' lives.

My mother's frantic eyes met mine, and she puffed out her chest in a final charade of bravery. "I'm fine," she said.

I put my arm around her shoulders and began leading her through the crowd. "Leave her alone!" I said to no one in particular.

My mother was trembling, almost violently. I wrapped my hand around her wrist and checked her pulse. She was tachycardic, her heart rate close to one-fifty.

"What were they doing?" I asked.

"Trying to frighten me." She swallowed hard and nodded. "Pretty good at it, too. I kept thinking about some of those abortion-clinic doctors getting shot, about the clinics that got bombed."

"Why does everyone keep comparing this to abortion? This is

about Elle. This is about the baby she's carrying. No one is having an abortion. I just wish these idiots would go away."

"Thank you." She squeezed my hand.

"I'm parked in the lot across the street," I said.

A few reporters were taking pictures, asking questions, following at our heels. I ignored them all the way to my car, beeped the door unlocked and deposited my mother in the passenger seat, locked her door, and rounded the car.

Once inside, no, once moving down Franklin Street, I said, "I don't want you to get hurt. But just because I pulled you out of there doesn't mean I've stopped being angry."

"I know. Where are we headed?" she asked.

"The hospital. You can get someone else to give you a ride back. Or you could drop the lawsuit, and we could be done with this shit. We could focus on what's important."

She stared out the window. "Elle's important."

"She is. Was. She's gone, though." My voice buckled as I stopped at a light. I gripped the wheel as tightly as I could, as if by doing so I could release the pain.

Mom softly rested her hand on mine. "I know. If it were you, Matt—if it were you in that hospital bed, what do you think Elle would do?"

"It's a ridiculous question," I said.

A horn blew behind us.

The light had changed to green, and I stepped on the gas too hard, lurching us into the intersection.

"Shit," I said. "You can't reverse the situation and ask what Elle would do. I cannot carry a baby. If I could trade places with her, even if it meant leaving her alone and pregnant, if I could die for her, I would."

"I know you think you're being noble. But isn't carrying the baby exactly what you're trying to do? Sitting there day in and day out? Aren't you trying to pull off the impossible?"

"Give me a chance to find out if it's impossible," I said.

Mom squeezed shut her eyes. "Jake may be clever with manipulating words, words from me, from anyone who testifies, but I know Elle. I'm the one she cried to about Alice. Ellie didn't want to die this way."

28

Day 10

Adam's bulk did what few could do; at six eight, he dwarfed me, and I was happy he looked uncomfortable with his long legs stuffed behind the witness box. Evidently Klein thought Adam had a lot to say because they were almost an hour into the endless drone of his testimony.

"Did she ever discuss having an advanced health care plan?" Klein asked.

"Yes, she did."

"Can you tell us a little about the circumstances?"

I had discovered that courtrooms were *not* very exciting places. The questions and answers followed the formula of a long math proof. Enter A. Enter B. Add. Take the sum. Divide by the product. Despite the tedium, I could discern patterns and understand complicated conceptual facts. Medicine also requires logic. For doctors, we prove things with research, and I was damned shrewd about what made a study valid or not. In the case of Adam's testimony, it was missing out on key variables: one baby and one mother's love.

Adam shifted in his seat again. "Elle was the mission specialist assigned to the Hubble Telescope repair team. After the *Columbia* disaster, we weren't even certain if the shuttle program would resume, but when NASA issued the green light, Elle decided she had to get her affairs in order. In case. She went to an attorney and prepared a will. That night she came home with the advanced directive. She told me she'd named me as her decision-making agent if anything should happen to her."

The testimony went back and forth. Adam read the document aloud. Much as she'd done in the living will my mother produced, Elle dictated certain specifications. If there was no hope of a meaningful recovery, she wanted nutrition and hydration withheld. She did not want a ventilator to make her breathe. She didn't want much of anything except a peaceful death. Adam scanned down the page. "In essence, Elle told me to pull the plug. She told me that the way her mother died was morally reprehensible."

"Dr. Cunningham, when was this dated?"

"On May nineteenth, 2003."

I leaned over and whispered in Jake's ear. "They split up a month or so after that—June or July of 2003."

Jake's thin lips lifted into a snakelike smile.

Klein took back the document and passed it to Judge Wheeler. "I'd like to submit P-2 into evidence."

"Does the respondent have any objections?" Judge Wheeler asked.

As Jake stood to speak, I took a swig of water. Without realizing how hard I was squeezing the water bottle, I crushed it and water erupted like a volcano and came down all over Jake's papers.

He glared at me, pulled out his handkerchief, and passed it to me as if he were prepared for any occasion.

I blotted while he spoke. In the gallery the blond reporter from this morning was snickering. Bitch, I thought. She probably considered herself a feminist. Elle was a feminist. Hell, I believed a woman could do anything, pretty much anything, a man could do. Elle could do things I couldn't—walk in space for example. And more importantly Elle could carry this baby. I couldn't.

"Your Honor," Jake said. "There's no way to tell if this photocopy has been altered or if the original has been destroyed. Although Adam Cunningham and Elle were involved in May of 2003, they severed their relationship within a few months. Odds are she destroyed the original. I move to exclude."

Klein had been watching me mop up the mess I'd made, but he stood. "Your Honor, I am attempting to contact the attorney who prepared the advanced directive to find out if she has the original."

"If you can produce the original, Counsel, I will enter it." The judge spoke to the clerk briefly, then told Klein to continue his direct.

"When did you last speak to Elle?" Klein asked Adam.

"A few months ago. She called when my mother passed away. My mother had Alzheimer's and was sick for a long time—even when Elle and I were together."

"Did you discuss Elle's advanced directive during this call a few months ago?" Klein asked.

"Not specifically, but we talked about our mothers and how difficult their deaths were. Elle said something to the effect that my mother was at peace now, and that's all any of us could ever want in the end. We discussed dying with dignity. Her views hadn't changed."

"Why would you travel all the way here from Houston to bring this document to the attention of the court when you are no longer an active part of Elle Beaulieu's life and haven't been for such a long time?"

Adam looked at his hands, feigning humility like the Pharisees postured righteousness. "I didn't want to get involved in this mess, but I respected Elle, and I want to make certain her wishes are upheld. Matt isn't doing that, so my conscience compelled me to step in. She wouldn't want to be kept alive on a respirator. She would hate this. Her greatest fear was dying a protracted death the way her mother did."

When I entered Elle's room, Hank looked up from reading the newspaper aloud to her. "How did Adam's testimony go?" he asked.

I leaned over and kissed Elle's forehead while I thought about how much truth Hank could handle without heading off to the nearest bar. I summarized the newly produced advanced directive, then I looked for an angle that would put him at ease. "It was almost entertaining watching Jake go after Adam on cross-examination."

"What do you mean?"

"Jake got Adam to admit he was *irrelevant*."

Hank's eyes widened. "How?"

"Jake and Adam were talking about why Elle prepared a will and an advanced directive before her *Atlantis* mission. The *Columbia* disaster wasn't long before. Astronauts get their affairs in order, blah, blah, blah. Jake asked if she didn't think she would survive a *Columbia*-type disaster, and neither *Columbia* nor *Challenger* had survivors, then why did she need to prepare an advanced directive? She probably wouldn't survive at all if something went wrong. Adam replied that she didn't necessarily think the advanced directive was relevant at the time. To which Jake said, 'So she designated you to do an irrelevant job?'"

Hank belly-laughed. "I'm starting to like your opinionated friend."

"Jake has a few virtues," I said, "but don't tell him I said so."

After Hank left, I replayed how Adam really reacted to Jake's cross. "I misspoke," Adam said. "I *don't* mean she thought it was irrelevant in general to have an advanced directive, but she thought she would die fast if something happened on her mission. For her, that made facing the danger easier because she was afraid of dying the way her mother did, the way she is, in fact, now dying."

I looked at Elle now. What the hell was I putting her through?

✦ 29 ✦

Day 11

Watching myself stoop to name-calling with the local newswoman over and over on CNN wasn't making me feel any better. I shut off the TV just as Mike entered Elle's hospital room, carrying a grocery bag filled with what looked like envelopes. He dropped it on the wide windowsill. "I guess you've seen your appearance on the news by now."

"A couple dozen times. From now on I'm planning to tattoo 'no comment' across my forehead. If I'd kept my mouth shut, they wouldn't be playing her piece over and over."

"She said 'rape.' How could you keep your mouth shut?"

I looked up at my brother and shook my head. "Let's not talk about it." I started picking through the bag of mail.

"You know Dave Hopper, right?"

Of course I did. He was one of Mike's crowd in high school,

and now he worked for the post office. My brother didn't actually expect me to answer him; he never did once he started talking, so I didn't even look up.

"Anyway," Mike said, "he called and said your mailbox is overflowing."

One good thing about living in the same small town where you grew up is everyone knows you, knows your family, and chances are that when a disaster strikes, someone calls your big brother so your mail doesn't collect on the ground.

"Thanks," I said, taking the bag.

"There's more—at your house."

"More than this?"

"More mail than Santa gets in December." Mike's voice grew grim with irony. He swiped a couple of tears away when he looked in Elle's direction. "Some of them are from people Elle knows, folks in town, others look like NASA logos, MIT, Houston addresses. Some are from weird places like South Africa. I didn't bring those in. By the way, there's something from Carol."

"Wentworth?"

"You know any other Carols?"

I shrugged. None as well as I'd known Carol Wentworth. Before Elle and I got back together, Carol and I were temporarily engaged.

Mike and I spent a few minutes chatting about his boys and how they were asking if they could keep our dog, Hubble. About his job. About what had happened to Mom the day before in Lincoln Park. Even though I knew he believed Mom was right, I didn't want to fight about the situation, and evidently, neither did he because, after a couple of minutes, he said he'd stop by tomorrow. Did I want the rest of the mail?

Not now. I thumbed through the letters and immediately spotted Carol's distinctive handwriting.

Dear Matt,

 I was so sorry to hear about Elle's accident. I suppose, given the reports, saying "I hope she gets well soon" would be a little trite.
 Nevertheless, if there's anything I can do, any strings I can pull, let me know. You may recall my father has connections. One call, and he could get you the ear of the attorney general.
 I read you hired Jake. You can give him my number, and I'll put him into contact with my father.

Best,
Carol

 How much influence Carol's father had, I didn't know. I set aside her letter to dig out a batch of Elle's letters from that period and found the one she wrote after I told her I was engaged.

30

Six Years Before the Accident

The truth was, even when I started seeing Carol, I knew she was too slick for me. I knew it, but hell, when I was with her, I couldn't tell if I'd stepped into heaven or boarded a plane destined to crash. After a while it didn't matter. Neither of our residencies allowed enough free time to seek companionship elsewhere. I cleaned up well enough that her Park Avenue parents didn't object to my presence on her arm. She was a brilliant conversationalist, clever enough to outwit me, and good in bed.

I didn't need more. I didn't want more, but there were more perks. She'd grown up among the New York elite, and she introduced me to people and places I never would have dared approach. After a while, though, I started wanting a relationship that mattered. Call it loneliness or longing or a desire to love someone. She was beautiful and accomplished. What wasn't to love?

But we weren't a match. Not really. Whenever I tried to convince her to stay over at my place, she made excuses. No. That's not true. She never even tried to pretend that my digs met her standards. One night, as she pulled her blouse over her camisole, I played with her long black hair, cajoling her.

"I have an early surgery. I want a good night's sleep." She tipped her head to one side. "But I'll miss you."

"I'd rather not think of you out around the city at night."

"You're so provincial with your small-town-boy ethics," she replied, smiling.

"Stay. Sleep."

"I don't come here to sleep. I come here for your body." She stroked my inner thigh.

I laughed. "I feel so used."

She grabbed her designer handbag and stood at the door, waiting for me to unlock it. "And as much as I like you, this place—not so much. Get a decent apartment and I'll stay."

I'd like to say the disparaging remark didn't bother me, but it did when the one-upmanship turned from sexual banter to my lack of financial strength. I tried to shift the power balance, and the easiest, cheapest, and most predictable method at my disposal? Seduction. It didn't cost me a thing. I traced her collarbone then took her face in my hands. She moaned softly, and for a second I thought, however mistakenly, that I'd won.

But the telephone's ring interrupted, and Carol closed her mouth around my tongue for a moment, then broke away, and shot out the door.

Damn. I glanced at the clock and grabbed the phone. It was too late for my family to call. "Yeah, hello."

"Uh-oh. Did I wake you?" Elle said.

I locked the door and leaned against the wall. "No."

"Any chance you'll be home for Christmas after all?" Elle asked.

"I can't. I'm on call at the hospital." I tried to picture my family and hers, gathered around the dining room table of the house where I grew up. Mom would cook every artery-clogging dish known to mankind. My nephews would spill gravy on Aunt Beth's heirloom tablecloth. Everyone would catch up. And this year, once again, I would be absent. I missed that sense of belonging. But it was strange that even though neither Elle nor I lived with our families anymore, talking to her made me feel like I was home.

She stayed quiet for a few seconds but I could hear her smile as she spoke. "I have a surprise, and I'll probably wait to tell the family at Christmas. Four weeks. It may kill me. I'm bursting. But if you won't be home . . . Listen, I can't keep this inside."

Shit, here it came, the announcement she was finally marrying Adam. I tried to hide my contempt for the asshole. "Congratulations." A little flat, but at least I'd choked out the word.

"You don't even know what it is yet," Elle said.

"I can imagine. Adam's a lucky guy. He'd better treat you well."

"What? Oh. No way. I'm not getting married." Elle almost giggled. Not marrying Adam didn't seem to sadden her at all. "You're so funny."

Relief spread through me. "Okay. What's your news?"

"Something huge." The pitch of her voice rose. I thought I was supposed to guess, but before I had a chance, she said, "Space. The final frontier."

"No way. Seriously?"

"I got word this morning. NASA just assigned me to the *Atlantis* mission. It's going to take us two years to prepare, but we're upgrading Hubble."

"The telescope?"

"Yes. And, Matt," she said. "I'm doing an EVA!"

"What's a—"

"EVA. Extravehicular activity. A space walk. Can you believe this?" Her voice was as bubbly as champagne.

I rubbed my forehead, absorbing it. My pride in her. My joy for her. My concern for her safety. This time, when I offered congratulations, I did so with enthusiasm. "Peep, I'm *so* happy for you."

"Thank you. I haven't told anyone else yet."

"Except Adam?"

"Not even him. I'm supposed to keep it mum until they announce it at work next week. But I had to tell someone, and I wanted to tell you."

✦ 31 ✦

Five Years Before the Accident

A little more than a year later, on February 1, 2003, traveling at twelve thousand miles per hour, the Space Shuttle *Columbia* broke up during its reentry. As Houston waited for confirmation in silence, the television stations broadcast what usually went without note. I mourned for every one of the crew, but I felt grateful for Elle's safety. *Atlantis* was scheduled for the following year.

NASA grounded the Space Shuttle program while they investigated and concluded that a suitcase-size block of insulating foam broke off the external tank and damaged a heat tile on *Columbia*'s left wing.

As a spectator with a vested interest, I watched the news, popped onto NASA.gov every day, and covertly hoped the Space Shuttle program ended forever. But after the safety experts came up with a number of rescue scenarios, officials gave the program the go-ahead.

However, Elle's scheduled flight to Hubble remained problematic. Rescue would be impossible from the telescope's orbit. If the shuttle were damaged during takeoff, it would not have sufficient fuel to make it to the International Space Station to await help. Thus Elle's mission was scrubbed.

"So close to bliss," she said. "Adam thinks they'll assign me to another mission."

Screw Adam, I thought.

My relationship with Carol moved forward or backward according to how much our surgical rotations overlapped or conflicted. If someone asked me if I had a girlfriend that winter, I probably would have said no, instead categorizing our relationship as friends with benefits. But during the early spring of 2003 Carol and I began spending more time together. Our rotations were in sync, and so were we. I all but moved into her place, leaving a razor and toothbrush and a drawer full of clothes. There was nothing official, not even a key, and I didn't stay there in her absence, but sometime, somehow, we became a couple.

Dr. Shah told me to close as he snapped off his surgical gloves. He wandered back to the MRI and studied the film one more time while I put in the last few sutures.

"Get him to the recovery room," Shah said. "Write the operative note and postop orders, and I'll check in after I speak with his parents."

"Will do," I said, not envying Shah the task of delivering the grim prognosis.

As the team rolled our patient past OR 7, I saw Carol through the window. Both in the fifth year of our residencies, Carol's in pediatric surgery, mine—of course—in neurosurgery, we were both logging many hours in the OR.

Ten minutes later I was sitting in the recovery room, charting on the eight-year-old boy. And there wasn't a damn thing we could do. Sure the biopsy would determine the treatment, but he would still be dead before he reached middle school.

Carol smiled at me as she slipped into the chair next to mine, her surgical mask pulled down around her neck, her black hair still hidden beneath her OR cap. Her warm eyes met mine, saying something more than the hello she murmured aloud.

"I don't know how you do it, working with kids." I leaned back in the chair.

She pulled my chart over and skimmed my entry. "Damn. Brain-stem glioma. Poor little guy." Furtively, she glanced around then she took my hand in hers.

I tried to shift the conversation. "What kind of case are you coming from?"

"Oh, an easy one," she said. "A pyloric stenosis repair. Some things are easy to fix. Six-week-old comes in with projectile vomiting. I rehydrate him, find the cause, and after a quick in-and-out surgery, he goes on to live a normal life. Happy ending. Not all of them are, but I get a lot more happy ones than not."

"This one won't have a happy ending," I said, pointing at the boy's chart.

She pulled my knuckles to her mouth, kissed them quickly, and let my hand go. "That's outside your control." She ran her finger along my cheek. "You know what I love most about you? You genuinely care about your patients."

"So do you," I said, but my gut clenched on her words. What she loved most about me? Yes, we were . . . sexually intimate, but we had never—even in the heat of the moment—ever uttered—the four-letter word *love*.

The sound of the infant's wails split the silence of the recovery room; the smallest patient is capable of making the loudest sound. Carol jumped up even before the nurse summoned her.

"Dr. Wentworth? I need an order for pain medication."

"Be right there," Carol said. Then she turned back to me. "Let's stay home tonight and drive out to the beach in the morning."

"Yeah," I said. "Let's stay home." The word swung down like a pendulum finding its equilibrium, swinging back and forth, slowing at the center point. Home. The word. The word *love*. And I was at home with Carol, more and more. And oddly, I almost added, *I love you.* But I bit my tongue. The only woman I'd ever told I loved her was Elle.

Nevertheless, as I watched Carol cross the room, as I watched her write orders then stop by the crying infant's crib, as I watched her lay hands on the child to soothe him, I realized there were things I loved about this woman, too. And for the first time I felt like I could be happy if I allowed her to get close, if I let myself love her.

The next day we drove out to her family's beach house in the Hamptons for the weekend. Although I'd been there before, as we pulled up, I saw the place differently. In spite of my desire to move home after I completed my neurosurgical residency, I could see the appeal of the big-city lifestyle, at least Carol's socioeconomic version of it: an apartment with a park view and a doorman, a second home on the beach. Even with the late April rains, I loved the ocean. This wasn't so bad.

That evening, in the Wentworths' not-so-humble cottage, Carol and I were curled up together in front of an expansive stone fireplace. I thought she must have fallen asleep; she was so quiet and still. In the distance the sound of the surf pounding the beach and rain pattering on the roof could lull anyone into dream. This was good, I thought. I had everything I could want: a career and a beautiful girlfriend. I very quietly whispered the words "I love you." Maybe I was practicing, trying it on for size.

Surprisingly, Carol shifted and regarded me with her eyes full of insecurity. I never thought she required support from me. Yet her voice warbled. "What did you say?"

For a moment I hesitated. I didn't need to retract what I believed was the truth. "I said I love you."

She lit up. We kissed in a way that was no longer only about sex. It was as if she'd been waiting for those words, those three little words. The funny thing was it had never occurred to me that someone like her, someone so poised, so perfect, would need the validation of words. "You love me?"

"Yeah," I said, almost laughing, liberated by the revelation that had started in the recovery room the previous day.

"I love you, too. Wow." She took my hand and pulled me off the sofa. "Come on."

"Where?"

"I don't know. Let's run outside in the rain. Let's . . ." She threw her hands around my neck. "I don't know."

I kissed her forehead, then her mouth, and I started undoing the buttons of her blouse. "You are beautiful. I should have said how much I care about you sooner. And as much as I like running on the beach, let's not do that right now."

The story was in the *Times* the following Monday. That's how I found out that NASA gave Elle's mission the green light.

"Damn it, you could be killed," I said to Elle, who was on the other end of the phone line. "It's too dangerous."

"You don't understand how important Hubble is to the exploration of space," she said.

A moment of silence followed while I searched for a convincing argument to make her surrender her dream. I never would have made it as a lawyer. "The last shuttle crew are all dead, Elle. For most of the families, there was nothing left to bury."

Her voice took a solemn tone but one not lacking in conviction. "Actually they did find remains. And it was a terrible tragedy, but every one of *Columbia*'s crew knew *exactly* what they were risking. We all do. I'm going. I'm not afraid of dying up there."

I wrung my face as I stared out the window of Carol's Tribeca loft. The two of us, Elle and I, had each traveled a long way from our childhood days in Maine when we thought we were having an adventure walking the shoreline of the Harraseeket River.

"But—" I said.

"I know you worry, but I need you to be happy for me," she said.

"But—"

"But nothing, Matt. But nothing. Just be my friend. Wish me luck and say a prayer or two if you need to."

After my less than enthusiastic response to Elle's announcement about *Atlantis*'s launch date, our weekly phone calls fell off for a while.

On Memorial Day weekend, Carol and I stole a little time away from the hospital, a weekend in the Caribbean. There were a couple of children, a little boy and a girl, five or six years old, maybe twins, sticking their faces in the water with snorkeling masks and ogling the fish. And somehow Carol and I started discussing "our" children, what they would look like, and how we would teach them to swim. When we returned to New York, we picked out an engagement ring.

My mother came to the city in early June to meet the Wentworths, wearing her best off-the-rack dress from Macy's. Carol's mother wore something not off-the-rack. Something designer. Couture. Nevertheless, Mom looked great, better than she had when my father was alive. She'd shed her matronly pounds, started running, and taken up yoga; small town or not, she held her own with the future in-laws in their Park Avenue penthouse.

After dinner, we gathered on their balcony. My mother stared at the city lights, one finger pressed to her lips. She withheld the clichéd reaction to the Central Park view. Instead, she said something that must have sounded completely inappropriate to the Wentworths. "Elle would hate it here, wouldn't she, Matt?"

The sky glowed that urban pink, devoid of stars. I knew immediately what Mom meant. I'd thought it a million times about New York.

"Elle?" Elisabeth Wentworth asked.

"Oh, I'm sorry," Mom said. "The view is spectacular, of course. Elle's a family friend, my goddaughter actually, and she's like my own. She works for NASA now—in the astronaut program. She wouldn't be able to see the stars if she lived in New York. She's such a stargazer." Mom scrutinized my face.

Carol knew that Elle and I had been close as kids and that we still talked frequently. Carol also knew that Elle and I dated for a while in high school, but she didn't know about Celina or that I'd stuffed my feelings for Elle down into the toes of my shoes. All Carol knew was Elle was a girl who grew up next door, a woman who remained my friend.

Yet somehow, I hadn't found a way to tell Elle about my engagement to Carol, and my mother knew I wanted to deliver my own news.

Mom turned to Carol's parents. "I'm terrified because NASA's chosen Elle for one of the upcoming shuttle flights. Next spring."

"I thought hers was canceled," Carol said.

"It was," Mom said. "But they got the go-ahead a few weeks ago."

"I had no idea." Carol peered at me. "Did you know that?"

"I thought I told you." I smiled at my future wife, who was so radiant she would outshine just about any constellation. And all I could think about was Elle.

After Mom and I went back to my apartment that night, I lay

on the sofa, imagining how Elle would react. I dialed her number, and Adam answered with a throaty hello.

"Hi, it's Matt. Can I talk to Elle?"

He grunted.

I heard her whisper, "Who is it?" Sheets rustled. Her voice came directly through the receiver. "Matt? Is something wrong?"

"No, not at all. I have news. I'm getting married." I blurted it out. Maybe it was like downing bad-tasting medicine in one gulp, except I was spitting it at Elle instead.

"Oh my God," she said with a tone that conveyed more surprise than enthusiasm. "Just a minute." I heard more rustling of fabric and what sounded like a door clicking closed.

"Elle, are you there?"

"Yeah. Who? Carol? You're marrying her?"

"Yes."

"Wow. I didn't foresee that."

I almost said that I hadn't seen it coming either. As if it were something that had just happened to me. As if I were not a willing participant. But the truth was that in a spontaneous moment I allowed myself to be happy again. With Carol.

"I didn't think you were serious about her," Elle said. "But then, you've been seeing her a while, haven't you?"

"Two years," I said, noticing her lack of enthusiasm and the silence that fell between us before she finally asked another question.

"How did you propose? On bended knee?"

"No. Nothing that pedestrian."

Again, there was a pause, too much of a pause for the quiet to be comfortable. "Oh," she said. "Pedestrian, is it? Well, congratulations are in order. I—I don't know what to say."

Suddenly I remembered stopping at the beach and walking the length of it hand in hand with Elle. I remembered asking her words that I didn't exactly ask Carol. But with Elle, I did go down on bended knee.

"So . . . when is Adam going to make an honest woman out of you, Peep?"

She snickered. "You sound like my dad. Actually, Adam has asked. I'm not ready."

"Why? Didn't he ask you on bended knee?" I tried to make it sound as if I were teasing her.

She cleared her throat. "It's not that. I have . . . other career goals. And . . ."

"And what?" I suppose I hoped she'd say she hated him.

She whispered, "I want children. After I get married, I still want children."

"He doesn't?"

I heard a squeak, and I was uncertain if it was her voice or static in the phone line. "Anyway," she said, "why get married if you're not ready for kids?"

She hadn't answered my question, but I didn't pursue it. I didn't want a picture in my head of Adam and Elle toting around a kid. Then she flipped the circumstance, and in her reciprocal question, I heard a tense undercurrent. "Will you and Carol have children?" Elle asked.

"I guess," I said. That was Carol's and my plan. Get married. Have two-point-five children. And we would teach them to swim and snorkel in exotic locales. "It's strange to talk about this with you."

"I know."

I swallowed hard before I dug up the courage to speak. "I still think about our baby, Peep. Sometimes."

"Oh, Matt." She sighed, and I could picture her with her hand pressed to her mouth.

Adam's voice came through the receiver. "Elle, tell him you were occupied, and come back to bed."

"Oh God," she said softly. To me. Then she called to him. "I'll be right there. Just give me a minute. He's getting married."

"Married? Tonight? Come on, Elle. I'm lonely in here," he said.

Shit.

"Are you all right?" she asked.

Sure, I was fine, if feeling homicidal was fine. "It sounds like you were busy. Good night, Elle."

June 4, 2003

Dear Matt,

You incited a riot. Adam's almost as furious at me as I am at him. Of course, that isn't directly your fault. But immediately after I informed him of your nuptials, Adam proposed to me.

Again. Damn.

Hey, babe, why don't we get married?

I'm tired of "Hey, babe." I'm not a baby. And I don't want to marry him. So why am I still here? In the past when Adam brought up marriage, I said not until after I've left the astronaut program. This time he had an answer. We should get engaged now and married as soon as this mission is over.

Right.

Stalling, I said I didn't have time to plan a wedding. His response? He would plan the entire event.

Yeah. He'd like that. Control this. Control that.

So I replied that planning a wedding was the bride's job. An unfortunate choice of wording. He assumed I meant yes, I would be said bride. And to seal the contract, he pulled out an engagement ring. A ring!

I had to say no. How do you tell someone with whom you've shared everything for eight years that you never thought it would last forever? I suppose that makes me insensitive. He wanted marriage almost from the beginning. I told him I wasn't ready, but I should have said I'd never be ready. All he wants is his career. He doesn't want children. And I love my job, but I want babies, too. I want it all.

Last month when I was late, just two days late, Adam blew a galvanized gasket. It's not as if I was happy about the possibility now. The mission had just gotten the go, and I would have had to forfeit my spot. God, that would have killed me, but I would not have had a choice. Thank goodness, I wasn't pregnant. Still, I can't believe that a week later he had a goddamned vasectomy—snip, snip.

Talk about illuminating moments, epiphanies. Over the last few weeks I've realized how little respect he has for me. He didn't even say, what do you think about this? He just went off and came home sore, expecting me to wait on him. Right.

But I've said nothing. What should I say? That I want him to be the father of my children? Again. A lightning-bolt moment. No. I don't. He'd be a *terrible father. He doesn't like children, not even neighbor children. I don't want to marry him. So, I said nothing.*

In the beginning we were good together, and we're compatible for the most part. Shouldn't that be enough? Maybe if I didn't want a family, it would be. Why is this so difficult? I feel like part of me is surrendering. All this wasted time I've spent with Adam.

I foresee a point when I'll want to leave Houston, when I'll want to go home and teach at a college. And then I hear his words. <u>Teach? In Maine?</u> What a waste of your aptitude, Elle. Adam rails, and I shrink. He said I was too selfish to apply myself, that anyone could teach basic physics, but most people couldn't understand magnetohydrodynamic waves even under threat of death.

Okay, my brain is wired in such a way that I can. So? Does that mean I have to exist on a two-dimensional plane, focused on a single aspect of the universe? I want more. I want to teach. I like seeing understanding dawn in someone's eyes. Or is Adam right that I am not willing to make the sacrifices real scientific discovery requires?

I miss my dad and my brother. I miss snow and autumn. I miss kayaking on Casco Bay. I miss my life.

And I don't want to grow old and reflect that I could have had children, but my career mattered more. I'm going to walk in space. Nothing will top that.

Except holding a baby in my arms.

I thought someday I would get married. Someday I would have a household full of children.

It won't happen with Adam. This is not working. I have never seen him standing beside me forever.

God help me, I saw you, Matt. I saw an altar and a white dress. I know our chance fell apart a million years ago. But somehow—

Matt, you're marrying someone else. Someone else will stand beside you in a church—and in life. Carol. Oh God. I want to be happy for you, but I feel like I'm slipping into my grave.

What am I supposed to do with these feelings? I'm afraid I made the decision a long time ago. I don't have any right to still love you. But I do.

32

After Elle's Accident
Day 11

After testifying the day before, Adam had the balls to lumber back into Elle's hospital room. He glared in my direction without actually meeting my gaze.

Confounded, I stood. "What are you doing here?"

He acted as if he hadn't heard my question and bent down to kiss Elle's cheek. "Hey, babe."

"Adam, get out."

"Have a little respect. I recognize that isn't something you were ever good at, respecting my relationship with her, but perhaps you could take a walk for an hour or two and let me say good-bye."

"She said good-bye to you five years ago. As for respect, respect that Elle and I are husband and wife. And as for asking me to leave, are you out of your fucking mind?"

He straightened up, his full height reaching for the ceiling, a smirk crossing his face. "What? You don't trust me?"

"No. I don't. What the hell are you even doing in Maine? Her condition has nothing to do with you. She dumped you a long time ago."

He rolled his eyes. "Weren't you listening in court? I have her medical power of attorney."

"Oh, for Christ's sake. My mother stepping in, I sort of understand. She's wrong, but she's family. You? You haven't even seen Elle in years. What's this about? Control? Power? Riding her fame so you look like a big man? Height aside, you're such a fucking little Napoleon, needing to run everything."

"You were always an arrogant asshole, Beaulieu. I explained this all in court. We were together a long time, and I owe her this much. She was important to me." As he swallowed, the gulp could have been heard in China. "I loved her. I never quite understood what went wrong between us, but I suspected it was your influence."

"You're still in love with her. Jesus," I said, turning toward the window for a moment.

"I'm not—in love with her. Anymore. But . . . yes . . . I still care," he said, his voice petering out. "We were together a long time."

"You've been apart a long time, too."

"That's pretty damned ironic, coming from you. You were pathetic, all those years, sitting around, waiting for her, calling her, interjecting yourself into my relationship with Elle."

"We never talked about you. We were friends, long before you ever met her," I said.

"You were still in love with her."

I conceded the point with a nod. "So why are you here? You didn't continue on as friends. That crap on the stand about—"

"It wasn't crap. We talked, maybe not often, but we did. I didn't want to know she was pregnant. Once she had a child, it would be over for her." He shook his head, looked back at her, and muttered, "I didn't think it would be over like this."

And with that, I saw Elle again, not with the eyes that had begun to adjust, but the way I saw her that first time in the ER, that drop-me-to-my-knees way, the world-coming-to-an-end way. I zoned out. To see Elle. My Elle. Lying there. So motionless and so distant.

He was still talking, recapping, excusing his intrusion. "So I didn't call her back after she said she was pregnant last winter. But caring about her, that wasn't crap." And as if he'd concluded, he whisked out of the room.

For some bizarre reason I felt compelled to follow him. Maybe I'd missed something. Maybe he'd announced the next bomb he intended to drop. I didn't know what besides a long-forgotten advanced health directive he might produce, but uncharacteristically, he had surrendered.

He took the back stairwell, the one that emptied out by the emergency room entrance, the one with the helipad, the large expanse of asphalt between the behemoth of the hospital and the parking deck. The rain was pelting down and neither of us was wearing a coat. In less than the fifteen seconds it took to dash across the lot, I was drenched. He was drenched. Only as he pounded on the elevator button in the parking deck did he see me. "What? I'm leaving. What more do you want?"

"I don't get it."

He exhaled, his shoulders sagging. "I know you don't. But you ought to. You need to understand so you can stop this travesty." He swiped the rainwater off of his face. "Let's get out of here."

It wasn't like this was the first time I ever sat across a table from Adam. Over the years I'd had the displeasure, but there we were again, this time soaked through to the skin, sitting in vinyl booths, hunched over laminated menus in a local Italian dive where overcooked spaghetti and olive oil ruled.

"Not exactly vegan fare," he said.

"Get a salad. We're not here for the cuisine. Talk," I said.

He closed the menu and looked at his watch. "Okay. I have an hour before I have to leave for the airport, but don't think I'm giving up. I'm going back to Houston so I can find the lawyer Elle used to write that advanced directive, and I'll be back with the original copy before court reconvenes in ten days."

A chill ran through my bones, and not because I was soaking wet sitting underneath an air-conditioning vent.

He rattled off the story of how he'd met her, how young she was, how he even felt a little jealous of "the princess," because he'd worked two jobs, and at twenty-nine he was just still working on his PhD.

"Look, I worked my way through school, too," I said. "How you met her has nothing to do with what's happening now. Or more to the point, it has nothing to do with what she would want."

"Patience," he said, rolling his eyes. "My point is everyone misjudged her. Even I did at first. The only reason I ever talked to her at all was because we both wanted to work for NASA. So whenever we ended up in the same place, I made polite conversation. But before long it became apparent she wasn't such the little spoiled prodigy after all. Every weekend she was driving all the way to Maine and back so she could see her little brother."

"Yeah, well, Alice made her promise to take care of him," I said, using the paper napkin to blot a rivulet of water running from my wet hair down my forehead.

Adam laced his hands behind his head and leaned back. "And I suppose you don't see anything wrong in that? A teenage girl, a genius with huge promise, and she had to clean up her family's dysfunctional mess. You were probably like everyone else."

"No. I told Elle to go to MIT," I said. I argued that my parents would watch out for Christopher if Hank didn't stay sober. And he did stop drinking for good not long afterward. I even told her I would go to Boston University instead of Columbia so we could be nearby. But no, Elle had to be responsible. "I wasn't like everyone else," I told Adam.

"I tried to help her," he said. "It didn't take long for her to get to me. She was mesmerizing—brilliant. Really brilliant. But she was so naive and inexplicably ignorant of academic politics. She needed to be more aggressive with her research, and she was too soft, too distracted by her family—even driving up on a weekday once in a while so she could attend Christopher's school events."

"Elle's family is important to her," I said. "She couldn't walk away from someone she loved, any more than she would have turned off her life support under these circumstances."

"See, that's the point, Beaulieu. You're forcing her into something equally inequitable. This time you're asking her to accept torture to take care of some amorphous blob that isn't even a baby yet."

"No."

"Listen to me first. For once, just listen to someone else's point of view. I anchored her, helped her stand up for herself, to put her academic dreams first. I'm the one who convinced her to push for NASA even though it was so far away from her needy family. I made sure nothing and no one got in her way. She had the talent. She had the desire. But she had to prioritize."

"You aggrandize your role."

"Not really." He laughed once, a dry, humorless laugh. "I helped her clear the static so she could get what she wanted. Space. Stars. Hubble. I loved her, and NASA was what she dreamed about. You were a distraction. Her family was a distraction. Sometimes even I was a distraction. And as much as she resisted me sometimes, she wanted my help."

The waitress came to the table, set sweating water glasses down in front of us, and took our orders.

I shifted on the vinyl booth seat, squeaking in my wet trousers. I wanted to get this discussion over with; I wanted to get back to my wife. "Elle was never as weak-minded as you describe her. She knew exactly what she wanted. Always did. Yeah, she was well rounded, possessed compassion, and she loved her family. Hank and Alice made sure that, even though Elle was a genius, she had a normal childhood, played sports, and did chores. That wasn't a distraction. That's what makes someone human, being part of something bigger."

"Making her responsible for everyone else's lives made her a doormat."

"Tell that to the crew of *Atlantis*. Tell that to Jabert. That she should have left him to die. She's heroic."

Adam raked his hair and leaned forward. "Are you incapable of understanding what I'm saying? Elle deserves to have someone put her first. For once, think about it. Stand up for her. She left NASA for you. For once, do the right thing. For her."

I slammed my hand down on the table between us. "She wanted to leave NASA. You keep saying that I don't understand. The fact is you don't," I said. "You evidently have very little respect for Elle's independence. She didn't need to be led. I couldn't have led her anywhere. We were going in the same direction. We wanted the same things. Elle wanted children, maybe more than I did. Elle wasn't an egocentric megalomaniac. Did she make sacrifices? Yeah. And that was her choice."

His face filled with so much contempt he looked like he might spit. "Keep telling yourself that. She wanted more. I took care of her. I'm here to take care of her now. Believe me, I don't want to be in the middle of this. If you were even a halfway decent man, you'd let her die with dignity. Damn you for letting her die slowly." Adam stood up and marched out the door.

* * *

Keisha unfolded the jigsaw-patterned quilt in Caribbean blues, yellows, and pinks and tucked it in around Elle. "She always said this one made her feel happy. I was planning to make her a quilt this year for Christmas." The furrow between her brows deepened. "She won't be here, will she?"

A couple of responses popped into my head. Certainly I hoped Elle would still be carrying the baby at Christmas—and for a while afterward—but even if Keisha completed a new quilt, it wouldn't matter. Elle would never know about the love and painstaking hours put into stitching one of Keisha's masterpieces. Elle wouldn't even know if she was warm or cold. I hugged Keisha, this woman whose support had seen Elle through the loss of our son, whose own struggles Elle had supported in kind. "We'll have to see what happens," I said.

Keisha made a pitiful attempt to smile and eased back into the chair next to Elle's bed.

We made small talk for a few minutes before I began to vent about Adam, his visit, the rain, and his tirade at the restaurant. "I hate that son of a bitch," I said. "Did she ever tell you about him?"

Keisha blinked a few times before she spoke. "I knew she'd lived with someone, but I didn't remember his name. What is it you really want to ask me?"

Is he right? Was I placing an inhuman burden on Elle by asking her to try to hold on for months? But instead of saying that, I shrugged.

Keisha put her hand on mine in a consoling gesture. "Here's what I recall she said about him. He reminded her of you. Don't look so horrified, Matthew. She said he possessed some of the same qualities. He was smart enough to keep her on her toes, and they were friends first. But he *wasn't* you. And although the relationship was serious, it didn't have the substance to last. But that's not what you want to know either, is it? You want me to tell you that you are right and that he is wrong."

I lowered my gaze. "After talking to him, *listening* to him, I don't know anymore."

"Well, I do. I'm biased. I want the baby to live, but that is not enough for me to recuse myself," she said. "You see, I have a theory. Do you want the long version or the short one?"

"The middle-of-the-road one," I said. Keisha was a storyteller by nature, and sometimes she went off on dissertation-length tangents. Elle said it was a hazard of academia. Faculty had a captive audience in the classroom, so sometimes that led to the delusion that every story professors told kept their students rapt.

Keisha shifted in her seat, and I could see her composing her explanation. "Did you know Elle had a sixteen-year-old girl in her senior honors class last fall?"

I nodded. "Julie something. Elle said she was gifted."

"She's a little mousy but obviously she has a fine mind. She came into Elle's office while the two of us were chatting one day, and after some discussion and some rambling about an incomprehensible mathematical formula, Julie excused herself. Elle sat back in her chair and told me how in between worlds she felt at that age. Like Julie, she had the intellect to outwit most of her peers, sometimes her professors, but she never felt like an equal to the other students, not in high school, not in college, not even in graduate school. Particularly not with *Adam*. At least not for a long, long time."

I leaned forward. "She had a hard time fitting in when she was a kid," I said, "but . . ."

"Exactly—*but*—she started to grow up. She went to Princeton. She met a much older guy. And she liked him because was older, and he didn't seem to mind that she was a little naive about some things. He mentored her. She let him have the upper hand."

"Why are you telling me this?"

"Because she outgrew him. She matured and she became a confident woman who knew what she wanted and knew how to fight and achieve her goals. She is . . ." Keisha swallowed hard. "She was a whole person. All of those things I talk about in women's studies courses . . . Elle was the perfect example."

"Okay," I said. "But how—"

"How does that make you right and Adam wrong?"

I nodded.

"He continued to discount her opinions. She'd had enough. But she told me once that even when you were children, you respected her. I saw that. You didn't always agree on everything, but you always listened. Do you believe she would want to save the baby?"

"Yes," I said.

"And that's how I know you're making the right decision. For you, it is a matter of respect. Besides, I knew her, too. And she would never surrender—even like this."

✦ 33 ✦

Day 12

"The Mass has ended. Go in peace," Father Meehan said.

"Thanks be to God," we responded like a pack of brainwashed peasants.

Rote memory is a wondrous thing. I could make it through an entire Mass and not have to think once. I could recite prayers from my childhood. I could zone out during the homily and the Liturgy of the Eucharist, standing and kneeling in a tidal rhythm.

God. If it took God, I'd bow to God.

But afterward I felt depleted, and I sat there wondering if the good priest who was at the front of the church shaking the hands of the devoted noted that I'd fulfilled my part of the bargain—at least for this Sunday.

I stood, dusted myself off as if I'd grown roots into the hard oak pew, and then headed up to the altar to light a candle. I should do that. Twelve days. It had only taken me twelve days to become a hypocrite. I was looking for the taper to light the flame when I realized that, not only were all the candles ablaze, they were electric. What a sham. Should I flick off one and then relight it? It was stupid anyway.

"I can't even get altar servers these days," Father Meehan said, walking up the central aisle. "Good to see you here." Then he began snuffing out the real candles, the ones illuminating the altar. "How is Elle today?"

"The same." I pointed at the collection of prelit candles. "What am I supposed to do with this?"

"It's kind of like a gas fireplace, don't you think?"

"Or an electric one. It gives the illusion. It's all smoke and mirrors, isn't it?" *Did I say that last part aloud? Shit. I'm tired.* I'd spent most of the night replaying Adam's argument.

"You realize you don't need to light a candle to pray. It's simply symbolic," Father Meehan said.

"Right," I said.

"As for the smoke and mirrors, it's called faith."

"Sorry," I said. "I'm trying."

He took the wine and chalice back into the back room. "Come along."

I followed. Can you say "sheep"? The analogy was befitting. Sheep. Shepherd.

"I can run all the clichés past you," he said, as if he could read minds in this house of magic. "Ask God for help, and He'll answer you. I can tell you that faith is a gift. I can direct you to certain passages in the Bible. Instead I'm just going to tell you to try to open your mind. Have a conversation with Him. Or try to."

"Sure," I said.

"How's the baby doing?"

"Thirty weeks to go. In sixteen, we have a chance."

"That's what you're like, isn't it? You are a numbers man. You want measurable parameters for your life. Did you ever believe in anything that wasn't a number?"

"In Elle. My faith was in her."

He exhaled loudly. "Well, that's a start. You believe in love, and God is the purest love."

✳ 34 ✳

Days 14 to 21

Even when Elle was a kid playing astronaut, she never counted
down. She always counted up. "It's like saying you're fixed in the
past, and you're running out of time. Every moment is only the
beginning of something new," she'd say.

As much as I wanted to embrace her optimism, the steady de-
cline of her body belied my attempt. Yes, the baby was sixteen
days older, ten weeks gestation, and all indicators were that he
or she was thriving. But how? Elle wasn't the glowing pregnant
woman. She was counting down.

The reality was seeping into my emotional crevasses. I had to
keep busy. Phil told me not to worry about our surgical practice.
D'Amato's group was still covering, but I was taking call most nights
and the ER summoned me usually once or twice. ICU was easier.
All I had to do was walk out of Elle's room to check on patients.

I'd acquired one of the foldout chairs, which converted into
something of a bed, permitting me to recline. I rationalized I was
sleeping an hour here and there.

"Why don't you go home tonight?" Jillian Waters, the ICU nurse manager, asked me. "We'll phone if there's a problem."

I shook my head.

"You don't trust us to take care of her?"

"It's not that."

"What then?"

"I don't know," I said, but I did know. I was sleep deprived and grieving, and if I were in my right mind, I'd have told myself to leave; this paranoia was insane. No one was going to turn off Elle's life support in my absence. "I'm not seeing patients except on call. I have to give Phil a little backup," I said, not feeling even a little a bit guilty for my white lie.

"You're putting holes in walls, and the night shift says you *aren't* sleeping. You've spent fourteen out of the past sixteen nights here. You need to go home."

But I didn't go home. Our house wasn't home without Elle. Maybe I should sell the farmhouse. I couldn't imagine living there without her, and besides, I needed the money.

Our medical insurer was balking about coverage. Why should they continue to pay thousands of dollars a day for a woman certified as brain-dead? Depending on how much care she needed, a month in ICU could run close to a million dollars. True, Phil wasn't going to charge for his surgical services. And the hospital might give me some kind of professional courtesy, but I couldn't expect Clint and the other intensivists to forgo their fees. In eight months the bill could easily exceed—God, I didn't even want to think about it, especially if she had more complications. We had some savings, but nothing close to what I'd need. And although I knew Hank would help, I doubted he had that much in the bank.

The only asset of significant value was the house. A couple of years before, a developer offered to buy the land for over $3 million, but Elle and I refused to consider it. Damn. Elle would hate it that someone would rip down our house and smear our farm with ridiculously ostentatious McMansions.

Moot. It was all moot. Elle was unaware of anything.

For the next three nights I spent more time in other patients' rooms than I did in Elle's. Three kids came in with head injuries, and an AIDS patient came into the ER with a sinus abscess, and because of its position, the ENT wanted me there while he drained it.

Then the baby came in, a former preemie born four months early. As a consequence of his prematurity, his brain had suffered severe damage. Before the baby's hospital discharge, Phil and I put in a shunt to drain the excess fluid off his brain. Now the shunt was malfunctioning, and the baby needed to return to the OR.

The mother wept when I told her. In her eyes, I could see Elle. I could see the grief of a woman whose loss was immeasurable. As I looked down at the baby, I saw Celina and Dylan and the two other babies who never took a form. And I pictured the baby Elle was carrying.

"Excuse me," I said. Under the pretense of preparing a surgical consent, I sat at the nurses' station.

If we could keep Elle alive until Christmas, our baby had a chance, as much of a chance as the poor child with the malfunctioning shunt. What the hell was I doing? We had to do better. The baby wasn't due until March. We needed March.

I picked up the telephone and called Phil to come in. I wasn't in any shape to operate. Not emotionally. Not physically. I was too sleep deprived and too stressed.

Just as I was falling asleep, Pediatrics called me down for Mark Nguyen. He was having a grand mal seizure that wasn't responding to the usual anticonvulsant medications. By the time his seizure ended, we'd loaded him with so many pharmaceuticals we had to readmit him to the ICU. The MRI didn't give us a definitive reason for the episode. Yet he awoke a couple of hours later, lucid.

Another long night. I rationalized it was better than moping around.

But during the day I did mope. Phil came by a couple of times a day, often armed with care packages from his wife, Melanie.

Mike. Christopher. Hank. Just about every hospital bigwig made daily stopovers. Stopover lunch. Stopover rounds. I didn't really want to talk to anyone, least of all the powers that be. I wanted to drown in Elle's letters.

I replayed her last voice mail a dozen times a day, skipping over the messages from friends and family who each called at least once a day. I only wanted to hear Elle's voice. "Hey, it's me . . . Let's spend a little quiet time together this evening . . ."

I took her hand in mine. "Enough quiet time, Elle. Let's talk. Wake up and tell me this is all just the worst goddamned nightmare I've ever imagined. I need you."

I'd begun to avoid newspapers and the news channels on television. There were often blurbs about Elle's status. Everyone seemed to feel they had the right to an opinion. Should Elle be forced to stay alive for the sake of a pregnancy? Was she a saint or a martyr? What chance did the baby have under the circumstances? Was she being forced to be the vessel for my spawn? Who had the right to self-determination? Anyone but a pregnant woman? Feminists weighed in. Mothers weighed in. Feminist mothers. None of them knew Elle.

When Keisha came in or when Hank stopped by, I went for walks, oftentimes after dark. Other times I went into the on-call room to sleep. They were the only ones I trusted, the only ones who thought we should keep Elle on life support, but I was beginning to have more doubts, and more since the former preemie came into the ER.

During the moments in between all the other invasions, I read.

The early letters were, as Elle once told me, a teenager ranting about her lack of freedom, mostly her outrage that her parents didn't allow her to go on her own foreign-exchange-student adventure, about school, about how, with me away in Britain, she felt more of a misfit than ever.

And then, her mother's cancer disclosure with all its emotional backlash seethed up from the pages. I started skimming the entries, remembering I was looking for something that would say definitively what she would want in these circumstances.

Later, during Alice's months in hospice care, Elle's letters grew dark. She talked about the dullness in her mother's skin, the sour smell of her mouth, the bedsores that appeared no matter how often the nurses turned her.

> *But what gets me the most is how Mommy's fingers curl, like she's in pain. I can't stand that she's suffering, that we're allowing it, or that we aren't helping her. She's in a coma, and that supposedly means she's out of it. She isn't completely. This is merciless. She's in agony, she can't speak for herself, and we aren't helping.*

The afternoon sun was peeking in through the window and onto Elle's almost translucent skin. I adjusted the shades so the sunlight didn't strike her eyes. I couldn't help it. I had to even though I knew she was blind and deaf. I pulled my chair closer and rested my head on the pillow beside her. "You aren't in pain. Please tell me you aren't in pain. Tell me I'm doing what you'd want."

Standing at the door, wearing her scrubs, my mother cleared her throat. "Elle wouldn't want this, even if she's not in pain. But we can't know for certain what she's feeling."

"Ah, Jesus . . ." I stood, burying my hands in my pockets.

Mom stepped up to the bed, then bent down and kissed Elle's cheek. "Hi, sweetheart. Your face looks better. The swelling's gone down."

"I don't want to open the debate again," I said.

"I know. Please, just give me a minute to sit here with her." Mom slid onto the chair in the corner, staring at Elle. "I haven't seen you to talk since the incident at the park. Your help meant a lot to me."

I grunted. I hadn't wanted to help her. My own mother, and I had offered my help with reluctance, and I sure as hell didn't want to bond over the moment now. And Adam. She had allied herself with Adam. "You've seen Elle. It's time for you to leave. Go back to work."

"I'm worried about you, spending all this time here. You can't be getting any sleep."

"Look, I'm a grown man, a married man. It's no longer your place to worry about me."

"Mothers always worry. There's no off switch."

I drew a breath. "Maybe not. And I'm the father of the baby growing inside Elle and, strangely, I can't find an off switch either. You see, his grandmother wants to turn off the life support keeping him alive."

"It's not like that—"

"You even dragged Adam into this."

"I didn't. He called me."

"You should have told him to stay home. You shouldn't have been involved with this at all."

"Elle's like my daughter."

"Don't try to feed me that crap. Elle isn't your daughter. She never was, no matter how much you always coveted a girl. She's my wife, and this tragedy doesn't have anything to do with you. Your interference is out of control, you, Adam, those right-to-lifers, that reporter. This is insane. Everyone thinks they're protecting Elle. From who? Me?

"I didn't come to the conclusion to keep her on life support easily. And yes, the consequences of it are eating me alive. But Elle never backed down from having a child—even though she knew she could die. When she hemorrhaged, I almost lost her. Elle knew the risks, and she still wanted to try."

"You should have protected her. You shouldn't have gotten her pregnant again."

There it was, the accusation. This was my fault. As if I didn't realize it. "I thought she was using her diaphragm." I couldn't believe I was talking to my mother about Elle's and my contraceptive choices.

"Are you saying she misled you?"

"That's not what I'm saying. Go back to work."

Mom shook her head. "My nurse manager is giving me the rest of the day off, even suggested I might want to consider taking early retirement." She tried on a nonconvincing laugh.

I studied my mother, who had never once considered retiring early, who had probably never considered retiring at all.

"Yeah," she said. "Another patient refused to let me take care of her. Actually the husband sent me away this time."

"Funny how husbands want to protect their wives and unborn children from you." I knew my words were cruel, and I didn't care.

"Matthew!"

"Go away."

Tears formed in her eyes as she turned away from me and made an abrupt exit.

I slithered down into the chair. Shit. We would never repair the relationships that were coming undone.

✦ 35 ✦

Day 21
September

I hadn't braced for the McClure version of civil war; nevertheless, the first shots of anger rang out, bullets of accusations in the court-house. Maybe the altercation wouldn't have stunned me if I'd ever seen Hank behave as if he thought Christopher was capable of a misstep. But no one ever put Christopher in his place. Yet right there, Hank dug his heels into the marble checkerboard floor. "She was *my* daughter before she was *your* sister."

I didn't hear Christopher's response. Or maybe I thought he'd have none worth noting and instead I focused on the descending reporters.

I grabbed my father-in-law's elbow and pulled him toward the men's room, not a private venue but more private than the corri dor. "This way, Chris," I said, hoping he'd follow.

A reporter came out of the stall and regarded us with either wariness or piqued curiosity.

"Get out," I snapped.

"Jesus," the wannabe CNN anchor muttered.

Suddenly Jake's cautions that I ought to play the nice guy galloped out of my memory. Damn it. Time for a mea culpa. All I needed was to see myself all over CNN again. "I didn't mean to bark. Please. Give us a minute alone."

The reporter's angry expression didn't lift as he turned on the faucet and washed his hands in the low porcelain sink. He shook his hands dry and turned toward the paper-towel holder. "You know, I'm just covering a story and dealing with the call of nature. I don't need my head bitten off."

Hank was pacing behind me, his breaths coming in short spits. Christopher leaned up against the subway tile with his arms crossed.

"I know," I said to the reporter. "I'm sorry. Emotions are running high. And low. My wife . . ." My voice broke and that was something I couldn't permit in front of this man who would report whatever I said and however I said it.

Jake barged into the restroom. "There you are. Court's reconvening."

The reporter lowered his eyes and squeezed past Jake, exiting.

"What's going on?" Jake asked.

"That's what I'd like to know. What the hell did you mean, Christopher?" Hank asked.

Christopher glared at his father. "You don't want to listen. You never did."

"What's this about?" I asked.

"He thinks Elle will just wake up and be normal. Just like he thought my mom would suddenly wake up and be cured of cancer. That didn't happen, and this won't either. He thinks I was too young to remember, but I do. He's the one who doesn't remember what it was like. You were drunk all the time, Dad. *All* the time. Elle took care of me. Not you. So she's my sister, but she's also like my mom, and I refuse to let you do this to her. Elle didn't want to die this way. We used to talk about it." Christopher spun toward me. "And you, haven't you caused her enough pain?"

Jake stepped between Chris and me. Maybe Jake didn't trust me. Maybe he was trying to defuse the tension. God knows, I was incapable of reason at that moment.

"I'd never hurt Elle," I said.

"You got her pregnant again—after she almost died last winter. And you knew she was scared of dying the way my mom did, and here you are, fighting Elle's living will." Chris shoved Jake out of the way and got right up in my face.

"Believe me; I struggled over whether or not to keep her on life support. I'm still struggling with it, but she wanted a baby."

"Yeah, well, that didn't bother you when my mom was dying, did it? You didn't care that Elle wanted to keep that baby. Nope. You just made her get an abortion."

His words were like a match lighting tinder under my panic zone. My heart rate shot up in flame. I looked at my father-in-law, who, to the best of my knowledge, didn't know about Elle's teen pregnancy. Hell, I didn't realize Chris knew about Celina either. Whatever information he thought he knew was muddled. "She never had an abortion," I said.

"What are you talking about?" Hank asked. "What abortion?"

"Matt got Elle pregnant when Mom was dying," Chris said, like a simpering little tattletale. "Then he talked her into having an abortion. And now he's all holier-than-thou with his I-only-want-to-do-what-Elle-would-want bull. Well, I swear she wouldn't want to be lying in a hospital bed on life support."

"That is not what happened. There was no abortion. Not then. Not any other time," I said.

"That's why she was so desperate to have a baby now. She's always felt so guilty," Chris said.

"No," I said. "And it's not that simple, Chris. Besides, if she'd had an abortion and felt guilty about it, it would make my case all the more clear. I didn't make Elle get an abortion. I never would have done that."

"You got my daughter pregnant while Alice was dying?" Hank pounded into my chest with the heel of his hand. "Damn you. Elle was only a child when Alice died."

"She wasn't a child. She couldn't be a child because of you. *You* were the child. A lousy goddamned drunk. Yeah, she was young. We both were. And we messed up. But you weren't exactly taking care of your family back then. You abandoned them. You didn't even notice her big belly. That's how bad it was. But yes, Elle got pregnant. I got her pregnant—"

Before I had a chance to explain what happened, Hank stormed out of the bathroom.

I turned toward Christopher. "You don't get it. She didn't have an abortion. She miscarried. She was five months pregnant that first time. And it broke her heart. She felt guilty. Yes. But not because she aborted the baby. She felt guilty because she couldn't save our daughter. Every day of her life. Every child we've lost since. I'm telling you she would want to save this one."

I slid onto the bar stool next to Hank. In front of him sat a line of empty tumblers. In his grip, one half full. And one full to the rim waited off to the side. "How'd you find me?" he asked.

I shrugged. "This is the fourteenth bar I've been to in"—I looked at my watch—"three hours. Persistence, I guess."

The bartender, a redheaded girl, slicked-back punk and perky, stood in front of me and smiled as if by showing me enough dazzling teeth, I'd hand over a hundred-dollar tip. "What can I get you?"

"Corona, if you've got lime," I said, turning my attention to Hank. "Thought you were a beer guy."

"Only thing Alice let me keep in the house back then. She figured I'd get drunk slower on beer. She wasn't so bright in that regard. 'Naive,' maybe, is a better term. Alice was always an innocent." He bottomed up his glass, set it down hard, and nodded at the bartender for another.

She set down my beer. "Wait, haven't I seen you on TV, the astronaut's husband?"

"Pretend you didn't see us here, okay?" I said, setting down a twenty.

She slipped the tip in her pocket and stepped away.

I turned back to Hank. "You don't seem drunk."

"I can drink a hell of a lot before I seem drunk. Besides, this is soda."

I reached in front of him and pulled the tumbler filled with Scotch on semimelted rocks.

"All the others are plain Pepsi. The temptation is always there, real or imagined. Sometimes it's easier to look your enemy in the face." He turned as if to study me.

"First off, Elle never had an abortion. Second, I was going to tell you about the first pregnancy. I meant to. Because . . . I'm going to talk about it when I testify. But the short version is we were kids in love and stupid. And things were bad with Alice."

Hank nodded, picked up a stirrer, and then pushed away the Scotch. "I need to refresh this one. Take it and bring a fresh Scotch. On the rocks, please. I hate diluted Scotch."

The bartender glanced at me and then went about her assigned task.

"You know, I never even suspected you and she were . . . intimate . . . back then. Jesus, she was a baby."

"We were two teenagers, and a whole lot of horrible things were going on around us. We got swept up in the one good thing we had: each other. And she didn't want anyone to know because she didn't want to add to the trouble. Then she miscarried. Elle didn't abort. Chris got that part wrong."

"You were going to keep the baby?"

"I don't know. We talked about adoption, but I honestly don't know."

He bit his cheek. "And I was too drunk to even notice what was going on in my own house. Jesus. She was fifteen. You had sex with my daughter when she was fifteen. You should have known better. You were older."

"Yeah, but not that much. I was a kid, too. I'd be appalled if my fifteen-year-old daughter was having sex—especially after what happened to us—but when you're the teenager with your girl-friend, that's not what you're thinking. You're thinking you want her. And I did love her. I still love her. We messed up. She got pregnant. And then she wasn't."

He stared at me long and hard. "I thought Elle was a good girl. Sweet, you know."

"She was."

"Did Alice know?"

"I don't think so."

The bartender placed the drink in front of Hank, smiled at me, and then backed off again.

He sniffed it, and set it back down. "And I was too drunk for Elle to talk to me. You're right. I was a lousy father."

"No." I clapped Hank on his shoulder. "But for a while there you were a lousy drunk." I took a long swig of my beer. Getting sloshed would be stupid, although it was a damned tempting idea. To get lost. To forget. If just for a few hours. But I had plenty of problems already. I pulled out my wallet, took enough to cover his tab and mine, a little more to buy silence from the redhead, and slapped it on the bar. "Let's get out of here."

"Maybe Linney and Christopher are right," Hank said. "Maybe we should let Elle go."

Death comes with simple surrender, a word that allows the last breath to slip away. I stared at the black oak floor as if it were an abyss.

I could let go. I could let Elle go. I could let her be at peace. She didn't want to live this way. And then I could lie down and die—whatever that took, pills, a gun, stepping in front of a train. Our families could bury us together. And even if there was no heaven and no hell, there wouldn't be this agony of missing her. God. How could a benevolent God allow this to happen to my beautiful wife?

It had only been three weeks. I could never survive three months or three years. I couldn't survive without her in the world. I couldn't.

But there was a baby at stake. Elle's baby. Part of her could still live, and what did she say that afternoon? Life is about taking risks. And the baby was still alive.

"No," I said to Hank. "I can't let her go."

"Have you seen what it's doing to your family? That's what I have been sitting here thinking, not about Elle losing her virginity. Not about you taking advantage of her. We all thought you'd end up together. Me, Alice, your mom and dad. Not that that made it right, but we all figured someday . . . Besides, it's moot at this point, but . . . but, Matt, you're screwing this up the same way I did."

My head snapped toward him. "I'm not a drunk."

"I guess I deserve that, but it's not what I meant." Hank sighed. "Chris might be right. He begged me to talk you into discontinuing Elle's life support. Linney is a wreck. And if they're right, that there is no hope, maybe we should let Elle go."

"I am letting Elle go. I'm grieving, but I'm letting her go. There's no way in hell I can let the baby go. Not now. The baby has a chance. That's the only thing I can do for Elle. I owe her that. I owe her this baby. And no one, not you, not Christopher, not my mother or anyone else matters. If I lose everything else, if the baby lives, then . . ." I was going to say it would be all right, but I couldn't say all right. Instead I finished by saying, "I owe Elle and the baby everything. *They* are my family." Oddly, I realized after I'd phrased it that way, that the baby was my child, too. Not just Elle's. And I wanted it to live.

In pounding silence, Hank studied his shoes. I don't know what I expected him to say. I nodded, turned, and walked toward the door. Hank had done some bad things over the years, yet in some ways, I respected him deeply. Maybe because he struggled. Maybe because, though flawed, he loved his wife and his kids. After he sobered up, he'd been there for me, too, helped pay for my medical education, and made a point to keep in touch after my own father died.

I reached for the doorknob and realized Hank was at my side. "You're not alone, son. We are family. And I owe Elle, too. Let's head back to the hospital."

After I'd been away from Elle's hospital room for nine straight hours, the reality of her condition hit me hard, and my legs shook.

Hank pulled up a chair behind me. "Go ahead, Matt. Sit."

I did. How the hell was I going to fix this situation? I couldn't fix Elle no matter how hard I tried to figure out a way. And kidnapping her and taking her somewhere safe until after the baby was born didn't seem like an option.

Hank's voice snapped me back. "It's like looking at Alice," he said.

I nodded. I'd been trying not to see Alice lying in the living room of the McClure house, but I wasn't blind.

"Right now you're probably feeling like you don't want to survive this."

I looked up at Hank.

"Well, that's how I felt when my wife was sick. I'm not saying this is ever going to get easy. I loved Alice"—he paused and swallowed hard—"every bit as much as you love my daughter. Every bit as much as I love my daughter. It took me a while to figure it out, but she's still . . ." He patted his heart. "Go home and sleep tonight, Matt. I'll be here. I'll stay with my little girl."

I shook my head. "I've been gone all day because of the trial."

"And chasing me down, but, son, you need to sleep or you'll break."

✦ 36 ✦

Day 21

I drove for an hour, out around Back Bay, up along the Eastern Prom, taking time to look out over Casco Bay and to clear my head, and then I headed north to my house, where Jake and I planned to meet. As I approached the usually deserted road, I spotted more than a dozen cars and minivans parked along the side. Faces stared through my windshield at me. Some of the people held crosses, and others held signs of support. A local NBC affiliate news crew aimed their cameras at me. Yep, there was the blond newswoman. I gritted my teeth and avoided eye contact. *Do not make a scene.* I pulled down our winding driveway and parked in the barn.

When I came out, Jake was plodding down the slope with a soft-sided blue cooler slung over one shoulder and extending his other hand to me. He rolled his eyes. "It seemed like a good idea to meet here, but the media is all over the place. Let me handle them, though. Don't give them a statement again."

I shook my head. "Shit, no. I don't want to talk to them. Particularly not to that crazy witch."

"Remember what I said about watching your mouth. I want you to look like a choirboy, especially after you snapped at that reporter in the men's room. You're starting to look like a hothead."

"I could have said 'bitch.'"

"Not funny. I'm serious. The last thing you need is to come off as a misogynist right now."

Although I didn't appreciate being told to behave myself, I yanked open the back door and held it wide for him. "At least the property is big enough that they can't see the house from the road."

He preceded me into the kitchen and then the living room, where I dropped the duffel bag with Elle's letters and diaries on the coffee table.

"The oversize property is the only good thing about living out in the boonies," he said, opening the cooler. He pulled out two foil-covered sandwich-size blocks and a Caesar salad. "No one makes paninis like Yvette. Turkey artichoke." He turned on the oven and threw them on the top rack. "So update me. You said your father-in-law is sober when you called me to come out. Have you heard any more about the Pro-Lifers hassling your mother?"

"Some little stuff at the hospital."

A blank expression fell over his face and I supplied the details. "Seems some people don't want her to be their nurse. I can't say that I blame them right now."

He nodded. "That's too bad. I used to like your mother. I think I liked the care packages she sent you at college even more than you did. Does she still make those butterscotch cookies?"

I shrugged. "Doubt she'd bake you a batch right now."

"True. No matter. Yvette sent blueberry tarts. Just you wait." He pulled out glazed tarts that looked like they belonged on the cover of a gourmet magazine, and they smelled even better.

Everyone wanted to feed me, but I'd lost my appetite when Elle fell, and even incredible food couldn't resurrect it. We sat down at the table and I ate a little anyhow.

Jake twisted his neck from side to side making it pop like a chiropractor had just cracked it. "When I said it might get ugly, I didn't expect this already, but it might get worse. I hope not." He gestured toward the duffel. "Now, down to business. This is actually very simple; you hand me a stack of letters or diaries, and I read them. No associates, just one of your oldest friends, trying to save your unborn child." Jake reached for one of the journals, and I almost felt sick to my stomach, like there was a Peeping Tom watching Elle through an open bedroom window.

"Simpler still," I said. "I'll read them. Meanwhile, you go through the video."

"Video?"

"DVD. Our wedding. You said you wanted to see any video of Elle, to see if there was anywhere she talked about family. I think there might be some from her niece's Baptism, too, but Christopher would have that." I dumped a carton of Elle's books and notebooks in front of Jake. "And these are what Keisha found in Elle's office. She has notes embedded in the margins. Maybe there's something where Elle weighed in on abortion. I'll invest my time in her letters."

"You could trust me to be respectful of her privacy." He pulled out his glasses and sat down in the wing-backed chair.

I nodded once. "It's not a matter of trust, Jake. She didn't write the letters ever expecting anyone to read them."

By the time he'd gone through Elle's college notes, he found one or two notations that he thought he could use. While he watched our wedding video, I left the room. I figured I'd look at it later, preferably alone.

Elle wasn't much for public displays of affection, but on that day we did kiss to glass clanking. Both of us teared up during our vows. It was nothing unusual, nothing which proved anything other than we were in love.

I sat on a wicker rocker on the front porch and flipped on the light to read one of her entries. She opened it by writing about NASA and some new anti-micrometeor technology they were developing. But a few paragraphs in, I started paying attention.

Woo . . . there I go again, getting dizzy.

Elle's handwriting thinned out.

There, better now. I should tell you tonight. I'm a little worried about how you're going to react. You'll probably go into doctor overdrive, but it will be fine. I hope it will be fine. I don't want to lose another baby. It's happened so many times I feel like a murderer, like it's my fault. And it is—at least medically. But if I can bring this one into the world, maybe I can forgive myself for failing our others.

She dated it the day she told me she was pregnant with Dylan.

I stepped off the porch and walked through the darkness to the garden Elle planted after Celina died. For a week that spring we drove from nursery to nursery, finding the plants she wanted for the flower bed. In the years between, the lilac bush we planted had grown huge. The tulips and crocuses burst up out of the ground every spring. Irises. Peonies. Daisies and black-eyed Susans. Echinacea. Sedum. Mums. We buried Dylan's ashes there, too. Elle sublimated her grief by pouring her love into this garden.

I crumbled beside it and wept for the family we should have had.

The screen door creaked open. "Matt?" Jake called from the front porch.

In darkness, he couldn't see me. I cleared my throat. "Yeah?"

"What are you doing out there? You're not talking to a reporter."

"No." I pulled up my T-shirt and wiped off my face, then climbed back to the porch.

Jake dropped into the wicker rocker when I reached the steps. "You okay?"

"Sure," I said.

"The wedding video has something we can use."

"What?"

"It's nothing earthshaking, but I'd like the judge to see her talking, to see her as a real live woman with dreams and hopes." He paused. "When I married my wife, my mother-in-law staged a big production, doves, a horse-drawn carriage, about a thousand people."

"I remember," I said. Jake and Yvette married straight out of college—before he even went to law school.

"Your wedding was very simple," he said, "but it had something, I don't know, sincere. It was the real deal, you and her."

"Yeah. We love each other. I've had other relationships. Good ones even, but when Elle and I were apart, during the years our relationship was platonic, she was always the one. I know that sounds sappy."

Jake didn't say anything for a minute. "It doesn't. Look at Vette and me. We've been married for fifteen years now. We have a daughter. It's the best part of life."

"You two were young," I said, suppressing my envy of his healthy family.

He smiled. "Obscenely young. And not prepared, but once Janey was born, we were determined to make it work. And"—he knocked the arm of the rocking chair—"so far so good."

"How old is Janey now?"

"Almost thirteen." He pulled a picture of his daughter from his wallet and passed it to me.

The girl stood on a balance beam with the pointed toe and arched back of a gymnast.

"Lucky for her she looks more like Yvette," I said.

Jake bellowed a hearty chuckle. "Yeah. Very lucky. She's a good kid," he said as I passed the photo back to him. "And hopefully yours will look like Elle."

Jake's words kicked me back to the reality of the moment. "Yeah, like Elle," I said. Or like me. It didn't matter a bit as long as the baby was healthy. How many times do people say those words with no real grasp of how very precarious life is? But I hoped that someday I'd be the proud father showing off our kid's picture.

Jake must have realized the implication of his words because he didn't say anything else for a while, and I returned to reading Elle's journal, getting lost in her voice again, until finally he asked, "How many more of those diaries do you have?"

I shrugged. "She was prolific, chronicled everything from her time at NASA to the day she got a bad perm. I'm skimming most parts."

"Did you ever think she kept track of everything because she was planning to write a memoir? *The Adventures of an Astronaut Heroine?*"

"You don't get it. She wrote because she was private. These were her innermost thoughts. These are things she chose *not* to share. I knew most of this, but not every little nuance. Her mind could orbit around a situation and . . . I'm skimming most parts."

"Let me skim with you."

"You can see this one." I passed him the one passage about how delivering Dylan would have helped her forgive herself. "Can you use it? I'll make a copy of the page."

He scanned it. "Yeah. This is good. I need more like this. Let's refine your search. Home in on the times when life threw her curveballs—her mother's death, her previous pregnancies."

"I did. She didn't write then. I organized them, chronologically. Nothing for months after her mother died. Nothing from after Dylan's death either." I rubbed my eyes with my palms.

"Her first pregnancy?"

"Only the beginning of it. She was still writing letters back then."

"Well, that's when she would have decided on whether or not to abort."

"You don't want to see those letters," I said.

"Why? She considered having an abortion?" he asked, looking horror-stricken.

I swatted a mosquito. "Yeah. And it's weird because by the time she told me she thought she was pregnant, she had dismissed the idea, or at least she acted as if it was out of the question. In the last letter she wrote about it, she was leaning toward terminating."

"Any idea what changed her mind?"

"None."

"Too bad. That's the entry we'd need." He smacked his forearm. "I'm going inside. These mosquitoes are wicked. You got any gin?"

"No," I said, standing to follow him. "Neither of us drinks much." *Gin.* Gin made me think of Prohibition, and Prohibition made me think of Elle. Her great-grandfather ran whiskey during Prohibition all around Casco Bay. Elle said that was why there was a trapdoor in the attic. It was where he stashed his supply. The compartment was just one of many secret spaces we had stumbled upon. Elle discovered another just last spring in the butler's pantry. Maybe she kept the missing letters in some other hidden closet I didn't know about. *Damn.*

"Listen, Jake, I'm going to crash. It's after midnight."

He glanced at his watch. "Yeah. I'll see myself out. I want to meet you for breakfast before the hearing."

As soon as he was gone, I bolted up the attic steps. Where were the other stash zones? Not necessarily in the attic, but it seemed the logical place to start.

I tugged up floorboards. I moved the trunks and the dollhouse. Nothing—save the already discovered attic and pantry compartments. On impulse, I pulled out Alice's diaries and quickly bundled them up in a bag.

Where else would a bootlegger keep his bounty? Under the stairs? No. And by the end of the night, after ripping apart the attic, the basement, and the barn, I concluded that, if Elle hid her letters somewhere, she meant them to stay hidden. I slunk back inside, defeated.

At the top of the stairs, I stopped in front of Dylan's room, a room he never entered, a room I didn't think either Elle or I addressed in the time since. We simply closed the door. At least I did. Now I switched on the light. The crib was still situated along the inside wall. I could hear Elle say, "This old house is drafty enough. We don't want him near a window."

The morning light poured through the transom. Another night without sleep. Another futile night. The telephone rang and my adrenaline-driven heart leaped into a race with fear. No one called that early in the morning unless there was trouble. The caller ID said Longfellow Memorial, the hospital. "Dr. Beaulieu, this is Evie, your wife's nurse. You asked me to call if there were any changes."

"And?"

"We've had to increase her oxygen. Her blood gases deteriorated overnight. They're shooting X-rays right now."

"Jesus," I said, with sharp panic rising in my gut. "Make sure they shield the baby."

✦ 37 ✦

Day 22

I lost my bearings and stumbled at Elle's bedside.

Her attending physician, Clint Everest, eyed me. By way of explanation for my clumsiness, I said, "I haven't slept more than an hour or two in days. I want to see her X-ray."

Hank interrupted. "You went home. Why didn't you sleep?"

"We can talk about that later. You should have called."

"Once I understood there was a problem," Hank said, "I asked the nurse to phone you. I figured you'd have questions, and she could answer them better than me."

"Okay." I turned to Clint.

He shoved Elle's film up on the light box. "It's a lower-left-lobe infiltrate. See? Pneumonia. We started antibiotics."

"And the baby?"

He set Elle's lab work in front of me. "I called your wife's perinatologist. She's coming over to do an ultrasound after she delivers a set of triplets who don't want to wait. You're really pale, Matt. Go catch a couple of z's in the on-call room. I'll come get you if anything happens."

I kissed Elle's cheek, put my palm on her belly, and said a silent prayer. *Please, God.* I'd found myself doing that, heathen that I was. Smoke and mirrors. Self-delusion. Anything. *God, please.*

"Go. Sleep. I'll stay awhile longer," Hank said.

I woke two hours later when Hank tapped on the door. "Dr. Clarke asked me to get you. She's doing the ultrasound."

I didn't remember passing through the ICU to arrive at Elle's room, but my gut said the baby would have no heartbeat. Elle and I had done that dance before, and I was afraid this would be our last waltz.

Through the glass wall, I could see Blythe's white hair complete with the pink ribbonlike headband peeking over the ultrasound machine. Her conciliatory smile prepared me for the next words, but she didn't deliver the expected line. Instead she beckoned me over.

Keisha was standing close by. Her hand was pressed hard up against her mouth as she peered at the ultrasound's monitor. She was supposed to sit with Elle while I went to court today and she must have arrived while I was sleeping.

In the flash of faces I tried to ascertain the verdict. "Do you want to see him?" Blythe smiled at me.

Keisha took my arm and pulled me toward the machine. "Come see him," she said.

"See him? *Him?*" I asked.

"Well, it's too early to tell gender," Blythe said. "But he or *she* is awake, and evidently, he or *she* wants to be an acrobat. He's doing somersaults."

"That's my grandchild?" Hank pushed forward.

Blythe nodded.

Through the static, my child was indeed spinning around as weightless as his mother had once been when she orbited the earth. "He's alive," I whispered. It was as if Elle had taken my hand and placed it on her belly to feel the baby kick. I looked over at Elle's face, somehow expecting recognition. It wasn't there. And my sense of responsibility shifted to the baby. Our baby.

Hank squeezed my shoulder.

"It could as easily be a girl." Blythe popped a disk in the machine and hit record. "Seeing the sonogram might help the judge decide. Or to convince Linney."

"I love you," I said aloud. I meant the baby. I meant Elle. I would always love her. I loved Blythe, too, because she offered hope.

"You think I'm right?" I asked.

"It's not my place to say. You know that, but given Elle's reaction the night you lost the last baby, I'm pretty sure she would insist you try to save the baby." Blythe turned off the machine. "Her heart is beating, but Elle's already—brain-dead. Sorry, I don't mean to be brutal."

"It's all right," I said. Fate or God had already determined that Elle would not survive. The baby had to live. *God. Please.*

"Keeping Elle's body alive over the next months, few days even, is iffy, you know, this pneumonia—" Blythe pulled her pager from her hip and looked at it. "I'm sorry but this is a stat page. I have to go." She left the ultrasound machine in its place and darted out of the room.

Hank dropped into the chair, silent and pale. Keisha quietly retreated to the window side of Elle's bed and whispered something about being a mother into Elle's ear.

I checked the ventilator. Since I'd left Elle to take a nap, her oxygen requirement had doubled. Keeping her alive might take a miracle. Although I'd stopped believing in those the night of Dylan's stillbirth, I was suddenly willing to pray one more time. I didn't even care if it was smoke and mirrors—or electronic altar candles.

✦ 38 ✦

Eighteen Months to Six Months
Before Elle's Accident

Many women miscarry. Usually, though, once a heartbeat is evident, the pregnancy will make it. Elle's hadn't. We had heard all three babies' heartbeats and lost each one. Elle was thoroughly bereft. I needed to understand what was going wrong. Blythe discovered Elle had an autoimmune disorder called antiphospholipid syndrome, which caused abnormal blood clotting.

Elle said, "I don't understand why NASA didn't pick this up. I mean, they tested me for everything." She dropped her hands to her lap and laced them together, a gesture she used to control her trembling when she was afraid.

"It may be new or even pregnancy induced," Blythe Clarke said. "It is, however, very easy to treat with a baby aspirin once a day. I'm going to have you see someone who specializes in autoimmune disorders. He may want to put you on something more aggressive, but make sure you tell him you're trying to conceive. As soon as you get pregnant again, we'll put you on heparin."

"That's a blood thinner, Peep. And unfortunately it's a shot that you have to take every day," I said, knowing how much she hated needles.

Elle cringed. After drawing a deep breath, she said, "All right. Shots."

The OB bit her lip. "Actually, the heparin is twice a day."

"I was trying to break the news to Elle gently," I said.

Elle's eyes widened. "Twice? A day? Damn. Okay. I want a baby. We—" She met my eyes. "We want our baby to live, so I'll do anything, anything for that. Just—how big are these needles?"

I gestured about a foot.

She reached across the arm of her chair and grabbed my hand then squeezed her eyes shut. "Okay, no problem, but you are joking, right, Matt?"

"They're little. I promise," I said, almost smiling.

We lost a baby, but a little heparin would ensure a new baby would receive the blood supply it needed. We found our answer, or I thought we had.

Elle started taking a baby aspirin every day, and the next time we found out she was pregnant, her doctor put her on a heparin regimen.

"It's really not so bad," she said, although she flinched as she injected her thigh.

I assessed all the bruising she'd developed. Not only on the injection sites, but here and there, on her elbows, on her hip. "We need to make sure your blood-clotting times aren't getting too far out of whack," I said.

"I love it when you use medical terminology. 'Out of whack,' ha!"

"Peep, you need another test to make certain we aren't thinning your blood too much."

"Okay, that'll mean more needles, right?" But before I could answer, she added, "No big deal."

I didn't want her to hemorrhage, so I did what any controlling spouse with a medical degree would do: I watched her and her lab results, took her to the best perinatologist and best rheumatologist in the area. I made sure she didn't do one single dangerous thing, worrying that while on the blood thinner she could bleed from the most minor injury. Hell, I had Mike, my brother the mechanic, check the brakes on her car every frigging week.

"All good," he said, rolling out from the undercarriage. "You've got to relax, Matt. You're going to have a fucking heart attack before you're forty like Dad."

"No. I'm good. I watch my diet. I run."

"You stress."

I reached out my hand to him and pulled him up. "I'm healthy as a horse."

"The oldest in the family is supposed to be the control freak. You're the baby. You're supposed to be the comedian. What happened to you?"

I slapped him on the back and joined him for a beer in the kitchen.

Snow was falling lightly when I arrived home. Elle had just finished adding a log to the fire, which was snapping and hissing. She poked it and closed the woodstove's door. "Come here and feel this." She beckoned, reaching out with her hand. There was another black bruise.

"Peep, Jesus, what happened?"

"Nothing, I just bumped it. It doesn't even hurt. Forget about that. Here, feel the baby," she said, grabbing my hand. "He's jumping all over the place."

I placed my palm on her belly. "In nine days, we'll get a face-to-face, kiddo. Your mother wants to call you Vladimir because of all the blood she's had sucked out of her on your account."

"Shush, don't tell him that. Dylan. We want to call you Dylan after the poet from Wales. Your daddy saw his house and lived in Swansea for a while."

"Sit down." I tried to lead her to the couch, but she stopped in the middle of the room, clenching my hand so tightly the bruise on her hand blanched. "What is it?"

Elle answered, "My back. It's killing me today. Since I woke up this morning. I must have slept badly."

"But you stopped all of a sudden. Is the pain coming and going?" I thought of preterm labor, but I held back. Those were the days when everyone was telling me to relax and to stop worrying. Even I knew I was on the brink of a neurosis.

"No, not really. It's more like when I move certain ways. It's muscular. I'm so fat; everything's out of alignment."

"You're not fat. You're in your eight month." I smiled at her. I didn't enjoy seeing her in pain, but I was so grateful we'd come so far this time. "Come over here. I'll rub your back. Lie down."

We walked to the seat by the bay window. She loved to read there on the wide bench, and I thought she would enjoy watching the snow fall. I had her lie on her side, and I massaged her lower spine for a long time, settling against the wall beside her. After a while Elle's breathing became regular; she'd fallen asleep.

I rose and covered her with an afghan.

The wind had picked up and the petal-soft flakes had morphed into pellets that battered the windows. I stoked the woodstove while I considered how much snow had already fallen. A few inches, maybe more.

I tromped out to the barn and tugged the snowblower outside, but it wouldn't start. Instead of having my brother fix all my mechanical problems, I needed to learn how these things worked.

I played with the spark plugs. And fiddled with the primer. I checked the gas, which was full. Nothing worked. It was dead. Time of death, I looked at my watch: 10:43. In a halfhearted effort, I cleaned up the stairs and threw rock salt on the walk. My father had his first heart attack on a night like this with wet snow. That's why I'd bought the blower; but it looked like I'd have to clear the driveway the old-fashioned way this time in the morning.

I went inside to wake Elle for her shot, but she wasn't there. I assumed she woke up and went upstairs to bed.

"Matt!" she called out through what sounded like gritted teeth.

I rounded the corner and found her lying on the kitchen floor, wrapped in the granny-square afghan. Doubled over, she was pale as our white cupboards.

I knelt beside her. "Did you fall?"

"My water broke—just a minute ago," she said, gasping.

I pulled back the cover. Dressed only in a nightgown, and her legs were saturated with amniotic fluid and blood.

The baby was premature, and he might be in trouble if he was born so soon, but that wasn't my only concern. Elle was supposed to stop taking the blood thinner before a planned delivery. If she delivered tonight, she could hemorrhage to death.

I dialed 911. "Breathe, Peep. It will be fine." But it wasn't.

Miracles don't always happen.

✦ 39 ✦

After Elle's Accident
Day 22

Elle needed a miracle if she was going to survive this pneumonia. Jake said he'd make an excuse to the judge for my absence in court, downplaying Elle's current medical crisis. However, today was the day my partner, Phil, would be testifying, and he'd probably tell the judge Elle was dying. Her body was dying. She was already gone.

But inside her, the baby was still doing somersaults. I was holding on to that glimmer of life, replaying it over and over in my head while the nurse was doing Elle's trach care.

I heard a sputter and looked up. Elle was coughing. I jumped up. The nurse eyed me. "What's wrong?"

"She can't cough. She lost that reflex," I said.

The nurse adjusted Elle's oxygen upward. "The cerebral edema is down. She has some spontaneous respirations, too," she said. "Not enough to sustain her, but some. Maybe once we get the pneumonia under control, we'll be able to wean her off the vent."

Jesus. I reached into my pocket. "You have a penlight?" I asked the nurse.

"Sure." She pulled one from her scrubs and passed it to me.

I flicked the light across Elle's eyes. Nothing. Her pupils remained fixed and dilated. I checked her corneal reflexes and her deep tendon reflexes. She did not respond to painful stimuli. *Jesus.* With just the smallest hint of hope, a cough, I flew into denial again. I needed to talk to Phil. I needed to talk to Blythe about the safety of doing an MRI on a pregnant woman. But cognitively I knew Elle's brain damage was irreparable—and global.

Was she in there somewhere? I wanted her to live long enough for the baby to be born. Hell, I wanted her to wake up, but that wouldn't happen. If she did, she'd be profoundly disabled. She wouldn't want to live—for years—in a vegetative state—not after the baby was born.

The baby inside her was flipping around—our baby.

I could still see Elle in her family's driveway, telling me she would want to die if she were ever in her mother's condition.

"I'm going to try to catch a little sleep in the on-call room." I grabbed my duffel bag and walked out of Elle's room, grasping the implications of what I was doing to her. But—the baby.

The on-call room was smaller than a freshman dorm. A set of bunk beds and one small desk outfitted with a computer for charting. I fell back on the bed and stared at the springs of the mattress above me. Instead of hearing my heart pound *lub dub, lub dub*, it was pounding *calm down, calm down.* As I lay awake in a frantic haze, I reached into the duffel bag for Elle's journals and somehow pulled out one of Alice's diaries instead. For a moment I flipped through it, fanning the pages. The writing almost looked like Elle's, but Elle wrote letters and in composition books. I snapped the book shut and dropped it on the top of the pile. On the back cover, enclosed in a heart, Elle had scribbled the words:

Elle loves Matt

I whipped the book back up. The first date inside was December 25, 1988.

Dear Matt,

Mom did her Christmas shopping before she got so sick she couldn't. Can you believe it? She knew I'd been writing these letters as a sort of journal, and so she bought a hokey-pink version, as though I'm a little girl. I'm not. I don't know if I've ever been like that. I'm certainly not now.

Daddy hit me last night. It was an accident. He didn't even see me there. When you saw the bruise, you went after him. Fortunately, your dad pulled you back. Then in the scuffle, Dennis got a little better look at my expanding waistline and figured things out. It's Christmas, but I'm not Mary, and you're not Joseph. And now your dad knows I'm pregnant.

Merry Christmas. It's more like a Christ-mess.

Peep

January 20
Celina

January 21
  Celina

January 22
  Celina

Every day for weeks after the miscarriage, that's all Elle wrote, Celina's name. You could see where she'd left the pen point pressed into the paper at the end of the *a*, like she'd paused and considered writing more. The name looked so lonely there, and it occurred to me, I'd never seen the name written down. It occurred to me that it could have been spelled with an S instead of a C. It occurred to me that I, too, had always pictured it with the letter C.

Then Elle began to talk about her mother again. I flipped the page.

February 16, 1989

Dear Matt,

  I was talking to Linney and said I had a head-ache. She told me to get some Tylenol from the medicine cabinet. That's not the only thing in there. I found the leftover Percocet—from when you broke your leg. And I thought, I could give these to my mom. Only Linney walked in and yanked them out of my hand.

  I begged her. I begged her. She won't help. She said they were only for the person they were pre-scribed for.

February 17, 1989

Dear Matt,

   I can't stand it anymore. Too much has gone wrong. They're going to put Christopher and me in foster care. We'll probably get split up. Linney said she'd try to get custody of us, and she got a temporary order tonight. She swore, at the very least, she'd manage to get Christopher. Me? Well, that's more tricky because of you. I guess she's right about that. I'm scared. And I want to be with you, too. Really with you. But we can't. What if I got pregnant again? I wanted to keep Celina. I loved her.

   And there's Mommy. I don't want to leave her to go to a foster home. I should be here. No one else fights for her.

   I begged Linney to help my mom.

Peep

February 18, 1989

   Mom is dead.

   I keep saying the words out loud, but they don't make sense.

   She's dead.

   Finally. After months, my mom is dead.

   I didn't want her to die, and I don't want her to

be dead. But it's better, right? She isn't suffering anymore. God, how she suffered.

I thought we should help her—ease her pain. I begged the nurses. I begged Daddy. I begged everyone to give her more pain medicine. No one would do it.

Last night, after we came back from the social workers, Linney brought me back to my house. She doesn't want me to sleep at her house because she thinks you and I will have sex again. Maybe we would. I want you to hold me right now. I need you. But Linney brought me home. And Mom was moaning. It's worse at night. Linney could see that. The nurse had some problem with her husband and Linney said she'd stay until the nurse could take care of it. Linney gave Mom more pain medicine. Extra. Your medicine, Matt. She showed me how to crush the pills if I needed to give my mom another one later. And maybe it's sick, but I was grateful that you had broken your leg last summer. That's terrible, right?

But then the nurse came back. And Linney left. I stayed with Mommy all night. She got quiet, and it was like for the first time in forever she seemed comfortable. I drifted off to sleep with my head resting on Mommy's pillow. When I woke up, she'd stopped breathing. She just stopped breathing. It was my fault. Mine.

I don't know anymore if it was the right thing. She's not suffering. But she's dead. And I'm never going to see her ever again. I miss her. So much.

I need her. Christopher needs her. And Daddy. Oh God. Did the extra medicine kill my mom? Did I kill her?

Peep

I stared at the page. Holy shit. There were no more entries in the diary—only blank, yellowed pages.

I had to think this through, absorb it. Elle didn't kill her mother. Alice had been dying for months, long agonizing months. If giving an extra dose of pain meds hastened Alice's death, that probably made Elle more saint than murderer. Hell, if I'd remembered pills were left over from my broken leg, I would have dosed Alice myself. What bothered me was that my mother did it and left the house, left Elle alone, left Elle to blame herself.

I took the diary and returned to Elle's hospital room.

The nurse was suctioning Elle's trach. "She's doing okay. More secretions, but she's okay."

Elle silently coughed again.

"I'm going to write for an EEG." I went to the desk, stared at Elle's chart, and scribbled down the order. I stared into her room, and after some minutes of numbness I realized I still had the diary in my left hand.

In the morning I could lock it away in my safe-deposit box. I could tell my mother about it, and convince her I was desperate enough to stoop to blackmail. *God.* I stood up and wandered out to the parking garage. Had my mother participated in a mercy killing?

It was an act of mercy.

I found my car, popped open the trunk, and saw the dried-out sedum and hardy mums. I'd bought them at a nursery Elle liked in Yarmouth the day before the accident. I'd come home, planning to surprise her. She met me at the car with the mad idea of seduction and baby making, not knowing she was already pregnant.

We started arguing instead. She wanted a baby, and I was afraid of losing her. When Phil called me to come in and assist him with an emergency, I bolted. The last night we would ever share, and I left. No. *I bolted.* I didn't get home until after midnight, and then we watched the Perseids, putting the rest aside. I forgot about the flowers in the trunk of my car. Now the plants were deader than dust—like all my good intentions.

I dropped the diary into the trunk, opened the driver's door, and sat in the car. I was planning to blackmail my own mother. I was trying to keep Elle alive when this was the one thing—the only thing—that truly terrified her. Who the hell was I becoming? A father, I hoped.

After a while I returned to Elle's side. The nurse was right. Two, maybe three times a minute, Elle took spontaneous breaths. It wasn't enough to sustain her.

I repeated Elle's neuro exam. Nothing else had changed. No miracle was coming.

Or maybe there was a miracle—waiting and doing somersaults.

I settled in again, watching the ventilator make Elle's chest rise and fall. She'd take a breath on her own. Then the ventilator. Again the ventilator. Still the ventilator. Then her.

Phil entered the room and sat down beside me.

"How was court?" I asked.

He shrugged. "I said she wasn't in pain, and she wanted children."

I looked up at him. "She's taking a few breaths."

"I heard," he said. "Her brain stem didn't herniate, but I told you what her cerebrum looked like. She'll never have any meaningful quality of life."

"You don't think she's feeling any pain," I said.

"No, Matt," he said. "No pain."

I closed my eyes, and we sat in silence for a few minutes. He went through the motions of doing another neuro exam on her, no differently than I had done not long before. As he checked her reflexes, he said, "In court, I didn't say any more than I had to about how she believed that the quality of life trumped the longevity by miles."

"Okay." I didn't have enough energy left to get into the debate of whether or not I was wrong again. It might not be ethical to sacrifice one life for another, but morality be damned. My heart was breaking, truly breaking. The thickness and heaviness in my chest was something that could only be heartbreak. I said, "If you think I'm indifferent to what this has done to Elle, to her dignity, you're wrong."

"No. I don't think that. I thought I should tell you what happened there. Listen, I had to come back to the hospital anyway. I have to take the Nguyen kid back to the OR. He's developing hydrocephalus from the accident."

"Shit."

"I know, but I can fix that. I wish I could fix Elle."

✦ 40 ✦

Day 24

Two days later, with Clint leaning against the sink, I digested the lab report. Elle was going into kidney failure. There were two possible causes: the APS could have thrown a blood clot to one of her renal arteries or the antibiotic treating her pneumonia had seriously damaged her kidneys.

Elle was damned either way.

"It's probably the antibiotic," he said. "I changed it. We can hold off on dialysis for a while."

The word *dialysis* gave me that kicked-in-the-balls feeling. Even if her body were healthy, the odds against saving the baby were staggering.

"The good news is the antibiotic is doing its job. The pneumonia is resolving," he said.

Medical treatment had substituted one form of execution for another. I couldn't trust my voice to utter a single syllable.

"I'll keep you posted," he said as he left.

Despite my efforts to stay awake, I found my head in an odd

upright kink against the wall or the window more often than not. In my REM sleep, I dove into blackness, where I dreamed of stacks of cartons falling on an empty baby crib, Elle's body in a casket, an urn with her ashes, and holding a shotgun in my mouth.

I pulled into a parking slot along Back Bay next to my mother's car. Mom opened her door, slammed it shut, and climbed into the passenger seat of my Taurus.

"I was so happy to hear from you, honey," she said.

I called her just hours before and suggested we meet, but I still didn't know quite how to blackmail her.

"Are you going to tell me what's on your mind?"

I stared at my hands. "I needed to get out of the hospital," I said, thinking I didn't want to have witnesses overhear our discussion.

"I've taken a leave of absence," she said. "I was thinking I could come in and relieve you, so you could take more breaks."

My heartbeat throbbed in my ears. "I don't trust you near Elle."

"I'd never hurt her." Mom averted her gaze.

"You aren't coming near her. You got that?" I snapped.

"I have a responsibility to her." She hugged her purse to her chest. "This is killing me, fighting with you, trying to make you face such a hard truth. It doesn't get easier, being a parent."

"Why don't you give me a chance to find out for myself?"

"Oh, Matt. Under any other circumstance." She stared straight ahead and blinked. "You have to be realistic."

"Blythe says—"

"She's wrong. Blythe is wonderful, as good as they get, but she doesn't have a milligram of pessimism in her. And no matter what you think Elle would have wanted under these circumstances, she was just so damned terrified of ending up like Alice."

"It's not the same. Elle's not in pain."

"Maybe not, but she didn't want this. I love Elle as much as if she were mine. I do. Not more than I love you, but she's like my own. I doubt you remember this, but Alice spent a couple of weeks in the hospital when Elle was a baby."

"I know. You love her. You've always loved her. You took care of her when she was a baby. None of that's relevant. The fact is Elle is *my* wife. That's *my* child." I considered how I was about to commit blackmail against my own mother. This was a line I thought I'd never cross. "I have a diary Elle wrote. From the day Alice died."

Mom shifted, her head cocking to one side. "That must have been difficult to read."

"You killed Alice."

The blood drained from my mother's face.

"You used the Percocet they prescribed for me when I broke my leg the previous summer, and you spiked Alice's feeds with it. I'm not completely horrified, but let's face it, Mom; you killed her, and you left Elle alone to watch her mother die."

Mom shook her head. "You don't understand."

"I understand everything. If you don't withdraw your petition to remove Elle's life support, I'll go to the authorities with this."

"You wouldn't. I didn't kill Alice. I—"

"You put her out of her misery? Okay, I'll buy that. The police might not."

Mom stammered before she found words. "I didn't do it. But maybe I should have. No maybes. I should have, but all I did was crush one pill and add it to the feeding. One. I showed Elle how to do it. There were eight pills left. I told her she could slip one in every six hours as Alice needed them—if the nurse had gone to the bathroom or stepped out for a smoke."

"You're saying Elle overdosed Alice?"

"I don't know. It may just have been time. Elle said it was her fault that Alice died. I was always afraid to ask what happened to the last seven pills."

"I don't believe Elle would have done it. And it says in here that *you* gave her the Percocet. Not Elle."

Mom stared at her hands. "I don't know. During the night Alice stopped breathing. Maybe it was a coincidence. Maybe it was from the one pill. Maybe it was just time. God knows, it was long overdue."

I rubbed my temples, not wanting to believe that either Elle or my mother intentionally killed Alice. Their purpose was to make her comfortable. These days in hospice care, it's routine: we make the patient comfortable.

"You have to accept that Elle didn't want to live like her mother."

"No, she didn't. But Elle is *not* in pain. No pain. She isn't feeling anything, and even if she were, she would have done anything for her child. I would do anything for this child."

Mom shook her head. "It's so early. It's almost impossible that she could hold on long enough to give birth to a living child. Not with her history of miscarriages. Even when she was pregnant with Dylan, she went early. She gave me her medical-decision-making powers, and then she gave them to Adam. She never asked you, did she?"

Now it was my turn to shake my head.

Mom covered my hand with hers. "I know what I said in court, but she must have known deep down, you'd never be able to pull the plug. Matthew, if you love her, and I know you love her, you have to let her go."

Maybe my mother was right in one regard. I had never let go of Elle.

✦ 41 ✦

Five Years Before Elle's Accident

When Mom set the loaf of still-warm corn bread in front of me, driving through nine hours of traffic became worth it. She plopped down at the head of the table. "How's Carol? I was surprised you were coming home without her."

"She's working this weekend." Which meant Carol was pulling an on-call stint for three straight days. I scarfed down a buttered slice of heaven. With my mouth still half full, I mumbled, "It's hard getting up here together with our schedules."

Mom's lips tightened, and I expected another snarky remark about Carol, the city girl, as Mom called her. Instead Mom changed the subject. "Elle was home from Houston, but she's gone."

My head snapped up. "I haven't seen her in ages." Or talked to her since I told her Carol and I were engaged—although I'd tried. There'd been a few e-mails, a few voice mails. "Elle's been a little distant lately, busy preparing for the Hubble mission."

My mother grimaced as she stirred her cocoa. "I'm so proud of her, but after the *Columbia* disaster the idea of her climbing into that shuttle terrifies me." Mom forced a smile onto her face. "She was driving to Acadia tonight. It's too bad you missed her."

I shrugged as if it didn't matter while I calculated the odds that I could find Elle if I drove the three hours up to the national park. The last time I was up there, cell-phone coverage was virtually nonexistent, so I concluded it unlikely.

"She's homesick," Mom said. "She's planning to move back here in the next few years."

"Really?" Elle hadn't told me that, although I suspected a move home was more about how Mom interpreted Elle's words. Mom probably said, "Don't you want to move home, Elle?" To which Elle probably replied, "Of course I do."

We all wanted things we couldn't have.

"Unfortunately," Mom said, "Adam loves NASA."

Right. Adam. Pain in the ass as usual. "If I could talk Carol into moving to Maine, I would."

Mom seemed to roll her words around on her tongue for a moment before she actually spoke. "It'd be nice to have you two close enough for Sunday dinners." Carol and my mother in the same town, sharing recipes. Now there was an image.

A change of topic was in order. "Do you want to know something funny? There's this guy, Phil Grey. He's finishing his neurosurgery fellowship this month. He's from Brooklyn. You know, he has the swagger, the New Yorker attitude. Yankee fan." I shook my head, that I, an avid Sox fan, would befriend a Yankee fan. "Brilliant doctor, though, fantastic surgeon."

"You've mentioned him."

"He heard me talking about Maine and how much I love it, so he and his wife decided to come up here on vacation last year. Three hours in, they decided this was where they should settle. A neurosurgical group offered him a position—Welsh and Sanders.

Phil's moving to Maine, and I'm spending the rest of my life in the Big Apple. Ironic, huh?"

"So he's the one taking over for Sanders?"

"No. I think he's replacing Welsh. Welsh is retiring. Sanders is only fiftyish; I talked to him before I began my neurosurgical residency."

"Yeah, but Sanders has cancer. It's bad. I heard through the grapevine his prognosis is grim. Your friend may need another partner if Welsh wants to retire, too. You should make nice with Phil. Maybe the two of you could start your own practice."

I scratched my head. It was a shame about Sanders. He'd let me follow him around for a couple of days when I was still in med school. Nice guy.

I indulged myself in a brief fantasy where I convinced Carol to live in Portland, but it was indeed a fantasy. There was no way. She'd already bought a beautiful apartment on the Upper East Side. Hell, she had a preschool picked out for our future kids.

The farmhouse, an unpolished and aging Victorian with peeling clapboard, reflected the morning sun, and the unyielding steadiness of the place comforted me. The garden appeared recently tended. Whenever Elle came home, she took care of it as her first order of business. If she didn't make it up from Texas, it sometimes filled with crabgrass and dandelions. Mom weeded here and there. Sometimes I even spent an hour or two yanking up roots. But it was Elle's place, Celina's place.

Most of the plants were perennials. This time home, Elle must have spent hours augmenting them with annuals. New Guinea impatiens in hot pink and petunias in white tumbled over the edges. The garden looked like a fat wad of cotton candy.

A creaking door opened across the field. "May I help you?" Elle called, sounding tentative.

I spun toward her and waved, the pinwheel in my hand catching the summer breeze.

Wrapped in a long moss-green cardigan that matched the color of her eyes, Elle paused for a moment. Then the surprise in her voice rose over the anxiety I'd heard moments before. "Matt? Matt, what are you doing here?" Elle crossed the field, her step springing into a gallop, until we were hugging, not as lovers but as the friends we had become over time.

"Mom said you'd gone to Bar Harbor," I said.

"I was planning to, but I, well, please don't tell her, I exaggerated how soon I was driving there. I wanted to spend last night, watching the stars—alone."

Elle's cheeks and nose wore a barely sunburned glow. She shaded her eyes from the sun, which had broken through the trees to hit her face. "I didn't know you were coming home."

"I wasn't. But I had this urge to see the ocean. Carol suggested Long Island. I wanted Maine."

"Is she here?" Elle's gaze shot up to the driveway and my car. "I'd love to meet her."

"She's on call this weekend. I have to go back tomorrow."

"Oh, too bad." She tugged on my sleeve. "Come up to the house. I'll make you a cup of coffee."

I only held Celina for a few minutes, yet I'd carried her with me every day since. Pausing, I scanned for the rock-circled patch of moss and pushed the pinwheel into Celina's marker. Elle watched with silent intensity. I shrugged, and neither of us said more about my gift.

I'd never quite gotten over what Elle said about naming Celina, that her name would be the only thing we would ever give her. The day we buried her I felt compelled to leave some kind of token and the only thing I had in my pocket was a package of Bazooka bubble gum. I slipped it underneath the urn. Stupid, I know, juvenile even. I was a kid. Both Elle and I were. But ever since, I left a trinket here, a marble there, a wind chime, a ribbon, something. Almost fifteen years had passed and the only real thing we ever gave her was the name and even that was only etched in our memories.

Elle didn't say a word but scooted down and blew the wind toy, making the wheel spin around, then she placed her palm down on the pocket of moss for a moment.

"The garden looks *very* pink," I said, mustering a grin.

She cocked her head to the side. "Something wrong with a pink garden?"

"Suppose not."

Elle shook her head. "You won't believe this. Christopher and his girlfriend came out here. He thought he was doing me a favor, dug up everything except the lilac bush and moved the garden over by the house. He said it would make the lawn easier to mow. I had to replant everything."

"Shit. Did he find her urn?" I asked.

"No. The moss was undisturbed. Thank God. It would be too difficult to explain after all this time."

In the bright sunshine, I could read her body language. Neither embarrassment nor shame had kept her from telling her family. She still felt like it was her fault Celina died, and I wanted to tell her again that she shouldn't blame herself. I didn't. "Did you ever tell Adam about Celina?"

"No. He wouldn't understand. She didn't belong to him." Elle lowered her eyes. "But enough of that. Tell me your plans for today."

After a beat to regroup, we went inside. Not much had changed inside the kitchen. It still had one of those rounded-off Frigidaires from the fifties, as indestructible as the generation who made them.

"You look great," I said.

She tousled her hair and pulled it away from her face. "If I knew I was going to see anyone, I'd have tried to make myself a bit more presentable."

"You look great," I repeated.

She leaned against the old sideboard, appraising me. "You, too." Elle darted over to the blinking answering machine, picked up the receiver, and listened to the message.

"Something wrong?" I asked.

"I keep missing Adam. We haven't talked for a couple of days."

"I talked to him Thursday night."

"You did?"

"I was calling to talk to you."

"Did he sound okay?"

"A little distracted, but that's nothing new. He didn't even say you were in Maine. What's up?"

She shrugged. "The opportunity to take a few days off came up suddenly. I left him a note saying I was going home because it was now or never before the mission chance. Anyway, I think he might be angry, but it's hard to tell. Lately, he's been so tied up with the safety issues on the orbiter that we barely see each other. We live together, but we only bump into each other at night."

That could have a couple of different meanings. As much as it bothered me to think of her with him, they did live together. Still, I didn't say anything. I considered her my best friend. I often told her things I didn't tell Carol, like how I had doubts about my neurosurgery residency, how I often wished I'd stuck with general surgery, how much I missed home. But our love relationships were forbidden topics.

We took the coffee out to the gazebo and sat on the wicker rockers, looking down at the high-tidal river. We talked about her father, her brother, about New York and Houston. We laughed the way we used to, and I felt more comfortable with her than I had with anyone in a long time. There was never pretense, only acceptance.

"You're no longer the child prodigy. Now you're just a smart-ass," I said, grinning at her. "Are you feeling any trepidation over turning thirty next month?"

She chuckled. "No, just the opposite. I finally feel—normal—like I fit in."

My stomach growled loud enough for Elle to hear.

"Hungry?" she asked.

"Lunchtime."

We piled into my car, initially heading somewhere for lobster rolls. When I cranked the engine, it squealed.

"You need to tighten your belts," she said.

I glanced at my waistband.

"Under the hood. The car hood," she said. "How could you grow up with Mike and never learn the most basic things about engines?"

She was right to some degree. My brother loved cars as much as I avoided them. "I hung out with you," I said as we pulled onto the road.

"Oh no, you can't get away with that. I watched Mike every time he was fixing something. I know basic auto mechanics."

"You know quantum mechanics."

"They're not quite the same thing." She grinned.

"Yes, Einstein, I know." I was trying to draw attention away from the fact that the only thing I could do with a car was pump gas into its tank. "I fix brains."

"Yeah, yeah. Big brain surgeon. It helps to know how to fix a flat. I paid attention, and it's pretty useful now. When part of the Space Shuttle breaks loose, you sort of have to know what to do. Damned heat tiles."

"You knew some of the *Columbia* astronauts, didn't you?"

"Yeah." She stared out the passenger-side window.

"Are they training you how to fix the tiles if they come loose again?"

She turned away from the window to look at me. "They train us for every *contingency*. I think it's their favorite word. Don't worry. You're like an old woman sometimes. At least, if you die on a mission, you die fast."

"That's comforting." I refused to conceal my sarcasm.

"Listen, today I don't want to worry about what is going to happen up there. For the next ten months I can do that. Every day. How to do this maneuver, how to do that one."

"You never told me how the Vomit Comet ride went," I said, trying to break the tension.

She chuckled. "You'd lose your cookies."

"And you think this, why?"

"Remember the roller coaster at Funtown? You were greener than the Hulk when we got off."

"No." I denied it to salve my macho ego.

"Yes. Like a lizard."

"No." I denied it to save face.

"Like a lawn on the PGA tour."

"No." I denied it because she was on a roll.

"Want to go to Funtown right now, get on a coaster, and redeem yourself?"

No, but we did. We took Route 1 to Saco. Funtown was like a microversion of Great Adventure, but it had a roller coaster, an old wooden one for the purist.

Forty minutes and the cost of admission later, Elle was rubbing her hands together like the villain in a silent movie. "Choose wisely, my victim. It may be your last ride."

I pointed to Excalibur, the wooden roller coaster. I needed to, in Elle's words, redeem myself.

Elle practically danced backward, luring me onward with her finger coiled and her smile nearly as big as the dip in the rail. The *clickety-clack* of the cars going over the tracks could unnerve Rambo, but when we reached the line, she said, "You don't have to prove anything to me."

"Methinks thou art trying to get thyself off the hook by making it sound like this young page wants to chickenshit out."

"Ha!" She crossed her arms.

"It's all right," I said, rubbing her neck. "If you want to surrender and admit that roller coasters don't scare me, I won't make you go on," I said, hoisting up my bravado in the hope she'd leave my ego intact.

"Yeah, yeah. That will be the day."

After ten minutes in line we climbed into the first car on the tram. I started to sweat, not because I was nervous, but because I felt strangely cold, as if my body was having a paradoxical reaction to the blazing sun.

"Matt, seriously, we don't have to do this," Elle said, her eyes glimmering. "You look um, green."

"Don't be ridiculous."

The chain clicked and began to pull us along the upward slope. I was going to die for my pride. Elle was sitting beside me, and she took my hand. We reached the top, and Elle cawed, "Woo-hoo!"

"Yeah!" I yelped back. Surely, she didn't notice my voice cracking like an adolescent boy. If I'd had the brains to go on a steel roller coaster, it might not have been so bad, but as we cornered and swung up and down along the creaking structure—I swear I could see wood rot on every railing—it took everything I had to hold the guttural death cry inside my chest.

As we pulled to a stop and the attendant opened our car's door, Elle let go of my hand. She stood with grace and smiled over her shoulder. "I offer my sincere apologies. You're fine, not green at all."

"Then how come my legs won't support me?"

She smiled brightly. "Why, Dr. Beaulieu, you must have suffered a spinal-cord injury. I just happen to know a brilliant young neurosurgeon. Would you like his number?"

"Funny," I said, rising on my wobbly legs that felt like disconnected stilts.

We were walking the length of Pine Point, a wide beach with soft, powder-white sand and icy water with our pant cuffs rolled high, our feet bare, testing the flat hem of the waves. We laughed, we bantered, and we commiserated about how complicated our professional lives made our personal ones.

About a mile down the beach, she dropped on the sand and sat cross-legged. "I haven't been here in years, not since that day."

"Which day?"

Sadness slipped over her face. "When we found out I was pregnant."

I sat beside her, scanning the beach and remembering.

She scooped up a handful of sand and let it run through her fingers like an hourglass while she studied me. "I'm so homesick."

"Mom said that, but I thought it was wishful thinking on her part."

"No. Homesick. Knowing Gramps's house is still up here waiting for me is pretty seductive when it's a hundred and ten degrees with a hundred percent humidity in Houston." She grabbed more sand and let it fall through her lightly clenched fist. "Can I change the subject and be morbid for a minute?"

"Okay."

"I made a will, in case something goes wrong on the mission," she said.

"You are *not* going to die."

"It's unlikely, but the risks are high, and everyone accepts them as part of the bargain. I won't belabor this, but there was something I didn't want to put in the will—in case my dad reads it. He never knew about Celina. If something happens, would you see to it that her ashes are buried with whatever remains of mine are found?"

My mouth gaped, and while I regained my composure, she continued speaking. "The house would go to Christopher, and neither he nor my father would understand if they found the urn by accident."

I felt sick but muttered, "Jesus."

"You wouldn't have to tell Carol. You and your mom could take care of it quietly."

"Why my mother?"

"I named her as executrix."

"You didn't name Adam?"

"No." She paused for a moment. "No. I figured I'd need an executor who at least knew about the baby, and I'd rather not leave any posthumous surprises. This is a little neurotic, maudlin even, but I need to have her buried with me."

"Stop talking like you're going to die." I stood and marched down to the water, my mind replaying the video footage of *Challenger* blowing up, drifting, and falling into the sea.

A couple of minutes later she arrived at my side and took my hand. "Just promise me, you'd take care of her."

Elle was acting like this was a shared custody arrangement. In all these years we'd barely talked about Celina, and now this. "I will ask one thing in return," I said.

She nodded. "Anything."

"Don't die."

She looped her arm through mine. "If I *live* up to my end of the bargain, you won't have to live up to yours, and strangely, I can deal with that."

"Elle, I mean it. Don't go."

"I have to. I want to. I'm so happy I can barely stand it. And I fully intend to come back—alive. But if it goes wrong . . ." For the briefest moment Elle rested her forehead on my chest. "Celina was a real person to me; I don't want to leave her there in an unmarked grave. I asked your mom, but she dismissed me, like talking about Celina all these years later was an emotional indulgence. And maybe it is. But I need this one thing. Will you do it for me?"

I swallowed the acid in my throat. "Okay."

She exhaled. "Thank you. We don't have to be morbid anymore. I'm prepared now, and if you're prepared, the evil spirits don't dare land on you." She let go of my arm. "Now, I'll race you back to the car." She took off down the beach.

I watched for a second or two, waiting for my soul to catch up with hers. I was powerless to stop her, but I could try to follow her example. "Hey, no fair, Peep!"

We weren't supposed to kiss good night, but we did. There's something about first love. There's something about loving a woman that never goes away. There's something about night skies and shooting stars and the way Elle beamed every time she looked up at them.

Did it start as a peck on the cheek, innocently, inadvertently, softly? Perhaps. I don't know if she kissed me or if I kissed her, but it happened down by the riverbank in the light of stars from a million aeons past. Before I cognitively grasped what we were doing, need took over. I wanted to climb inside her skin. I wanted to steal her up to the widow's walk and make love to her like the first time.

I wanted to make the fifteen rotten lonely years in between then and now disappear like rain into the sand on a beach. I wanted to start where we belonged. Together.

Her voice was husky when she said my name. "Matt."

I was kissing her neck, pulling down the shoulder of her T-shirt, trying to get closer.

"Matt, wait." Just those few inches she stepped back were like a slap across my face, shoving me into the reality of a world where I was engaged to Carol, and Elle was living with Adam.

"Oh, shit," I said.

"Right. Oh, shit," she murmured. "What are we doing?"

We were loving each other the way we were supposed to. "Give me a minute so I can come up with a good answer, maybe one that can bulldoze away all the reasons we shouldn't be doing this," I said.

"Please come up with a very good answer; one which will appease my guilty conscience," she said. "God. You're engaged, Matt! And I'm with Adam."

"Well, he's a prick," I said. "But yeah, Carol." She didn't deserve this.

"I thought you liked him," Elle said.

"About as much as Hitler. Are you kidding me? I hate him." I started pacing, something which is not easy to do on the slope of an uneven hill. It was hard to get a rhythm there. I needed a minute or two. Shit. Carol was back in New York. Carol, who probably stayed up most of the previous night and all of this day taking care of sick kids. And I was up here, trying to get Elle into bed, trying to justify my actions. Did Elle ask me to come up with a good reason? How about I still loved her? God, I still loved her.

"And all this time I thought it was just Adam who hated you," she said.

"He hates me?"

"Oh, yeah," she said. "He hates you."

"Because he doesn't want you to have friends." I didn't know why I said "friends." Adam was jealous, plain and simple. He wanted to control her. I was Elle's first lover, and I was pretty certain that bugged the shit out of the Southern Green Giant.

She released a short snort of a laugh. "No. We have friends." She sighed. "It's just that he's very protective of me."

"Protective? Of what? I'd never hurt you."

She shook her head slightly. "Of course you wouldn't, but you did—hurt me. Once. You broke my heart. I've forgotten about it, but he hasn't."

I didn't see the windup coming. And the guilt and the realization that she could never completely forgive me hit me hard. I stood there a little dumbfounded. In the moment we kissed, I believed we could dig our way through the wreckage that split us apart. "You haven't forgotten."

"I have mostly. He just knows we have history and that for a long time I was bitter. And he blames you for my inability to commit."

I nodded. "Is he right?"

"I don't know how to answer that question." She wet her lips. "Matt . . . he doesn't understand how symbiotic you and I are, how at ease, how you make me laugh." She squeezed her eyes shut and her voice grew so soft that I had to lean in to hear. I sensed she was only half speaking to me, half realizing something, daring, maybe for the first time, to utter the words aloud. "He doesn't understand that I don't need anyone to protect me anymore. I'm a big girl. I know what I want."

"What do you want?" I asked, hoping she would say me. Clinging to the hope she would grant me complete redemption even if I did hurt her once. So long ago. I wanted to kiss her again, to persuade her we belonged together, but she stepped back.

"We can't," she said. "It's . . . lust. Besides the friendship, there's a powerful dose of lust between us, isn't there? God. Under the circumstances, maybe you'd better leave. It's not what I want you to do, but—I don't hate Adam. And you don't hate Carol. This is a mistake."

"Elle—"

"It's just"—she hesitated—"lust, Matt. I know you. You would never have asked her to marry you if you didn't love her."

I stood with my mouth hanging open. I did love Carol. Even so, I wanted to say that there was love and then there was the kind of love I felt for Elle. I wanted to say that my feelings for Elle were all-consuming. I wanted to say I hadn't exactly asked Carol to marry me. But somehow I did ask. Or she asked. Or we simply decided together. But I couldn't say any of that because Elle was making other points, valid points.

"Go home," she said. "We can't do this. I won't cheat on him. It's a terrible way to end a relationship. It's such a betrayal. When you cheated—oh . . ." Her voice trailed off, and I knew she was thinking of how we had ended. "I didn't mean to bring that up again."

"It was a hazing, Peep. I was drunk out of my mind. I did it without intention. I never meant to hurt you or to end it between us. I loved you. I still love you. You're my best friend. Elle, I wasn't trying to end our relationship. That was the mistake."

"I know you didn't mean to. But this is a mistake, too. One we can't make. Please. You should leave. Before you say something or do something you'll regret. Because right now, if you try to ratio nalize this thing that we almost did, this thing we still want to do, you will be betraying her. So go home. Not because I want you to leave. But because you're an honorable man."

It wasn't my good character that made me walk away that night—no matter what she thought. It was my need for Elle's respect, her faith, and her trust.

* * *

In the month that followed, the only time I heard Elle's voice was on her voice-mail message, but she'd sent e-mails. The *Atlantis* crew had begun their training in earnest, and they were spending hours and hours in the Neutral Buoyancy Pool, working on a full-size mock-up of Hubble. I kept trying. I dialed her cell and left another voice message, then called her home number, expecting the usual "Leave your message at the beep."

Instead Adam grumbled, "Elle? She isn't here." It wasn't his words. It was his tone. He sounded pissed off, and I wondered if she told him about what almost happened.

"Well, let her know I called," I said.

"Tell her yourself. She has a cell phone," he said, before the dial tone sounded.

I didn't like how he sounded, like he might slug her if she dared to enter the same room. "Right."

I tried her cell again.

"McClure," she answered this time.

"Wow, you're alive. I was beginning to doubt it. How are you? Are you still at work?"

"Nope, I'm home."

"Then why didn't Adam pass you the phone?"

A long pause followed. "You talked to him? Listen, I have a new home number. Ready to jot it down?"

"What do you mean? You two have separate lines?"

"Very, very separate. Can you hold on for a minute?"

"Yeah." My eyes darted around the loft as I tried to figure out what was going on.

In the background, I heard Elle speaking to someone, and then a door shut somewhere.

"Sorry about that," Elle said. "I have a new apartment, and it has a very active Welcome Wagon. People keep dropping by. I planned to call and give you my new address."

For a beat, I didn't know what to say. She'd left him? They'd split up. After we almost— What did she say? Betrayal was a terrible way to end a relationship. "What happened?"

"I let Adam off the hook. Evidently, I have commitment issues. He thinks I should see a shrink, and I think he deserves someone who will love him for who he is. Long story short: I moved out."

I raked my hair. "Elle—"

"Don't even go there, Matthew. You had nothing to do with it. Period."

How the hell did she know what I was about to ask? "Are you sure?"

She exhaled, and when she finally spoke, her voice was so soft, almost consoling. "I already knew it wasn't working between Adam and me. I had a hard time letting go. Then you and I kissed. Gramps's farmhouse, you and me, sweet memories from long, long time ago. And if we hadn't kissed, I still would have left him— eventually." She tried to laugh, but sounded anything but jovial. "Anyway, I'm certain it's not your fault."

I glanced up at the sound of Carol's key in the door. "Fault? That sounds as if you think leaving him is a mistake."

"No," Elle said. "It was time."

The loft door swung open, and Carol called to me before she saw me with the telephone at my ear.

"Carol's home?" Elle asked.

"Just came in."

Carol smiled at me and slipped her arms around my waist. God, she smelled good. And I never felt as awkward in my life. She mouthed, "Who are you talking to?"

"Elle," I answered.

"What?" Elle asked.

"Oh, let me talk to her." Carol took the phone out of my hand. "Hi, Elle. It's Carol." She paused. "Listen, I was wondering if you could do me a little favor." Pause. "No, I have a ten-year-old patient who wants to be an astronaut. The kid has spent most of her life in and out of hospitals. Is there any way I could get you to send an autographed copy of something NASA?" Pause. "That would be so great. Her name is Camilla Rodriguez." Carol spelled the name, said good-bye, and handed the receiver back to me.

The air in the room was as sparse as water in the desert. "Hi," I said.

"Hey, I have to go. I'll send that picture of the crew along."

"Peep—"

"We do it all the time. It's part of the PR end of NASA. How are you doing? The wedding plans?"

"I, uh, Carol's handling that mostly."

Silence. "I want you to be happy," Elle said.

"Are you okay?"

"Sure, but I have to hang up. I'm not ready to sound brave right now."

"Wait. What do you mean, brave?"

For a beat she didn't say anything. "I have a lot going on here. A new apartment with no curtains, not that it matters. I'm not home much. It's just life feels a little bare. As full as it is with the mission, it feels a little empty. And . . ." Elle's voice broke. "I suppose being emotional is normal in the wake of relinquishing someone you love. Talk to you soon."

42

After Elle's Accident
Day 25

As I said good-bye to Father Meehan, I'd actually asked the priest to pray for the baby. How was that? Progress? Or was I slipping into deeper desperation? If there are no atheists in foxholes, there are none in critical care hospital rooms either. The funny thing was I'd never thought of myself as an atheist. I was a lapsed Catholic, perhaps, with a little agnosticism thrown in for good measure. I was a man of science and a man of little faith, a man who loved his wife and behaved within the confines of whatever was and whatever would be.

"Of course, Matt," Father Meehan answered. "I'm praying for both Elle and the baby already. I'm praying for you, too."

I shook his hand and walked off. I'd parked on a side street, knowing it would be easier to make an escape quickly after Mass. Freeport used to be the quintessential New England town, lined with Victorians and farmhouses, until the upscale outlets arrived on the heels of the town's only real business, L.L.Bean. Now it had become a small town with every shopping opportunity known to mankind. Three blocks off the main street, I slipped into my car and drove toward my house four miles away, where rural America still teetered along in its time-forgot-us way.

I didn't bother to park in the barn. I wouldn't be staying long enough. I just needed a little fresh air, a little time, as Father Meehan said, to listen, to converse with God. Strangely, God seemed to be the strong silent type, and He didn't say a hell of a lot. Well, maybe He didn't say a *heaven* of a lot.

I snickered at my own dark humor.

His silence might be an answer of sorts, although not quite what I was looking for.

Celina's garden was thick with dead stalks of black-eyed Susans and every other living thing. Dead things, and dead seemed appropriate in my grief.

I would have to dig up the urns. I would have to—bury them with Elle. She asked me that five years before, and we'd never discussed it since, but I knew. I knew Elle hadn't changed her mind about that either.

I hadn't gone to the farm to prepare myself to bury her, but I needed to. Her kidney function was marginal, and the pregnancy would put a strain on them. The odds were bad. For a few minutes I sat on the grass and stared at the garden. Not here. Elle needed to be in the small family cemetery next to her mother under the trees in the pine forest she loved so much, and the babies would have to be with her.

"I need to be morbid for a minute," she'd said that day on the beach. She was preparing herself for space back then—a kind of heaven in her eyes.

We never talked about where she wanted to rest for eternity, only that Celina should be with her. And that meant Dylan, too.

I headed across the field and up through the woods. Ten minutes later I came to the family cemetery on the ridge. Mostly because of a rainy summer, I hadn't been up there all year. It was unkempt, straggly, and a little lonely. Alice was buried over there in the corner. Elle's grandmother had died in a car accident when Alice was still a child, and Elle's grandfather died the summer Elle and I fell in love. The rest of the stones bore names that were only names to me. But even as a little girl, Elle had all of their names memorized.

I could still see her kneeling in the cemetery, pushing the white-blond hair out of her eyes as she prepared to do the rubbing of her grandmother's gravestone. Elle at nine, the intellectually precocious tomboy. "It's so tragic," she'd said. "All my grandma left behind was an epitaph. My mom doesn't remember her at all. A few words on a headstone isn't much."

It was an odd thing for a kid to say, odder perhaps that I recalled it, but her words stuck with me. Elle was intriguing, not that I would have admitted it back then. She was a girl, after all, the kid next door, a convenient playmate in a crunch. But she was a girl, and I hadn't yet stopped hating girls, at least publicly.

Without a word, she crossed the patchy lawn, skirting the graves, as if afraid that stepping on a plot of dirt would rile a ghost. Then she traced the words written in stone of ancestor after ancestor. "All the ladies in my mom's family died before they turned forty. Look. This one's the oldest."

A few years later, Elle's own mother, shy of her fortieth birthday, died of cancer.

And now Elle. I had lost Elle.

In the morning stillness, I stood in the same bitter place, a family graveyard with nothing but lichen-covered stones marking the dead, marking the lost lives of the women who all died too young.

I was no longer a boy fascinated by the towheaded, little-girl-child Elle. I was her husband, and as incomprehensible as it was, I would have to bury her alongside her mother and grandmothers. Yes, all the women in her family died young. But I was determined an epitaph would not be the only legacy Elle left behind.

There wasn't much sunshine beneath the trees, but enough that a few shade-loving plants could grow. Bleeding hearts bloomed in the springtime, and hostas in late summer. There should be a garden for Elle; she loved flowers. Over by the back near the fence, the sun peeked through. Even if I had to take down a couple of trees to bring in enough light, I could do that.

"Please, God," I said. "When it happens, take care of her." I lumbered over the ground thick with the blanket of pine needles, my legs feeling heavier with the reality of grief, and I lay down on the dank ground where she would rest and let my tears flow like rain. There was no comfort in the promise of heaven or God's grace, at least not yet. Maybe not ever.

"What do you want from me? You want me to thank you for this? You want me to come closer to faith by stripping me of the only person who I ever believed in?"

My faith was in her, in the love we shared, that it was as durable as the light coming from a distant star, crossing space, enduring through the void expanses of time.

Time we lost.

"Time you stole," I yelled.

I was angry at God—if He existed. And for the first time, maybe in my entire life, I was pretty certain He did. I had the entire mumble jumble circling in my head. God's plans. Trust in Him. Miracles happen. Lazarus. God so loved the world. Resurrection. Christ.

But I needed her. And the baby needed me.

"Please, God," I whispered. "Please."

✦ 43 ✦

Day 26

Clint Everest shifted in the witness stand. "The mother's blood clots and causes circulation to the placenta to stop, and the baby dies. During pregnancy, that's the basic pathology, the very basic pathology, of how APS causes miscarriages."

"Is it likely Elle Beaulieu will miscarry this time?" Jake asked.

"Probably not because of the APS. We're treating her with heparin, a blood-thinning agent. When diagnosed, the women rarely miscarry as a result."

The subtext of Clint's words was that Elle could miscarry because she suffered a devastating brain injury. For Christ's sake, she couldn't even blink. As I'd left her hospital room that morning, the nurse was putting ointment into Elle's eyes to prevent them from drying out.

Clint and Jake were explaining the basic issues complicating Elle's pregnancy. Was the APS dangerous to Elle or just to the baby? Yes. Maybe. Not yet. APS could shut down any of her organ systems. Of course her brain injury could do the same, was, in fact, more likely to start shutting down her body systems.

I hated all of this prancing around in the courtroom. I wanted to get up and make the judge understand that my child had a right to fight for his or her life, without Jake, without Clint, without anyone intervening.

But I focused on the nuances of the testimony, on the reactions of the judge, and on key words. There were two forms of the disease, basic and catastrophic. Elle had basic APS, but *catastrophic* is an emotional word. In catastrophes like earthquakes, floods, and tornadoes, didn't we focus on that miracle survivor, the one pulled from the rubble a week later? Well, I was digging through the rubble of Elle's life, trying to save our child, her child, my child.

"And if she developed the catastrophic form, could it be treated?" Jake asked.

They were already treating her preemptively.

"How likely is it that the catastrophic form would cause Elle's death prior to the point her baby was ready to be born?"

"APS mortality rates in pregnancy are not well documented," Clint answered. "But with it, she has an increased risk of pre-eclampsia, which might require premature delivery. She could develop blood clots in her legs or her lungs, that sort of thing."

"But these are just risk factors?"

"Yes," Clint said. "Risk factors."

"Thank you. That's all." Jake sat down and leaned over to whisper in my ear. "Whatever damage your mother's attorney does on cross, I'll fix on redirect."

I nodded. If only I could fix the damage done to Elle.

"Mr. Klein, do you have questions for Dr. Everest?" the judge asked.

"Yes, Your Honor." My mother's attorney stood, and after tapping two pencils like drumsticks on his stack of papers, he said,

"Doctor, during Elle's last pregnancy—which ended February second of this year—she had complications from her APS, didn't she?"

Clint studied his hands. "She was admitted to the ICU for two days because she lost a large volume of blood, but I don't believe it was from the APS directly. She was taking blood-thinning agents. Unexpectedly, she went into preterm labor and delivered at home. Because of the blood thinners, she hemorrhaged."

"Actually, she nearly hemorrhaged to death, didn't she?"

I drew a breath, remembering. On that night, on our kitchen floor, I saw more blood than I'd ever seen outside of a hospital.

Jake put his hand on my shoulder. "You okay?" he whispered.

I nodded and tried to stay present in the courtroom. I looked up and saw my mother staring at me. And unlike Jake, she didn't look concerned. Her expression was pointed, almost accusatory.

"Her blood loss easily could have been fatal," Clint said.

I followed Jake to a high-rise down in the Old Port. The contemporary exterior contrasted with the gentleman's-club decor of the inner offices. Leather-bound law texts lined the shelves.

"The cross-examination didn't go well," I said.

Jake hadn't fixed the damage Klein leveled on cross-examination, and I couldn't sit still while we reviewed the past two hours. Instead I paced the generous expanse between his desk and a conference table at the other side of the room.

"It could have gone worse," he said. "If she hadn't gotten pneumonia or kidney problems already, it could have gone better."

"Klein made it sound like Elle . . . Hell, everything he pulled out of Clint was the truth. It's been twenty-six fucking days, and she's already had pneumonia and suffered kidney damage. We need another fourteen weeks, twenty weeks would be better. The APS could kill her or the baby—"

"Stop. I realize you're worried about her medical challenges. But the primary legal issue is what Elle would want done on her behalf. We don't have the best evidence to make our case on that point. We need something substantial in writing that backs up your contention. Have you found anything in her diaries?"

"Nothing besides what you already know. I decided to fight for the baby based on our conversations over the years."

Jake studied his hands. "We need more. We're out of time. You have to let me help you go through the diaries."

I wasn't about to tell Jake that either Elle or my mother might have done a Kevorkian on Alice McClure. He might find another confession of matricide. "I don't know what happened to the baby ones."

"Matt—"

"They. Are. Private." I glared at Jake, letting him know I meant business. "Besides, I don't think there's anything in them."

"Your life is already front-page news all over the world. Under the circumstances, maybe you should forgo your First Amendment right to privacy and let me see them." He offered an engaging grin, making me think that First Amendment bullshit was supposed to be his idea of a joke.

I shook my head.

His office phone rang and he picked up the receiver. "Yeah. Put her through. Dr. Clarke, we're expecting you to testify in thirty—" Pause. "I see." Jake gave Blythe the phone number of the courthouse and instructed her to call it once she was free.

"What?" I said.

"She's tied up with a complicated delivery. And another of her patients was just admitted with preterm labor or something."

"She can't get to court?" I asked.

"No. And I want her to testify before you. We set up possibility. The judge sees the ultrasound of a baby. Then we hit him with how much you love your wife and how much the two of you wanted a child," he said as he laid out index cards in order. "Then I want to set the framework for the fetal guardianship issue. Timing will be important; otherwise, it would smack of desperation. I want it to be a deliberate card we play."

"Meaning?"

"After I question you, I'll call Father Meehan. The Catholic Church teaches life begins at conception, and you and Elle are Catholic. Therefore, fighting for this baby becomes part of your constitutional right to practice your religion. I then ask the judge to give you guardianship of your unborn baby, protecting that life, acting on Elle's behalf to protect her unborn child, exercising *her* right to practice her religion. It's a little transparent, but constitutionally, it could work. At the very least it would be grounds for an appeal. We could also base an appeal on the Texas advanced directive. There's no way the judge should be considering it. In Texas, the law prohibits the removal of a pregnant woman's life support. If the appeal fails, we can file a cert petition. And that's all we need. If it goes before the Supreme Court, chances are we'll have time for that baby of yours to be born alive."

"What if the Supreme Court denies the cert petition?"

Jake smiled and shook his head. "Did anyone ever tell you you worry too much? Have a little faith in me. I told you, I can pull this off. Let's go back to court and see what we can do about Dr. Clarke's absence."

"One more thing, I forgot to tell you I got a letter from Carol Wentworth. You remember her?"

"Of course."

I slid the letter across the desk to him.

He picked it up and scanned it. "The *U.S.* attorney general?"

✦ 44 ✦

Five Years Before the Accident

If I ever marginalized a woman, it was Carol, but I didn't intend to and I didn't believe I was doing it at the time. I honestly thought she and I could have the kind of marriage that was built on mutual respect. We were good together. Nevertheless, I didn't tell my fiancée that I'd run into Elle in Maine, and that my few hours with her cast doubts on my decision to get married. Carol didn't need to know. I would only hurt her if I eased my conscience by confessing that I'd kissed Elle.

Besides, we didn't do anything, not really, and a few doubts were normal. Logically, I could recite a dozen reasons to marry Carol. Emotionally, my tether to Elle unraveled them one by one, but I convinced myself this connection was simply a remnant of childhood and, as she said, lust.

All right, I loved her.

Over the next few months Elle grew more distant, almost detached. When we spoke on the phone, she avoided talking about herself. Hell, she didn't even ask many personal questions about me. We talked about work, hers and mine. If I mentioned Carol, Elle seemed to find reasons to get off the phone. I told myself we were growing apart, and that maybe we should; after all, I was getting married. Still, I hated that marriage meant cutting Elle out of my life. Or worse, that maybe she was cutting herself out.

In December, Phil Grey paged me at work and asked if we could get together while he was in Manhattan. I was on call all weekend, but first thing Monday morning he met me at the hospital. He shook my hand. "You didn't tell me winter in Maine came on November first."

"Trust me," I said. "You won't see real winter until February and March."

"March is springtime."

"In Maine, *May* is springtime," I said.

"So, you wouldn't be interested in joining the practice with me?" He wagged his head toward the door. "Let's go get breakfast and talk. I'm buying."

In a diner not far from the hospital, Phil launched into a prepared list of reasons why he was recruiting me to join him as soon as I finished my residency. One, the junior member of the practice died three months after Phil joined it. Two, the one he was hired to replace was diagnosed with an early onset of Parkinson's, and the guy hadn't done surgery in four months. Phil had done every surgery since he moved north. In essence, he was the solo surgeon. He could continue for a while, but not forever. In spite of his crack about the weather, Phil and his wife loved the area, and she was pregnant, so they wanted to make a nest and line it.

I told him Carol was vehement about staying in New York, and he said that he understood, but, hey, just go talk it over with her anyway. I was his first choice. He gave me a week to decide.

Seven hours later Carol came into the bedroom and flipped on the light. "You didn't sleep all day, did you?" she asked.

I grabbed her waist, pulled her down on the bed with me, and kissed her with sincerity mixed with more than a moderate dose of lust. "I spent most of the day running along the reservoir and thinking. Phil Grey stopped by this morning."

"Phil? How is he? Wait, let me guess, he got sick of that sleepy little town already, and he's in the city to look for a job." She pulled away and walked to the closet. "Here," she said, tossing me a pressed shirt. "Dinner with my parents tonight, remember?"

I stayed put, watching her slip out of her skirt. "Come to bed and play."

She smiled and studied me. "So tempting," she said. "The mayor will be there."

I rubbed my eyes and yawned. We'd met the mayor before. The first time I was a little starstruck. The second time I found myself disagreeing with him and called him on a couple of things, which hadn't sat too well with Carol or her father. The mayor was a regular visitor at the Wentworths', and although he had power and position, he wasn't any more fascinating than some of my patients and their families. That Carol needed to be a courtier to power brokers annoyed the crap out of me.

I rose and pulled on a pair of sweatpants. "I don't want to go tonight. I want to talk about something."

"Is it important? We said we'd be there."

"How many guests are your parents hosting? A dozen? Two dozen? We won't be missed." I came up behind her so I could kiss her neck. She was sensitive there. "Listen, Phil offered me a position up in Portland, and I want to take it. I did a little checking. There are only a couple of pediatric surgeons in the area. You could—"

"Matt, we've already been through this. I'm not moving to Maine."

"No discussion? You aren't even willing to consider Portland? It's a beautiful small city. It has an art museum—"

"You cannot be serious. I'm a New Yorker. Beautiful? Sure, Maine is beautiful for a weekend, especially a weekend when we're there to be tourists. But I don't want to live there. We can visit; we can vacation, but I am not moving there to practice medicine."

"I want you to give this more than an unchecked dismissal this time. Anything you can get in New York, you can have there, too."

"I know you're serious, but so am I. I love New York's energy, its people, its diversity. Right outside your door. I don't want to live in a small town. I can't. The people are all so narrow-minded."

"I grew up in a small town. *My family* lives a small town."

She drew a deep breath and sat on the edge of the bed. "I didn't mean to generalize. I didn't mean *your* family. And I certainly didn't mean you. Besides, you've been out in the world. And you're brilliant, and rather easy on the eyes." She could be elitist, and she was insulting people and places I cared about. She kissed me, and I pulled away.

Her chin jutted out. "Please get dressed. I don't want to be late for my parents' party. After which, if you so desire, I'll remind you of how indispensable I am to you."

Indispensable. The word echoed around my head. I thought about it. Who was indispensable to me? My family. Carol. Elle. Not necessarily in that order. Surely not Carol's parents or this dinner with their wealthy socialite friends. Her parents were gracious and polite, but I'd never once felt any real warmth from them, not toward me. Maybe toward Carol. They were no doubt proud of her. She reflected well on them, and I would be a socially acceptable partner for her, a graduate of an Ivy League school, a neurosurgeon. I didn't see us being chummy.

"I'm going to skip it tonight," I said. "Tell them I'm beat from work. Tell them I'm on call. Tell them anything you feel will save face, but if you aren't even willing to consider going to Maine with me, I don't think I can play your command performance." I pulled on a shirt and a hoodie and marched out of her loft.

Over the next few days Carol and I stopped talking. She wasn't speaking to me because I'd stood her up. On the other hand, I had begun to wonder which I wanted more, her or the job in Maine.

I called Elle and reached her machine. I called my brother Mike. He said I shouldn't make any rash decisions. I called Phil and asked for more time.

He gave me until the first of the year.

Carol and I were going to Maine for Christmas. Actually I was going home. She was coming so we could go skiing. It would always be this way, I realized. Maine was a destination of interest, not of affection, for Carol. In New York, we would live her lifestyle and I would become accustomed to it—not that living her lifestyle would cause me any hardship.

If I wanted to change things, I needed to do it soon. So, shortly after we arrived in Maine, I left Carol with Mom to do a little shopping in the local downtown boutiques, and I went into Phil's office, met Welsh, who I liked immediately, talked seriously about the practice, and accepted their offer.

I didn't tell Carol. I decided to wait until we got back to New York. She had six months to get used to the idea. If she couldn't, one of us would have to buckle. I'd have to stay in the city, or she'd come to Maine, or we'd have to call off the wedding.

Far too much bickering followed, and a few months before the wedding, with a stack of save-the-date notices piled high, I stood in front of Carol, shaking my head. "If you're not even willing to try it up there, then I don't think you should mail those," I said.

Carol wrung her hands. "You're picking a job in the middle of nowhere over me?"

I cleared my throat. "It seems like you've made your own decision. You're choosing New York over me."

She turned away and crossed her arms. "What do you want me to tell everyone?"

I didn't know if she was angry or shaken. And although I didn't want to hurt her, we needed to break the tie before it became disastrous. "Irreconcilable differences," I said. "We don't want the same kind of life."

✴ 45 ✴

Four Years Before the Accident

The Galveston restaurant sported a tiki-hut motif, very tacky and very fun. Fortunately Hank, who was hosting the extravaganza, had reserved the patio for the Beaulieu and McClure clans to congregate. My brothers' boys were causing generalized mayhem, darting around and drinking out of coconuts—correction, spilling out of coconuts—and causing too much hubbub to be in a public space. Meanwhile the adults gathered around an Olympic-pool-length table that overlooked the expansive beach.

In the time leading up to Elle's space flight, my entire family decided to attend the launch. Any excuse for a Florida vacation sounded wonderful in the dead of a Maine winter, but then Elle informed us she would be quarantined at the Johnson Space Center the week prior to her flight. It seemed that even the common cold would be bad news for an astronaut in orbit. "I'll wave from the launch pad," she said, "but the last time I'll be able to see you in person will be before I go into quarantine."

After some discussion, Hank moved the good-luck-party venue

to Texas. A few people balked that Houston didn't sound nearly as fun as Florida until Hank suggested staying at the beach on the Gulf of Mexico. "A beach is a beach," he said. "And we'll all be ready for some sun by the end of April."

So only a few weeks after breaking up with Carol, I sat staring out over the Gulf. I hadn't told anyone yet. It could wait until afterward. Elle deserved to have everyone's focus on her, and frankly I didn't want to field the how-are-you-doing-with-your-broken-heart questions.

In the distance, oil rigs loomed on the horizon. The air was warm and sweet and calm in the way that lulls a man to sleep, and I was looking forward to seeing Elle.

My brother Mike dropped into the chair next to mine and slapped me on the back so hard he almost knocked me out of my seat. "Okay, your wedding's in what—four months? You want a stripper for your bachelor's party? As your best man, I have to plan this thing and I need a little lead time since it's in New York."

I coughed, suddenly realizing I'd have to let everyone know tomorrow morning so they didn't make plans or, God forbid, buy wedding gifts. "No, ah, don't worry about that tonight," I said. This was Elle's night, and thankfully, since Carol had never planned to attend the gathering, it seemed reasonable that I could dodge questions about her for few more hours.

At that moment my four-year-old nephew did it for me. He grabbed Mike's shirt. "Dad, you gotta come see the bird." The kids were all looking at a pelican about a dozen yards from the deck.

"Guess I ought to go be a parent. Want to come?" Mike asked.

"Sure," I said. He swung his son up onto his shoulders, and we trudged over to the railing to get a better view.

Fifteen minutes later Elle finally arrived, wearing a sleeveless blue-and-white sundress. She was glowing with excitement and grace, her lifelong dream days from realization. Elle laughed a little as she searched our faces. "Ya know I'm just going to work for a couple of days. It's not that big a deal."

I nodded at her, and her eyes held mine. She half smiled as if we were sharing a secret with no one else around us. That's how it had always been, the two of us alone although surrounded by our families.

Toasts buzzed around the table, all in her honor, until it came to her brother, who had brought his girlfriend. Christopher stood and held up his goblet. "To my big sister, who has always been there for me. I want to ask you if you would do me one more huge favor."

Her eyes shifted back and forth. "Huge, huh? Well, maybe I'd better know what it is first. The last time you asked me for a *huge* favor, I ended up writing a term paper for you."

The group cackled. Christopher was bright, but he never shared Elle's academic prowess. He glanced at his girlfriend, as if to apologize. "That wasn't one of my prouder moments," he said. "This is. Arianne and I are hoping you'll be—and don't take this wrong, Elle, but would you be my best man? Arianne and I are getting married."

Elle's mouth fell open, and she jumped up and ran over to hug Christopher, and then pulled in Arianne, too. "Oh my God! Really?"

Maybe it was sour grapes on my part, but I thought how very like Christopher this was. Elle waited her entire life for this moment. She put off school to take care of him when she was just a kid herself, and once more, Christopher selfishly turned the attention to himself.

"Wait, what do you mean 'best man'?" Elle's eyes narrowed. "I wore a dress tonight 'cause I can't wear one in zero G, and still, I'm just one of the guys. Jeez, I can't win."

"I want you to stand up for me," Christopher said.

"Can't do that in zero gravity either."

He pretended to strangle her. "You can wear a dress or a monkey suit as long as you promise me you'll be there." And releasing her neck, Christopher kissed her cheek. "Please?"

Elle's stance softened, and she hugged Christopher. "You know it, baby brother. I won't miss it."

Maybe Christopher was making her swear to come back to Earth, and I wanted her to keep that promise, but after his announcement no one talked about Elle. The toasts turned to him. Cacophonous conversations rounded the table and then circled back and forth.

As one of the last hangers-on, I waited for my good-bye and grabbed a quick hug. "The next time I see you, you'll be in the history books, Peep."

She batted me. "NASA doesn't make the books anymore unless it's a disaster. Just say 'good luck.'"

"Good luck," I mouthed, but really I was whispering a prayer.

"Will you keep me company and walk the beach for a while? I have to stay up late. They're trying to move our sleep cycles around for the flight."

"Absolutely," I said.

We crossed the street and took the stairs to the beach. She pulled off her sandals, dangling them by the straps. "Quite a party. I can't believe your whole family came."

Following her cue, I removed my Docksiders and let the coarse sand scratch between my toes. "You're an honest-to-God astronaut. Everyone wanted to come. I was kind of surprised Adam didn't show."

She paused for a beat then resumed walking. "I see him still at work. He's met someone, so that made it easier." Her pensive expression made me wonder if she was over him, which once again resurrected my old green-eyed monster.

"Are you seeing anyone new?" I asked. Not that someone new would make me feel better.

She wet her lower lip. "I've been a little too busy."

"You've been a little closed off," I said. "I'm still waiting for you to return my last call, from, um, *two* weeks ago."

She shoved into me. "I needed to focus on the work. I appreciate that you've gone with the flow."

"It's not as if I had a choice." Without thinking, I slung my arm around her shoulder and kissed her temple.

She shrugged away and crossed her arms as if I'd trespassed. "You're getting married," she said. "I had to back off."

"Elle—" I hesitated only for a second before I blurted out everything. "I'm not. Carol and I split up a couple of weeks ago. I took the job in Maine, and she wouldn't even consider moving there. There were other issues, too, but I called it off."

Elle stared at me for close to a minute, blinking. Maybe there was even a hint of a smile.

"Why didn't you say something?"

I glanced away. "I haven't told anyone yet, not even Mom. I didn't want to steal your thunder with my shitty news—like your brother did."

"He didn't—steal my *thunder*." Elle touched my elbow. "Are you doing okay with the breakup?"

"Yeah. Yeah, absolutely." I took her hand, patted it, as we began walking again. There we were, for the first time in sixteen years, without anger or partners between us, and I didn't want to discuss Carol.

An hour later we were still talking by her hotel room. She leaned against the open doorjamb while I stood by a little awkwardly. Her room had the typical layout: bed, café table, armoire, couch, and minifridge. "Want to come in and play cards?" she asked.

"You forget that I know you cheat."

"I do not."

"You count the cards. You can get thrown out of Vegas for that."

Her eyes narrowed. "It's a strategy. I have a good memory. Sue me. We won't play blackjack."

"Okay. Strip poker." I wagged my eyebrows and strolled past her. I wasn't serious, but it seemed like a good comeback line.

She chuckled. "I'm not up for anything quite that risqué tonight."

Okay, maybe I was half serious. "Only because you're not as certain you could win."

She shook her head. "Rummy, then."

We plopped down at the table. I dealt first. She must have been letting me win to prove she *never cheated* because, after a dozen hands, I had ten times more points. It grew very late, but I was having difficulty making myself leave. I eased back in my chair to watch her contemplating her next move. She added a queen of hearts to a straight and discarded an ace. Then she rose and grabbed a couple of sodas. "Cheers."

"To your flight. Nine days and what—three more hours?" I said.

She glanced at her watch. "Two hundred nineteen hours and twelve minutes, but who's counting?"

And then she was planning to strap herself to a stick of dynamite. Actually, the Space Shuttle was closer, in my opinion, to a nuclear bomb with a half-million gallons of rocket fuel as a detonator. I stood and pulled her up into my arms. I wanted to try one more time to convince her not to go, to tell her I couldn't survive if *Atlantis* blew up like *Challenger* did on takeoff, or disintegrated like *Columbia* did on reentry. Instead I said, "I always knew you could do it," which was equally true.

Her eyes crinkled up at the corners. Actual lines tracked around her eyes. When had she grown old enough for a few lines on her face?

She followed, as she always did when complimented, with a non sequitur. "Can you believe my little brother is getting married? Arianne is sweet, but he's so young."

I fingered the fabric of Elle's dress at her shoulder. "I don't want to talk about Christopher."

"I'm glad they told me. What if it goes wrong?"

"It won't," I said as much for my sake as for hers. "Are you scared?"

"A little. Don't tell anyone." She laced her fingers with mine and rested her ear against my chest as if she were listening to my heart. "I'll be fine. And for the record, afterward, I'm planning to make a radical transition—from rocket ship to rocking chair. After this mission I'm determined to land a teaching job back home, hopefully at Bowdoin, and then I will grow old, watching sunsets on my grampa's porch. Maybe, since you'll be nearby, I'll even beat you now and then, playing a game of rummy."

"Strip poker," I whispered into the crown of her head.

"Flirting with me again, huh? After being asked to be the best man, I suppose I should be grateful."

"You don't need to worry. You're sexy as hell." I ran my hand down the back of her dress, which wasn't revealing, but still she curved in all the right places.

"If you think this is sexy, you should see me in my space suit." She stepped away and winked. "Now, there's a look that makes astronauts hot and bothered."

"Yeah, right." I picked up the deck from the table and fanned the cards like a Vegas dealer. "I'm pretty sure I'd prefer you naked. Come on, one hand of poker. Winner takes all." I permitted myself a quick visual sweep of her body.

Elle's face turned crimson. "What are you doing? Is this one of those games of truth or dare? A joke?"

Before I answered, I considered my words carefully. "It's not a joke or truth or dare, although maybe it's both. The truth is that, on the surface, I only meant to put you at ease, make you laugh. But you have to know I could never take you to bed and not have it mean more. Last summer you minimized what happened by saying it was lust. Sure. But not only lust. The real truth is I love you, Elle. As a friend." I paused. "And more deeply. Much more deeply." I thought I should leave; this was not the time for a re-evaluation of our relationship, so I pecked her cheek. "Come back to me safely." I turned and reached for the doorknob.

"Wait. You can't say something like that and just breeze out the door." She grabbed me by the elbow. "Tell me what you want."

"Okay. There's the dare." I drew air into my lungs and then exhaled. Why not tell her? I stared straight into those hot green eyes of hers. "I want you. I want another chance. I have never stopped wanting *you*. And after wearing my heart on my sleeve for five years, I finally made a decision. I could handle the scraps you gave me in the form of friendship; as long as you were part of my life, I could manage. Now it's my turn to ask: Is friendship enough for you? I need to know if there's a chance you still love me."

She stood before me with a charged stillness, silent, pensive, searching my face. "Yes," she finally said. "I still love you. Oh God. Even when you broke my heart, I wanted you. Even then. Please don't walk out that door. Don't marry someone else. Don't *ever* marry anyone else. Please. Just stay with me. Please."

"I'll stay. I want to stay," I said. "And I would have married you when I was seventeen."

"We were too young back then." She swallowed then nestled herself in my arms.

"We aren't too young now," I said, stroking her hair.

A smile crept across her face. "Definitely not."

I tipped her chin up and kissed her. "This time we'll get it right."

Although I hadn't planned to attend the launch, I had to now—for my own sake as well as hers. Even before I returned to New York the following afternoon, I was on the phone calling in favors. I needed time off, and for once everything fell into place. Almost everything. Prior to the launch the astronauts meet with their spouses for one last visit at a beach house along a NASA-owned, twenty-five-mile stretch of ocean. Elle told me it was a beautiful place and that she wanted me to come. But NASA wouldn't allow me to be her significant other. They said that working in a hospital exposed me to too many pathogens, and I could make her sick. So the next time I saw Elle it was from a distance as she followed the mission's commander to the bus, which would take the crew to the launch pad. No matter what fetish astronauts joked about, Elle's orange flight suit was not nearly as sexy as the sundress I peeled off her nine days earlier. She was smiling and searching the crowd for me. When our eyes met, she tapped her chest with her fist. God, I loved her.

Beautiful stars on a balmy night promised the flight to be everything Elle had hoped. And I thought of little Celina. Her name meant goddess of the moon. Surely, I didn't believe in gods or goddesses, yet it seemed fitting that a full moon hung like a spotlight over the launch pad.

I imagined that inside the orbiter, Elle was counting up as the announcer counted down. The engines fired, and at zero, *Atlantis* lifted off. My heart pounded louder in my ears than the damned booster rockets. Booster rockets I didn't trust. Booster rockets, which were known to explode.

They didn't. *Atlantis* rumbled up into the night sky with spectacular grace. We all waited on the bleachers as the shuttle disappeared from sight.

Ten days later, buried in the medical library—all day—I missed the announcement. One of my friends paged me. After a couple of strained questions: "How are you doing, Matt?," "Are you okay?" he finally said, "You must not have heard. There was a terrible accident on the Space Shuttle. It's all over the news. Elle McClure was on her space walk and something happened. They got the other guy inside, though he's in bad shape, but—"

I didn't hear the rest of what he said, I was flying out the door, careening down the hospital corridor, in search of a television and news footage and reality. I shook as I pulled out my cell phone, running headlong onto a surgical floor and smack into Dr. Shah, my direct supervisor.

"Easy, Matt. Hey, are you all right?"

"I have to find out what's happening with *Atlantis*."

His pity shot me right between my eyes. "That's right; you went for the launch. You knew one of the astronauts."

I barged into a patient's room, an old guy with an oxygen mask. "Mind if I turn on your TV?" I asked, but I didn't wait for his reply.

He pulled the oxygen away from his face. "Nothing's on 'cept that astronaut who got killed. They got to land in someplace in Sweden. Can't even wait to get to the good old USA. Guess the other guy's in a bad way."

I flipped channels until I got to CNN. The footage of the crew going into the bus in their orange flight suits crossed the screen, Elle beaming as she passed. The voice-over said, "Dr. McClure was a mission specialist. Jabert and McClure were six and a half hours into their EVA—that's extravehicular activity—when a micrometeor punctured Jabert's space suit. McClure spotted the gas venting and immediately tried to get back to the orbiter along with fellow astronaut Jabert. At this point we are uncertain about the condition of Dr. McClure. Jabert is said to be in critical condition. They are expected to land within the next twenty minutes.

"Again, if you are just joining us, the Space Shuttle *Atlantis* is making an emergency landing in Arlanda, Sweden, after a micrometeor penetrated one of the astronaut's space suit during the Hubble upgrade. Here to explain this is Darlene Kruger, former NASA engineer."

The woman, who looked like the principal of a Victorian girls' school with her hair tied back in a severe bun, sat next to the CNN anchor. "This has long been one of NASA's concerns, and it is why we minimize the time the astronauts spend outside the vehicles. Although space is a virtual vacuum, it is not empty. Particles as small as specks of dust travel at speeds upward of sixty kilometers per second, passing through just about anything due to their velocity. In order to minimize the risk, the astronauts' suits are lined with Kevlar, and they try to work in the shadow of the shuttle, and in this case, Hubble's shelter wasn't enough."

The CNN anchor said, "NASA representative Adam Cunningham is going to make a brief statement."

Adam strode up to the podium. I hadn't seen him in a year or two. His hairline had receded slightly, and he looked strained. "Thank you. I'm going to read a brief statement and take a few questions. At thirteen twenty-three EST, mission specialists Dr. Elle McClure, an astrophysicist, and Dr. Andre Jabert, an aerospace engineer, were on an EVA, having just completed repairs to the Hubble Telescope and were preparing it for release. We believe a micrometeor, perhaps two, penetrated Andre Jabert's space suit, rendering him unconscious. He was on personal jet pack. Elle McClure, who was on tether, recognized his situation, untethered herself, and managed to get him into the air lock before his suit fully depressurized. We're not sure how the miscommunication occurred, but the media has reported that Elle McClure was left outside the shuttle and slipped off into space. That did not happen. She's safely inside *Atlantis*. First of all, the outer hatch is *never* closed with a crew member outside, because in the event of a hatch failure, we would be unable to bring the crew member back into the shuttle." Adam shuffled the papers in front of him.

"Jabert, however, is critically injured, with a serious chest wound. The flight surgeon is stabilizing him while *Atlantis* prepares for an emergency landing. Medical personnel are awaiting the shuttle on the ground. The crew is currently expected to land at eighteen-forty EST."

I dropped into an empty chair.

"Are you all right, Matt?" Dr. Shah asked.

"Elle's okay. Hell, yeah, I'm fine."

Two days later, via satellite, Elle looked a little shaky as she approached a podium in Sweden. She wore a NASA-issued polo shirt and a pair of khaki pants. She cleared her throat. "I'm Dr. Elle McClure, mission specialist. You know the Mark Twain quote, right? The news of my death was greatly exaggerated. Greatly. Those of you who saw me walking in here might have noted that I was a little unsteady. I'm still readjusting to gravity. Nothing more. Let me get straight to the real issues. Andre Jabert is awake and talking—and joking about the landing being so smooth he barely remembers it. However, I assure you the rest of the crew always will.

"What occurred is something NASA has considered to be one of the major risk factors for space walks for some time. Space exploration is an inherently risky endeavor, but those of us involved believe it is worth the risks. We are passionate about our work and its necessity. Each of us takes our love of space with us when we leave Earth's atmosphere. Although some will point to this day and say we endangered more lives, I see this more like the *Apollo 13* mission. We overcame the obstacles, and we *saved our crew*. We'd practiced for this very contingency and were able to complete our mission. When Andre was injured, everyone immediately geared into action, and we released Hubble in working order."

A British-sounding reporter said, "Dr. McClure, you're being hailed for your heroism. Do you care to comment?"

Elle chuckled, but she looked uncomfortable, shifting her feet. "Heroism? No. I did what needed to be done, what I've been trained to do, what we *all* learn to do. The entire *Atlantis* crew brought us inside. Our commander did a fantastic job of coordinating the rescue. Hubble is working, and I'm repeating myself here, but we're alive." Elle smiled broadly and then a sober expression fell over her face. "I do apologize for the worry the false reports of my death caused my family."

"Speaking of your family, have you spoken to them?"

"I've only talked to my dad. I promise I'll try to reach the rest later. Matt, if you're listening, I'll get ahold of you soon."

"Who's Matt? Your husband?"

Elle grinned. "No. Not yet."

✦ 46 ✦

After Elle's Accident
Day 27

Blythe Clarke told me that when Paul Klein interviewed her, he grilled her for nearly three hours, asking very specific questions about Elle's obstetrical history. Although I was still hoping he would be blindsided by what she would reveal, I was dreading her testimony today.

Jake started out with the usual questions, establishing Blythe's formidable qualifications. After he reviewed Elle's history of miscarriages and the diagnosis of Elle's autoimmune issues, he proceeded into the current world. This world. Elle's physical status, the likelihood she might deliver this baby—alive.

Jake entered into evidence—with a few overruled protests from Klein the ultrasound of this baby, doing somersaults. Watching the two-minute video gave me a brief reprieve of peace, and even Mom looked moved; at least she tried to make eye contact with me, which I avoided.

Jake took a long sip of water then approached the witness stand.

"Dr. Clarke, would you tell me about the phone call you received from Dr. Beaulieu on February second of this year?"

Blythe nodded once. "Yes. As I said, because of my professional relationship with Linney and Matt's position on staff, I did something I very rarely do: I gave them my home phone number. I knew that Matt was very concerned about Elle, but I also knew he wouldn't make a pest of himself. On February second, he called me in the late evening and said Elle was in trouble. She'd gone into preterm labor, and her water had broken. You see, the protocol with APS dictates we keep the woman on the blood thinner heparin for the duration of her pregnancy to prevent abnormal blood clotting. We schedule the delivery early, usually by week thirty-six, because we see a higher number of complications at the end. First we admit the mother to the hospital and take her off the blood thinners. That way, her blood will be able to clot normally during delivery. Then we induce labor once it's safe. But Elle went into labor while still on blood thinners, and she was hemorrhaging."

Blythe paused, and Jake told her to continue.

"Matt said he'd called an ambulance, and the 911 operator was trying to talk him through a normal delivery, but the baby's umbilical cord prolapsed, which in and of itself was dire."

"Dr. Clarke, I'm showing you what's marked as Respondent's Exhibit Fifty-one. Could you please identify it?" Jake asked.

"It's an obstetrical diagram of a prolapsed umbilical cord." Blythe rose and walked over to the cross-section poster now displayed on an easel. "You see, the umbilical cord supplies the baby with oxygen. When the umbilical cord comes out before the baby does, it's an obstetrical emergency because the baby can lose his lifeline. In the hospital, we would have taken Elle straight to the OR for an immediate C-section. We would have had her under anesthesia within five minutes. And even then, we might not have saved the baby.

"Matt had a little OB experience and was able to determine the baby was breech, which means the baby was coming out with his feet first instead of his head first. Another problem. Breech deliveries are more risky for a number of reasons. And finally, Elle was bleeding heavily. Matt wanted me to tell him what to do."

"What *did* you tell him?"

"He put the phone on speaker so I could talk him through it. Initially, we knew the baby was all right because the umbilical cord had a strong pulse. If we could get Elle to the hospital before the blood supply in the cord was cut off, we could save the baby. I wanted Matt to keep the baby from compressing the cord by manually pushing up on the fetus. Not exactly pretty, but he was trying. Unfortunately, when Elle had her next contraction, the baby came down into the birth canal and cut off his own oxygen supply. This was a precipitous delivery, which means very hard, very fast contractions. The pulse in the cord stopped. Matt's a smart guy. I didn't have to tell him we were losing the baby. He asked me to tell him what to do, but what we needed was a miracle."

"What did you tell him?"

"What he already knew . . . I said if they were in the hospital we'd do a cesarean section. But at home . . ." Blythe shook her head. "I told him he just had to try to get the baby out as fast as possible."

"Could you hear what was going on at the Beaulieu household?"

"Yes," Blythe said. "Elle was crying, and she told Matt that he should operate on her."

"At *home?*"

"Elle begged him to save the baby. Matt said he couldn't do it because he wasn't an OB. He couldn't operate without anesthesia. He told her that she'd bleed to death."

"How did she respond?"

"She said there were sharp knives in the kitchen and to just get the baby out—even if it killed her."

A collective gasp slipped out of the courtroom gallery. Jake's eyes widened, and honestly, if I didn't know that he'd already heard the story, I would have believed his reaction was completely unrehearsed.

"Obviously," Blythe continued, "he said no, but Elle continued to beg him to save the baby—to put the baby first."

"What did you say?"

"I was calling to Matt, but he didn't seem to hear me. He was telling Elle to calm down."

"But he didn't . . . cut her open?" Jake asked.

"No. Of course not. He told her to push. And she did. But it took nearly ten minutes to get the baby out. And then it wasn't good. And worse—because Elle was bleeding profusely."

"Was she conscious?"

"Objection," Klein said, jumping to his feet. "Your Honor, the witness was not even present. This is all hearsay."

"Could you hear what was transpiring?" the judge asked.

"Yes, sir. Your Honor. I was on speakerphone," Blythe said.

"Overruled. You may continue your questions," Wheeler said.

My mother was sniffling, swiping her cheeks from tears, raking her hair away from her face.

"Was Elle conscious?" Jake repeated.

"In and out. Matt kept telling her to try to stay awake." Blythe shook her head. "The baby had no pulse, so Matt had started CPR. The ambulance arrived within a minute or two after the delivery." She glanced in Klein's direction and added, "I could hear them."

"Could you also hear Elle's reaction while Matt was doing CPR?"

"She was crying, praying really, and she sounded very weak." Blythe picked up the water glass and took another drink. "Matt told Elle to lie down, but apparently she kept trying to get up to help Matt save the baby. That's when she passed out, the EMTs said."

"Objection," Klein said.

"I'll be happy to call the EMT as a witness, if you like, Mr. Klein," Jake said.

"Withdrawn," Klein said, looking defeated.

"You may continue," Wheeler said.

"Even though she was hemorrhaging," Jake said, "she tried to get up to try to help the baby?"

"Yes," Blythe said.

I cradled my face in my hands. The memory flooded back at me, and I found myself holding my breath again, remembering my hands wrapped around Dylan's tiny chest, compressing his sternum with my thumbs, blowing puffs of air into his lungs, looking up at the pool of blood collecting on the kitchen floor, Elle turning whiter and whiter.

Jake put his hand on my shoulder. "You need a recess? You look sick," he whispered.

"I'm okay." I didn't feel okay, but didn't want to admit that my emotions were sucking the air out of the room, that I didn't feel like I could breathe.

"Dr. Clarke, were you at the hospital when the ambulance brought Elle, Matt, and the baby into the ER?" Jake asked.

"Yes. I drove in. The roads were bad that night. Snow. I was at the hospital almost thirty minutes before the ambulance arrived."

"When the ambulance reached the hospital, what were the conditions of Elle and the baby?"

"The baby, Dylan . . ." Blythe looked at me as if to say she remembered the name we'd given him. "Dylan was dead. Elle had lost a lot of blood. An IV was started in the field, but she was in and out of consciousness."

"How premature was Dylan Beaulieu?"

"He was thirty-four weeks gestation. By definition, an infant is term between thirty-seven to forty weeks gestation, but as I said we deliver infants of mothers with APS a little preterm because we see more complications during the last few weeks. So Elle was scheduled to be induced nine days later, just before her thirty-sixth week."

"Excuse me, Doctor, but what do you mean by 'induced'?"

"We would have admitted her to the hospital, taken her off the blood thinner, and then we would have given her a medication, Pitocin, to kick-start her labor."

"Are you saying she was almost ready to deliver?"

"Yes, and he probably would have been fine if his cord hadn't prolapsed."

"Prior to the premature labor, and other than the APS—for which you were treating her—did Elle have any other complications during that pregnancy?"

"No. She complained of a little dizziness at the beginning, and a little morning sickness, a few extra bruises from the blood thinners, but otherwise she was the definition of the glowing pregnant woman."

"One more thing, Doctor; did you see Elle sign her hospital admission form stating she had no advanced health care directive?"

"No."

Jake showed Blythe a form. "This is Respondent's Exhibit Fifty-four. Can you identify it?"

"It's Elle Beaulieu's intake record to my practice."

"Where would she have said she had an advanced health care directive?"

"Here, but she left it blank."

"So she didn't say she had an advanced health care directive when she was asked?"

"To me, a blank there means no, the patient did not have an advanced directive."

"After Elle lost the baby, did you see her again?"

"Yes, for follow-up care. She said she wanted to conceive as soon as possible. I wanted her to wait six months and said it would be feasible to try one more time—if we proceeded very carefully."

"And since that follow-up visit, had she been in?"

"No, but my receptionist told me Elle had called the morning of her accident for a prenatal appointment. It was in our appointment book."

Elle knew she was pregnant?

"Nothing further." Jake sat down beside me and whispered, "You look seriously sick. I'm going to ask for a recess."

Shaking my head, I poured a glass of water.

"Would you like to cross, Mr. Klein?" Judge Wheeler asked.

Drumming his pencil on the table, Paul Klein pulled off his glasses. "Yes, Your Honor."

For nearly an hour Klein asked question after question about what could go wrong with this new pregnancy. The truth was everything could go wrong and Klein milked every potential complication.

"Dr. Clarke," Klein said, rolling an unsharpened pencil between his palms. "You said that Elle Beaulieu was in shock when she was admitted to the hospital on February second. Is that correct?"

"Yes. Hypovolemic shock from blood loss," Blythe said.

He took a document already marked into evidence and showed it to Blythe. "Do you recognize this document?" he asked.

She examined it for a moment. "It's a consent for a hysterectomy. Elle was hemorrhaging, and I thought I might need to remove her uterus to save her life, but I was able to stop the bleeding without taking her uterus."

"Who signed the consent?"

"Her husband, Dr. Beaulieu. It's customary for next of kin to give consent during an emergency."

"I see. Why didn't you ask Elle?"

"As I said, she was in shock—in and out of consciousness and not in any condition to give informed consent."

"For clarification, in Elle's condition, she would not have been able to understand the implications of what was written on this consent?"

"Probably not."

"But she did sign the hospital admission form that asked if she did or did not have an advanced health care directive?"

"I did not witness her signing that."

"But as a physician, you would not allow her to sign a consent for her own surgery. Is that correct?"

Blythe's jaw tightened. "Yes."

"I have no further questions, Your Honor," Klein said.

I looked at Jake for his reaction. His eyes were closed and his mouth tight. He turned toward me and whispered, "I still believe we can get the Supreme Court to hear the case if we fail all our other options, but this may be a long, hard ride."

Mom grabbed my arm at the recess as I rounded the corner. "I have to talk to you," she said.

"I can't. Not again. Not now." I shook her loose as a photographer's camera flashed in my face. I was already feeling dizzy, and the flash was pushing me to the brink. I made my way through the crowded corridor.

"Dr. Beaulieu, you're scheduled to testify next," someone holding a microphone called out. "How can you in good conscience say that your wife would want to be kept on life support when she had an advanced directive?"

Jake was still inside the courtroom, and even though I knew he would advise me to utter the ubiquitous "no comment," I turned toward the reporter and realized she the one who always baited me.

"My wife, the woman I love, the woman for whom I am grieving to a depth I doubt you can understand, the woman I know better than anyone else in the world—trusted me. And I would never, ever, ever do this unless I believed— My son or my daughter is still alive. Elle's son or daughter is alive. My child. And I have to fight for my child. No matter what anyone else says."

"Even if Elle didn't want it? You'd put her through hell to save—"

"Elle would want me to do whatever I could to save our child." I pushed past the reporter.

"Matt, please . . ." Mom said.

Just before I slipped into the men's room, I saw the reporter corner my mother and shove a microphone into her face.

Mom shook her finger at the reporter. "Don't you dare imply he doesn't love her."

After the recess Jake put me on the stand and asked the preliminary questions, then he offered the wedding DVD as evidence. "Your Honor, I'd like to show a short section to the court and then ask Dr. Beaulieu a few questions about it."

"Go ahead, Counselor."

Jake's baby-faced associate rolled in a flat screen on a cart, popped in our wedding DVD, and clicked it on. It was the reception, held at a banquet hall of a local inn.

I knew I was in for something when Elle's dimple appeared. She only had one, off to the right side of her chin, and it only bubbled up when she had mischief on her mind. She bent down and whispered in my ear: "Remember, I love you."

Looking as elegant as a princess draped in white silk, she lifted her champagne glass and began her toast. "I was the girl next door, the little squirt trailing behind the golden son. All right, all of the Beaulieu boys were golden sons, but Matt was the one I adored." She winked at me. "But years came and went, and four months ago when we finally decided to marry, can you believe every Beaulieu came up to me in private and asked with the most serious of tones, 'Come on, Elle, you know this is a mistake, right? I mean, Matt? No way.'

"But you know what I told them? I said, 'Yeah. I made a bet with the high school cheerleader he used to date that I could get him to the altar before she did.' Yup. I bet her a bottle of hair gel. Now—" Elle patted her very smooth straight blond hair so carefully coiffed for our wedding day and then continued: "I haven't used hair gel since the big-hair days of the eighties disappeared, so that is not the real reason I'm marrying Matt." She met my eyes. "I'm marrying him because I admire his intelligence and his compassion. I'm marrying him because he's part of me already. Because he's the one person who has always known my heart. Because I would trust him to know what I needed if I couldn't figure it out by myself. Because he loves me, and I love him. And I need him." She bent down and kissed me. People clapped.

I had pulled her onto my lap, taken her face in my hands, and held her close. I wished that moment had never ended.

Jake stopped the film but the last frame stayed on the screen. Elle sitting on my lap in her wedding dress; me, in my tux. The absolute ache of the emptiness of my arms crushed me. First down my left arm. Then in my jaw. In my chest.

Jake stepped toward the judge, blocking my view of the screen. "Matt, was that speech by Elle rehearsed?"

Jesus. I didn't feel right. I must be getting sick, but I had to get through this. I had to convince the judge. "I assume she planned on saying it, but I hadn't heard it before that moment."

"How long have you known Elle?"

I cleared my throat and tried to draw in more air. "Our entire lives, and with the exception of a couple of years after we had a huge blowout, we were close, the best of friends. Even while she was with Adam, we were always in touch and talked almost every week. Sometimes more often, sometimes less. Even when I was engaged to someone else, we talked. Elle trusted me. I trusted her." I kept staring at the screen, at her face, to keep my focus on her, not on how bad I hurt.

I didn't even realize what was happening to me; my light-headedness seemed like the grief making landfall. Then I felt a crushing weight in my chest. That's when some basic understanding clicked; I was having a heart attack. I opened and closed my left hand and stared at my wedding band. I could see my father's face. Not much older than me now. I could see him lying in his casket. Dead. Of a heart attack. And suddenly I was afraid. I needed Elle. I needed to know I would see her again. I shifted in my seat so I could see her face—one last time. God, please. Instead I collapsed, and I saw nothing but blackness.

✦ 47 ✦

Day 27

Burning ripped through me, a jolt that boiled my blood. My body spasmed as if it were being smashed up against an unknown force. Then I lay in darkness. The crushing pain in my chest was the only real attachment to the world. Then nothingness.

Stillness.

Ecchymotic light.

Tumbling.

And sound returned. *Beep, beep, beep, beep*, blending into one long, reverberating note. Panic filled me as if I were submerged in a tank of water, desperate for air.

Elle stood over me, wearing an EMT uniform, her light hair toppling over her shoulders like a halo. "Matt, you have to keep the oxygen mask on. Calm down." But her silky voice sounded low and sonorous. Maybe the tracheotomy had damaged her vocal cords. In front of my hazy vision, a burly guy took her place.

My mouth tasted of bitter aspirin. "Elle?"

"Shush, Matt. She's fine. She's in the hospital," a woman's voice said, but still not Elle's voice. It was Blythe's voice.

"She was just here. I saw her here," I said. The panic surged through my veins like a cyclone. I had to find Elle, but the pain was so densely piled on my chest I could barely move.

"It's okay, Matt. You were dreaming."

"It hurts." I squirmed around under the weight crushing me. God, my chest hurt. What happened to me? I was strapped to a gurney—in the back of an ambulance—which explained the jostling sensation. We were rolling up a Portland street. And I had an IV in the crook of my elbow and EKG leads stuck to my chest. I tried to sit up. I needed air.

Blythe said, "Stay calm. It looks like you've had a heart attack. I may have to charge you for a house call. A courthouse call." Her chuckle sounded forced and tethered to her need to soothe me.

The courtroom. Testifying. Elle's face on the screen. God. Elle. She had fallen, and I'd had a heart attack. My father. My dead father. Dad. And again, I was afraid. I wanted my wife, even though I knew she was lying in a hospital bed with a severe brain injury, wasting away. Even though I knew all of that, I still asked, "Where's Elle?" I batted at Blythe and at the burly EMT. Elle was here. I'd seen her.

The ambulance came to a halt just as an elephant landed on my chest again. I couldn't breathe. I couldn't.

For a few minutes or a few hours I lay on a gurney in the ER or in the Cardiac ICU. I don't know which or what, just that I was someplace. Narcotics eased more chest pain but muted my vision beneath a frosted blur. The heaviness in my chest bound me to life. And then it didn't. The code cart ground closer to my bedside, and I heard the frantic undertone in a familiar voice say, "Let's tube him."

And as the world around me fogged up, I realized I needed to tell someone that Elle would still want the baby to live. I needed the baby to live even if we both died.

Aside from the time I broke my leg when I was seventeen, I'd never been on the sick end of a hospital bed, and even then the hairline fracture didn't keep me in the hospital for more than a few hours. During my professional career, I had spent a lifetime of nights wandering hospital corridors, examining sick people, cutting into other people's flesh. As a family member, I'd watched my wife dying in a hospital bed for what felt like aeons.

But this view was different . . . confusing, narrow in its scope, and out of focus.

"Easy there, Matt. I'm going to remove that tube from your throat. On three, I want you to cough," some guy in a white lab coat said. "One . . . two . . . three." He yanked the endotracheal tube from my airway as I gagged, and horrible burning in my throat and the ongoing ache in my chest competed for top billing in my litany of discomforts.

I sputtered and wheezed. "What happened?"

He slipped a nasal cannula into my nose. "I'm Randall Zane, your friendly cardiothoracic surgeon. I don't believe we've met before. Here's the long and short of it: you collapsed, then you went into V-fib—or maybe the other way around. It looks like you had an anterior wall infarct, so you're hooked up to all the usual suspects: lidocaine drip, fentanyl, nitroglycerin, the works. You've been a little out of it, probably because of the fentanyl. We had to restrain you." He released the belts from my wrists. "With your family history, you should have been keeping an eye on your cholesterol. It's sky-high."

"How bad is the MI?" My voice sounded weak and tight, raspy like someone with laryngitis.

"Bad enough, but it looks like a small infarct. Your cardiac cath, though, that showed you've got a ninety-five percent blockage of your right coronary artery. You need a cabbage."

"Eat more cabbage, right." In my drug-induced stupor, I thought he was referring to how my diet affected my cholesterol.

"No, Matt, a C-A-B-G. It's pronounced 'cabbage,' but that's an acronym for 'coronary artery bypass graft.'"

"Oh, shit. I know. I went to med school. I'm groggy as hell. What are you giving me through this IV?"

"Again, it's the fentanyl. You've been a little out of it." He chuckled. "I promise I won't tell your colleagues you've forgotten the basics." Then he was suddenly more serious. "We're taking you to the OR in a couple of hours, and I'll fix you right up."

"Where's Elle? Does she know I'm here?"

There's a kind of silence in the pity that falls over the face of a doctor when he knows something his patient does not. I know; I've worn that expression.

"What is it?" Fear coursed through my veins again. "Elle? Where is she?"

A long pause preceded his answer. "I don't know your wife's condition. You're in CICU. Cardiac ICU."

And then it hit me again. Elle. She couldn't come to me. God, she was in the ICU, in another area of the hospital. But the part of Elle that counted, the part that was my friend, the part that made me feel whole and human and male, that part of her no longer existed, and my aloneness nearly swallowed me. I needed her more than I ever had, and she was gone.

"I need her," I said aloud. Like a boy crying for something he could never have. And I wept, all my inhibitions pounded into submission.

From the corner of the room, I heard my mother's voice. "Oh, Matty, honey." Then she was by my side and cradling my IV-bearing hand. "I know you want Elle; I know, but you have to rest."

"It's bad," I said. "Elle. Oh. I can't. Maybe we were supposed to die together. Maybe—"

"Don't you dare give up." She set her jaw firm, although I noticed she was trembling.

My mother seemed no more real to me than Elle did when I saw her in the ambulance— It was as if my mother, too, might disappear, or at the very least step out of my line of vision. As powerless as I felt, it would take no more than that for everyone I knew to slip away.

"I need to see Elle," I said.

"I'll check on her."

"No, don't you go—near her." My voice cracked as I tried to get out of bed. The baby. Mom couldn't be the only one speaking for Elle now.

"Matt, honey, listen to me. I understand how much you love her. If she could be here, she would."

"Alice, the diary about Alice." I began gasping for air.

Mom cupped my chin so I would close my mouth and get the oxygen flowing into my nose. "Breathe, honey. Deep breaths. It's all right. I understand. No one will take Elle off life support. No one. That's what I wanted to talk about with you—at the courthouse— after Blythe testified. I think I understand what you've been trying to tell me. How Elle was with Dylan. But right now, come on, just breathe through the cannula; you have to get better. Then we can talk it through. Together. We'll figure out what Elle would want, and we'll work it out together."

I pushed away Mom's hand because my air hunger was growing fierce.

"You'd better leave, Mrs. Beaulieu. I don't want him agitated," Zane said.

"Don't—" I tried to yell, *Don't go, Mom*, but I was hoarse from the tube, and the only sound that came out was a pathetic squeak.

I was a frightened little boy with my painful heart pounding inef-fectually. I was cowering from what my powerful mother might do and for what she might now understand. I was crying for my mother to hold my hand while I died. "Help me. Elle. God, Elle."

"Easy, Matt," Zane said. "Let us take care of you, and we'll check on your wife. I'll see if someone from ICU can give you an update." He looked up at a nurse. "Let's get him on a non-rebreather mask."

The nurse slipped my cannula out and put an oxygen mask over my face.

Mom, I thought, *come back*. I drew oxygen and stopped thrash-ing as my mother tiptoed out the door and past the nurses' station, glancing back at me. I lifted the mask. "Blythe Clarke. I need to talk to Elle's doctor."

"I know Blythe. She's a good doctor," Zane said. "I'm sure she's taking very good care of your wife." Then he leaned down and spoke conspiratorially to me. "Listen. I've heard you have a one-track mind, that you're very focused, so I want you to focus on this: relax. Let me fix that heart of yours. Now use the oxygen mask or I'm going to have to reintubate you."

I pulled up the mask. "I can't have surgery right now. I have to see Elle. She's pregnant."

He put it back on me. "This can't wait. I'll see you in the OR."

"Stop. Give me a second." I tried to break through the fog of the drugs, shaking my head like a punch-drunk fighter. "I don't want the surgery."

Zane's patronizing expression said, *Idiot*. "Given your reaction to the medication, you may not be capable of giving *informed* con-sent. I'll ask your mother to act on your behalf."

"No. Not her. I want to see my attorney, Jake Sutter."

"Attorney?" Zane said. Lawyers drive the fear of malpractice into the pocketbooks of doctors. Even in my dopey haze I knew that much.

"I need to write an advanced directive and make sure no one can challenge it. And I *have* to see my wife. Roll me down to ICU. Treat me in ICU. I have to see her." I needed to make sure Elle was still alive, because if she wasn't alive, if the baby wasn't alive, I didn't have any reason to live.

His lips thinned in disapproval.

"If you don't take me down there, and I know you can do it, I'll check myself out against medical advice."

"That would be stupid. Besides, you wouldn't make it to the door."

"So humor me," I said as I had trouble ordering my words into a cogent sentence. "I may be—dying, but I need to see her before—you cut my chest open."

I floated in and out of sleep; my sense of time befuddled from the narcotics they'd given me for chest pain. A hand jostled my arm. "Matt? It's Blythe. Your doctor said you wanted to know about Elle before your surgery."

My vision was not wholly focused, like looking through a block of ice, but the pink ribbon clung to the side of the white blur of Blythe's hair. "How is she?" I asked.

"The same. Fairly stable."

"Her kidneys?"

"You need to stop worrying about her."

"Is she worse, Blythe?"

"Not worse. If we can pull Elle through this, that baby is going to need *you*."

I drew oxygen through the tubing in my nose. "You saved my life."

"First time I've done CPR in years. You're lucky I keep my Advanced Life Support certification current. You're also lucky they had an AED in the courthouse. We had to shock you."

"Thank you, but no matter what happens to me, please, please, save the baby." The baby. Somersaulting in Elle's belly. Kicking, although she'd never feel it.

"Listen to me. You're the one who has to take care of the baby."

After Blythe left, I fell into dreams about Elle on the widow's walk, staring up at the night sky. I dreamed about holding her. I dreamed about long ago when we were children swimming in the river by her grandfather's farm, and I had nightmares about her turning her back on me when I betrayed her. I kept pleading, "Come back."

If Jake Sutter looked any paler, I'd have gotten off the bed so he could lie down in my stead. He had never even come in to see Elle, but there he was at the foot of my hospital bed.

"Ah, how is the, ah, chest pain?" Jake swiped his forehead.

The drugs tempered the ache. I drew a deep breath through my nasal cannula. "Tolerable. My mother said something about working this out with Elle. But I don't know if she's just saying that because—"

"Because you dropped dead in the courthouse."

"I didn't die."

Jake cocked his head. "Close enough for me. Until your, ah, crisis is over, we shouldn't assume anything, but you're right, she might stop the litigation."

"You aren't convinced?"

He pressed his thin lips together. "No. She's your mother. She wants you to live."

"I need to make certain she doesn't have any legal rights over my health care."

"I don't think you have to worry that she'll pull the plug on you."

I shook my head. "No, but she might try to have me declared incompetent or something. She's my next of kin under the circumstances."

"That would take a judge, but all right. For the sake of your peace of mind, you'd prefer one of your brothers?"

"Things can go wrong in the OR. This is major surgery. I'll probably be walking out of here in a few days, but if I can't, my brothers won't stand up to her. I want to set up an advanced directive, and I want you to be the decision-making agent."

"Me? You want *me* to make *medical* decisions for *you?*" Jake rubbed his temples. "In a hospital?"

I nodded.

"Are you sure you wouldn't prefer a family member?" He was shaking like a man about to be hanged.

"You can stop my mother from taking Elle off life support."

"Designating me with your medical power of attorney won't give me the power to stop your mother from acting on Elle's living will. Or on the one Adam Cunningham produced. Good Lord." He muttered something unintelligible. "Legally, that's a separate issue from an advanced directive." His eyes grew a bit wider. "But you could give Elle's father your power of attorney. Then, God forbid, if something happened to you—he is her father, so he has standing and he could fight to keep Elle on life support until the baby is born."

A baby I might never see. That Elle would never see. "Just until the baby is born. Afterward, you have to make sure Hank lets Elle go in peace."

The Mass has ended. Go in peace, flitted through my mind like a chanting chorus.

Jake lowered his eyes and nodded. "In case something happens to you, you should make a new will, name an executor, a guardian for the baby, and set up a trust. And I'll serve you in any capacity you think is appropriate. But, Matt, I gotta tell you: *don't die.*"

"My father died from a heart attack." My father, dead and cold in his open casket. I could be as dead and cold, leaving behind not four grown sons, but a newborn one. I couldn't leave my kid alone.

"That doesn't mean you will," Jake said.

It might. I had to make certain someone would take care of the baby, would fight for him or her. "My brother Mike and his wife would take care of the baby—if I die. I have a will already. And we made Hank the executor because he's good with money. He can have my power of attorney, or whatever it takes. I know Hank will fight for the baby."

"I'll write it all up." Jake glanced away from me. And unless the drugs were distorting my vision, he was tearing up. I had to be hallucinating.

A nurse entered my room. "You're having more runs of trigeminy, Matt, so your cardiologist wants you to rest."

"What's trigeminy?" Jake asked.

"An arrhythmia," I said. "Irregular heartbeats." And it wasn't good. Damn, I was in trouble.

Before I could protest, the nurse injected my IV port with a syringe. "I'm giving you a sedative," she said.

In less than the time it took to wrap my mouth around the words "I need to finish," the flush of the drug was running through my system and I was spooning around my Elle. I was dreaming with her head nesting in the crook of my arm and her soft hair brushing against my face. I hungered for her and pulled her closer. We were in a hospital bed together, a Salvador Dalí–like bed, warped and wide. In my drug-induced confusion, it made sense that they'd put us together. It made sense that we would heal better this way.

I tried to root myself. Was this the ICU or the CICU? It was neither. We were in our own house, in the attic with the doors to the widow's walk opened wide as the fall air circled us, ripe with the tidal river flow.

"Don't try to make sense of it," Elle whispered. "This is our time. For all time."

"I died?" Strangely, I didn't feel afraid. If I was with her—

"No," she said. "You're sedated. Your mom probably put them up to it. To keep you from having Jake—never mind any of that. You're here, with me, and I miss you."

I pushed back her hair from her face, memorizing her like this again. She was alive, and for weeks I'd only seen her becoming more and more still. "Are you a ghost?"

"You don't believe in wraiths, or ghosts, or anything you can't see."

"I believe in you," I said.

"You're dreaming, sweet little dreams. I'm here. You're here. But—" She sat up abruptly and the sheet slipped down to her waist. She was nude, noticeably pregnant. "Did you hear that?"

I listened. Hospital sounds.

Someone said, "Clear."

"They're defibrillating someone," she said.

"Me?" I was afraid, but less afraid because she was holding me. I could stay with her.

Her eyes shifted back and forth. "No. You're all right. You're looped on whatever they gave you, but that's probably for the best. Your sense of self-preservation has taken a nosedive. It's funny. You always said I was the reckless one."

"Not really reckless. You didn't value your safety as much as I valued you."

"Hmm . . . I never took all that big of a risk."

"You shouldn't have gone up on that ladder. You knew you were pregnant."

"You've got a point there, but there's a certain poetic irony. I walked in space just fine. On Earth, I fell off a ladder. I'm not so glamorous." She kissed my forehead, the tip of my nose, my mouth.

I ran my hands over her body, the swell of her breasts, her abdomen. Her belly so much rounder with our child than it had been just moments before. "I want this baby to make it," I said.

"She has a name."

"She? Do you know something I don't?"

"I know everything you don't." Elle smirked. "It's a girl."

"A girl? Celina?"

"Not Celina. This one is our hope, a miracle, a reason for you to keep believing. Put your hand here. She's kicking. They can't feel her yet, but you can. You saw the ultrasound. She's alive. Doing somersaults. And no one will fight for her if you don't live."

"Peep—you let me feel the baby kick."

"Of course I did. This is our baby."

"Our baby. Yes. Why didn't you tell me about the advanced directive? Why didn't you name me?"

Elle shrugged. "You're off topic." She pressed my palm to her belly, which suddenly looked full term. I felt the kick again. It was so real, so certain.

"She's the only part of me that's alive, Matt. She's *all* that matters."

I squeezed my eyes shut. Elle mattered. To me. Elle mattered to me, and I couldn't let her out of my sight. Not ever again. Not even to blink. When I opened my eyes wide, Elle was holding a newborn baby, all swaddled in pink. "Don't you want to know her name?"

The baby had white-blond hair and Elle's pointy chin.

"Her name's Hope," I said.

"Do you want to hold your daughter?" Elle beamed at me.

"Yes. God, yes." I reached for the baby, our baby.

"Then you have to live." And just like that, they both melted away.

✦ 48 ✦

Days 32 Through 35

I couldn't bear witness to what occurred over the next five days although I've read my chart. In simple terms, I did my damnedest to die. I arrested again before they got me to the OR. I hemorrhaged. They even had trouble restarting my heart when I came off bypass.

Did I see a loving, white light? No. I saw Elle, a dream, a hallucination, or endorphins flooding my brain. Whatever it was didn't matter. I'd never believed in bullshit like that before, but now I wasn't so certain.

Sometimes it's a matter of what a man chooses to believe. Father Meehan called it faith and my faith was always in Elle. I didn't see any reason to change course. I wanted to believe in her and that we'd had a way to say good-bye.

Father Meehan came to visit me, and when I told him about seeing Elle, he asked why I assumed it wasn't real.

Because—these things didn't happen.

He reminded me my Confirmation name was Thomas, the

Doubter, and said I'd chosen aptly. "But remember, Matt, in the end Thomas believed. He was the one who first proclaimed Jesus as 'my Lord and my God.'"

Sure, I thought with a heavy dose of skepticism, but maybe, just maybe, there was something to the smoke and mirrors.

Dr. Zane told me to call him Randall as he removed the dressing from the zipperlike scar over my sternum. "You're good for another forty years or hundred thousand miles, whichever comes first."

"Only a hundred thousand? I put that on my car in three or four years," I said.

He snickered. "Then this go-round, you'd better watch the kind of oil you put in your engine, unsaturated and no trans fats."

"Great, a comedian with a scalpel."

"Yes. I kept everyone in stitches while massaging your heart. Stitches, get it?"

"Okay." I laughed, holding my incision. "Now that is painful."

"The entire surgical team earned our fee, keeping you alive, Beaulieu."

"And I appreciate it," I said.

My heart attack and subsequent near death made headlines, something I should have become accustomed to but wasn't. As if I'd deliberately added to the drama, some people condemned me and others drew me as a tragic hero. Although neither of us tried to kill ourselves, I was suddenly Romeo to Elle's Juliet. But all I knew was that when I regained consciousness, Elle had woken up.

She hadn't really awoken, but that's what the papers said. That's what the Pro-Lifers contended. And that was what Hank believed at first. "I told you my little girl would come out of this."

Not exactly. She started to breathe on her own again, but her gag reflex was still gone. She still had no corneal reflex, and she didn't respond to painful stimuli. She was in a different kind of persistent vegetative state, more like the one that made it to the press with Terri Schiavo seemingly smiling.

Elle, however, did not smile, not even once. I couldn't say she grimaced or that she appeared to be in pain, yet it was harder to look at her in this condition when she appeared to be conscious. I wanted her to respond to me; the nonneurosurgeon part of me still expected her to respond to me.

"But," Hank said.

I shook my head from my own hospital bed. "Elle is still gone. She isn't suffering. And the baby has a better shot now. This is good."

Hank turned to my mother. "Linney, don't you think it's possible Elle might continue to improve? You changed your mind."

Mom averted her gaze and shook her head, too. "I know Elle's your baby, Hank, but no. We have to accept that she's gone, but we're going to try to save your grandbaby."

"Your grandchild, too, Mom," I said.

"That's right. This baby is all of ours."

For two days the nurses let me see Elle on a webcam, an idea Jake came up with. Thank God for Jake. He had soldiered through the hospital days, signing consents on my behalf, making health care decisions about things that went well beyond any lawyerly duties he anticipated when he signed on.

Once I was well enough to leave intensive care for a telemetry unit where they could monitor my heart rhythm constantly, they moved Elle into the same room with me. She was doing well enough that she no longer required ICU either.

Always bossy, my mother insisted it would be stressful for me to be in the same room with Elle, but it wasn't. I could look across and see her, then be assured that she and the baby were safe and secure because they were close. I could finally sleep.

* * *

Keisha snapped the green-and-brown quilt in the air, and it settled over me like a loon landing on a northern lake. "There," she said.

I didn't know quite how to respond to the gesture. When Keisha brought the other quilt in for Elle, I knew it was a way for her to do something when there was nothing to be done. "Thank you," I said.

She nodded, barely looking my way. I sensed something was bothering her, but I was three and a half hours into my pain medication, I'd just finished walking the length of the corridor twice, and the ache was escalating. In thirty minutes I could ask for more. I closed my eyes for a minute, longing for the reprieve of sleep and figuring Keisha was here to visit Elle, not me. Besides, the burden of small talk fell on the visitor.

"Will the baby be all right now?" she asked suddenly.

Or her question felt sudden because I had dozed off. "I don't know," I mumbled, rubbing my eyes.

"I need a happy ending," she said. "I'm sorry. It's just . . ."

"What's wrong?" I asked, raising the head of my hospital bed.

"Nothing." She feigned a thin smile, then, with an uncomfortable twist, she added, "Guy doesn't want to try to have a baby anymore. He says enough is enough. And he doesn't want to adopt."

The four of us, Elle and me, Keisha and Guy, had founded something of a wannabe-parents-lonely-hearts club, although mostly Elle and Keisha commiserated while Guy and I talked about whatever sport was in season in front of the TV. But he said he wanted kids, and I was a little surprised he'd given up.

"Sorry to hear that," I said. I blinked a few times while I tried to come up with words Elle might say to make Keisha feel better.

"Elle told me you kept pushing her to consider adopting a child," Keisha said.

"After Dylan, yeah." I looked over at Elle. "I didn't want to lose her. Maybe that's what Guy is telling you. He doesn't want you to have to pump any more fertility drugs into your system or to be disappointed every goddamned month. In our case, every time Elle miscarried. Guy doesn't need you to produce a kid. He just needs you. At least that was how I felt. I wanted to forget the losses. And if we adopted . . . but . . ."

"But what?" Keisha asked.

"The wait. It can take years. And birth mothers change their minds sometimes after they see the babies—pretty often, we heard. I just wanted her safe. I wanted to be happy again."

"Did you ever tell her that?" Keisha asked.

I pictured Elle the day before her fall, standing on the lawn. She said we should make a baby. *I wish we hadn't argued.*

"I tried to," I told Keisha, "but I don't know if I said it right. I don't know if she was listening—the right way. Next time you talk to Guy, listen to what he means. He'll listen, too. You can work it out. Elle and I would have worked it out."

Jake entered my room with a little more color in his face. "The doctors are releasing you tomorrow."

"I know. Now that I'm semiliving again, they tell me these things. I appreciate that you acted on my behalf, though."

"You'll get my bill." He snickered. "Don't look so worried. I'm not charging you for acting as your health care agent. That I did as a friend."

And I wondered, were we friends?

"You think I'd spend the better part of a week walking the halls of a hospital for a regular client? Only for a friend or family," he said.

Maybe I had suffered hypoxic brain damage during my multiple cardiac arrests because I could swear Jake was reading my mind.

I swung my still-sore, vein-harvested legs over the side of the bed. "Okay, *friend.*"

He rolled his eyes. "The point is, once they discharge you, you shouldn't be alone, and the farmhouse is too remote."

"Probably not for a couple of weeks, anyway. I'm trying to figure it out. Mike offered to let me move in while I recuperate, but he's in a three-bedroom with four kids. My mother wants me to stay with her, but I don't see it. I'm still pissed. Not as pissed since she withdrew her participation in the case, but—"

"You can stay with us. In fact, Yvette insists. We have a guest room on the first floor, and we're two minutes from the hospital. No arguments. It's all set."

"Seriously?" I asked. A guest room in Jake's nineteenth-century Georgian would be considerably more comfortable than sleeping on my nephews' bunk beds even if it required me to make small talk with Yvette. "Thank you."

"Of course I'm charging you rent." He winked. "Are you up to talking about the case?"

My head jerked up. "But my mother dropped the suit, right?"

Jake nodded but grimaced. "I have bad news. Adam Cunningham has produced the original of his advanced directive. And Christopher is still insisting that Elle be taken off life support."

"Oh, shit."

"Yeah, so we continue on. Cunningham has filed a complaint. I haven't heard who's going to represent him."

"Not Klein?"

"No. Klein is out. It would be a conflict because he represented your mother, who is now siding with you." Jake began to whisper. "But since Elle's breathing now, it becomes much more difficult to withdraw her life support. Death from dehydration is slow and inhumane."

Tension seeped into my muscles, burning my already raw flesh. That Elle had started breathing on her own made the baby's survival more likely, but it also meant Elle could live on in a vegetative state indefinitely—against her wishes. It meant even if the baby lived, even if, God forbid, the baby died, Elle could linger forever.

"Are you okay?" Jake asked. "Should I call a doctor?"

"I'm fine. Have you found Elle's diaries?" I asked.

"No one's seen them," Jake said.

"Damn. I swear I left them in her hospital room. When's the next court date?"

Jake looked at his Rolex. "In an hour."

"What?" I couldn't get discharged and to court in an hour.

"Wheeler strongly discourages you from walking into his courtroom *ever again*. Well, maybe not ever, but until you're well, so don't get any ideas. When you went down on the floor, Wheeler froze. The press corps noticed and mentioned something about 'his impotence on the bench,' which was absurd. It had nothing to do with his competence as a judge. He was just taken aback."

"I'm sure you could relate."

"Yeah, but I managed to dial 911 while Blythe and your mother took over pounding on your chest." Jake looked at me as if I'd come back from the dead, which, in a manner of speaking, I had. He shook his head. "I have to leave for court."

"I want to come with you."

"In your dreams. I'll report back. I'm putting Father Meehan on the stand. You know what he's going to say. After that, I'll file the petition for fetal guardianship. I'm hoping the judge will give that its due consideration, that he won't dismiss it outright. But if he does dismiss it, we've got grounds for an appeal on constitutional grounds. We're looking for time, time for the baby to grow. We only need three months, and I can't imagine that anyone would turn off her life support with a viable baby on board."

"Three months isn't enough." The baby needed more time or she could suffer from a million health issues of her own—blindness, lung problems, brain damage.

"Elle will be twenty-five weeks pregnant."

"That's still extremely premature."

"That's why the judge will wait. We hope."

Hope—I was clinging to mine with more determination than ever.

After Jake left, the evening-shift nurse, Ava, took my vital signs, listened to my lungs, and checked my wounds. The visible ones.

Ava was a five-foot-tall powerhouse. Although my patients didn't often land on the telemetry floor, from time to time I found myself making rounds on a patient who warranted a bed on that unit. She and I had met on entirely different terms. She was formidable and reminded me of Elle in some ways, but not in her appearance; Ava, like Elle, exuded confidence and still managed to be as warm as melted butter.

"Am I going to live?" I was half serious, half sarcastic, with a pinch of challenge thrown in.

"Looks like it. The question is whether or not you're going to sleep. Rumor has it lack of sleep over in ICU was part of what landed you in this situation."

"High cholesterol. Familial."

She glanced over at Elle. "Not to mention a little stress." Ava set about assessing Elle, doing her vital signs, changing her trach dressing. "So, Elle is sleeping like a little lamb. What are we going to do about you tonight?"

Elle wasn't exactly sleeping; however she did appear to be at rest—whatever that meant when you don't wake up—when you were never going to wake up. At least she wasn't in pain.

"You have an order for a sleeping pill if you need it for bedtime. Or I can give you Percocet," Ava said.

"I'll take the pain pills. Wouldn't mind having the Percocet now, actually," I said.

"And I had one other thought. What if, just for tonight, I pushed the two beds together. Bet you're used to sharing the bed with your wife. Would you sleep better that way?"

I had a momentary urge to hug Ava. "Oh, yes," I said. "Most definitely, yes. Thank you."

She unlocked the wheels on Elle's bed with a kick and rolled her near me. I took Elle's hand in mine. "Peep, I'm right here." I slipped my hand onto her belly. "Right here, kiddo. Dad's right here."

There is an interlude in the hospital after visiting hours are over and before the night shift arrives when there is quiet. Not silence. Quiet. An occasional call bell rings. Footsteps continue to pad up and down the corridors, but there is a calm certainty, ever briefly, that for now Death is not in charge.

I was sleeping in such conditions, lulled by Elle's proximity and by the dampened awareness of the narcotic analgesic. I ignored the disinterested and distant clinical sounds. I didn't hear Christopher enter the room or pull the squeaky chair over to his sister's side of the bed. In fact, after I finally awoke, he told me he'd been there for hours and that he'd come long before visiting hours had ended so we could talk. But I slept, and slept restfully with Elle close. He allowed me that quiet time. For that, I was grateful.

Christopher possessed one gift his sister did not, a sense of pitch. He was singing a lullaby to Elle. Softly. It was one I remembered their mother singing, *Too-ra-loo-ra-loo-ral. Too-ra-loo-ra-li.* His voice possessed a gentle tone, rich and mellow.

I opened my eyes and searched the near darkness. Only a slit of light broke from the bathroom.

"Hey, Matt. How are you feeling?"

I grunted and reached for a glass of water on the over-the-bed table. Hospital air is directly imported from the Sahara.

He circled the bed, took the cup, and bent the straw to make it easier for me to drink.

What the hell? "Thanks," I said. "What are you doing here?"

"Visiting Elle. And visiting you."

"I'm trying to sleep."

He nodded. "And I let you. I was thinking about leaving you a note, but since you're up now, I just wanted to tell you I'm glad you're okay."

I didn't respond. I had nothing to say.

"I wanted to talk to you about something," Chris said.

"You can talk to my lawyer. I'm not in any condition for a fight."

"I don't want to fight, and we don't need lawyers. You almost died, and even if we're on opposite sides of this, I want you to be okay. You're my brother-in-law. Linney said you're going home tomorrow."

"They're discharging me, yeah."

"I wanted to let you know I brought Elle's car back to your house today. And I didn't want you to go home and see it, not expecting to. I mean, it might be weird. I keep going to call her, and then I remember I can't. It hurts, you know? I don't want to stress you out any more than I have to. The car's at your house. I just wanted to warn you for when you get home."

"Yeah, sure. But I'm not going back to the farm. Not yet. I'm planning to stay with Jake for a while."

"That's good, I guess. By the way, I heard you were looking for the duffel bag that was in Elle's room."

I pushed the button on the rail to raise the head of my bed. "Do you have any idea where it is?"

"I got it at home. You had the heart attack, and one of Elle's nurses said it was yours. I took it for safekeeping."

"Did you look inside?" I asked.

"Yeah. Elle's diaries."

"Did you read them?"

Christopher shrank a little and snickered. "I wanted to, but I couldn't. You know, when we were kids, she used to keep a lock-box under her bed so I couldn't get to those diaries, so no, I didn't read 'em. You've been looking through them, though, huh?"

"Yeah, I am. I need answers. And I miss her, Chris. I really miss her." I reached across and touched her hand.

"Me, too," he said. For a minute or two Christopher leaned against the window ledge and stared across the darkened room at Elle. Then he looked at me again. "You know, when you collapsed in the courtroom, God, all I could think was, not you, too. You've always been like my big brother." He stopped talking and took a long breath in and then exhaled, just as slowly.

"You're wrong about Elle, Matt. But I don't want anything to happen to you." He scratched the back of his head. "That's all I came to say. Get well. I'll let you sleep."

He crossed the room to Elle's side of the bed and kissed her forehead before walking out the door. "I'll drop off the duffel bag."

"Chris?" I called out.

He stopped and turned around.

"What do I need to do to convince you?"

He shook his head. "You can't."

✦ 49 ✦

Day 36

Jake drew the curtain so the sunlight wouldn't hit me in the eyes as I sat on the edge of my hospital bed. "Adam Cunningham is one arrogant, self-important idiot. He's representing himself. Unfortunately, he's also pretty bright. Doesn't know the law—at all—but he seems to have a facility for deductive reasoning."

"What happened?" I asked.

"I'll give you the short version," Jake said. "After Father Meehan's testimony, I submitted the petition for fetal guardianship to Judge Wheeler, who then hauled me and Adam into chambers. I cited religious freedom. And Wheeler, taking pity on Adam and his lack of legal expertise, cited no existing statutes for guardianship of a nonperson. I cited the Unborn Victims of Violence Act of 2004. I cited the First Amendment. I listed the states which will not remove a pregnant woman's life support. Wheeler's going to take it under advisement. I wouldn't hold my breath, but we can appeal and, if necessary, we've got grounds, as I've said all along, for a cert petition. This could be very interesting."

"I don't care about interesting," I said, lacing my Nikes. I was grateful my brother brought in clothes for me to wear home from the hospital, but bending over to tie my shoes hurt like hell. I needed old-man loafers. "All I care about is—"

"Yeah, I know. This baby. Let me ask you this, when you get some medical mystery, and you have to figure out how to fix it, don't you find it *more interesting* than, I don't know, your run-of-the-mill appendectomy?"

"I don't do appendectomies. But if I did, I wouldn't tell my patient with a teratoma growing out of his cerebellum that I thought his case was more interesting than a routine appendicitis case. Did you ever hear of the Chinese curse 'May you live in interesting times'? I don't want interesting."

Looking duly chastised, Jake leaned up against the windowsill. "Whatever the heck that means—tera-whatever thing—point conceded."

"Did you talk to Carol, about the attorney general?"

"Yes. She told me to instruct you to get well."

"And?"

"The attorney general and I had a scintillating ten-minute conversation. It should come as no surprise that Elle's tragedy is a hot topic down in D.C. in both conservative and liberal circles. Nevertheless, there is nothing we can do there until we've exhausted our legal options on this level. And the appeals level. Maybe not even then."

"Do you think Wheeler will go for fetal guardianship, or that the Supreme Court will hear it?" I asked.

"Hard to say. I hope so. I think so."

"When do I finish my testimony?"

"I'm not sure I want to put you on the stand again. Who's going to pay me if you die?" He shot me a grin and replaced it with the stern face of a schoolmarm. "Seriously, I don't want you to testify again."

"I need to tell the judge what was in Elle's letters."

"I know. But you collapsed on the stand, Matt. Instead of you, I'm putting Keisha up this afternoon, and she's quite compelling."

"I want a chance to tell him my side."

"How about you do a little recuperating first?"

After a wheelchair ride to the front of the hospital, followed by a two-minute drive to Jake's, he escorted me up the three steps, cradling my elbow as if I were an invalid. The irony that I was taking my first steps toward the future by moving in with my old college roommate didn't escape me. Still, I had to admit that the quality of his digs had vastly improved.

"Would you stop looking at me like I'm going to drop dead?" I said as we entered the two-story marble-floored foyer.

"Only if you don't drop dead *again*, you idiot."

His wife, Yvette, said, "Jake, don't say things like that."

"It's okay, Vette," Jake said. "He understands what I mean."

She looked at him as if she were appalled and then back at me. "Don't listen to him, Matt. Can I offer you something to drink?"

"No, I'm good. Thanks for opening your home."

"Oh, please . . ." she said as she swept out of the foyer.

Jake's gaze followed her. "She has one sister and no brothers. Her family never bickers, never even banters. Ever. Now sit on the sofa, and let's talk." Jake set his briefcase on the Louis XIV side table.

Instead, I chose a chair with arms because I didn't think I could get up off the low seat where he directed me.

"Elle's doctors want to discharge her, put her into a nursing home," Jake said.

"Yeah. I'm not happy about that. I'd like to take her home, instead."

"You can't do that. You're not in any condition to take care of yourself, much less her. Any thoughts about an appropriate place?"

The idea of a nursing home made me cringe. All I could think of was the smell, the bedsores, and, too often, the neglect. "I'll work on it."

He studied me. "Are you okay?" he asked. "Because if you die in my house, my property value will nose-dive."

"I'm fine. Thanks for the concern. If I feel any chest pain, I'll try to make it over the threshold."

✳ 50 ✳

Day 37

Mom showed up at Jake's door, carrying a suitcase full of my clothes and literature on three local nursing homes. Hank was a step behind her, muttering and grumbling. A number of people had thought my mother and Hank would hook up after Dad died, but the idea was absurd. Dad and Hank were great friends. Mom and Alice were great friends. Mom and Hank were more connected by circumstance.

"How'd you get into my house?" I asked Mom, trying to take the suitcase from her.

"Oh, no. Don't even try it. You're not lifting a heavy bag." She pulled it aside and nosed her way around Jake's downstairs until she found the room off the kitchen, a onetime maid's room, converted for my sake into a guest room.

She set down my suitcase, tossed the nursing-home brochures on the bed, and began opening drawers, loading them with my underwear, socks, and clothing. I paced, albeit more of a shuffle than my usual rapid gait. "You didn't tell me how you got into my house, Mom."

"I have a key."

"You gave me your key."

"I gave you *one* key. I had another." She offered me a wink.

"How come I never noticed what an interfering busybody you were prior to this?" I asked.

"Having a key to your house doesn't mean I ever used it to check out things or that I ever imposed myself on you or Elle. I don't know how or why I got a second key, but it's a good thing I did because someone has to look after the place right now, and you need clean clothes."

"Screw the house key," Hank said. "Let's decide which nursing home is best for Elle."

"That will depend on where there's an available bed," Mom said.

"Not necessarily," Hank said.

I dropped into a chair and grunted. The pain burned from my incision to the muscles down my leg. I rubbed my stitches, feeling how little held me together. "What do you mean, 'not necessarily'?"

"I've been thinking about this since the doctors took her off the respirator and said we would eventually be able to move her out of the hospital. Nursing-home beds are scarce, right?"

"Exactly. That's why we can't be picky," Mom said.

"We can be picky," Hank said. "There's a shortage of nursing-home beds in Portland. I'm a businessman. If I were running a nursing home, I'd be looking to expand."

"I'm not following you," I said. "We don't have time to build a new nursing home."

"No, not a new one. I'll offer to finance an addition." Hank waved his hand like a magic wand.

"But that won't help us—" I said.

"It will. Not the addition itself, but if the owner's shrewd, he'll give us what we want in exchange."

"Which is?" Mom asked.

"The stipulation will be that at least one room—not one bed—one *room* will be made available for Elle for as long as she needs it. The last thing we need is to have to tiptoe around a roommate. Besides, after your heart attack, you can't be camping out in a chair day and night. And at my age, I can't do it for months on end either. So I will stipulate that Elle gets a private room for as long as she requires one. There's always some turnover in nursing homes. She moves to the top of the wait list. And as a second room becomes available, we will get that one, too. Two side-by-side rooms in exchange for a new wing."

Mom and I exchanged a look. I couldn't speak for her, but I was thinking that Hank had lost his mind.

"I'll buy the place if I have to," he said.

Mom's mouth hung open.

"That's a very generous plan," I said. "But do you have any idea how much something like that costs, not to mention the regulations involved?"

"Of course I do. I broker a hell of a lot of commercial real estate. These days that's most of my business. I've even sold a few nursing homes. Now, which one of these places has the best reputation?" he asked.

Mom glanced at the brochures on the bed and narrowed her eyes skeptically. "I know you've been successful, but—"

"She's my daughter, Linney. I can afford to take care of her. Believe me." Hank stood a little taller as if to show he was man enough to keep his word.

"But—" Mom tried to argue.

"It won't even break me, Lin," Hank said.

Mom nodded, but I could see she was choked up. We were all riding close to the edge of emotional overload. Even a sense of relief could drive us to give in to a catharsis of tears. Even my pragmatic mother. She pointed at one of the brochures. "This one's close to the hospital."

"And it has excellent rehab facilities," I said. Elle would never recover, but a good physical therapist could help prevent complications from immobility, and Elle did not need *any more* complications.

"No one there probably knows diddly-doo about OB," Mom added.

"So, that's where you come in," Hank said, leaning back in his chair. "You spread the word that we need a few good OB nurses to moonlight for a few months. We'll pay them double what they would get anywhere else if they will do private duty for Elle. We want to give her round-the-clock care."

"Great idea," I said. "But insurance won't pay—"

"Matt, for a brain surgeon, sometimes you're a little slow. You think I watched the real estate boom without investing in property myself? I have money. Trust me. It's the least of our problems."

My eyes locked on my father-in-law's. I couldn't believe this, and yet I knew that if he said he could do it, he had the means.

"How fast can you make it happen?" I asked. "They want to discharge her in the next couple days."

"Give me a few hours, and I'll let you know." Hank stood in apparent preparation to head out the door. "Let me go do my job and hope it's as simple as I anticipate. All you have to do is rest up so you're well enough to do midnight feeds in a few months." He clapped my back, obviously forgetting I'd recently had my chest split open.

My eyes filled with pain and with gratitude for his optimism. "Thank you."

But I knew we still had to deal with Adam and Christopher. And I whispered one more prayer that Elle would not miscarry.

✦ 51 ✦

Day 38

I yanked open the duffel bag's zipper.

"I didn't take out any of the diaries, if that's what you're thinking." Christopher played with the Indian shutters in Jake's study. "Man, if Jake ever sells this place, I want the listing. I love the architectural details. Look at that crown molding. It's gotta be eighteen inches thick. Where is Jake anyway?"

"Boston. His daughter has a gymnastics meet this weekend," I said, looking at a picture of Janey on Jake's desk. Their house was covered in family photographs. The beach, Halloween, and birthday cakes were backdrops to a family who often were caught in the middle of spontaneous fits of laughter rather than in tightly posed-for-the-camera happiness.

"He left you alone?" Chris asked.

When you're thirty-seven years old, you generally don't expect two things: the need for a babysitter or to have open-heart surgery. "My mother stayed here last night, but she had to go into work

today. Mike took me over to the hospital for a while to see Elle.
And Jake will be back tonight."

"You need anything else?"

"A chauffeur. I'm not supposed to drive for a few weeks. But
it'll wait."

"Where do you need to go?"

"Home. I need to pick up something."

"I can drive you."

The gray sky hung over the Harraseeket River like a shroud, low
clouds but not quite ground fog. Chris pulled into my driveway in
his SUV. Elle's car was parked exactly where she always left it, by
the back door. Chris was right; it would have startled me if not for
his warning.

"Are you up to taking the stairs?" Chris regarded the porch
steps as if they were a gauntlet I had to run.

Seven stairs, a half flight—I could do it. "I'm really not an invalid. Considering everything, my heart muscle sustained very
little damage."

"That's why you kept dying." He still looked at me as if I might
keel over.

"Well, there was that, but hey, what's a near-death experience
from time to time?" I grinned, but somehow the power I'd always
felt over him had shifted. He was the stronger one, the more powerful player now.

"Glad you haven't lost your sense of humor," he said.

"I'm fine. More or less." *Less being the operative term.*

His eyes narrowed in a skeptical salute. "Let's just get what you
need and take you back to Jake's."

We entered the house through the back door into the mudroom
and kitchen. The air was stale inside, as if the house knew Elle and
I no longer needed to breathe. On the counter, Elle's bag, a canvas

tote, sat as if she'd just come home and dropped it there. A note from Christopher lay beside it.

"Her wallet's inside. I didn't want to leave it in the car," Chris said.

I used to tease her that she carried half the world in that stupid bag. She'd stuff a towel in it and go to the beach, or pack a lunch and come to my office to kidnap me for a picnic. She kept student papers and her laptop. Now all that was left were her wallet, sunglasses, a package of sugar-free gum, and her car keys. God, I missed seeing her walk through the door and shed her keys here, her shoes there. As bright as she was, she could be a little scattered and forget to take care of the details in life. Why the hell did that stuff bug me?

"Where did you leave the rest of the letters?" Chris asked.

"Check the dining room table."

"I could have picked this up without you," he said, heading through the butler's pantry.

"Yeah, probably." But after having died, I wanted to see if the world had changed, transubstantiated, developed depth and color. Looking out the window, I saw the lawn certainly had transformed into a field, but the world hadn't developed deeper hues. If anything, it looked a little flatter, paler, emptier. The reality of Elle's accident had set in. It was autumn. Everything was dying away. A wave of pessimism broke over me as I scanned our empty kitchen. Then I told myself that new life came in the spring and the baby was due in spring. I wandered into the living room.

"Got them," Christopher said, returning through the doorway.

"I just need a minute."

On the fireplace mantel, there was a snapshot of Elle and me that someone had framed as a wedding gift. I was probably eight, and Elle was five or six. Our families had gone camping together.

Alice, who had loved black-and-white photography, shot us with fast grainy film. We were backlit by the campfire, and sitting nose to nose, we were silhouettes, cameos. Except for our eyes, which caught the light, a spark between us even then.

"Carrie looks like Elle," Chris said from behind me. His four-month-old daughter did indeed resemble her aunt.

"Tell her that when she's old enough to understand."

"Of course I will." Christopher's voice broke.

I turned toward him. "This baby might look like Elle, too."

"That's low, Matt."

"What do you mean?"

"It's manipulative."

I sat on the arm of the sofa. "Why? It's the truth. Elle's carrying a baby, her baby, a part of her that could live on. The baby won't be Elle, but you know how much she wanted a child. Just think about what Elle was like. She took care of you when you were a scared, motherless, little boy. She put off her own dreams for you, Chris, for you. She took herself off a tether in space, going seventeen thousand miles an hour, three hundred and fifty miles above the earth, to save another astronaut. She would do anything to save someone she cared about." My voice cracked. "She would have loved this baby. She would even stay on life support for her child."

"I don't know." He rubbed his eyes with the heels of his hands. "I don't know. One of my clearest memories is of Elle crying. Mom was sick. And Elle was sitting with her. Then suddenly Elle got up and ran into the kitchen. She kept saying that it was wrong, that we were torturing my mom, and there was no point to it."

"There's a difference. Your mother was going to die no matter what happened, and the only thing to come out of keeping her alive was that she suffered longer. Elle is pregnant. There is a point to keeping her alive until the baby is born. What about the baby? Doesn't the baby matter? And Elle isn't in pain. She doesn't know what's happening to her body. And afterward . . ." I paused, trying to find a way to wrap my tongue around the words. "I'll make sure she finds peace. I'll petition the court to discontinue her life support." *Or,* I didn't say, *I'll slip something into her feeding tube so she never will feel pain or suffer again.* I dropped my head into my hands.

"Let's not fight about this. Let's just go," he said. "You're okay, right?"

I nodded. I wasn't having another heart attack, but I needed another minute more, so I stalled. "Do me a favor. Walk through the upstairs. Make sure the windows are closed. I probably shouldn't go up a full flight yet."

"Sure." He took the front staircase two steps at a time.

"Show-off," I muttered as I lumbered back into the kitchen. I removed Elle's car keys from her bag and went outside, planning to move the car into the barn. I thought I could manage that much.

I couldn't say I slid into the driver's seat. My body was still moving like an old man's, but I hated that I needed a chauffeur. I crawled inside and closed my eyes while I waited for the muscles to stop hurting. When I slipped the key into the ignition, out of the corner of my eye, I spotted something purple on the passenger seat. No. Not purple. Indigo blue, faded from the sunlight through the windshield to purple.

"Jesus," I said aloud as I flipped it over. It was a baby book. And a ballpoint pen was stuck inside it like a bookmark.

I read the page and knew this was exactly what I'd been searching for.

"Matt?" Chris called.

I rolled down the window. "I'm here. Come read this."

✦ 52 ✦

Day 40

Adam approached the bench with the intensity of a bull charging a matador, and the court officer stepped between him and the judge.

"Order!" Wheeler said. "Dr. Cunningham, you do not approach the bench without my permission. Do you understand? I realize that you have not retained counsel, but you still have to obey procedure. I don't want to have to hold you in contempt. This is your last warning."

"Yes, Your Honor, but why haven't we heard about this baby book prior to this? Did you ever hear of discovery?" Adam directed at Jake.

"You address the court, Dr. Cunningham," Wheeler said. "That means you don't speak directly to Mr. Sutter. You ask if you can speak to me. This is a serious matter, not traffic court. As I said before, you *should* retain counsel."

"Right. I'm sorry, Your Honor."

Jake turned slowly toward Adam, wearing a condescending smile. "Your Honor, we didn't know about the baby book until this weekend. It was in Elle's car, which had been sitting in her brother's driveway since the day of the accident. My client was a little too preoccupied with his wife's illness, and more recently his own, to think about her car."

"Or, perhaps, you were concealing evidence?" Adam snapped.

"To me," Wheeler said. "You address your remarks to the bench."

Jake's lips tightened in a parental-type purse. "As I was saying, Your Honor, Elle's brother moved the car to Dr. Beaulieu's house last Thursday. Dr. Beaulieu was still in the hospital. On Saturday, he went to move the car into the garage and found the baby book. We haven't been concealing anything."

"I'm going to allow this," Wheeler said. "You may continue questioning Dr. Beaulieu, Mr. Sutter."

Adam sat down, all the while aiming a seething glare in my direction.

"Thank you, Your Honor." Jake returned to the witness stand and handed me the baby book. "Do you recognize Elle's handwriting in the book?"

"Yes. It's Elle's."

"Would you please read what she wrote?"

I recalled the message I found a few days after her accident, the scrawled words on the steamed-up bathroom mirror. This was what she meant. "It's dated August thirteenth," I said, and then proceeded to read aloud the passage that Elle wrote:

> *"You are the sweetest thing . . . a little miracle.*
> *Dear Sweet Thing, that's what I'm going to call you*
> *until you have a real name."*

[I read, hearing Elle's voice and not my own].

> *"About an hour ago I found out you're inside me. The very first thing you should know is that your mommy already loves you. Your daddy will, too, as soon as I tell him tonight. We have always wanted to have children. We have always wanted you."*

I drew a deep breath and wondered how I would have reacted that night if she didn't fall off the ladder and instead we had taken that long walk on the beach she suggested in her last voice mail. I would have been afraid for her—and for the baby. I would have worried for months. I wished I had those troubles instead of sitting here pleading for our child's life.

"Matt," Jake said, "please continue."

> *"We didn't plan to wait so long, but sometimes things happen that mommies and daddies don't expect."*

I took measure of my voice as I glanced at the judge.

> *"None of that matters now. You're coming into this beautiful world. Oh, I have so much I want to share with you. So much I want you to see and know. The world is a big place. And a small one. Someday I'll tell you about how I had the privilege of seeing it the way few had seen it before me. But for a baby, probably the only thing you need to know is love. You need to feel safe and warm, and day by day your world will grow. You*

just need a chance. And time. And love.
　"We will give you that. I promise."

I promised the baby, too. I would love this child enough for both Elle and me.

　"You will be born healthy and strong. I'll eat right, stay on bed rest for the next nine months— if necessary. I'll—groan—take shots—I'll tell you about that later when you're older—how Mommy is afraid of needles—but I'll take the shots. I'd do anything for you. Anything at all.

　"Oh, baby! Boy? Girl? A girl, I think. Why do I think you're a girl? But maybe you're a boy. A boy would be as perfect as a girl. Whatever you are, whoever you are, you're loved.

　"I could sit here all day, talking to you, but I have to go to your uncle's house for a couple of hours. Tomorrow we'll go see the baby doctor, and then there will be shots. For me. Not you! Not yet. And don't worry if I say 'ouch.' It's really not that bad.

　"Everything is going to be fine. I promise you. I'll make sure of it.

Love,
Mommy"

I had read and reread the note. These weren't her last words. But they were the last ones that mattered.

The baby book had to be enough. I studied the judge's face. He was hard to read; still, something softened in the set of his jaw.

I glanced around the courtroom. Mom sat behind Jake, snif-fling. Sitting next to my mother, Chris rubbed his eyes. After he read the baby book on Saturday, he finally agreed with me that Elle would do this for the baby's sake.

Jake was staring at the judge, gawking really. "I have no further questions," Jake said.

The judge reached up under the sleeve of his robe and played with his cuff for a moment. "Dr. Cunningham, do you have ques-tions for Dr. Beaulieu?"

Even Adam looked a little shaken. "May I have a few minutes first, Your Honor?"

"We'll reconvene in ten minutes," the judge said.

We all stood as the judge swept out of the courtroom.

I'd become somewhat oblivious to the court reporters, stopped feeling conspicuous as they scrutinized me. Thirteen days post–heart attack, cardiac arrest, and open-heart surgery, I stepped down from the witness stand. Phil emerged from the gallery, fell into step with me, and grabbed my wrist to check my pulse. "Any chest pain?"

"I'm just a little tired."

He grunted. Worried about me taking the stand again, Phil had gone so far as to enlist a few paramedics to come and sit outside the courtroom. "You evaded the question. Chest pain? Yes or no."

"No, Doctor. You can have your friends stand down now. I promise I won't die, but convey my thanks for having them spend their lunch hour here."

"It's too soon for you to be doing something like this."

"You've said that already, but if this convinces the judge, my stress level will ease considerably."

"All right." He clucked his tongue. "Sit down over here, and let me take your blood pressure."

I gritted my teeth and rolled up my sleeve. "This is not necessary."

"Are you okay, Matt?" Jake asked.

"Fine. Please, everyone, stop hovering."

Phil patted my shoulder. "Your pressure's good. All right. By the way, I was wrong. The passage convinced me."

I met his gaze. "Thanks. But it's the judge it has to convince."

Mom set a water bottle in front of me.

"Thanks, Mom." I took a long draft.

A short time later the court officer said, "All rise."

So we did like a well-rehearsed band of dancers—up, then down.

Wheeler made eye contact with me for the first time, then he lowered his eyes as he sat. "Are you ready to proceed, Dr. Beaulieu?"

I walked up to the front of the room, hoping Adam couldn't pull apart my testimony.

Adam looked a little leery as he approached the witness stand. "Did Elle ever ask you to make health care decisions for her?"

I rubbed my chin. "Well, I signed medical consents for her before, when she was admitted to the hospital last February. She needed a blood transfusion. And they took her to the OR because of the hemorrhaging. I signed that consent. She didn't have an issue with it."

"But she never officially made an advanced health care plan, naming you, did she?"

"Not so far as I know."

"When she wrote her will, did she write a new advanced health care directive, which named you to make her health care decisions?"

"No."

"She didn't trust you, did she, Matt?"

"Actually, I believe she did—with everything. Our money. Our hearts. I was her best friend. Even when she was living with you, Adam, I was her best friend. She was mine." I shrugged my shoulders. "But I think I know why she didn't make it official."

"This ought to be good," Adam said.

"Dr. Cunningham, and Dr. Beaulieu, refrain from personal commentary, please." Wheeler shook his head.

"Yes, Your Honor." Adam turned to me. "Could it be that she didn't think you'd do what she wanted?"

"No, I didn't even want to make a will. I resisted it. I procrastinated. She knew that I worried a great deal about her health after we found out about the APS—even though the odds were we could have a child with minimal risks. But as a physician, I've seen too many bad things happen. She knew I couldn't face losing her. I didn't even want to face my own mortality. The last few weeks have been a real stretch for me."

There were a few grim-looking smiles in the gallery.

"I'm not a brave man, not brave the way she was anyway. You never would have found me applying to become an astronaut. I'd never strap myself to the rocket boosters. And she did that."

"Yes, thank you," Adam said.

"Please let me finish, Your Honor."

"Dr. Beaulieu, we have procedures we have to follow," Wheeler said. "The attorneys, er, the opposing side, asks the questions. You answer them."

"All I want to say is that she was a selfless person, not that she didn't have her own dreams, but—"

"Your Honor, you just told him to stop talking and he's—" Adam said.

Wheeler's gaze rested on Adam. "What you say is 'move to strike,'" then he paused for a moment. "So stricken."

"It takes a brave man to make tough decisions, doesn't it?" Adam said.

"That's not where I was going," I said.

"And she knew you couldn't make a tough decision, didn't she?"

"I make tough decisions every day."

"But you couldn't make the decision to let Elle die in peace, could you?"

Jake stood. "Objection, Your Honor? The witness—"

I interrupted Jake. "I'd like to answer that question, please."

Wheeler's eyes narrowed. "Go ahead, Doctor."

"She knew I could make life-and-death decisions. I'm a neurosurgeon. I was going to let her go. Then I found out she was carrying our baby. I was thinking about what Elle would want me to do. Let me see if I can explain this . . . Elle signed an organ-donor card. She was willing to donate her organs to save a stranger. If she'd do that, certainly she would let her own child use her organs for a few months. Elle's gone. She's already gone. She's not in any pain. She has no awareness of her surroundings. The pain and the idea of feeling trapped was what scared her. She watched her mother suffer. We all did." I took measure of my voice again. *Steady*, I thought. "You heard what she wrote. She would have done anything for this baby, stayed in bed, taken shots. I realize that isn't the same as staying on a ventilator, but knowing Elle, she would have even stayed on life support. She was a brilliant woman, and to a court of law all that matters is what she would have wanted to do, and I knew her. I believe she'd have sacrificed herself for this baby who she called the sweetest thing."

Adam's summation was surprisingly eloquent. He didn't speak to me afterward, he just sat there in court, wearing a suit, staring straight ahead, a little grief bearing down on him, too. Later Adam gave an interview to Barbara Walters where he portrayed Elle as heroic. It wasn't a bad tribute, nor was he completely off base. Skewed by his opinion, but still, he said some things for which Elle should be remembered.

I was asked to talk to all sorts of people, from Katie Couric to Oprah. I never did. For me, this was personal, and Elle was never a public person—even after the Space Shuttle accident, when she appeared on the cover of *Time* and *Newsweek*, she never spoke about anything personal. She would have hated that her life had become the subject of public discussion.

When Wheeler delivered his ruling, I thought my heart would stop, not something unprecedented as of late.

His robes billowed as he sat. Everything seemed exaggerated, from the way the sun shone through the transoms to the musky smell of my own sweat and the dryness of my mouth.

"In the matter before the court, I am denying the petition for fetal guardianship. The state of Maine has no statute for guardianship of an unborn child, no legal precedents. A guardian cannot be appointed to a fetus. And there's no precedent to apply the First Amendment's right to religious freedom to a situation like this."

I tried to keep breathing in and out while I scribbled on Jake's legal pad. *Can we still appeal?*

Jake focused on the judge as he nodded.

Wheeler continued: "Regarding the advanced health care directive, which named Dr. Adam Cunningham as Elle McClure's health care agent, I must disregard Texas law. Maine does not overturn an advanced directive during pregnancy unless specifically stipulated. Moreover, I question if she revoked the 2003 advanced directive somewhere, sometime, because of her signature and initials on the February second hospital admission form, which stated she did not have any such advanced health care directive." He leaned back, and we waited for him to continue. "It's also possible that since she was in shock on February second, she initialed that document not knowing its meaning. Elle Beaulieu had long since severed her relationship with Dr. Cunningham and had maintained no significant personal relationship with him afterward. And Linney Beaulieu is now in agreement with her son."

I drew a breath and held it.

"It is not the job of the court to make moral judgments. We are here to determine what Elle Beaulieu would choose if she were competent to do so. From the notation in the baby book she wrote the morning of the accident, I believe she would want this pregnancy to continue."

Jake put his hand on my shoulder.

"However," Wheeler said, "she also made it clear to everyone who has testified that she did not want to continue on if there were no hope of a meaningful recovery. I am instructing her caregivers that her life support continue until such time as this pregnancy ends."

"Thank you, God," I whispered.

"Dr. Beaulieu . . ." the judge said, turning toward me. "I admired your wife. And I am very sorry for your loss. I do hope that the pregnancy brings you a healthy child. I wish your family well. At such time as Elle Beaulieu gives birth or miscarries, a hearing will convene to determine the terms of the cessation of her life support. Court adjourned."

I hugged Jake. And Hank. And every person who came my way. But Adam sat alone, staring out the window.

✦ 53 ✦

Day 160

When Elle's mother was sick, I remember thinking that the dying was taking too damned long. Every groan and every gasping breath tortured Elle, and I finally realized that Alice's illness hurt Christopher, too. And Hank. Watching Elle this way was like being scourged, but I kept in mind that every day she lived was another chance for the baby.

The ultrasound at the end of October indicated the baby was a girl. The one at Thanksgiving confirmed it. There is uncertainty in hope, but even with its tenuous nature, it summons our strength and pulls us through fear and grief—and even death. So I named my little girl Hope.

But she wasn't out of danger yet. Elle's blood pressure was becoming increasingly problematic, and Blythe was now ultra-sounding the baby daily to determine if Hope was tolerating Elle's deterioration. I tried to be there each time, but that day I was running late. One of my patients suffered a slight complication with his anesthesia that morning, which messed up my schedule. I crossed the snow-covered parking lot to the nursing home and then raced through the lobby full of the wheelchair-bound, fragile-skinned, white-haired women—and a few men—who had lived long enough to end up in a place like this one.

Our family had taken over the two rooms down at the end of the north wing of the Seashore Nursing Home. Most nights I slept there. Hank spent most days reading aloud to Elle. She couldn't hear her father, but I never discouraged him.

I missed her, and the only way I could cope was to write my own letters, *Dear Peep.* Maybe one day Hope would want to know the story of her parents' lives together. But for now the letters were a way to keep me sane.

Blythe was cleaning the ultrasound wand off as I entered Elle's room. "It's time to take down the Christmas decorations. January is over tomorrow."

"Elle loved Christmas," I said, but I meant, this was her last Christmas. "How's the baby?"

Blythe turned away from me as she spoke. "Not too bad, sucking her thumb, actually. Elle, however . . . Matt, she's slipping. Her blood work is worse. I want to move her back to the hospital today. Her kidneys are shutting down, too, and her blood pressure is up. Even though I lowered the dose of her heparin yesterday, her morning labs showed her blood-clotting time is way off. She could hemorrhage. I could go on, but you get the idea. It's not good." Her pink ribbon fell out of her hair, and she bent to pick it up. "Did you notice the petechiae?"

"No. Where?"

Blythe pointed to small hemorrhagic pinpoints, another indicator of abnormal bleeding, on Elle's forearms, her belly, and her forehead near her hairline.

"It's still early to deliver the baby," I said.

"The odds are pretty good at thirty-one weeks. And under the circumstances, the odds are better for the baby outside, but we'll try to give her twenty-four more hours. I want to give Elle one more round of steroids for the baby's lungs first," Blythe said.

I pulled up a chair to Elle's bedside and took her hand in mine. "When do you want to move her?"

"I already called for transportation. The ambulance should be here within the hour." She slid a lab report at me.

Elle's levels were far worse than I thought. "But the baby is okay?"

"She's holding her own, but she's not growing as well as I'd like. We can't wait. It could go bad fast. I'll give you a few minutes alone." Blythe closed the door behind her as she left.

I rested my hand on Elle's. "I love you, Peep. God, this is it?"

Silence can be deafening. She left so long ago.

"I miss you."

I bent down and kissed her belly. "It's okay, Hope. Daddy's here, and Mommy wrote all kinds of letters, and I'll make sure you know all her stories."

Sometimes, my mind takes stills, pictures that seem frozen instead of running film. As the double doors to the labor room opened, we passed by the admissions desk, where a man sat holding his wife's white-knuckled hand. A consoling smile on his face, concern in his eyes. I don't know why I only saw his expression and not hers. It was as if she were a ghost.

Usually people anticipate new life on the OB floor. That was my expectation, too. But I was also anticipating grief. I was afraid. Afraid for the baby, afraid for Elle, afraid for the distilling moment when her body would eventually die, and I knew that time was racing toward us. I was afraid for how empty I would feel without any part of Elle left in this world.

The routine things happened next, a transfer from the gurney onto the hospital bed, the placement of the fetal monitor, the starting of an IV in Elle's hand. Elle, who was once afraid of needles, did not flinch.

The less routine things followed. My mother's face appeared in the doorway of Elle's hospital room. We both wept when I explained Elle's body was spiraling down, slowly perhaps, but in the irreversible way that water runs down a drain.

I was pacing the eight feet of floor space. Two steps one way, two back. My mother hugged me, anchoring me, holding me still. But stillness was uncomfortable. Stillness was death. Stillness was Elle.

"Let's take a walk, honey," Mom said.

I shook my head.

She squeezed my arm the way she used to when I was a kid, the way that made me pay attention to her without raising her voice above a whisper. She wasn't making a request. She was telling me. "You have to take care of yourself. The baby needs you, and worrying about Elle won't help the baby. You can't afford another heart attack now. Nothing's going to happen for hours. Let's get something to eat."

I followed my mother out of the room, but not before I looked back. I would always look back.

As though she'd heard my thoughts, Mom said, "You have to think about the baby, not about Elle. You have to look forward."

My mother was right. I didn't want to remember Elle like this. I wanted to see her as I did the morning before the accident, backlit by the blue sky and the sun reflecting off the river. I wanted to remember her strong and healthy. I wanted to have her back that way. Elle was giving our daughter life. And I wanted to give Hope the memories of Elle—the way she was for thirty-five years, not the memory of her dying in a hospital bed.

I followed Mom to the coffee shop, not exactly the best place for a heart-healthy meal. The smell of bacon filled my nostrils, but I ordered a bowl of vegetable soup. I hadn't had an appetite for months and I'd dropped weight. The only reason for eating these days was to appease my mother. We both made calls. I left voice messages for Keisha and Jake. Phil said he'd cover the hospital.

Mom's cell phone rang, and after a minute of monosyllabic grunts she clipped it closed. "Christopher doesn't want to be at the hospital any longer than necessary, but he said to let him know when they take her in to deliver the baby. He will be there in the waiting room."

I tapped my foot, reminding myself that if Elle were still here, she'd remind me Christopher was doing the best he could, that he was just a kid when Alice was sick, that it scarred him, too.

"Hank was in a meeting, but he'll be here soon," Mom said.

Although the sound of Hope's amplified heartbeat steadied me as we returned to Elle's room, I didn't notice how slow it was. The chaos must have distracted me. A respiratory therapist was using an ambu bag to move oxygen in and out of Elle's lungs. She'd been breathing by herself since I'd woken after my surgery. And now she wasn't.

I strode into the room. "What's happening?"

One nurse was hanging blood and another was starting another IV. "Her blood pressure dropped. We're taking her to the OR for a stat C-section."

"How low is her pressure?" I asked.

"Sixty over twenty-seven." Meaning Elle was in shock. The nurse, whose name I couldn't recall, turned to Mom. "Blythe's scrubbing."

I pushed past the others in the room and made it to Elle and kissed her forehead, noting that the little petechiae had grown more pronounced in the forty minutes we were gone. "Hang in there, Peep. Just a little while longer."

Mom was pulling out the fetal monitor strip and examining it. "How's the baby?" I asked.

She blanched. "Come on, Matt. Out of the way. Let them get Elle to the OR." She took my arm and pulled me out to the hall.

"The baby? Mom? What's wrong?"

"Bradycardia. The fetal heart rate is only in the sixties."

That's when I realized it. I wasn't hearing the rapid fetal heart rate. Hope's was slower than my own. And if a baby's heartbeat was that low, she warranted CPR.

"I'm going to change into scrubs," I said, starting down the corridor.

"They aren't going to let you in the OR, Matt."

"*Yes*, they will."

Mom's eyes filled with tears. "Not like this. Elle is going to die in the next few hours, or maybe sooner in the OR."

"I know. That's why I will be there. For her. For Hope," I said as I ducked into the men's locker room. I needed to know that even though I couldn't save Elle, I never abandoned her. Less than a minute later I emerged wearing blue scrubs in time to see them pushing Elle's gurney through the double doors to the C-section room. I followed at a breakneck speed, slowing at the outside door to don a surgical mask, cap, and shoe covers. Fully garbed, I stepped to the side as they positioned Elle on the OR table.

The anesthesiologist stripped off Elle's hospital gown and put lead wires on her naked chest, just before they buried her under a mass of sterile drapes. Then he shoved a tube down her throat to suction out the contents of her stomach, but instead of pulling up her tan-colored feeding formula, what looked like old blood was coming up through the suction catheter. The anesthesiologist's eyes widened as the color changed to bright red. Elle was hemorrhaging.

Her heart monitor alarmed. "She's throwing a lot of PVCs and odd-looking cardiac complexes, and she's having a GI bleed. You better get that baby out fast, Blythe," the anesthesiologist said.

"Hang lidocaine for the arrhythmias," Blythe said.

My mother came in behind me.

"You sure you want to be in here, Linney?" someone asked.

Mom took my hand in hers, leaned into me, and summoned her voice. "Yes."

The NICU team shoved in, three of them—a neonatologist, a nurse, and a respiratory tech. They checked the resuscitation equipment for the baby. "How's the baby's heart rate?" one asked.

"We lost it about a minute ago."

My head started to reel, and a stool was pushed behind me. "I should take you out of here," Mom said.

"No," I said, putting my head down between my knees. "No."

The OB resident dumped Betadine, an orange-brown antiseptic, on Elle's belly, and without leaving time for the disinfectant to kill a single bacterium, Blythe cut into Elle's abdomen with a deliberate swipe of her scalpel. "Suction. I need more suction," she said. The blood was pouring out as if Blythe hit an artery. She hadn't. This was a combination of the blood thinner and possibly the preeclampsia doing its damage.

One of the neonatal people, not recognizing that I was there, said, "Call for backup. This is *not* going to be good. Start drawing meds. I want a bolus of saline ready and . . ." He continued on.

One nudged the other. "Shush, that's the father."

"What's he doing in here?"

Blythe was cutting fast. Another doctor was tugging on a retractor so hard that he nearly pulled Elle off the OR table. More blood gushed out and onto the floor.

Then, with strength and tenderness, Blythe reached into Elle, practically elbow-deep, and pulled out my blue, limp daughter. It was like seeing Dylan again.

The NICU team put her on the radiant warmer and closed in around her.

Please, God, save Hope.

I stood and crossed to where the anesthesiologist was at Elle's head. I knew him. He knew me. He looked away. Certainly I shouldn't have been there at that moment, but it was as if they had all turned blind eyes.

Blythe was operating frantically, cauterizing bleeders. As if it mattered now, as if it was still possible to save my wife.

I dropped to my knees beside the operating table and matched my fingertips with Elle's. *Please, Elle, know how much I love you.*

"She's in V-fib," the anesthesiologist said to Blythe.

"Matt, what do you want me to do? Do you want me to resuscitate?" Blythe asked.

I hesitated for a moment. I had promised to respect Elle. "Do not resuscitate," I said. "Let her be at peace."

This was anything but peace.

Everyone had said it was impossible, but I told them to save the baby anyway. I told them to try. I wanted the baby no matter what it cost, but I hadn't thought it would be like this, with them violently ripping Elle open. And the baby dead, too. The NICU team was there, trying to resuscitate Hope, but she looked like Dylan did when he was stillborn, pale and limp.

"Do you have Apgar scores?" Blythe asked.

"Six at one minute. Not quite at five minutes for the second one."

Apgar of six?

"Heart rate one-sixty," a female voice said.

"Come on, breathe," the neonatologist said. "That's it. That's better. She's coming around."

I jumped to my feet.

"She's pinking up," the neonatologist said, turning to me slightly.

And suddenly my tiny daughter cried, a big whelping scream.

"There you go," the nurse said.

Mom had pushed her way in by the NICU team. "Matt, she's beautiful."

I took my own breath, maybe the first real breath I'd taken in months. "I need to see her."

The respiratory therapist stepped aside, and my little girl, smeared in blood but decidedly pink, was bawling.

I turned back as the anesthesiologist turned off Elle's heart monitor.

Blythe spoke softly, "Time of death, one-thirteen."

Come back to me in dreams; that I may give
Pulse for pulse, breath for breath:
Speak low, lean low,
As long ago, my love, how long ago.
~Christina Rossetti~

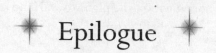# Epilogue

Four Months Later

During the past year I've come to think of grief as a tidal wave. It unexpectedly rises from the depths of my being, carrying with it the debris it's picked up along the way. Sometimes I wake angry that Elle wasn't more careful. Some mornings I reach out for her, still denying she's gone forever. Then I lie there pleading with God, begging Him that I would do anything if He would just make the damned nightmare go away. I have wept. I have accepted the love and support of family and friends.

And I have experienced joy because my daughter is thriving. I peek inside Hope's room.

Our Lab, Hubble, appointed himself her guardian angel the day I brought my little girl home, and now he lifts his head off the carpet as if to acknowledge he has his post covered.

Inside the crib, she sleeps, her arms stretched out wide, her chubby baby fingers splayed. How much she has already grown astounds me. She weighed less than three pounds at birth; she has already more than tripled her weight. She has her mother's white-blond hair and pointy chin. I see myself in her other features. Her eyes grow darker with each day, brown like mine. She is both of us. She is her own little person.

Hope shows no indication she plans to wake up soon to help me procrastinate. She's probably storing up on sleep. Her Baptism is tomorrow.

Everyone will come, Mom and Hank, my brothers and their families, Chris, his wife and daughter, Phil and Melanie, Blythe—and even Judge Wheeler. And because of Jake's role in saving Hope, Father Meehan is allowing my non-Catholic best friend to be her godfather. Officially only one godparent must be Catholic, and Keisha is.

Keisha is very excited these days—and not just about godmothering Hope. Keisha and Guy decided to try foster-parenting an older child, one who is likely to become available for adoption soon. Last night she called and said they'd passed their home study, so it shouldn't be too long of a wait. I'm happy for them.

"Sleep a little longer, baby girl," I whisper to Hope as I turn to go. "Big day tomorrow."

On the way to the stairs, I pass Hank's room. He moved in with us—"for the time being," he says. He takes care of Hope while I work and nights when I get called into the hospital.

Mom helps—in her own way, too. She made a big fuss about

painting Hope's room pink. I said it was too "girlie." And Mom said, "What other color should it be?" She tells me I know nothing about raising girls, so I have conceded certain points, but not the hot-pink room. Still, Mom has stuffed Hope's closet full of ruffled dresses—which I'm pretty sure Elle would hate, and my mother, Grandma to Hope, babysits two days a week—which I'm pretty sure Elle would love. Everyone is pitching in. Evidently it takes a single dad and *a village* to raise one nine-pound baby girl.

But before the celebration, before the sacrament, I have something I have to do.

The decision to bury Elle here on the farm was not a difficult one, but it turned into something quite complex. An ordinance passed that only allowed burials in professionally run cemeteries, and the town refused to give us a variance for interring the casket up in the family plot. The only concession they made was that if Elle were cremated, then I could bury her ashes anywhere on the property, not a real concession at all.

Our family didn't like the idea of cremation, but Elle convinced me it was best when Celina died. And when Dylan did. "They were stardust," she said. And no falling star ever shone more brightly than Elle.

Now that the ground is no longer frozen, I will fulfill the promise I made so long ago. Celina's ashes will rest with Elle—and of course Dylan's. Certainly she would want him with her, too. But there's something else. After the two other miscarriages, the ones which came too early for shape and gender, Elle needed a way to commemorate our "babies." So she purchased two small meteorite fragments, and we buried them in the garden inside a small box made of elm. "Stardust," Elle said. This morning I dug up the two urns, Celina's and Dylan's, and the meteorite fragments.

And there, buried in the garden, I found the baby diaries in a sealed glass canister. These Elle did not address to me but to them.

Celina was "Dear Angel." The second was "My Little Darling," the third was "My Tiny Star," and Dylan . . . he was "My Little Love." I will read the journals then bury them again. I suppose she placed them in the garden as the babies' epitaphs.

I lay newspaper on the kitchen floor and then bring the three urns inside and set them down. I have not felt this hesitant about anything since I made my first surgical incision. I kneel, open Elle's urn, and shudder. I console myself by saying, "Stardust. You have no idea how much I miss you, Peep." I open Dylan's and transfer his ashes, combining them with Elle's. "I love you, kiddo. Rest with your mother." I drop the two meteorite fragments in, then stare at Celina's urn for a few seconds longer. "Celina, you'd be all grown up. We loved you, too." I glance inside and see something.

My first thought is that after all this time her ashes have clumped together, but on closer inspection I realize it's a plastic zip bag with an envelope rolled up inside. I swallow and retrieve it, carefully brushing Celina's ashes into Elle's urn.

In Elle's handwriting, the envelope is addressed to me.

Dr. Matthew Beaulieu

I tear it open:

Dear Matt,

This is what NASA calls the contingency letter. Usually during the quarantine, astronauts write good-byes to the most beloved people in their lives. As I write this letter I'm still at the farmhouse, but my heart is full of you. We spent today riding a roller coaster and walking on the beach. I want you to know I treasured every moment. Those hours were our real good-bye, but I need to leave the words behind. In case. I know what you said on the beach. You don't want to hear that I could die. But I might. And if you're reading this, I did.

I don't want to put you in an awkward position with your fiancée. I know you love her, and I don't want to leave you a letter that might raise questions and complicate your life, so I'm tucking this missive away where I know you'll find it discreetly. You made me a promise, and I know you'll keep it. I know you have kept it because that's how you found this letter. At the same time, if you want to tell her, it's fine. You have my blessing.

I understand the risks of what I'm about to do. Space travel is dangerous, but some things are worthy of sacrifice. This is one of them. I'm happy—elated even—to take the chance—to bring the stars closer—to touch a little piece of heaven. How few people experience sheer exultation? I am so very blessed that I have the opportunity to fulfill my dream.

I love you, Matthew. I don't remember a time when I didn't. You've always been my dearest friend. You were my first love. And the father of the only little baby I'll ever have. I loved her even though I wasn't ready for motherhood. We were too young. Thank you for being so good to me then. And thank you for bearing the burden of burying her with me now.

I probably shouldn't be telling you any of this. After all, you are marrying someone else. But I know a part of you feels the same way about me, *and I want to tell you these feelings are not wrong. We have our history together, one which preceded anyone else. It's not a betrayal of her that you are mourning for me now.*

I will take a part of you with me on this mission. You have made me stronger and kinder and more confident. You made my life richer, and I believe I have given you an equal share of my heart.

I'll still be with you in your memories. Someday you'll tell your children about this girl you knew who loved the stars so much she flew on a rocket ship intent on fixing an ailing telescope.

You are a tender and kindhearted man. You will make a wonderful husband and father someday. I want you to have a full life. Promise me one more thing. Promise me you will be happy.

All my love,
Peep

Promise to be happy? Jesus. I reread the letter in its entirety again. Obviously Elle wrote it before her mission, when I was still engaged to Carol. Like other things, like the damned advanced directive, she got her affairs in order and left the remnants behind.

It takes me a while to get up off the floor. Another reading. Now I want to tell Elle I never married Carol. I want to tell Elle that Celina was not the only baby she would have. I want Elle to come upstairs and stand at Hope's doorway and ooh and aah over our sweetest thing. Even now I hold on to my sanity by dipping into denial.

I shake my head. She is gone. I read the letter yet again. It is still the last line that has me in its grip—another promise she is coercing me to make, a promise to be happy.

Hubble pads down the stairs and whines. Hope must be stirring, but she's not crying yet. I put the dog out into the yard then slide the rest of Celina's ashes from her urn into Elle's. "Ashes to ashes, stardust to stardust," I say.

Upstairs, Hope starts to squawk. After washing my hands, I go to her. "Hey, baby girl," I say, lifting her out of her crib. She quiets immediately. Little charmer that she is, she knows once she has my attention I'm rapt. She smiles. She glows. She is lightness and happiness. "Okay, Elle. Okay. I promise."

A diaper change and a warm bottle later, Hope settles into my arms out on the back porch. It's a radiant spring morning and the scent of lilacs fills the air. The tide is high and the river is full and glimmering. New life comes in the spring. A new life.

I put Hope up to my shoulder for a burp and walk down the steps, scanning the landscape, the garden, the lawn, and the forest. Perhaps it's a trick of the light, but for a second I see a transient figure among the trees, Elle backlit and smiling. And then she is gone. But she's still here. In my memories. In my heart. And a part of Elle is in our daughter.

"Hope," I say. "Once upon a time there was a girl who loved the stars so much she took a ride on a rocket ship . . ."

Author's Note

Historical Note: I watched the *Columbia* Space Shuttle disaster with great sadness, and I greatly admire the bravery and dedication of all space explorers before and since.

However, for the sake of this story, I placed Elle's fictional *Atlantis* mission in May 2004, fourteen months prior to the actual resumption of the Space Shuttle program. In reality, the Space Shuttle *Discovery*'s crew made their intrepid return-to-space journey on July 26, 2005. Although NASA did use *Atlantis* to repair/upgrade Hubble, it did not do so until 2009, and fortunately the crew's mission went relatively smoothly.

Finally, it is true that micrometeorites are a risk for astronauts during space walks, but what transpired on Elle's mission and the rest of the story are fictional events.

In terms of the legal matters presented in this story, laws governing advanced directives and pregnancy vary from state to state. Some forbid the removal of life support when a woman is pregnant. Some base the laws on the viability of the pregnancy. Some do not mention how the matter will be handled at all. I encourage you to find out what the statutes are in your area.

Acknowledgments

Truly, I could never have written this novel without the love and support of my family. My husband and sons encouraged me when I wanted to surrender. They gave me time to pursue my dreams. They celebrated my victories and hugged me when I needed to be held. I am a truly fortunate woman to have you as my husband, Tim. Robert, Cole, and Ethan, you are my joy. I love you all.

My sisters, Sherron Small and Lou Symington, each helped with little details in this book. But you both know I owe you for your friendship and strength.

I am indebted to my literary agent, Laney Katz Becker. Her wisdom, insight, and faith made me reach deeper than I thought I could. Thank you so much for your guidance through this process.

I want to express my thanks to the following people: Linda Retstatt, Carol McPhee, Judi Romaine, Verna LaBounty, Deborah Nemeth, Kathleen Lutter. You've all taught me so much about writing. And Amy Nathan and Catherine DiCairano, thank you for being early readers and giving me your encouragement and your honest feedback. Maria Imbalzano, thank you for your legal expertise and logical writing mind. Any bumbles made are mine, not yours. Thank you, Mary Otis, for answering my adult ICU questions. I also want to send a shout-out to Dr. Leroy Chiau, who answered a few astronaut questions for me.

I have also depended on the fabulous Backspace Writer's Forum. Thank you, Karen Dionne and Chris Graham, for creating that community. It has been a haven for me.

Finally, I want to thank my wonderful editor, Emily Krump, for her keen understanding of my characters and their world. Thank you to Julia Meltzer, Martin Karlow, Juliette Shapland, and all the people at William Morrow for their support and enthusiasm.

About the book

About the author

Insights,
Interviews
& More . . .

Read on

Reading Group Guide

MATT BEAULIEU AND ELLE MCCLURE share a lifelong love, but after an accident leaves her with severe brain damage and no hope of recovery, he agrees to take her off life support until he finds out that she is pregnant. Not everyone believes it is possible to save the baby Elle's carrying, and some believe it is morally wrong to keep her on the ventilator because she has an advanced health care directive that states that she would never want extraordinary measures taken to extend her life. Matt still wants to try.

1. As a neurosurgeon, Matt immediately realizes that Elle's brain damage is severe. Why do you think he lets Phil operate? Do you think he betrays Elle by letting Phil do so? What about when Matt decides to keep his wife on life support?

2. Do you think Linney is overstepping her bounds when she opposes Matt's decision to keep Elle on life support? How much of Linney's behavior do you think is motivated by her experience as a nurse? Or by guilt over her decision not to intervene when Alice was dying/suffering?

3. As teenagers, Matt and Elle find themselves about to have a baby. What do you think would have happened if Matt had approached his parents for help? Why doesn't Matt's dad, Dennis, do anything when he finds out Elle is pregnant? How do you think Hank would have reacted? Do you think Matt could have gone to one of his older brothers?

4. When Elle miscarries the first time, she says a name is important because it is

the only thing they will ever be able to give the baby. Do you think it's important to give a name to grief?

5. Matt wants to keep the court case private, but it becomes a media circus. How much influence does the media have on events like this? How much should they have? Is their involvement an expression of freedom of speech or is it an invasion of privacy?

6. Matt keeps talking to Elle while she's in the hospital, even though he knows she can't hear him. Why do you think he does that?

7. Elle says women are stronger because they can discuss their sadness and men feel as though they have to mask their pain and insecurities. Do you think that's true?

8. Matt describes Adam as a controlling prick, but at another point Matt describes himself as a controlling spouse with a medical degree. Why would Elle choose two men who, on the surface, are quite different from each other? Or are they more similar than Matt believes?

9. Do you think Elle or Linney actually hastened Alice's death? Do you think Matt would have actually gone to the authorities with Elle's diary? Would you have given Alice an extra "dose" to relieve her suffering?

10. Matt tried desperately to resuscitate his and Elle's stillborn son. How do you think that loss affected Matt? Elle? And, as a doctor, was Matt's "failure" to save the baby a deeper loss for him?

11. Matt does not hold Christopher in high esteem. What do you think the origin of Matt's animosity is? Do you think Christopher is aware of Matt's feelings about him? Was Elle?

12. Why do you think Elle never gave Matt her medical power of attorney? Have you made an advanced directive? Who would you designate to make those decisions for you?

13. At the end of the story, Matt sees a fleeting figure in the trees and for a moment he thinks it is Elle. In the aftermath of loss, have you ever briefly forgotten that your loved one is gone? Do you believe some part of them stays with you forever?

14. In some states, pregnancy invalidates a woman's advanced directive. Are you familiar with the laws in your state? Would you want to be kept on life support if you were pregnant? ∾

A Conversation with Priscille Sibley

The Promise of Stardust is a family story, a love story, and a story that deals with tough—at times unimaginable—moral issues. What inspired you to write this novel?

I love being a nurse, but it isn't an easy job—not physically, not technically, and certainly not emotionally. We see people in crisis every day, but some situations are worse than others. Years ago I took care of a child who had been in a persistent vegetative state for an extended period of time. He did not respond to his environment. He had no spontaneous movement. He did not breathe or even blink. I don't think he was suffering, but I didn't believe that keeping him alive was in his best interest. My understanding was that the family had dissolved under the tension. If they ever visited, I never saw them. While I certainly don't remember every patient I've ever cared for, I'll always remember him. Nurses will all tell you we carry some patients with us forever. He is one of mine.

Sometime later, in 2004 and early 2005, the headlines were filled with stories about Terri Schiavo, a young woman in Florida who fell into a persistent vegetative state after suffering a cardiac arrest. Her family tried many therapies, but she remained unresponsive. Eventually her husband requested that she be disconnected from her feeding tube and be allowed to die. Her parents objected. A heated court case ensued. Pictures of Terri Schiavo looking like she was smiling were held up by the right-to-life advocates. At the same time doctors showed her CT scans, which indicated that Terri's brain had severely atrophied. The entire situation disturbed me because, again, I found myself thinking about the child who was unaware of the feel of human contact.

I knew I would not want to live like Terri Schiavo or like that child, and I felt frustrated and sad. What possible good could come from this? What, if anything, could make this worth it? Then I had a "what if?" moment. What if she were pregnant? Of course in Schiavo's case, it was impossible, but I found I couldn't ignore my "what-if?" question, and I started to write a story about a man, the wife he loved, a terrible accident, and a family divided by the ethical dilemma of keeping a pregnant woman on life support.

The political issues in the book—right to live, right to die, a mother's rights versus her unborn child's, who speaks for the voiceless—are divisive and highly controversial. Did you have any hesitations writing about such timely yet explosive issues? Did this impact the way that you approached the book?

Controversy is definitely inherent in this premise, but I didn't set out to write a political statement. I set out to write a human story. People get caught up in real ethical dilemmas every single day. What is right or wrong is not always as clear as a pundit's sound bite. These kinds of decisions are affected by relationships and human frailties and love and denial and the need to hold on to what's left after a tragedy. And sometimes the answers are not as clear as our principles. I'm not trying to be funny or disrespectful when I say the opinions expressed by my characters are not necessarily my own. They are there for balance. And yes, at times it was difficult for me to write those words. The opinions are there to pose the question: What would you want if this were you? So I created a cast of characters who could speak to different sides of the dilemma. Linney loves helping women give birth to babies, and she loves her son and her daughter-in-law. Yet she's in a position of having promised her goddaughter—her Catholic goddaughter—that she would never let her languish near death. Matt loves his wife, and he wants to do one last thing right for her. He wants their child. He's clinging to the very unlikely chance he can salvage something from his and Elle's life together. Adam is still trying to protect Elle. Jake has a cause he believes in and an old friend he wants to help. But I'm not even certain if there is a right or a wrong under the circumstances in which Elle's family and friends find themselves. Matt picks a course, but I don't think he's completely convinced that he has done the right thing even in the very end.

Writing experts often advise people to write what they know. In writing **The Promise of Stardust,** *did you follow this rule? How did you follow this rule, and how did you break away from it? In the cases where you were writing about something new, how did you go about researching and learning about your characters' worlds?*

Ah, the rules! Because this is a work of fiction, I did not know everything my characters would need to know if they were real people. For example, I am not an astronaut. And thankfully Matt, the narrator, is not either. However, Elle was and I needed to learn a little bit about NASA. When my kids were young, I watched an endless number of videos about space, one of which talked about how a micrometeorite could potentially compromise a spacesuit. And so that became fodder for Elle's adventure. I found the web site and e-mail of an astronaut online. I sent him a question and he kindly responded. (I have to say I love research sometimes. That was one of the coolest things I ever did.) ▸

A Conversation with Priscille Sibley *(continued)*

And although I'm a registered nurse, I am not a neurosurgeon, so I went back to the books to learn more about neuro exams and brain death determinations. I work with sick newborns, who really don't have myocardial infarctions from years of unhealthy living, so I needed a refresher and update on heart attacks. Back to the books I went again. Google became a close friend. I spent hours in the medical library. I posed questions to other health care professionals. One of my writer friends is an attorney. She repeatedly sent me back to rewrite scenes. It was fun. It was frustrating. It turned into a book.

As a woman writing a male character like Matt Beaulieu, did you face any challenges in capturing his perspective or keeping his voice authentically male?

The challenges were significant, at least in my mind. If I could have told the story from any point of view other than Matt's, I would have. But I wanted a reader to feel what was at stake for him. I wanted to show Matt and Elle's love story, and since she could no longer voice it, Matt had to speak for both of them. Fortunately, I am surrounded by men. I'm raising three teenage boys, I have one husband, and I have six brothers-in-law (if no actual brothers). Men speak and see the world a little differently than women do. They banter with one another. Their one-upmanship is usually affectionate, not mushy, and when things are difficult, they try to solve problems rather than commiserate. Men are interesting characters. But I did spend a lot of time second-guessing everything from his reactions to his word choices.

There are four types of love—storge (familial love), philia (love between friends), agape (unconditional love), and eros (romantic love)—all of which appear and are important in The Promise of Stardust *whether it is between Matt and Elle, Linney and Elle, Matt and Linney, Matt and Jake, etc. Do you think all love is equal?*

This is an interesting question, but it is one for which I don't have a simple answer. I didn't want to make anyone in the story wholly right or wholly wrong. They see Elle's condition from their own perspectives, and I messed with the typical dynamics. Elle and Matt are almost a family from the very beginning of their lives because they live next door to each other and their parents are lifelong friends. Matt could have easily seen Elle as more of a sister than a lover. They are childhood friends, first loves, and eventually husband and wife. After her accident,

I do think he demonstrates his love for her has become unconditional, and I believe true love, be it for one's parents or friends or lovers or children, is unconditional. It must be unselfish to be real.

Matt and Elle have been in love with each other for a long time, but they do break up and date other people. Do you think it was important for them to break up in order for them to ultimately be together?

Here's the romantic in me: Matt and Elle's love was more powerful than either of them was prepared to handle when they were teenagers. It almost swallowed their dreams. It might have if Celina had lived. Then what would have happened? Would they have been able to stick it out? Having the chance to concentrate on their demanding careers instead of each other made it easier for them to attain their individual dreams. Of course, Jake and his wife married fairly young and stayed married. He gave up his political ambitions though, and Yvette didn't have a demanding career. So there are examples of young love *working* in the story, too.

After Elle's accident the Beaulieu and McClure families are forced to make decisions for her, and Matt and Linney have very different ideas about what this means. Do you think it's possible for one person to completely know another person?

That's a question for the ages. I'm not even certain we know ourselves as well as we think. Linney loves Elle like a parent, and she loves her son. One of the limitations of telling the story from Matt's point of view was that I couldn't get into Linney's head. If I could have, she would have shared some interesting insights into Matt and his denial. He is a fairly reliable narrator, but he only sees the story from his singular point of view. There were things he did not know about Elle, either. On the day they went on the rollercoaster, he said he often told her things he said to no one else, but they didn't talk about Adam. They didn't talk about Carol. Some things were out-of-bounds. No, I don't think we know everything.

Many first novels are semiautobiographical. Is this the case for The Promise of Stardust? Do you see yourself in any or all of your characters? If so, which ones?

It's not a story about me or my family or anyone I know, and I've never witnessed this scenario in the workplace. That doesn't mean the story

A Conversation with Priscille Sibley *(continued)*

didn't emanate from me. As a nurse, I have had a front-row seat to terrible suffering; my first nursing job was in a burn unit. I have taken care of children with fatal diseases, and I've taken care of babies who were born with problems which made it impossible for them to survive. At times, I've wondered if we (health care professionals) were trying too hard to extend life. I still wonder that some days, and in an oblique way I'm asking that question in *The Promise of Stardust*.

And I did borrow little details from my life here and there. One example is that Matt and Elle grow up in Freeport, Maine, a town I've loved since I was a kid. Their house is down on Wolf Neck Road, which is a real place, although their house is a figment of my imagination. There's a lovely state park on Wolf Neck, a forest with hiking trails. Casco Bay is on one side of the peninsula and the Harraseeket River on the other, and I envision their property as part of the state park I've wandered around in so many times.

Another (bigger) thing I borrowed from my life was that my own mother died when I was fifteen. The circumstances were very different than Alice's death. My mother's illness was short (no hospice care was involved), and I did not go through a teenage pregnancy. (If anything, her illness made me more of a goody-goody than I was before.) But when I needed a reason for a young, healthy woman to be adamantly opposed to being kept on life support, I pulled that one out of my bag of tricks. Even seeing my mother on life support for a short time was enough to put a dreaded fear into my young soul. I thought the motivation would be sufficient to send Elle charging off to write an advanced directive.

What books and authors have inspired you? Are there any books that you continue to go back to?

I don't tend to reread books. I might pull one off the shelf again to savor a passage or two, but I don't reread books in their entirety very often. I do love stories of redemption. I loved *Les Miserables*. I also think Jodi Picoult does a great job of building tension. In *The Pact*, Picoult tells a devastating detail on the first page, but several hundred pages later I was yelling at the book, "Don't do it!" as the characters were replaying what happened on page one. I mean, that's just fabulous when a writer can evoke that kind of emotion from a reader. Alice Sebold had me yelling at *The Lovely Bones*, telling one of the characters to get out of there. In *The Murderer's Daughters*, Randy Susan Meyers had me saying "Just let someone love you." Whenever a writer can get you to shake your fist at a character's stupidity, cry, or laugh, they've pulled off something great.

If you could choose a dream cast to play your characters in a film, who would you include and why?

Oh, my. I barely described what Matt looked like other than to say he was tall, and in the epilogue he says his eyes are dark. For me, he's telling the story. He has a confident sense of himself, but I don't think what he looks like is important to him. How he sees Elle is important though, and I tried to make his perception of her intimate. She's the center of his world. I pictured Claire Danes when I thought of Elle, mostly because I'd seen her grow up on screen. Initially I saw Linney as Tyne Daly, an actress who can portray an opinionated and simultaneously tender character. I can't say I mentally cast anyone else with actors. ❧

Meet Priscille Sibley

© DiGiovanni Photography

PRISCILLE SIBLEY is a neonatal intensive care nurse who lives in New Jersey with her husband and three teenage sons. Her short fiction has appeared in *MiPOesias* and her poetry in *The Shine Journal*. She is a member of Backspace Writer's Forum and Liberty State Fiction Writers. *The Promise of Stardust* is her first novel.

Sources

OVER THE COURSE OF WRITING *The Promise of Stardust* I needed to do research to learn about Matt and Elle's world. Here are a few things that I found particularly helpful and revelatory:

Books

Bizony, Piers. *The Space Shuttle: Celebrating Thirty Years of NASA's First Space Plane.* Zenith Press, 2011.

Devorkin, David, and Robert Smith. *Hubble: Imaging Space and Time.* National Geographic, 2011.

Giffords, Gabrielle, and Mark Kelly with Jeffrey Zaslow. *Gabby: A Story of Courage and Hope.* New York: Scribner, 2011.

Kübler-Ross, Elisabeth. *On Death and Dying,* New York: MacMillan Publishing Co. Inc., 1969.

Rees, Martin, ed. *Universe: The Definitive Visual Guide.* Covent Garden Books, 2009.

Sawyer-Fay, Rebecca, and Lynn Karlin. *Gardens Maine Style, Act II,* Down East Books, 2008.

DVDs

Cruise, Tom, James Arnold, Michael J. Bloomfield. *Space Station 3D.* DVD. Directed by Toni Myers. IMAX and Lockheed Martin Corporation in cooperation with NASA, 2002.

Neeson, Liam, Meredith Eder, Pierre de Lespinois, Fran Lo Cascio, Stephen Jay Schwartz. *Inside the Space Station.* DVD. Directed by Pierre de Lespinois. Family Home Entertainment, 2000. ❧

Highlights from the Space Shuttle Timeline

MATT LOVED TO WATCH ELLE stargaze and, in the story, she took a fictional ride on *Atlantis*. In reality, the Space Shuttle program flew 135 missions between April 1981 and July 2011. The shuttle fleet consisted of six orbiters: *Enterprise, Columbia, Challenger, Discovery, Atlantis*, and *Endeavour*. Two flights ended in disasters and the loss of their crews: *Challenger* STS-51L and *Columbia* STS-107, but after each tragedy brave men and women returned to space.

Here are a few highlights from the Space Shuttle timeline:

August 12, 1977
First Space Shuttle test flight: *Enterprise* rode aboard an airplane to test its flight and landing capabilities.

April 12, 1981
Columbia made its first launch carrying astronauts Bob Crippen and John Young.

April 4, 1983
Challenger conducted its first spacewalk.

June 18, 1983
Sally Ride was the first American woman in space.

February 7, 1984
Astronaut Bruce McCandless tested a device that allowed untethered spacewalks.

January 28, 1986
Challenger disaster: a short seventy-two seconds after takeoff, O rings on the rocket boosters failed and exploded. It was the twenty-fifth Space Shuttle mission. Seven astronauts including teacher Christa McAuliffe, a civilian, were killed.

September 29, 1988
The Space Shuttle *Discovery* made the first return to space after a major disaster. Seventeen years later, it would once again launch into space after a terrible tragedy.

April 24, 1990
The Hubble Telescope was launched by *Discovery*.
    For more information about Hubble visit: http://hubblesite.org/

December 2, 1993
Endeavour returned to Hubble to replace its flawed vision.

June 29, 1995
Space Shuttle *Atlantis* docked with the Space Station Mir.

October 29, 1998
John Glen, seventy-seven, the first American to orbit the earth, flew again aboard the Space Shuttle *Discovery*.

December 4, 1998
The International Space Station began with *Endeavour*'s delivery of the first U.S. component, *Unity*.

February 1, 2003
The *Columbia* disaster occurred when it broke up during reentry. Insulating foam fell off the external tanks during liftoff and damaged the heat-resistant panels on the left wing of the orbiter. On reentry, the hole caused the ship to rip apart. All seven aboard were killed. The program was grounded during the accident investigation.

January 2004
George W. Bush called for the retirement of the Space Shuttle program. Although he called for a new program to take us back to the moon, that program was later canceled.

July 26, 2005
Discovery once again made an intrepid return to space.

February 24, 2011
Discovery made its last flight after thirty-nine missions, two of which followed disasters.

May 16, 2011
Endeavour made its last flight, docking with the International Space Station.

July 21, 2011
Atlantis made the final Space Shuttle flight, the program's one hundred thirty-fifth mission. ◌⬳

Meteor Watching:
A Few of the More Prominent Annual Meteor Showers

BEFORE TRYING TO WATCH *a meteor light show, get away from city lights. Find an open field or a beach. Moonlight can also block out a good showing. If the meteor shower conflicts with a full or gibbous moon, watch before the moon rises or after it sets. Take along a blanket to lie on and another to wrap yourself in. A reclining lawn chair is a good idea. Even a late-summer night can be chilly. And in the winter, bring warm clothes and a thermos with hot chocolate. You're looking for fire in the sky. Have a late-night picnic. Have music. Have fun!*

(Listed below are the usual peak dates for viewing.)

January 3, 4—Quadrantids meteor shower. About forty meteors per hour. Look around the constellation Boötes (northern sky).

April 21, 22—Lyrids meteor shower. About twenty meteors per hour and are known to leave dust trails that are visible for several seconds. Look at the constellation Lyra (visible in the northern hemisphere, almost overhead, spring through autumn).

May 5, 6—Eta Aquarids meteor shower. This is a light shower with only about ten meteors per hour. The best viewing will be after midnight. Look for the constellation Aquarius in the east, far away from city lights.

July 28, 29—Southern Delta Aquarids meteor shower. Look toward Aquarius again. The best viewing is usually after midnight.

August 12, 13—Perseids meteor shower produces about sixty meteors per hour during its peak. The debris is from the comet Swift-Tuttle. Look for the constellation Perseus (toward the northeast).

October 21, 22—Orionids meteor shower. The Orionids produces about twenty meteors per hour. The best viewing will be after midnight in the east.

November 17, 18—Leonids meteor shower. One of the better light shows. In the northern hemisphere, look for it coming from the constellation Leo after midnight.

December 13–15—Geminids meteor shower. This is considered one of the best showers and produces up to sixty multicolored meteors per hour at its peak. Look toward the east and toward Gemini after midnight.

Don't miss the next book by your favorite author.

Sign up now for AuthorTracker by visiting www.AuthorTracker.com.